# The Seeding II Virgin Landfall

## Allen Dionne

Books by Allen Dionne

*The Seeding Seven's Vision*
*The Seeding II Virgin Landfall*
*Duhcat, Mystery and Legend Unfold*
*A Summer in Mussel Shoals*
(available January 2013)

Front cover art: Dave Archer, Copyright ©1986
Spine art: Allen Dionne, Copyright ©2012
Copyright ©2012 AD by Allen Dionne

Cover design, editing, graphics, layout by Integrative Ink
My heartfelt thanks to Stephanee Killen

ISBN: 978-0-9853979-1-3

*The Seeding II Virgin Landfall* is entirely a work of fiction.
Names, characters, places and incidents are a product of the author's imagination and dreams.
Any similarities to the real world, people, places and things are purely coincidental.

Printed in the United States of America by Lightning Source

*Intrepid Souls flying free
and those who dream
of what could be*

For Ayn Rand

# ONE

Tay rose early. The warmth of his blankets called to him as his feet touched the cool wooden floor, but his resolve pried him away from the bed's promise of comfort, despite his aching muscles.

He had been cutting hay for days. The weather was sunny and hot, so the drying would go well if the monumental task could be finished before the rain came. With good fortune and sixteen grueling hour's labor a day, the barn would soon be full of hay—that valuable winter commodity.

Tay had no intention of selling the tall, golden grass once it was dry. His plan was, instead, to trade it to the herd of wild horses, to strike a bargain with them in midwinter, when empty bellies would lend more patience to their temperamental and often flighty personalities.

He made a coffee and fried some eggs. Then, holding the coffee in one hand as he scarfed an egg sandwich, he walked to the barn.

The scythe, to which he was enslaved for a few more days, was hanging inside the door. He stuffed the final bite of sandwich into his mouth and grabbed the tool from the wall in the same motion.

The day was cool, and sun-up was still an hour away. Hanging his straw hat on the garden fence he walked through the entered field, which was nearly half-cut.

Tay had planted twelve acres of high-grade orchard grass along a sweeping bend in the river where the dark, loamy soil ran deep. It had headed up with grain. The tops danced lazily in morning breeze. The sweet scent of it drying soothed the aching muscles in his arms and back.

As he lay into the standing grass with long, sweeping motions of his scythe, he quickly lost track of time. Fluid strokes back and forth flattened the tall grass. To someone watching Tay's smooth motion, it might have appeared an effortless task, yet it strained the limits of his endurance.

After a time, he stopped for a short rest and a drink of water. He wiped beads of sweat off his forehead with a shirtsleeve, looked down river, and saw him: the striking young stallion he had named Eclipse.

The elusive charcoal-grey horse was making his way down the far side of the field, not looking towards the sweating man. Something else was on his mind.

Tay took the beast in visually, remembering a dear friend he had left back on Seven. Seeing this horse was a trip back in time, to the days of his youth before Shadow had grown grey, to a time when Shadow had been full of himself and had legs like loaded steel springs.

Tay was surprised to see the dark horse heading towards the cabin and barn. Normally the animal was skittish and unapproachable, but now he was clearly headed for Tay's home—while Tay was far away, out in the middle of the field.

*What is he doing?* he thought.

Not taking his eyes from the animal, he watched the horse's flawless movement, a motion filled with graceful power. The young beast was poetry in motion, Tay thought, as the horse approached the garden fence, grabbed the straw hat in his mouth, and ran straight back out into the field, towards him.

Stopping a hundred feet away, Eclipse began bobbing his head up and down, his large, dark eyes filled with intelligent humor.

"Give me that, you bugger!"

Tay began walking towards the horse, hoping to save the hat before it was ruined.

As soon as he was near, Eclipse skirted him and ran a bit farther away, letting out a shrill, short squeak.

Tay experienced a stunning sense of déjà vu. Shadow had always made a game of eating his hats, to the point where Tay had quit setting them down and instead wore them on a string, so they could be taken off and rested against his back when not in use. Even then, Shadow would still sometimes make off with them, always letting out the shrill squeak and then playing his humorously frustrating game of keep-away, just as Eclipse was doing now.

Eclipse squeaked again, obviously enjoying the man's frustration. They were close to the river. Mist curled up from the water and rolled ethereally towards them. The horse kept eating the hat. He wasn't actually swallowing, Tay saw, just chewing and bobbing his head up and down, taunting the man as if this were some immense and very funny practical joke.

Tay said, "Wait till this winter when you're starving. I'll remember this!"

The horse turned suddenly, as if spooked, and ran to the water's edge, where it stood hip-deep in a surreal white mist that ebbed between them.

Then he saw her. She was walking upslope from the river's bend, appearing ghostlike out of the mist, gliding through the waves of tall, golden grass. Her haunting eyes—like violet, green, and blue pools—drew upon his soul, compelling his steps to falter so that he stood frozen in place, hypnotized.

She moved towards him and paused next to the horse, which stood still as she took the hat from his mouth. When she moved toward Tay again, Eclipse followed her. Her long, multicolored hair swung with the fluid movement of her hips.

She was here, he thought.

She had come to him before, just as she was walking to him now. The look in her eyes drew his heart into a knot. It beat so loudly Tay feared it might burst.

The horse and the enchantress were steps away. She reached out her arm, offering the hat. The scent of Eclipse's sweat, the aromatic smell of freshly cut hay, and her mystic presence so close he could almost touch her: it was all so familiar. *I have seen her before, in my dreams,* Tay thought. Then, in that moment, Tay started awake.

The shadows of the steel bars cast a familiar, depressing pattern of stripes onto the walls of his cell. Tay counted down. *Four days,* he thought silently. *Four more days.* It was the promise that allowed him to hang on.

# TWO

WITHIN a moon vast distances from Tay' beloved home, the maximum-security prison held him and Alex. It was home to the worst culled from Seven Galaxy society. As in any culture throughout history, some prisoners were innocent of the crimes for which they had been convicted. In the prison, all were observed. Every word was recorded. Out of necessity, Alex and Tay had developed their own personalized sign language to use aboard *Independence*. They spoke verbally of mundane issues, but, in moments of chance, they signed discreetly, developing their plan whenever possible even though they saw each other rarely. Often, they spoke and signed at the same time; multitasking had become an absolute way of life.

Alex had learned that the penal colony's computer system was antiquated and not interfacing well with the newer Seven Galaxies system. He had offered his expertise to help upgrade the aging computer network.

The warden, who knew that Alex's background was intertwined with the historical modifications and upgrades of the Seven Galaxies system, happily consented, especially considering the prison's ever-short budget.

Alex was paid next to nothing and was soon very busy working programming wonders. New and necessary hardware was requisitioned and installed. The system began to work flawlessly, much to the appreciation of the entire colonies' administration body.

As so many savvy programmers have done throughout computer science's thousands of years, Alex programmed in certain system failures. Most of the time, these were minor administrational issues of no great importance, but they created a dire need for his expertise. Many programmed failures were tied to the central timekeeper so that Alex knew exactly when to expect a necessary service call and how to repair it quickly. The reason for this blueprint of system failures had a long-reaching goal.

First and foremost, no other programmer could possibly figure out the deeply buried control language that Alex had written, most of which was secured by encrypted passwords known only to him. More importantly, the colonies administration soon came to realize Alex's indispensability as chief computer tech, and Alex was given great latitude of movement.

All locking systems in the facility had digital keypads with system overrides controlled by the central computer. Fire suppression, food dispensing, indoor garden lighting and watering, and atmospheric control of the many underground levels—along with a host of other functions—were controlled by the central computer: Alex's new friend. Very little was left to chance or to the carelessness of human nature.

Soon Alex had garnered enough favor that he was granted time to visit with Tay. In the early days of their incarceration, they had been separated and held in different parts of the prison. In the new freely allowed visits, they communicated discreetly about Alex's progress with the security systems and his knowledge of Seven Galaxy prisoner transport ships, including the ships' configurations, class, routes, and times of arrival and departure.

Time passed, as did many transport ships that did not meet Tay's criteria for escape. The ship he was looking for needed to have Deep Space jump drive, Full Stealth Cloaking potential, particle acceleration transfer, and a propulsion system that could accommodate magnetic-velocity enhancement.

Eight months went by.

Just when Alex and Tay had become disillusioned with their escape plan and its many complex criteria, Alex came to visit Tay with good news.

Recently he had gleaned information from the penal colony's computer system indicating that an older war-class frigate of some renown had been decommissioned and replaced by a newer vessel. The ship had been relegated to prison transport duties.

"Is she war class?" signed Tay.

"Yes," Alex answered silently.

"Then she has the capability of Deep Space jumps?"

Alex assured him it was true. "Not only Deep Space but also all the necessary components to convert her to mag-grav."

"When will she arrive?" Tay signed.

"First delivery is scheduled to arrive here from Seven Galaxies Seven in three weeks."

"That doesn't leave us much time."

"No. The problem is that although we can take control of the prison transport ship and lock everything down here for twenty-four hours, we will have to do so before she unloads, meaning any prisoners on board will have to be transported along with us to whatever secret destination you chose."

"Will the prisoners be in space sleep?" asked Tay.

Alex nodded. "Yes. It's standard policy to transport them that way; they cause a lot less trouble when they are sleeping like babes."

"Will profiles of their backgrounds be available?"

"Yes. Full psyche and records from earliest childhood until present."

"Then we depart in three weeks. Make all necessary preparations."

"And where are we off to?"

"Our final destination will only be known to me. However, we will be stopping by Seven Galaxies Seven to roust some old and not very dear friends."

"You mean the Twelve?"

"Exactly."

"Will they be accompanying us on our Deep Space jump?"

"Yes. I plan to escort them on a little vacation to a place beyond their wildest imaginations."

"You have been spending way too much time alone thinking about the Twelve, my friend."

Tay ignored Alex's joke. "Will our mission necessitate full Stealth Cloak?"

"It would be more than handy!" added Tay

"And do you foresee any problems?"

"If we can take the prisoners on board with us, none."

"Then we must take them. See it through, Alex."

"Tay, my old friend, I must ask: where can we possibly run that they will not find us?"

"You get us on board that ship with Full Stealth Cloak and magnetic-gravity-enhancement drive, and then ensure there is a break in the legislatures' personnel shields so we can grab our twelve friends. Let me worry about the rest. I assure you, I memorized our plot to the destination long ago."

"Okay, amigo, I am at your service. Your wishes shall become reality."

"By the way, I almost forgot to ask, what is the name of our new ship?" Tay asked.

"*Intrepid One*," signed Alex, smiling.

"The *Intrepid One*?"

"Yes. She is an old craft. Admiral Gor commanded her as a young officer when he was thrown into the Twenty-Seven Years War, not long after graduating the Academy."

"Yes, I am very familiar with the history of *Intrepid One*. TyGor directed the defeat of Xeries Eight in the final battle. *Intrepid One* came in under Full Cloak after lying in wait behind a planet's moon. In the split second when the Nesdian shields faltered, he launched a five-directional barrage and annihilated the enemy. Such strategic accuracy and timing had never before been accomplished in the history of war."

Both men smiled, as if reliving a moment shared with the admiral. The young men felt honored to have worked with him.

"We served under him, Tay," signed Alex, a slight sheen of moisture in his eyes. "He would not want us rotting away here."

"It was the admiral who gave me the location for our new safe haven," Tay signed. "A place where we will be safe and never found."

"You have to be shitting me?" Alex's hands could not fly fast enough to ask the necessary questions.

"Not in the least. The admiral has opened the door to our freedom," Tay responded. "Just get us out of here."

Alex's eyes brightened. He signed, "Three weeks."

"Tell me, Alex, what recent upgrades does *Intrepid One* possess? Surely in the past two hundred and ten years, she has been retrofitted?"

"Yes. Two years ago, in preparation for the expectation of a long drawn out Nesdian war, she was brought completely up to modern specs. Her configuration is slightly old fashioned, but that will in no way affect her speed under mag-grav."

TayGor thought of his grandfather's old ship, and how his grandfather had laid out their course and destination in the manner of a riddle. *You're watching over me,* he thought. *I can feel it. Thanks pa.*

# THREE

Alex had planned the trip to freedom flawlessly. When the transport ships delivered prisoners that would live at the facility, they were in deep sleep, and the pilot and navigator would disembark the vessel and visit with the administrators and guards in the main command center for a while.

Any small emergency malfunction in the complicated air-supply system or in the water, fire prevention, and lighting systems would automatically sound an alarm. All prisoners would then be quickly locked down, and those who were in jeopardy due to the system failure would be moved into safe blocks while the problem was diagnosed and repaired. When this happened, all guards had free time and would converge in the control center as well.

The facility ran on a system of set rules, and Alex intended to use this system to his advantage.

Once *Intrepid One* had docked and the pilot and navigator were free of the ship, a system-failure alarm sounded. Fortuitously, Tay's block was one of those where the prisoners were considered in danger, and so the prisoners in that block were diligently moved to a block much nearer the loading bay to the ship. After the guards had finished the chore of moving the prisoners, they went to the command center to make good use of free time and socialize with the others.

At once, the locks on all doors between the blocks clicked tight. The command-center doors auto-bolted as well.

For some odd reason that no one but Alex could figure out, the system failure had affected the locking mechanisms facility-wide. For a brief second, the door lock on Tay's block snapped open. Tay, who knew what to expect, was standing by the door. He stepped out and closed it quickly behind him before the bolt went back into auto-lock mode. The ship was a hundred meters away, with no one but Alex in the space between. He was beaming.

Tay broke into a dash and grabbed Alex's arm as they moved towards the air lock. Before the door closed, they turned and waved to the group of astonished guards and administrators locked behind the bulletproof glass of the command center. Many of their faces were purple with disbelief as they pounded frantically on the windows. Many mouths could be seen aping words, but little sound emanated from the enclosure.

Aboard *Intrepid One*, Tay waited until they were clear of the prison-bay loading lock and then called, "Clear! Hatches closing! Secure and prepare; deep jump in eight seconds."

Alex clambered into the engineer's seat and quickly strapped in.

As the eight seconds counted down to zero, Tay thought, *A ship's helm has never looked so good.* One moment the prison was off the starboard side, and the next it was gone.

"Full Stealth, Alex," Tay said. "Let's surprise the shit out of those slimy bastards."

The jump to Seven would take less than four hours. Alex had shut down prison communication and overridden all manual controls. All prison doors were locked down tight. Good fortune prevailing, they would arrive at Seven undetected before the breakout was reported.

Their timing was perfect. The legislative hall would be in session, and the Twelve would be in special chambers, isolated from the other politicians. Alex had managed to get session schedules downloaded and, fortunately, *Intrepid*'s arrival coincided with a very long one. The plan was to sweep by Seven, pausing momentarily to grab the Twelve, and then jump under Full Stealth Cloak to their final destination, some six years away.

Before he had become a prisoner, Alex had been involved in the design and implementation of the complex shielding programs that protected the legislative hall. Knowing the inner workings of the program from his old days gave him the ability to weave a strand of particle matter through the complex security web that was otherwise thought to be impenetrable.

If Tay and Alex's design worked, the twelve politicians who had taken over rule of Seven Galaxy's vast society and then wrongfully imprisoned Alex and Tay would no longer be in control. Instead, they would be taken along for the ride and then dropped in a carefully chosen area as fitting punishment for their crimes.

Alex ran a systems check throughout the ship, making sure that all was in order and that they would have no unexpected surprises. He gave Tay two thumbs up.

The plan was to broadcast Admiral Gor's retirement speech as they jumped from Seven's gravity. Gor had beseeched the populace to clear the wreckage and rebuild the Dome of Wisdom, but, upon the admiral's death, Ventras had ordered all work on the project to stop before it had even fully begun.

Tay felt that the admiral's desire to have the Dome rebuilt had been for stronger reasons than mere nostalgia. In an attempt to honor his grandfather's wishes, they would send the broadcast, and then run for their lives, with Ventras and his eleven cronies locked securely in *Intrepid*'s brig. Tay smiled to himself and prayed that all would play out without a hitch.

As the time to arrival at Seven raced by, Tay's mind raced as well. His eight months confined to a disturbingly small and depressing cell, only being let out briefly to eat and exercise, had given him thinking time—and lots of it. His grandfather, Admiral Gor, had dedicated his life to selflessly fighting to uphold the morals, laws, and freedoms of their vast society. Tay suspected that in the end, for everything he had accomplished, he had been murdered by a group of dirty, grasping politicians who lusted after power.

Tay, in the countless hours of his incarceration, imagined the spineless creatures salivating over his grandfather's death. With the guardian and protector of Seven Galaxies and the Fifteen out of the way, and the Dome of Wisdom leveled by the Nesdian's final assault—the manipulated asteroid strike—those corrupt politicians now possessed ultimate control. It made his stomach roll with sickness to think of it, but shortly those responsible would be his. He would have ultimate power over their destiny, a destiny they'd had a hand in creating through their despicable acts.

He remembered how his grandfather had wanted so fervently to retire and spend his last days on the farm with the woman from the reception and decorations banquet: the one with the striking blue eyes. Tay could still see the admiral and Serene walking through the crowded banquet, illuminated as by a brilliant ray of sunlight. They had seemed to shine from within.

The scene had been held as if in freeze-frame and played in slow motion countless times in his dreams and waking hours over the past year. One picture was etched indelibly into his mind: Tay's last glimpse of his beloved grandfather alive. Each time the priceless memory played in his sorrow-filled head, Tay wondered what had happened to her: that woman with the striking blue eyes.

# FOUR

Serene had spent eight months treading an exasperating path of misdirection caused by inept government workers, rules, and regulations. Yet here she stood; persistence had paid off. Soon, her promise to her beloved Admiral Gor, the last wish uttered upon his dying breath, would be fulfilled. In her hand, she held Admiral Gor's written order to transfer the dead Nesdian Regent Xrisen's property to Zuzahna.

It was not Tay who had transferred the fortune, as the charges against him stated. Why the attorney representing Tay had not been able to subpoena the document and present it as evidence, she could only wonder. However, with the evidence in hand, the charges of treason would have to be dropped. The judiciary was obligated to reopen the case and hear Tay's appeal.

In times past, as special assistant to the Ancient and to the Fifteen as a group, she had been swept into the special legislative chambers without waiting. But now, with the Fifteen missing and presumed dead, she had become just another citizen. Serene felt fortunate to be admitted at all.

She waited anxiously in the foyer outside the chambers. She had been admitted before to expound upon Tay's wrongful imprisonment, but not without many frustrating delays and postponements. Each of the other times, her requests to free Tay had been ignored. Today would be different, she thought.

The secretary called her name and told her that the Twelve could see her for a few moments only. The woman looked disdainful, obviously enjoying Serene's demotion of stature.

Serene kept her head erect. Technically, her position still held, even though the Fifteen were absent. The problem was that no one else in the current government realized or acknowledged that she remained special assistant to the Fifteen in absentia; without their force of presence, she was treated commonly.

The huge double doors auto-opened as she neared. She strode through the massive archway and stopped before the twelve politicians who now controlled Seven Galaxies.

Ventras scowled, and Derian's ferret-like eyes flitted nervously around the room. Belvidius, on the other hand, seemed asleep. His head drooped onto the massive folds of fat encircling his neck like rows of sweating doughnuts. The others appeared indifferent, some yawning, some reading papers or ignoring her completely.

Ventras spoke. "Serene, with all due respect, we have entertained your requests on two previous occasions. We are extremely busy and cannot keep seeing you. I am afraid we are obligated by law to deny your request to hear TayGor's appeal. He has been convicted of treason.

As a traitor and enemy of the people, his appeal is in vain. We cannot hear it."

"Dear sirs, I have with me today a certified copy of the order to transfer the dead Nesdian Regent's property to Zuzahna Duhcat," Serene said, brandishing the paper. "Admiral Gor ordered the transfer while still in Deep Space, in accordance with ancient Maritime Law. I assure you, Tay is no traitor; this document proves it. The supposed order was the basis for the many charges against him. With this evidence, his innocence is established. His appeal must be opened and the facts of the case must be re-scrutinized by a competent judiciary instead of a military tribunal."

"I regret to inform you," Ventras said, "that it is too late to present evidence at this time. The document in question should have been presented at his trial. It cannot be entered now, after the fact." Ventras' eyes narrowed, gauging Serene's reaction.

"Surely if you seek Truth and Justice, you will authorize the reopening of the case and look at the facts in the clear light of day! Seven Galaxy's Constitution demands it!" Serene spoke with authority; her belief in the supreme law of the land was unshaken.

"Serene, Seven Galaxies is changing," Ventras said. "Today is a momentous occasion. Before the twelve of us is a redraft of the antiquated and beleaguered document referred to as Seven Galaxy's Constitution. With the sweeping changes our signatures will momentarily be authorizing, the population of Seven Galaxies becomes not billions of individual sovereigns but a congealed mass that can be easily policed and—if necessary—forcefully controlled. No longer will unbridled freedom of speech prevail. No longer will the right to demonstrate openly or privately exist. Most importantly, we will be using a tribunal of justice instead of our outdated and senile judiciary. We, the Twelve, the new leaders of Seven Galaxies, will be in ultimate control." Ventras smiled, gloating over his apparent victory.

"With you, Ventras, as the new totalitarian dictator?" Serene asked, frowning.

Ventras fell silent.

"This is completely absurd!" she cried. "You can't possibly think the people will stand for this, can you?"

"Serene, I would be careful. We have allowed you your freedom, hoping that you would eventually come to your senses and drop this shortsighted quest. What is done is done; history has been set in motion. You cannot change what the twelve of us have worked so fervently to accomplish. Drop this folly. I will see to it that you are placed well and have some status. While your position may certainly be less prestigious than your former one, it will still yield a lavish and comfortable lifestyle for you."

"You wish me to sell out? To join you?" she said, already shaking her head in refusal.

"Joining us would be wise, Serene. You know the old adage: if you can't beat them…"

"I am special assistant to the Fifteen in absentia! Upon their return, I will report your treasonous conduct! Me, join a pack of vipers, the likes of which have not been assembled since ancient Earth? I hardly think so!"

"Serene, you forget yourself!" Ventras said, pounding his fist onto the table before him. "The Fifteen were pulverized beneath the Dome of Wisdom's ruins! Have you forgotten the asteroid? Are you losing your mind? I have warned you for the last time, woman. Calm yourself! Respect this governmental body and swear allegiance to us. It is time to quit your confrontational stance."

"Never! Take my life, my voice, and my freedom! I will never swear loyalty to you, you usurping, filthy, grasping scum!" Serene was livid. Losing her normally cool composure, she swore the oath she had taken upon accepting her position within the Dome of Wisdom: "To the people of Seven Galaxies, and to their freedom and welfare, I dedicate my life."

Ventras called for a guard and then said, "Serene, you are under arrest!"

Suddenly, the hall began to flicker and fade. Startled, the Twelve looked at each other, right before they, and Serene, disappeared.

The guards rushed into the empty hall moments later. All wondered where the Twelve had disappeared to, but none came close to imagining the truth: the Twelve, and Serene, were all in particle-accelerated transfer. Momentarily, they reappeared, safely contained within the brig of Tay's new ship, *Intrepid One*.

# FIVE

Alex and Tay were both shocked at seeing Serene materialize along with the despised Twelve in the brig of *Intrepid One*. Alex deftly stroked the controls, and she disappeared and re-materialized for a second time between him and Tay.

The Twelve went ballistic, screaming colorful strings of profanity and shouting berserk insults and threats.

"Alex, activate the silence mode until the prisoners calm themselves."

Alex touched the controls again, and the commotion was silenced.

Tay turned to Serene and said, "I saw you with the admiral at the welcome banquet when we returned from the war against Nesdia. We were never introduced. I am Tay, TyGor's grandson. This is my partner, Alex."

Serene, obviously confused and visibly shaken, took a moment to gather her thoughts. "Your grandfather and I were very close," she finally said. "I was with him when he so suddenly passed. My name is Serene."

"What happened, Serene? He was so healthy?"

"The death was explained to me as a cerebral hemorrhage, but when I investigated further and read the coroner's report, I found that there was severe cerebral edema, an unexplained swelling of the brain. Normally, that would be associated with trauma, such as a massive and brutal impact to the head. In my opinion, the explanation of your grandfather's death is not complete." Serene broke down in tears.

Tay held her for a moment in consolation, his eyes watering as well. Attempting to change channels and move from the dark mood that had settled upon the three, he asked, "Serene, what were you doing in the special legislative chambers?"

"Upon your grandfather's last breath, he asked me to promise I would do everything possible to free you. I was in the hall asking the Twelve to reconsider your appeal, because new evidence not made available at your trial has proved that your conduct was in no way treasonous. The Twelve had just refused my request when we were taken from the hall. What is all this about, Tay? How did you get here?"

"We've escaped, and we are taking the Twelve with us. You must come too. We left Seven's orbit minutes ago, and now we are in a Deep Space jump, heading to a place far away, where we will be safe. I cannot risk going back to Seven; we could be arrested again. We can't go back, so you must come with us. I'm sorry," he said, feeling genuinely bad for this unexpected circumstance.

"Tay, I have nothing holding me on Seven," Serene said. "With the Dome of Wisdom destroyed and the Fifteen missing, my position is no longer recognized. I have no family, and my soul mate has passed from the physical plane. I am mourning his loss and feel lost myself." She began weeping again.

"I understand your grief," Tay said, trying to console her.

Struggling to speak between broken breaths, Serene said, "You look so much like your grandfather! When you held me a moment ago, it was as if I were in his arms again. Oh, how I miss him!" Her anguish was evident.

"You are not alone, Serene. All within Seven Galaxies mourn his loss. Of course, some of us feel it much more deeply because of our intimacy with him." Tay turned to Alex. "Show Serene to the Diplomatic Quarters, and see that she is comfortable. Then come to the bridge. I wish to broadcast Admiral Gor's farewell address to all of Seven Galaxy's people. Perhaps they will remember and honor their promise to him and rebuild the Dome of Wisdom in our absence."

Alex nodded and led the sobbing Serene to quiet quarters.

Tay walked up to the cell holding the vile Twelve. "Welcome," he said, looking Ventras square in the eyes.

Ventras looked frightened. The drastic change of events was beginning to sink in, and it would continue to do so over the hours, months, and years to come. Tay spun crisply and walked towards the bridge, smiling softly.

# SIX

VOLTRANS watched the break in transmission with astonishment. Moments before, he had received an unbelievable report from the security task force delegated to protecting the special legislative chambers: the special Twelve had just disappeared, along with one "Serene," who Voltrans knew, from vast past experience, was the Ancients' personal assistant. At least, she had been before the Dome of Wisdom was destroyed.

Pondering the dilemma he now faced watching a haunting vid-clip of the late admiral, who was beseeching the vast populace of all of Seven Galaxies to give the sacred bond of their word and dedicate themselves to rebuilding the Dome Of Wisdom. Ventras had halted work on the project the morning after Seven Galaxies learned of Admiral Gor's untimely death. As Seven Galaxies mourned, the promise of a combined consciousness had been lost in the midst of tears, sorrow, and darkness.

There seemed too much coincidence in the new turn of events. Ventras had gripped control, wringing it until there was little to do but follow the powerful man's orders. Voltrans, attempting desperately to break out of the chaos and re-establish order after the Nesdian's manipulated asteroid strike, had been at his wits end. He had worked untiringly, as had his staff. The planet was operating as a stifled shadow, a fleeting memory of what it had once been. All this flashed through his mind.

The dome had not been rebuilt. The wreckage had not been cleared. Now, with the disappearance of Ventras and his pack of cronies, Voltrans had become the leader of not only Seven but also the union of Seven Galaxies. Voltrans sank down into his favorite chair and contemplated the meaning of the disaster that could, in the blue light of day, be turned into very favorable circumstances to help Seven and her galaxies beyond.

Voltrans thought of Mick, his beloved and trusted friend who had saved Seven by breaking the potentially planetary-fatal asteroid into many small shards. The Nesdians had hoped the asteroid would completely destroy the cultural, spiritual, and governmental hub of Seven Galaxies, but Mick had played a key role in preventing this annihilation.

Who better than Mick, thought Voltrans. He knew instinctively that Mick was the one. Mick had been born into action, but now he was a man devastated by his handicap.

Given the opportunity to rebuild the Dome of Wisdom, Mick would once again have purpose. Surely, Voltrans thought, that would bring his best friend out of the depression he had been spiraling down into ever since he'd lost his legs.

As Voltrans contemplated the possibilities, a knock came at his closed office door.

"Yes?"

Dadian walked in and closed the door behind him. "Sir!"

"Dadian, good morning."

"You have word of the disappearance of the special Twelve, and of Serene?"

Voltrans nodded.

"And the admiral's speech?"

"Yes, Dadian, I watched it."

"We have no idea where it came from, sir. None of the networks had control of their systems until the message was delivered. What do you make of it, sir?"

Voltrans seemed to be in deep contemplation and did not answer immediately. Dadian was surprised by his commander's reaction. Behind Voltrans' normally stoic mask, Dadian saw the fleeting glimmer of emotion. Was it joy? Sorrow? Relief? Happiness? Or all four. His eyes seemed to be far away.

"There is more, sir."

"Spill it."

"Sir, moments after we received the transmission of the admiral's retirement speech, a distress signal was received from the penal moon. It seems, sir, that there has been an escape of gigantic proportions. Two prisoners apparently working in concert were able to take control of the colony's computer system. They locked down the complex and escaped on a transport ship that was bringing a full load of convicts to the facility."

"Which transport, Dadian?"

"*Intrepid One*, sir."

"Shit!"

"Is she still fully capable?"

"Yes, sir."

"Triple shit!"

"It gets better sir."

"Oh *really*?"

Dadian broke into a smile and paused for effect.

"Tell me! Don't just dangle a fragment of information. You know how I hate that!"

Dadian's smile transformed into a suppressed smirk. "Sir, from the info we received, there were two people responsible for the break-out. These were the only two to leave the facility. It appears that one was responsible for the computer and the other for piloting the ship."

"I can see from your expression that you have the answer to this riddle. Will you now grace me with the conclusion?" Voltrans said, impatient.

"Sir, TayGor appears to be piloting the vessel. Alex Delanport is the other person who went aboard."

Voltrans' forehead wrinkled in shocked disbelief. "Are you sure of all this?"

"Yes, sir. We just received the report."

Dadian handed the brief to his commander, and Voltrans quickly scanned the document.

"Kind of interesting, don't you think, sir? TayGor escaping aboard his grandfather's command vessel? The same vessel responsible for the defeat of Xeries Eight in the final days of the Twenty-Seven Years War?"

"Very!"

"Also interesting is that those responsible for Tay and Alex being imprisoned have vanished from the special legislative chambers. Considering it is a hardened facility, sir, that should have been a feat of impossibility."

"Yes! So it would have seemed. Where is the ship now?"

"We glimpsed her at the same instant the Twelve disappeared, and then she vanished, sir—without a trace."

"That young man ... he is a bit too much like the admiral," said Voltrans. "I hope, with all deference, that Seven hasn't seen the last of him. And I *also* pray he's not too pissed off! Do you understand what a man like him could do with a ship like Intrepid One?"

"Just about anything he wanted to, sir."

"Yes, that's what concerns me."

"Sir, I believe Tay is running for his freedom. He is loyal to Seven and his grandfather. I don't believe he would ever stoop to harming Seven Galaxies. He *has* what he came for: the Twelve."

"Yes. I find that I pity those twelve scurvy bastards, even though I should feel nothing of the sort after the games they played with the reconstruction fund. Seize all their assets! I don't want word of this out. We can't have their family members attempting to play another shell game with the credits. We will conduct a comprehensive investigative audit and release what is rightfully due to their heirs."

"Heirs? Sir, do you believe the Twelve won't be coming back?"

Voltrans said nothing. He only looked at the smiling Dadian like a father about to reprimand his son. Lifting an eyebrow, he said, "Get back to work, you smart ass! You already know I believe they won't be back."

Voltrans looked at his watch, scribbled a memo to the warden of the penal moon, and thought again of Mick. He decided to go and see him straight away. He left his office and hurried down the stairs to the parking level below.

As his autocar streaked out over the city, Voltrans looked down on the massive reconstruction project underway. The project of repairing the asteroid's damage was just getting started. Work was evident nearly everywhere—everywhere except for an elevated area of land: the hill the Dome of Wisdom used to command. On the hill above the city, it was still and silent. The rubble lay as it had for nearly a year, undisturbed. *Not for long,* Voltrans thought, as he slid the craft deftly towards the ground in front of Mick's place.

He climbed from the vehicle and strode towards the door, which was ajar. He knocked lightly, walked through, and closed the door behind him. Glancing around the room, he saw Mick out on the veranda, sitting in the wheelchair with his back towards Voltrans. At the sound of the door closing, Mick spun the chair and took in his friend without saying a word. His eyes were lackluster. He had grown a beard on his normally clean-shaven face.

"Hey, Mick, how you getting on?"

"Not worth a shit, Volt! Oh, I got my medal and my pension. I got people coming to visit me regularly, all with the same pitying look on their face ... a look I understand. A look that says I'm worthless. Hell, if I had the means, I'd roll this piece of crap chair to the highest cliff and take to flying. That's how I'm doing."

"Well, I have a project for you. Something that may perk you up. Want to hear what it is?"

For the first time in their short meeting, Voltrans saw a spark of the old Mick. Then it faded.

"Mick, I want to rebuild the Dome. Ventras and the special Twelve have disappeared. TayGor has escaped from the penal moon with *Intrepid One*. We caught a flash of her for a nano when she dropped shield above Seven. Then the Twelve were gone!"

"Don't shit me! There's no way to escape that burg. Never been done; can't be done. And the special legislative chambers are shielded. No way a strand of particle matter could rise from there."

"Well, Mick, it happened. Alex Delanport is with Tay-Gor. Evidently, he was working as *the* computer-tech at the prison. They managed it, and they have *Intrepid One*!"

"She's a sweet ride, Ventras. I supervised her retrofit. You better hope to hell Tay isn't gunning for your ass." Mick started laughing and kept on for a long time. "He's gotten to the vile Twelve! He's taken *Intrepid One*? Shit, that boy could be the damndest pirate if he was inclined. I don't envy Ventras; he's probably pissing blood out in the great black vacuum right now. Christ, I wish I could have seen the look on that bastard's face when he realized his jig was up. Hoo boy! Delanport's with him you say?"

"Yes."

"That kid! Hell, he's so damned gifted … I've never seen anyone like him. He worked under me for a time while we were developing mining-techno. Those two! What a team!"

"The project, Mick."

"Project?"

"The Dome."

"The Dome of Wisdom?"

"Yes."

"Volt, I appreciate what you're trying to do, but what good would I be? I can't climb a ladder; I can't deal with rough ground. I understand you're trying to get me out of the funk I've been living in since the … accident, but—"

A knock sounded at the door. Both men looked towards the sound. Mick said, "What in the hell now?"

"Mick, all I've told you … it's Red under Black. Should I get the door?"

"Yeah, let's see what they want to sell me today."

Voltrans walked through the apartment and quickly opened the door. Mick followed him.

A man with dark wavy hair stood outside. His eyes were piercing—deep pools of brown flecked with gold. In each hand, he held a long composite case, too long to be mere briefcases.

"I have some articles for Mick Mullowney. May I come in?" He spoke confidently. His voice carried an old world inflection of someone well-traveled, and his words were spoken formally, with the slightest hint of aristocracy.

"Whatever you're peddling, I ain't buyin', so there's really no point," Mick said. "Might as well take it down the street."

The visitor smiled disarmingly. In that moment, Mick softened, glanced at Voltrans, and said, "Come. Sit down."

Voltrans thought that with *that* smile, the man possessed powerful persuasion and would immediately be offered the most generous hospitality anywhere in Seven Galaxies.

"Thank you both," the visitor said.

They moved to the veranda, and the stranger sat down in a chair next to Mick. Voltrans and Mick were silent.

"I have a gift for you, Mr. Mullowney."

"Call me Mick … please."

"Very well. Mick, I have something for you." He bent gracefully and opened one of the cases. When the lid rose, it exposed the surprise within.

Voltrans and Mick stared at what appeared to be a well-muscled human leg and foot. It was a right leg. At the upper thigh was a dark hole, as black as an unlit tunnel. The stranger opened the second case and there lay the matching leg, ankle, and foot.

"These were made for you. They will fit perfectly. I am giving them to you, along with a lifetime service contract. It is my way of thanking you. For what you did … for breaking the mammoth 'stroid and saving this planet and its people. Here, if you don't mind, I will show you how they are worn and how they operate. It is really quite simple."

The man slipped the artificial limbs over the stubs of Micks legs and pushed a button on the top and the side of each. The legs shrunk slightly over his thighs and melded almost perfectly with the color of his skin.

"Do they hurt you at all?"

"No. Not a bit."

"Will you stand for me please?"

"Will they hold me? I haven't walked in over eight months."

"I assure you, they will."

Mick stood up easily, and the stranger held one of his arms to steady him.

"These limbs are state of the art robotics. They will signature to your movements automatically; no calibration is necessary. You may begin walking now."

"Are you serious? I've tried some of these new-fangled contraptions from physical re-hab, but they left me on my face every time. I finally gave up and have been sitting on my butt ever since."

"I will steady you until you are okay on your own. A few steps please. They take a moment to program themselves, so we will take it easy. No tap-dancing . . . yet."

Mick took a few steps and broke into a giant grin. "Hey, these are really something! Pinch me, Volt; I know I'm dreaming!"

Voltrans reached over and pinched his friend's arm.

"Hey, that hurt! Did you have to be so rough?" Micky laughed good-naturedly. "Let me try a few steps on my own."

The man released his arm. "Yes, of course. I believe you are ready."

Mick walked easily around the veranda and then stopped abruptly and looked at the stranger who had brought him freedom from the chair.

"I don't believe this! These things are great." He took a short little hop and began laughing like a child. As soon as he ran out of steam, he asked the stranger, "Where in heaven's name did you get these?"

"I made them . . . for you. It was the least I could do. I love this planet dearly, and you stopped the asteroid. Without your efforts, this planet and all on it would certainly be dead. Thank you, Mick."

"You . . . *you* made these?"

"Yes."

"I am at a distinct disadvantage, mister. I don't even know your name."

The dark-haired stranger smiled, his deep brown eyes reflecting the sunlight. A bit of grey showed at his temples, adding a distinguished look to his youthful face.

He bowed lightly, formally, and straightened again. "Enricco Duhcat. The pleasure, I assure you, *is* all mine."

Silence fell. It was a quiet so complete, each man could hear his own heartbeat.

"I have a favor to ask of you two: please, clear the south wing first. Once the rubble is removed, fence off the area and post three guards around the clock. No one is to go in or out of the enclosure. The guards must remain on the outside of the fence. Do you understand?"

"Of course," Mick and Voltrans said, echoing each other. "But why?"

"I expect some old friends of ours to appear there. I believe they are safe on the other side of the portal."

"The portal?" Volt asked, confounded.

"Yes. The portal the Dome of Wisdom was built to protect. It is . . . sacred. It must not be entered by those who have not been accepted into the Dome. I am entrusting you both with its safety until the Dome is rebuilt and the Fifteen rule Seven Galaxies once more. I must take my leave now. If your new limbs act up, I will know. They will be corrected from afar. General Voltrans, a pleasure indeed." Duhcat shook Voltrans' hand firmly. "Mick," he said, shaking Micky's hand before making his way to the open door.

Mick and Voltrans stood in baffled silence.

# SEVEN

One of many tasks Tay had delegated to Alex was the scan of all prisoners aboard *Intrepid One*. Afterwards, he was to compile a brief summary of their backgrounds and create a list of potential candidates for rehabilitation. These people would join their small party upon landing the Virgin. The project would take days.

During Alex's speed-scan of the prisoner's names, two surprises jumped off the screen. The first was Zuzahna Duhcat. Alex's heart leapt. Tay had been feeling ever guilty about Zuzahna's imprisonment and about Ventras' promise that Tay and Zuzahna would spend their lives in the same penal colony but never be allowed to see one another. Alex couldn't wait to break the news to Tay.

The second prisoner who caught Alex's attention was Denali—no last name: the prisoner convicted of assassinating Admiral Gor. Alex couldn't believe his eyes. What would Tay do if he knew his beloved grandfather's killer was sleeping aboard the ship? Alex didn't know what kind of reaction to expect from his friend. Struggling with the quandary, he took a break from his desk and went to Denali's sleep chamber to look upon the admiral's assassin.

Alex physically started when he saw her. The sleeping woman was absolutely mesmerizing. She had red-blond hair flowing about her shoulders, wide-set eyes—closed due to her forced slumber—and a few freckles on her fair white skin.

*How*? he thought. How could such an enchanting creature, who looked like an innocent farm girl, be so utterly coldblooded? In that moment, Alex determined to investigate deeply the record of her past experiences, and whatever threads had woven her life. He desperately desired to understand this woman.

Alex went to Tay and told him of Zuzahna's presence aboard the ship. Tay's face lit up like a child on Christmas morning. "Where is she, Alex? Let's go and free her right now!"

They walked the decks and corridors towards Zuzahna's sleeping chamber as Alex contemplated the best way to mention Denali. He feared that if Tay knew of Denali's presence on board, he might possibly, in a fit of grief-filled rage, dispose of her. Alex chose to bury the knowledge of her existence aboard *Intrepid One* for now and keep her crime to himself. He would tell Tay when he knew more about her past.

The two of them did not speak as they walked side by side towards Zuzahna. Both were deep in thought: Alex was sorting through the quandary of Admiral Gor's killer, and Tay seemed overwrought with joy at the news of Zuzahna being on board.

They stopped before Zuzahna's sleep chamber. Tay looked upon her, eyes wide in disbelief. "Isn't she something, Alex?"

Alex, his mind still on Denali, was brought back to the present by Tay's question. He answered distractedly, "Oh . . . yes, she surely is."

Tay dialed up the hibernation mode, and soon Zuzahna's chest began to rise and fall at a normal rate. Her heartbeat on the monitor climbed, and within ten minutes, the flutter of her lashes had Tay perched on the edge of a fantastic coincidence of destiny. They had been reunited by a force much greater than themselves. Perhaps, Alex thought, it was the powerful and extreme desire to see each other that had created this event—the magnetism that had drawn the paths of their lives together once more.

Tay keyed in the code for the security curtain, shutting it down. He reached for Zuzahna's hand, still cool from the lower heart rate. Zuzahna stirred at his touch and opened her immense dark eyes. Even in the dimness of the sleep chamber, Alex could see the golden flecks. They sparkled like jewels.

In a fit of utter disbelief, Zuzahna called for him, her voice dusty from being unused.

"Tay . . . ? Darling? Am I dreaming again or is it really you? Please, oh please do not leave me again! Speak! Caress me like you once did. Tell me this is not another dream."

"It's me. We have escaped. We took this transport ship and found you aboard," Tay said.

"What?" She appeared confused and suspicious, as if she expected the man before her to be a fleeting apparition of subconscious desire, not warm flesh and heated emotion.

"Alex and I took the prison transport ship. We have escaped the penal moon. Alex found you among the roster of prisoners. He is right here beside me."

Zuzahna looked from Tay to Alex, and immediately her eyes welled full of tears, her entire body quivering from a mixture of disbelief, relief, and doubt.

"I have dreamed of you, Tay, near constantly," she said. "Sometimes in the visions, you come as you have now. Invariably, you are taken and I am left with my heart swept into a blackness that engulfs me totally. If not for my forced sleep, I would have walked to an airlock and jettisoned myself! How dark my days have been!"

"There now," Tay said. "All is well; I am here." With that, he slid his arms beneath her and lifted her from the sleep chamber. He carried her away, towards his private quarters, not bothering to look back at Alex's shocked face.

Alex, in a tumult of dazed thoughts about all that had transpired in the past fifteen minutes, found himself drawn, as if by a magnetic pull, towards Denali's sleeping form. He could not help himself. *I must look at her again*, he thought.

# EIGHT

Time passed aboard *Intrepid One* as her speed increased daily, pulled by Mag-Grav. Alex had calculated the journey to be six years; without the innovative drive system, it would have been twelve.

Alex had started studying Denali's backstory out of interest, but this soon became an all-consuming passion that approached an obsession. Reading of her childhood trauma at the hands of a perverted foster father, Alex was shocked. Her subsequent retribution against the man and his wife opened his eyes wide in disbelief.

In her ninth year, a dear friend of Denali's had unexplainably fallen to her death from the orphanage's rooftop. A few days later, an older girl from the same institution was found floating, apparently drowned, in the nearby river. An accident? he thought. Or could the girl's death have been tied to Denali's trademark vengeance.

A footnote at the bottom of the account read: "The orphanage's administrator reported that one of the girls was suspected of possessing a key to the rooftop; this key had previously disappeared from a janitor's keyring. The rooftop door was always locked. The mystery is in how Issabell, a child so small, could have fallen over a solid railing wall higher than herself. Could Denali have taken revenge for her young friend's suspicious death?"

Alex learned that Denali, as a young woman, excelled in sports, physics, computers, and science. He also read of the curious death of four other young women, bred on the streets and incarcerated in the same block as Denali. The four young street toughs had allegedly been brutally assaulted by Denali. After that, the record was blank. Denali had mysteriously disappeared, vanishing both from sight and from all government records.

The mystery stimulated Alex to look further, even without authorization. He would hack secure government sites if necessary. He checked *Intrepid One*'s data bank and found, to his great surprise, records unaltered from her time as a warship. She had, in the bowels of her memory, clues and secrets—pieces of a puzzle still incomplete yet taking shape.

The hidden period of Denali's life became Alex's primary focus when he wasn't working on official duties aboard *Intrepid One*. Tay remained unaware of Alex's obsession.

Denali lay in forced sleep, unaware that the admiral's grandson was walking by the sleep chamber on a daily basis. She slept fitfully, her subconscious fighting the inevitable and looking for avenues of escape. She had been trapped and then funneled into incarceration. Her life had been lost to a lonely cell where she would spend endless months and years, kicking herself for having been blindsided by Ventras so easily.

Alex, in hopes of finding something more on Denali, had entered the Seven Galaxies UIA files: the source of tightly guarded information accessible to few. After coming up with nothing, he took off his glasses and rubbed his tired eyes with the back of his hands. Thoughts and hunches rubbed together. Something nagged at him. He put his glasses back on and returned to his dogged search. He kept thinking of the mysterious Duhcat, a man about which little was known, yet who seemed to be some sort of ancient Patriarch of Seven Galaxies.

Perhaps, Alex thought, Denali was somehow tied to Duhcat. Could it be possible? The man was a vapor-trailing legend. No one even knew if he were still alive. Some said he was immortal, others said he had sold his soul to the dark side, still others said that he held the keys to life-rejuvenation and had lived over three millenniums. All farfetched, Alex thought. However, as he searched the UIA file on Duhcat, the legend became more believable minute by minute.

Extraordinary, Alex thought. Duhcat was a man whose intellectual property had first allowed Deep Space jumps more than three thousand years ago. He was a man whose innovations in deep-space mining and catapulting had won him a fortune greater than any previously known. A man who had ancient Earth begging for strategic minerals and precious metals previously depleted and necessary for Earth's sustenance at that time in history. A man who milked the evil billionaires of ancient Earth for their wealth in exchange for youth. A man who then invested that unheralded wealth in a dream he had long held fast in his amazing mind: Duhcat's dream had become Seven Galaxies. Duhcat had become a legend; his exploits were legendary.

Alex began searching for anything that would string the two mysteries together. A moment later, something flashed up on the screen and sent his mind reeling. The article began: "Nothing has been found that would support the suspicion that Duhcat has his hand in these cleansings, yet the unmistakable flair of each press release smacks of his signature."

Alex followed the trail backwards.

Apparently, over the course of the past fourteen and a half centuries, certain ruthless and powerful people had been slain. Many of the dead were mob types, crooked politicians, or industry moguls who were polluting the environment, colluding to create monopolies that would suppress cleaner technology, or simply abusing a workforce—wringing fortunes from the unfortunate and mistreated workers.

Moments after the deaths, an untraceable break-in transmission would be broadcast advising Seven Galaxy citizens of the erasure, or in some cases of the multiple erasures. Then would come a list of crimes perpetrated against the peoples of Seven Galaxies and the proclamation of a death sentence being carried through. The message would then encourage all citizens to be honest, hardworking, and generous, and never to forget that all people within Seven Galaxies are brothers and sisters. The message would end with no one taking credit for the assassinations, which were always done swiftly to avoid unnecessary suffering or the harming of innocents.

Could it be, Alex wondered, that Denali's disappearance had been her entrance into this cleansing squad? If so, how could the murder of Admiral Gor be explained?

Alex quickly compiled a list of all the incidents he could find since Denali's disappearance some fourteen years past. He found over two hundred and forty "cleansings" within Seven Galaxies over this period. Certainly she could not have been involved, he thought, while his fingers keyed a request for all records of interplanetary travelers through ports of entry two weeks before until two weeks after each slaying. He also checked some other monitoring stations and video records that were unknown to the average citizenry.

Keying in photos and Denali's physical signature, he let the computer work the search, and then went to look in upon the sleeping woman while he waited.

Denali lay peacefully, her chest rising and falling like clockwork, five times a minute. Her stats showed on the sleep chamber monitor. She possessed startling characteristics: she was a physical specimen of perfect symmetry, and the denseness of her musculature was extraordinary. The bone was much more dense than average as well. It was as if she had been bred a woman but carried the strength and speed of a man. However, there was certainly nothing masculine in Denali's appearance. Alex's yearning to know more about this woman had become a growing infatuation.

When he returned to his computer, he found the search was complete. In no less than 165 incidents, Denali had passed through entry ports or had been on the planet of the slaying before and after the deaths. Sometimes she had been incognito—wearing a wig, glasses, or padding to change her outward appearance. The complex screening program Alex ran sifted through the smoke and identified her by voice signature, iris identification, and DNA bone scans.

So, she was one of Duhcat's elite, he realized. Duhcat's plan to rid Seven Galaxies of vermin—the types that had cast ancient Earth into a downward spiral until all that remained was a stinking, bankrupt slave ship mired in the cesspool that industrialists and bankers had created—had been running successfully. Denali had apparently been responsible for over half of the carefully targeted deaths during the past fourteen years.

But why kill the admiral? The question reverberated in his mind. Had she done it, or could she have been framed for it? Had she gone crazy and become some sort of renegade? Alex's mind raced through endless possible explanations. The only way the truth would come to light, he thought, was to attempt to gain the knowledge from Denali herself.

The record of her trial before the tribunal showed her standing mute. She had not defended herself, as if she knew there was no hope and so didn't waste her breath. Was it because she was guilty of the crime? Alex knew his questions would never be answered unless he could speak to her and gain her confidence. But how could he possibly get a machine of death like her to trust him?

# NINE

Alex had not slept a bit during the night. Denali had lain upon his mind like a pillow over the face. Try as he might, he could not forget, could not take his thoughts from her story, could not help but wonder about her sanity, and her remorse. Could such a hardened veteran of death and suffering feel remorse? The questions came and went, flashing through his mind like lightning. After a fitful, sleepless evening, resolve finally came, shakily at first and then gaining strength until the foundation of his decision was unbreakable.

For the short term, he would not tell his best friend and commander. Alex's reason was twofold: first, he was afraid that Tay would jettison the killer of his beloved grandfather in a fit of rage; second, he felt Denali deserved protection, but not only that, by protecting Denali, he was also protecting Tay from making an emotional decision he might later regret. In his mind, Alex had justified his secret: he was the guardian of both Tay and Denali.

Rising without showering or eating, he walked to the sleeping woman's chamber. He dialed up the metabolic controls, bringing Denali's heart rate, breathing, and body temperature up to a threshold just below consciousness.

He knew that what he was about to do would be construed by some as unethical, yet he felt his actions were not selfishly motivated. He told himself that he was attempting to protect *both* Tay and Denali, and that this was necessary for the good of both. Alex prayed silently that he could be successful and not be severely burned.

Watching her breathing quickening, her body temperature rising, and her pulse gaining momentum, Alex's vital signs began to mimic hers. His heart raced, and he flushed warmly.

Time passed as Alex watched. At last, Denali's eyelids twitched lightly. He knew from her vitals that she was in that state of semi-consciousness where she would be dreaming and yet also conscious of what was going on around her. He began to speak in a soft and gentle tone, barely a whisper, so as not to startle her.

"We are your friends who have rescued you. You are asleep aboard the transport ship. We have taken control of the ship and are heading for a safe haven away from the penal colony. You can be free."

Denali's eyelids fluttered. She was obviously trying to decipher the words, perhaps attempting to sort her dream-state from her consciousness.

"Denali, my name is Alex. I am your friend. I am here to protect you, to see that no one harms you. You cannot be awakened completely. I know your history ... where you've been, what you've done. I have studied your childhood, and I believe you are not bad or evil. Events in your life led you down a path of darkness, a path you now regret."

Denali heard a kind, benevolent voice saying she was good, that she deserved protection. Her subconscious had been struggling for months with many troubling thoughts: her killing of Admiral Gor, which she had been forced to accomplish against her will and all common sense; the arrest and trial; and the prospect of life in a prison where suicide was made impossible. If death had been an option, she would already have chosen that path. Denali knew instinctively she was being offered a choice, and that there were conditions. All this she understood in an instant.

Alex watched the semiconscious woman. The wide-set eyes squeezed tightly shut for a moment, as if in convulsion, and the pale, freckled chin wrinkled and quivered. Her chest trembled, and tears began to flow down cheeks that had flushed red, perhaps from embarrassment and shame.

Alex felt compelled to do something that was completely against the rulebook. He switched off the electronic security curtain and reached for Denali's trembling hand. Her grip was fierce but not unfriendly, as if she had been starved her entire life for someone to give her a bit of softness or the whisper of love, someone who believed not just in her lethal qualities but also in her humanity.

A buzz that felt like electricity ran from Denali into Alex. He was stunned. He had never before experienced a magnetism so strong. He barely restrained himself from embracing her. With emotional difficulty, Alex reached with his free hand and dialed the metabolic controls back down to the full-hibernation mode.

"You must go back into full sleep," he said softly. "Know that you are safe. I will protect you from harm, I swear to you. I am your friend and guardian. Rest peacefully now and do not fear. I will come to visit you again soon."

Denali, feeling the touch of warmth from Alex's hand, knew she was not dreaming. For some unexplainable reason, this person—an angel—had come. As her heart rate and breathing dropped, she tried desperately to squeeze the hand in gratitude, but, in the overpowering weakness of sleep, her hand went slack.

Alex drew his hand back reluctantly, switched the security curtain back to its *on* position, and took another long look at Denali. He thought he could see the faintest trace of a smile on her perfectly formed lips.

# TEN

After she was awakened from the forced slumber and seeing Tay, Zuzahna, still exhausted, had collapsed into a more natural but fitful slumber. Tay had stayed by her side. Whenever she woke in fear, he consoled her. It had taken forty hours of nearly unbroken rest before Zuzahna's subconscious had accepted the unbelievable: she was free from prison, and really, truly with him.

Finally, instead of starting awake and jolting fearfully bolt upright in bed, she opened her eyes languidly and surveyed the room. Her eyes quit roving and lit upon him. He was watching her. This time upon awakening, she was not full of apprehension. Her old confidence had returned.

Zuzahna looked at Tay with sleep-filled yet knowing eyes. They mesmerized him. She had a bit of dried drool on her cheek, her hair was mussed from sleep, and wrinkles from the pillow had been etched into her striking face, and yet he found her unbelievably compelling. Instead of the perfectly poised courtesan, she had become human, touchable—no longer a haunting apparition but here, in his bed.

Her eyes—those immense, dark, startling eyes flecked with gold—were unlike any he had seen in his life. Tay's lonely heart had discovered love in them. Her sweet scent filled and overflowed his senses.

She spoke softly: "Love, come to me."

Tay, longing for her to ask, to consent, to acknowledge that she felt the same, let his clothes slip to the floor.

The softness and warmth of the covers welcomed him into Zuzahna's domain. Unbridled by cloth, her heavenly scent engulfed him. Those remarkable, extraordinarily dark eyes—whirlpools whispering of love—swept him away.

Zuzahna thought, *Finally!* Smiling confidently, she caressed the young man into an unfettered emotional and physical free-fall. Softly, the talisman of her touch swallowed him in undulating waves. She longed to grasp and hold his very being.

Zuzahna carried him on a journey far and away, into a place where, possessed by her unfathomable talents, she believed that Tay, was completely hers.

Zuzahna smiled with immense satisfaction. She had learned to possess men and hold them with the shackles of her will and her talents in the bedroom. Tay was, at long last, completely and utterly hers.

# ELEVEN

Alex had seen little of Tay since Zuzahna had been woken. Just as well, he thought; Tay's preoccupation with Zuzahna gave him the necessary freedom and time to spend with Denali. The visits were frequent, and the intensity of the feeling between them was growing.

Alex had not woken Denali completely. Fearful of her power, he chose instead to visit with her while she remained under light hibernation. Thus, he had yet to ask her the difficult questions that must be answered before he could reveal her to Tay. Instead, he learned more of her through visual observation as he talked of many things.

Today, the sleeping Denali no longer looked hunted; she looked at peace. It was as though these visits had consoled her troubled spirit. Dialing the metabolic controls up, he waited as usual for her to reach semi-consciousness.

Tay left his quarters. Zuzahna had been in fine form, teasing, joking, cuddling him, and exuding irresistible charm. She left him desiring to be with her whenever duties called him away. As he walked down a corridor near the sleep chambers, he noticed Alex at one of the compartments, evidently checking on a prisoner. He had noticed Alex at the very same sleep compartment earlier, when he had passed on his way to see Zuzahna for lunch. Tay made a mental note of the chamber number and slipped down the corridor without being seen by the preoccupied Alex.

Tay thought it odd for Alex to be spending so much time with one of the inmates, yet he had delegated to him the chore of sifting through the rabble of life prisoners to find those suitable for inclusion in a small settling party. They would need others: people who could be trusted, perhaps ones who had been wrongfully imprisoned like themselves, or people who at least were not the degraded human filth that comprised the bulk of the prisoners on board. Tay decided Alex was probably just taking care of the task. He shrugged off the situation and walked on, leaving the matter to his competent best friend.

When Denali's metabolic rate had risen and she was in a semi-conscious state, Alex said, "Good afternoon, Denali. It's good to see you. I hope you are feeling well."

Her eyelids fluttered slightly, as if in answer to his inquiry.

"I hope by now you have accepted me as friend and not foe. I am here because I care about your wellbeing."

Again, the flutter of lashes. Her eyes did not open, but the slightest quiver of her lashes showed him that she could hear and respond. Alex was excited that she was cooperating and willing to acknowledge him.

"Denali, I know you worked in Duhcat's cleansing squad. I know the people you took out were a nasty, filthy, corrupt bunch of slime."

The lashes quivered again.

"But what of Admiral Gor?"

Immediately, Denali's heart rate spiked. Her face flushed and her eyes squeezed tight, as if she were trying to wring the memory from her consciousness. Tears streamed down her cheeks and her mouth formed a grimace of suffering. Her entire frame trembled, as if in anguish.

Alex was sure that she regretted the slaying of Tay's grandfather, yet he wondered what had compelled her to do it. His mind raced. He continued. "Denali, you didn't want to kill Admiral Gor.... Were you forced?"

The lashes fluttered frantically.

Denali's happiness at being befriended by Alex evaporated as she was cast back into the deep abyss of despair. Here was a person attempting to befriend her, and yet he was asking about the very act that had driven her to the brink of suicide. She was absorbed by shame and guilt at having committed the unforgivable crime of taking a life so revered throughout Seven Galaxies. Her bruised and battered psyche rolled in a tumult of blackness. She prayed silently in her semiconscious state for a miracle, for that golden act we all crave when we have done something terribly wrong: forgiveness.

Alex watched her body language and facial expressions. Even in sleep, they spoke to Alex of her disgust with having taken an innocent life—one of a hero revered across all Seven Galaxies.

"One day, Denali, would you explain to me the unexplainable?" he said. "Will you tell me why you took our dear and *beloved* Admiral? We all miss him. There is a great void in Seven Galaxies without him. We are fleeing our treasured home because of it."

Denali's troubled face, already wet with deep-seated emotion, poured forth more tears. Alex cried also.

"I must go now, Denali. I don't believe you wished to destroy Admiral Gor. I believe you were somehow forced into the act. I cannot pretend to understand what you did, but perhaps someday when you meet me in conscious state, you might attempt to explain it to me."

Her wet lashes fluttered desperately, saying, *yes*! She would try.

# TWELVE

Alex walked down the corridor towards Denali's sleep chamber and turned the corner. He stopped suddenly when he saw she had another visitor. Tay was there, standing before her.

Alex watched, curious, wondering why Tay had stopped there when there were so many other prisoners. He was standing as if transfixed. One of his hands moved to the metabolic controls.

Alex approached quietly, out of his friend's line of sight. He saw Tay begin to dial the life support system to zero.

Alex placed a hand on Tay from behind and said, "What are you up to, my friend?"

Tay started, stepping backward slightly. Alex palmed the controls deftly up towards awake mode while distracting his friend and commander with conversation: "What are you doing here?"

"This bitch killed my grandfather. She killed *our* admiral!"

"I know what she did."

"And you kept it from me?"

"Yes."

"Why? We're best friends and partners in this migration. Best friends don't keep secrets from one another! And certainly not you and me!"

"I was planning to tell you when I found out more about Denali!"

"Oh! She's Denali now, not inmate number 173650! What the hell are you thinking, Alex? Why did you keep this from me?"

"I'm conducting an investigation into the cause and effect of her actions. I'm trying to find out why she took Admiral Gor's life."

"Cause and effect! The why isn't important. What she did is all that matters to me! I'm going to drag her scurvy, treacherous ass to the airlock and Deep Space the bitch!" He reached over and keyed in the shutoff code to the security curtain.

Alex was astounded. "You can't play God, Tay! You can't ditch her! You're going against maritime law and everything that's decent!"

"Watch me! You should have told me, Alex, instead of keeping me in the dark! What am I to think?"

"That I was looking out for you, so you wouldn't do something stupid like what you're talking of right now!" Alex said.

"I'm not talking, buddy! I'm dead serious. This trash is going to the dump port."

Alex grabbed hold of Tay's arm. "Tay, stop! You have to listen! I've found out so much about her. You don't know!"

"I don't know because you've kept your little *redheaded* secret here, safe and sound—but not for much longer!"

Alex pulled the much larger Tay away from the sleep chamber with all his might.

"Let go of me before you get hurt, you little geek!" Tay shouted.

"I won't let you do it, Tay."

"You think you can stop me?"

"I have to!"

"You mean this murdering wench means more to you than me or the admiral?"

Alex had never seen Tay in a state like this. *I know what he's doing,* Alex thought. *Blaming her.* The loss of his grandfather, and their imprisonment, could easily be blamed on Denali. Without the admiral to fight on their behalf, they had been railroaded by Ventras' tribunal. No wonder he was half out of his mind.

"Tay, calm down. It's more complicated than you think," Alex said. "The tribunal gave her a life sentence. You don't have the power to change that into a death sentence."

"I'm in command here! I can do whatever I want!"

"The Tay I know and love would never speak like you are now." Alex lowered his voice, trying desperately to calm his friend.

Tay faltered for a moment, and Alex stepped in close. "Please let me explain," he said. "I protected her from you because I thought that in the heat of emotion you might do something impulsive—something you would later regret!"

"Get out of my way!"

"I won't."

"I swear if you don't step aside, I'll throw you aside to get at that bitch."

"Don't, Tay. Don't."

"Get the hell out then!"

"I can't," Alex said, shaking his head. "I can't allow you near her in your present mental state! You have no right to take her life! Don't you see? If you do this thing in your crazed state, you will blacken all your grandfather taught you. You will erode your perfection. You will no longer be the unparalleled person I have looked up to since we were eight years old, when you stood against those bullies on my behalf. Don't you see? Everything you are, everything you can be in the future, now hinges on this crucial moment and the decision you make! You take her life, you step into the dark side, Tay!"

"Move or I'll move you, and you won't like it!"

"Don't you see? I'm standing up for her as you did for me so many years ago."

"Trying to protect the woman who murdered my grandfather! Our Admiral!"

Tay spun, breaking from Alex's grip. He moved towards Denali's sleep chamber, but Alex tripped him from behind. It was as if Tay had fallen on a huge coiled spring. He came flying back to his feet, more enraged than before. Alex stood his ground on the piece of deck that separated Denali from certain death and Tay from the worst mistake of his life.

Tay, propelled by anger, grief, loss, and confusion, came rushing at Alex, his eyes glazed and face crimson. Alex sidestepped as he had seen Tay do while working out, and the enraged commander went hurtling by. Alex positioned himself in front of Denali's chamber.

Tay spun and rushed at Alex in a blur of speed, preparing to use a double strike and foot-catch to send Alex flying backwards and out of his way. A nano before he was upon Alex, Denali shot from the chamber as if from a cannon. The sound she made the moment she engaged Tay reminded Alex of a wild, feline super-predator. It was a shrill shriek that made the hair on the back of his neck stand up.

Tay was hurled in an arc across the corridor. He bounced off the bulkhead, spinning a circle and a half, centrifugal force the only thing keeping his feet beneath him. He came to a halt and sized up the strange woman, whom he hated with passion.

Denali looked at Tay and said calmly, "Never lay a hand on Alex in anger. I am his guardian. I'm *truly* sorry I killed your grandfather. My hand was forced, but I take full responsibility. I could have chosen certain death instead. Looking back, it would have been the better decision. I'm truly sorry! Please, dear God, forgive me!" Remorse filled her eyes. She looked towards Tay, hoping for forgiveness.

"Sorry! You think that makes everything all right?" Tay shouted. "It's not that simple! You will be sorry when I space your worthless ass! When you're flying through Deep Space without a suit, your eyes popped out and your precious bodily fluids flowing—*then* you will be truly sorry!"

Tay was a madman. He had completely lost it.

"Tay!" Alex screamed. "Stop this! Stop it now!"

Tay rushed Denali, forgetting one of the first lessons taught to him by Sifu so many years ago: remain emotionless. Anger clouded his mind and vision; he hated his opponent.

She easily deflected his blows and stepped to the side, leaving only a foot in his path.

What Tay had expected was contact, the undeniable pleasure of impacting the murderess' flesh. What he got instead was several deflecting blocks and a free-fall through thin air.

Tay rolled into a summersault, came up on his feet, and paused for a nano, taking in the woman who had so effortlessly cast him into the air, twice.

He came at her again, this time more cautiously, engaging without losing control of his footing. Alex's untrained eyes could not follow the blur of blindingly fast blows.

The two opponents seemed to be acting out an intricate ballet of martial arts movements; it looked as though they had practiced this dance a thousand times. No blows met their target; Denali effortlessly deflected Tay's onslaught.

In the minutest opening, Denali struck. The fingers and thumb of her right hand were pressed tightly together. Her arm appeared to be the neck of a powerful bird, her fingers, the beak. In a blur, her arm and hand snapped, driving the point of her fingers into the center of Tay's forehead with such force that he staggered backward, his legs not keeping up with his body. He tumbled onto his back in a heap, eyes rolling back in his head, and went limp as a rag doll.

Alex looked first at his friend and then at Denali in disbelief. "He'll be okay, won't he? You didn't kill him, did you?"

"No," she said, shaking her head. "He'll be out for a few minutes. Can we lock him up until he cools down? I don't want to have to hurt him again."

"Good idea! Help me drag him into your sleep chamber. We can activate the security curtain so he can't get out. Maybe when he comes to, we can talk some sense into him."

Alex looked at Denali closely. He had never before seen her awake or standing. Her red-blond hair was mussed from sleep and the fight, and her pale, lightly freckled face was flushed from excitement. She was taller than he was, and as he looked up into her wide-set, blue-green eyes, he thought, *She's the most fearsomely beautiful creature I've ever seen!*

## THIRTEEN

Alex and Denali watched their commander lying unconscious in the sleep chamber. Tay had not stirred since being knocked out several minutes ago, and Alex was starting to worry about his health, and his state of mind. He wondered whether Tay would wake up in the same wild frame of mind in which he had been when he fell unconscious.

Alex looked at Denali once more; he had been trying not to stare. "Are you sure he's all right?"

"He'll be fine. He should be coming up soon."

Tay stirred, and Alex's mind ran through the possibilities. How would he calm his friend? How could he convince him not to harm Denali? What was he going to do?

"Perhaps you should dial down his metabolic rate before he becomes completely conscious," Denali said. "This will allow us some time to formulate a strategy—a plan, if you will—for calming him down from the state he was in. Is he always so hotheaded?"

"I've never seen him like that. I think he lost it completely." Alex quickly dialed the controls downward, and Tay's heart rate slowed to nearly half-normal. "You have to understand, Denali, the admiral was not only Tay's grandfather but also the father figure Tay most admired. He was his mentor, and someone who was absolutely dear to Tay while he was growing up. He was also our commander in the recent Nesdian conflict. Tay was the admiral's first. Do you understand what we're up against?"

Denali looked at Alex, actually seeing him for the first time. In sleep, her mind had heard the voice and formed a picture of the man speaking kindly to her. Sometimes the picture was of a fatherly figure, the father she'd never had but dreamed of as a child. Other times, the voice belonged to a kind old man.

Now, as she studied Alex with the scrutinizing eye of a gladiator, she saw that his appearance was nothing like the mental picture she had formed of him. His stature was neither large nor small. His chestnut curls, a bit long, covered his forehead and ears. He wore large, dark-rimmed glasses on a nose that was neither outstanding nor unnoticeable. It was a fine, strong nose, she thought offhandedly, a bit distracted that he was kind *and* cute. She dismissed her previous preconceptions.

Then Denali took in his eyes. She realized they were not just hazel, a shade that nicely complemented his hair, but that the hazel was encircled by thin rings of blue fading into sea green. He had the enquiring eyes of a child. She knew instinctively that he wanted answers from her.

Her appraising eyes wandered over him. His posture suggested a curve at the shoulders, like so many people who hunched over computers, but he was standing erect, shoulders square and appealing. He was obviously attempting to stand taller, she thought, so that she did not seem so dominating, so intimidating. He was the type of man she would normally pass on the street and take no notice of, yet now she was overpowered by attraction, a pull that was for her the ultimate taboo.

Denali drew her emotions in, just as she had her entire life; she had no need for friendship, nor for affection and the complications it caused. She owed a debt to Alex for stepping in and going against Tay to protect her. That debt she would never forget. She had sworn to be his guardian, and so she would be—but, she told herself silently, that is where the friendship would end.

Denali pulled herself from her silent appraisal and said, "We should go someplace. Someplace where he can't hear us talk."

She didn't wait for his response; she just moved down the corridor. Alex followed and walked far enough behind to see her form in its entirety. Denali had the stride of a big cat, he thought. She exuded bridled power. Sinew and defined muscles rippled beneath the skin as her legs moved. She possessed the primeval sway of hips that man-beasts throughout the eons had involuntarily followed with awed eyes.

Denali turned and caught Alex watching her, enraptured. She smiled. It wasn't so much of a smirk as it was a smile of enjoyment at catching him.

He stammered, "I-I was just admiring ... there was nothing lascivious or ... or lewd in my thoughts; I was just taking you in, as I would a priceless work of art. Examining ... admiring ... attempting to understand ..."

"It's all right, Alex. You like this? What did you say: a priceless work of art?"

Alex could only nod; he was tongue tied in embarrassment and felt his cheeks flush.

"Well, don't get your hopes up. I am warning you. I don't want to send your sweet soul spiraling off in disappointment, but I swore off men long ago, long before I even grew into womanhood." She smiled. "I like you, Alex. Thanks for protecting me from Tay. But you need to keep your distance. What we have here is a very complicated set of circumstances: Tay wants me dead, I don't want to be dead, and you are stuck in the middle, between your loyalty to him and your desire to protect me. Do you have any ideas? Any ideas as to how the three of us can manage to live in close proximity aboard this ship without being at each other's throats?"

Alex could only look perplexed. "Honestly, Denali, you shifted gears while I was still thinking about the possibilities between you and me. You changed the conversation to what are we going to do about Tay and how he feels about you, but I can't switch like that. I don't understand. Are you saying that even though I'm mesmerized by you and think you are the most extraordinary woman I've ever seen—that I want to know you intimately—are you saying there's no chance? You don't even know me! I've never been fortunate enough to see a woman who comes close to your...poise, your striking looks, the way you walk, the force your presence carries. To be perfectly honest, Denali, you make me weak in the knees."

She looked at him again, seeing something she hadn't before, something that made her careful in how she chose her words. She did not want to hurt him. "Such honesty! I admire forthright thoughts. Too much of our true intentions must be read between lines or uncovered in outright lies. Thank you."

She smiled disarmingly—an effervescent smile on perfectly formed lips. Alex thought, *I've never seen her smile before.* She suddenly seemed much more approachable—almost friendly.

And then the smile was gone, as if a switch had been flicked. Her eyes—wide, blue, and haunting a moment before—were now half-closed. The woman before him had changed in an instant, and what he saw now sent a cool shiver down his spine.

"Alex, you know nothing of me. You've read some file, or more likely guessed, and now you think you have an idea of what I am. Let me assure you that *even* in your wildest darkest nightmares you may, for a fleeting moment, come close to what I am and where I've been; but you will never really know. Because when *you* awaken, the fear evaporates, and you get up from bed and continue your real life. You soon forget the dream, the fear, the brutality. For me, Alex, it is never a dream. I can never leave it behind. It will haunt me.... It will follow me.

"I have crept silently in the dark jungles and deceptive labyrinths of hundreds of evils, black tunnels of forgotten humanity, where quicksand swallows your heart. I have prayed for a miracle, to be rescued from its grasp when there is no hope. Finally, the engulfing wet sucks out your last clean breath. Cold, unforgiving darkness comes, stifling you. Your heart pounds in your ears and your blood races."

She fell silent for a moment, then said, "The other side took me, Alex. Darkness is my mantle. I will never be the same. The beauty, poetry, and lightness of life's best moments ran. It fled from the monster I've become. An unending wasteland of loneliness is my best friend. I look upon Earth's wonders with eyes that can no longer see or appreciate beauty. So do not ever think I can relent and be tender with you. If you allow yourself that hope, you will only end up in disappointment and misery."

Alex looked at Denali, shocked by her words. Her face was blank, the blue eyes dark—almost black. He shivered involuntarily. "Anyone can change, Denali," he said. "I can wait. I *will* wait, because when you become one with us, you will be part of a family. You have come home."

Denali looked back at Alex in complete and profound disbelief. "That's a bit oversimplified," she said. "Have you forgotten that your best friend and commander has sworn to Deep Space me? Perhaps we should concentrate on that dilemma, instead of on your hopeless desire for something I just explained to be impossible."

"You cannot slam the door in my face! You owe me more than that."

"Oh, so now I owe you? Never forget, I have sworn to be your guardian! In that oath, I have paid, and I will continue to pay what I owe. You can never suffer me to feel that I owe you more than that." Denali was livid. How dare he assume she would somehow be indebted to him for his act of kindness?

"You misunderstand my meaning. Don't read into my words something from your past. You can't cast away a new friendship because of things you experienced before we met. This is new! We are to become friends! Don't push me away!"

Denali looked to the deck.

"Look at me ... This is Alex, your friend! I care about you. And yes, I have mostly guessed at your past, but you have affirmed my suspicions. Still, I never judged you! I attempted to understand what changed such a remarkable young girl from something of wonder—a butterfly all admired—into something that had to be secreted away from view like an ugly deformity. I wondered. I studied. I spoke with you in your sleep. I befriended you when no one else would! And now you cast me off? You throw me away like trash into the jettison tube and hit the button so you don't have to smell my stench?"

Alex's eyes welled. No tears dripped onto his quivering cheeks, but he was close. He felt like he was being mistreated by the school bully again—by a grossly insensitive being who thought of nothing but selfish wants, not the needs or pain of others.

Denali looked up from the deck. She felt a small bit of shame but did not allow it to show. "Alex ..." She stopped, taking him in: a grown man who looked close to tears. His eyes were red; his face, twisted in anguish. It was his eyes that softened the iron callouses protecting her heart; the armor weakened just a little. "Alex," she said, her voice softer now, "we can talk of this another time. Can we do that, as friends?"

She had changed. The glacial frigidity had melted away, and he saw her humanity for an instant. Alex saw hope. "Yes. We can talk of this another time. I'll let it go now, if you give me your word we can discuss it in the future."

"You have my word."

Denali thought, *He's unlike anyone I've ever met. He's so gentle, so caring. I have to get the message through to him. Somehow, I must show him that I'm not worth the effort, that he's wasting his time, and that I can only bring him unhappiness because I'm broken. I was broken and never mended, so long ago ...*

Denali's thoughts drifted backward in time ... to her childhood love, to the dark night that stole Issy from her, to the crime that ripped something deep inside her ... to that moment in her past when she changed and when all her beauty vanished. The vacuum created in its absence, the void, had been filled ever since with ... what she had become.

Alex looked toward Denali while she reflected, circumspection bringing her past into the present. He glimpsed in that moment her distance. She had a faraway look in her eyes.

Denali, as if waking from a dream that had held her in the throes of something terrible, looked to Alex with a confused expression.

"Alex," she said, as she came back from the distance to which she had been mentally removed, "we need a plan for Tay. What shall we do?"

"First of all, Denali, I have to ask: why did you kill Admiral Gor?"

"I was forced. If I hadn't, they would have hunted me relentlessly. I would have been living in terror. I had been out of the cleansing squad for two years and had begun living life within a semblance of normality, and I had grown to love my freedom. I didn't want to give it up. I wasn't ready to die or to be hunted like an animal. So I took the safe way out. It was the worst mistake of my entire life. It causes me unspeakable anguish daily."

For a fleeting moment, the ice-cold warrior—the brutality—disappeared, and in that flash Alex glimpsed her humanity once again.

Then the icy, half-lidded eyes came back. The human had retreated and been replaced, forgotten, shuttered away.

"Who forced you to kill Admiral Gor?"

"Evil politicians who desired ultimate control; they said that Gor stood in their way."

"Do you know their names?"

"Yes."

"Tell me, Denali!" Alex said. "I have to know who they are. The information may help. If Tay knows you were only the vehicle and not the mind behind the assassination, he may forgive you. Don't you see? Tell me!"

She looked again to the deck, averting her eyes in shame. "Ventras, Belvidius, and Derian."

"Are you absolutely sure?"

"Yes," she answered, without emotion, still avoiding his eyes, afraid for him to see what lay behind them.

Alex's mind raced: with the twelve politicians locked away in *Intrepid One*'s brig, Tay had ultimate control of the criminals responsible for the admiral's assassination. And, with this information in hand, Denali had a chance of being forgiven.

If Alex could convince Tay she was only an instrument and not the driving force, and if she would apologize sincerely and beg forgiveness, then perhaps Tay would relent and redirect his anger towards the proper channel.

"Denali, we need to tell Tay the truth. Can you ask him from your heart to forgive you? Will you beg him if necessary? We must get him to understand that you were not the force behind this action."

She said simply, quietly, "I will."

"Let's go to him then and try to explain. Let me do most of the talking. I can bring him up to semi-consciousness first and monitor his reactions. Then we can see if there is a chance of him calming his anger towards you."

"Let's try, Alex." She walked slowly past him, back towards the sleeping chambers. Alex followed, praying silently that it would work.

At the sleeping chamber, Alex dialed up the metabolic controls. Tay's heart rate increased. Then he began talking.

Tay briskly walked the corridor towards the brig. The twelve were in a shared cell. There were other cells available, and Tay could have split them up and given them a little more privacy, but he didn't want them too comfortable.

Reaching the brig, he strode up to the holding cell and glanced in. Belvidius was asleep, his fat jowls sagging and vibrating as he snored like a freight train. Derian paced back and forth like a caged wolf. Ventras sat in a chair in the corner, glowering. When he saw Tay, he straightened from a slumping slouch in the chair and sat upright. Others lay languidly in their bunks. Hopelessness pervaded the tight quarters.

"Everyone comfy?" Tay asked, as if he had true concern.

Ventras rose and walked towards Tay. All eyes were upon Tay, except Belvidius' who kept on the rumbling snore. Derian froze in place, obviously taking in his jailer, searching for weakness and attempting to understand the man who would ultimately decide his own fate.

Ventras spoke. "Funny, Commander, very funny. Why have you kidnapped the twelve of us, and where are we? You know, you will *surely* be caught and sent back to prison, except this time it will be the Hole for your remaining days. Imagine: no light, only sour gruel to eat. No chance to shower the filth from your wretched body; only darkness and unending days that will pass one into one another until you lose count."

"Are you finished, Ventras?" Tay said.

"Not in the least! What do you plan to do to us?"

Tay remained silent.

"So you plan to kill us! Is that it?" Ventras finally said, unable to stand the silence a moment longer.

"Why would I want to kill the twelve of you?" Tay asked. "What have you done to deserve such brutality? Are your consciences bothering you?"

Ventras said nothing. No one spoke. The minutes ticked away.

Tay finally broke the silence. "I know you all conspired to have Admiral Gor murdered. I want you all to know I have honestly thought about taking each of you to the airlock to deep space you one at a time. At first, I thought I would gain some satisfaction from that: seeing the murderers of my beloved grandfather with their eyes popped out and body fluids leaking into Deep Space—to see each of you suffering an agonizing death. I thought that would soothe the sorrow within me." Tay paused for effect.

"Then I came to realize that such a death would be too quick. Also, I have no desire to play God with your despicable, filthy lives. I decided that I would not kill you. I have something much more prolonged and pain-filled planned. Our journey together on this ship is one of six years. You will all be living in this cell together for that duration. In the meantime, you can wonder where you are going and what your destination has in store for you." Tay turned to leave.

"Wait!" It was Ventras.

"Yes?"

"We are wealthy beyond your imagination! I speak for myself, but I'm sure the others would agree. We will transfer everything to you: all our material possessions! We are sorry; we were terribly wrong. Please forgive us! Take our wealth. You can live like a king for the rest of your days!"

Eleven heads nodded frantically. Belvidius was still asleep.

"What an offer! Riches beyond my imagination! Hmmm. Should I crave to posses the wealth you twelve have accumulated? A stolen fortune...a fortune blackened by murder and other unspeakable acts? I think I'll have to pass! Nothing any of you possess can give back my grandfather.

"Oh, I forgot to impart a very important piece of information: for most of our voyage, you will be in deep sleep. When you are awakened for short periods, it would be wise to exercise with frenzy. If you don't, you will be ill prepared physically for the rigors and the grueling adventure of your new lives when we reach our final destination."

Tay spun and walked away, leaving a variety of pleas and catcalls behind.

# FOURTEEN

*INTREPID One* continued the run to the Virgin at an unbelievable and ever-increasing velocity. A Deep Space voyage that would normally take nearly twelve years would be completed in less than six.

Most of the passengers spent the trip in suspended animation. None of the former prisoners chose animation but were kept in sleep involuntarily. The craft was not outfitted to carry so many passengers on a journey of so vast a distance; there was little else that could be done.

Over the duration of the journey, Tay and Alex had to decide on a few prisoners who could be depended on to become possible friends and allies. These people had to be sorted from the rest, who were the worst sort of humankind and who might, upon waking, attempt to kill their skipper just for fun, and then wonder how to pilot the ship. These were not casual criminals. The seriousness of their crimes had destined them to be life prisoners in the penal moon, a facility designed to contain those who did not deserve to see the light of day again.

Alex and Tay worked on the assumption that almost everyone aboard—with the exception of themselves,

Serene, Zuzahna, and, questionably, Denali—were deviant misfits, as the prisoner files indicated. However, they figured that others may have been imprisoned on false charges. Perhaps there were some on board who were not truly the wretched excuses for humans their records showed. It was Alex's duty to sort fact from fiction, if possible. It was a monumental task, but aboard the ship there was little else but time.

How to choose a small group that could be befriended and trusted to support the settling became a sifting process. Alex sifted through the facts and summaries, looking for something within the potential candidates that would show they had merit or moral fiber.

Over the duration of the six-year voyage, a selection of possibilities was awakened, one at a time, and then allowed certain guarded freedom aboard the ship so they could be known on a more personal level while being studied.

The candidates who made the final cut needed to prove they had an imminent desire to participate in a positive fashion and that they were dedicated to leaving behind whatever had led to their incarceration so they could become a moral force in the new world.

Alex designed a screening process to sort psyche profiles, childhood information, and severity of the criminal behavior of which they had been accused. The DNA of each prisoner was checked to ensure all prisoners aboard the ship matched their paperwork. It was in doing this that Alex made a chance discovery: he found Gresham and Velonice among the prisoners. They had served aboard *Independence* for the duration of the Nesdian conflict under Admiral Gor: Gresham as the admiral's second and Velonice as chief medical officer. They had been listed under aliases on the prisoner roster: their true names had been erased. No doubt, Ventras had wanted to keep their arrest away from the scrutiny of their families and the public.

At the time of their disappearance, their families had reported them as "missing with no contact." Alex checked the news flashes and found nothing but an unexplained silence on their arrests. The police reports from that time stated that they had most likely fallen victim to "the chaos that ensued after the asteroid strikes." There were no subsequent entries showing any form of formal investigation; they had simply been lost in the quagmire of a planetary disaster unprecedented in Seven's history.

Slightly out of breath and flushed from excitement, he rushed to the bridge. "Tay," he called out with a large smile. "You will not believe who I've found among the sleeping prisoners!"

Tay, Zuzahna, Denali, and Serene all stopped what they were doing and looked up with bewildered eyes. Life aboard the ship had settled into a fairly monotonous day-to-day passing of time. Any news was relished, and Alex appeared to have something important to impart.

"Who?" Tay asked urgently.

"Velonise and Gresham!"

"You are serious?"

"I would never kid about something like this, Tay. You know me better than that. I was checking the passenger's DNA against the prisoner records and came upon them both. They are listed under false names. That's why I never found them before. Shall we go and wake our new companions?"

Tay looked astonished. "Let's go," he said. He turned to the others, who did not know Gresham and Velonice. "These two were crew members aboard *The Independence* with Alex and me. They are old friends. I never knew they had been arrested. It will be interesting to find out what disaster befell them, and whether its name was Ventras!"

The five stood and followed Alex to his new and wonderful find.

They broke in two groups, one with Gresham, and the other with Velonice. When the two awakened, Alex began talking with Velonice. Tay spoke with Gresham. Before long, the two were coherent, and the group of Seven began walking to the bridge where they could more comfortably sit down to talk.

Gresham began: "Tay, when we heard you had been arrested, we knew it was absurd; we didn't know what to do. Then, upon the untimely death of Admiral Gor, we knew we had to do something. We began picketing with signs in front of the legislature, hoping to draw governmental and public attention to your wrongful imprisonment. I mean it went completely against the Constitution! Our signs said, 'Free TayGor! Uphold the Constitution!' Your arrest had not even appeared on the news, and they would not allow us to visit you at the jail, although we tried repeatedly.

"Well, we weren't in place with our signs more than ten minutes when a black van pulled up, and four armed thugs dragged us into the van against our will. I knew what was happening and began to fight, but they gassed me, and I passed out. The last thing I remember, Vel was screaming at the top of her lungs before everything went black.

"Next thing I know, I wake up strapped into a chair and there is this tall, thin, creepy-looking guy with steely blue eyes staring down at me. I asked where I was, and who he was, but he said none of that was important."

"Ventras!" Serene exclaimed.

"Yes. I found out who he was later. Anyway, I said I wanted to call an attorney, and the bastard just starts laughing. I mean, he laughed for a minute or two like he was a madman. It was freaky! When he calmed down, he asked why I thought I should have the right to call anyone? I told him it was my right under the Constitution, but he just started laughing again. Then the bastard says that Seven is under martial law, that the Constitution has been done away with, and that if I didn't agree to stop making a fuss about your wrongful imprisonment, I would be joining you!

"Well, I wasn't thinking clearly...I went ballistic. I was so mad, I was seeing many shades of red! So I gave the psycho a piece of my mind and the next thing I knew, I was convicted by a tribunal for terrorism. I wasn't even given a public defender. They threw me in a cell. That's the last thing I remember, until waking here with you. Where are we? And how did you find me?"

"We found you on the transport ship," Tay said. "They were sending you to the penal moon."

"Life? They gave me life in that godforsaken shithole for carrying a sign?"

"We are aboard the transport ship, Gresham."

"What?"

"Settle down. Let me fill you in. It is no longer a prison transport ship; now it's *my* ship! Alex and I escaped. Alex found you during a DNA scan of the prisoners. You were listed under a false name, and so was Velonice. What's your story, Vel?" Tay asked, turning toward her.

"Pretty much the same. Although, I *was* thinking clearly, and didn't mouth-off." She looked at Gresham. "That Ventras! He's a freakin' nutbag! He's taken over Seven since the Dome was destroyed. Before long, he'll be in control of all Seven Galaxies!"

Tay and Alex looked at each other and smiled, and Zuzahna and Serene joined in. Only Denali remained straight-faced.

"I don't think Ventras will be taking over anything from now on," Tay said. "Come. Alex and I want to show you something." Tay began walking, and the others followed.

Coming into the brig, Tay said, "Hey! I brought some friends to see you!"

Ventras rolled out of his bunk. He had a beard growing, and his hair was greasy and uncombed. His shoulders slumped forward, and there were huge black circles under his eyes.

Tay said, "I thought you'd be exercising! You know this is your only day to be awake this month."

Ventras glowered and said nothing.

Gresham exclaimed, "I'll be damned! How did you get ahold of him, Tay?"

"The story," Tay said with a crooked smile, "is quite long. Let's go back to the bridge. I'll get you two some food. You must be famished. I'll fill in the details while you enjoy a hot meal."

Denali stared, transfixed upon the apparition that had haunted her dream-sleep.

Tay took hold of her arm and said, "Come on, Denali. You must come!"

Tay pulled Denali away from the man who had forced her to assassinate Admiral Gor, then darted and raped her, and in final totality saw to her sentence of life in the penal moon.

Tay pulled hard. Denali seethed. She wanted Ventras in a fashion that made the hair on the back of Tay's neck bristle.

# FIFTEEN

After arriving at the destination, a tricky set of procedures had to be executed.

Tay and Alex concurred that the riff raff of on board prisoners should be jettisoned in various locations a long distance from their own group's final destination.

Some of the prisoners who had been aboard the transport ship when Tay and Alex took control of it possessed very dark skin, and Tay felt it best to drop them into areas that were closer to the equator of the planet and well within the established comfortable tolerances of their genealogy. Other life prisoners were extremely light skinned, and it was determined they should be placed in Northern climes where their skin would not suffer the ill effects of high-intensity radiation from the Sun.

Tay and Alex collaborated on the drop zones so that the nearest of the wild ones, as they had begun to call them, would be more than nine thousand kilometers away from where Tay planned to settle. They both believed it would take decades for the unfavorable element to migrate such a great distance. If and when they did manage to close the gap, by that time the enlightened cultures from Andarean's and Tay's separate ships should possess far superior technology and the wild tribes would pose no serious threat.

Tay, Alex, and the preferred few would be dropped at a location known only by Tay. He had been given the details for this place, the future settlement of Andarean and his people, in the last message from his grandfather; it had been hidden inside the Virgin Mary necklace that Ventras had smashed open when he flung it against the concrete wall of Tay's cell.

The area had a moderate climate, providing a long summer growing season and cool winters with a little snow at higher elevations. A wide variety of minerals and metallic ores were readily available, so rapid technological advances would be possible.

The area bordered on a vast salt-water sea where many inland estuaries and channels afforded easy watercraft transportation and plentiful fishing.

The areas selected for the radical criminals on board had also been carefully chosen. They were locations void of metal ores, meaning a warring or aggressive society could not fashion blades or powder-operated concussion weapons. Tay had not wanted to bring these people to the Virgin at all, and he had struggled to decide what to do with them for the whole trip. Logic said jettison them into deep space, to kill the enemy in their sleep and avoid letting them infest the Virgin. However, a similar yet more intelligent voice spoke to him of morals, ethics, and benevolence. His conscience finally convinced him not to play executioner to the sorry passengers on board, so the dark element was spared.

He had been wrongfully imprisoned, and some of the others on board might have been as well. Tay felt that bringing them to the Virgin was the only conscionable action allowable. He hoped that in the future he would not regret his benevolent freeing of these known undesirables. Tay had spent many diligent hours in choosing a special drop zone for the twelve vile politicians: a desert so barren and dry a man would normally last less than three days without water. For six years, he had dreamed of killing the bastards, yet his conscience would not allow him to. Instead, he had formulated a plan where the treachery of the twelve would make sure *none* of them lived.

Each man would be dropped with an eighteen-liter water ration, approximately twenty-three kilos in weight. The vessel weighed another two kilos. It was enough water to see the person 150 kilometers through the desert and out into an area that abounded with artesian springs, animal life, and edible plants. That is, if they could carry the cumbersome weight of the life sustaining fluid. Each person would also be left with a spear, proper clothing and footwear, but no food. The water, if carefully rationed, was enough to see them through the grueling five-day trek.

Tay honestly believed that none would survive. He knew that some would drink their water too quickly and then murder another to take their water. Others would exert themselves too swiftly, when only a measured and methodical walk could bring one to safety. Others had been out of condition even before they were captured from too much high living and lack of exercise; certainly some would die of heat stroke and cardiac arrest.

In the end, it would be their own greed and treacherousness that would kill them. Tay's hands would be clean.

Tay had been too embarrassed to share his plan with Alex, but as soon as the drop zone for the twelve was finally made clear, Alex smiled slyly and said, "I see what you have in store for our old friends. What an appropriate fate it will be!"

# SIXTEEN

THE twelve, in a sleep-induced stupor, were dropped just before sunrise. They woke in a barren and hostile climate and groggily took one another in.

Belvidius, an obscenely obese and very revolting specimen, was the first to speak.

"Where in damnation has that bastard TayGor dropped us?"

Ventras, still tall and lean, with wolf-like eyes, sized up the situation. "Well, you fat pig, if you would get off your monstrous ass and stand, you might have a better view of our situation."

"There is no need to be hostile, Ventras. Where are your manners?"

"I believe my manners were lost when my person was particle-accelerated out of the special legislative chambers; the place that you, head of personal security, informed our group on countless occasions was protected from such an attack. I believe you said the shields would make such displacement of our bodies an absolute impossibility!" Ventras shook with rage. His hate for Belvidius would have been obvious even to the assorted reptiles witnessing these strange new creatures, had they not been in partial paralysis from the waning evening's cold.

Ventras began going through the list of provisions, which was attached to the shaft of a spear standing upright out of the ground. "At least he left us supplies!" he said. "He was good enough also to leave us a map and compass."

"Wonderful. Just wonderful!" Belvidius said, rubbing the sleep from his swollen eyes. "I'm freezing. Did he leave us any bedding?"

"Eighteen liters of water each, a spear, and no food! That arrogant—"

"He could easily have killed us in our sleep!" Belvidius said, interrupting Ventras' tirade.

"That would probably have been more pleasant than what we are about to experience!" screamed Ventras, seething with hostility.

"What do you mean?"

"What I mean, Belvidius, is that in about five minutes you will no longer be cold; the sun is about to break the horizon."

"OH! Thank goodness; my teeth were beginning to chatter!"

Ventras laughed at the gargantuan tub of lard. "Imbecile! You will not be thankful for long!"

"Listen! Listen, all of you! The map our gracious admiral left attached to this spear says we have exactly 150.96 kilometers to the next source of water—that is, if we can all walk a straight line. If we wander or weave, it will be a much longer distance."

Derian, an aging man who appeared to be in good shape, said, "We should be able to walk that in a few days. I have hiked similar distances many times with no problem!"

"Were you carrying eighteen liters of water on your back?"

"No. But I did have a light rucksack."

"Was the temperature so hot you could fry an egg on a rock?"

"Well, of course not! Who would be so stupid as to hike in temperatures so extreme?"

"Well, Derian, prepare yourself for that very experience!"

"What do you mean?" asked Belvidius.

"In case you have not noticed, we are in a desert. We had better get moving while it is still fairly cool."

"Move now? I am still half asleep!" Belvidius whined.

"Then stay and die where you are. I am on my way!"

Grabbing a spear, one vessel of water, and the compass, Ventras set off towards blue-green hills in the distance.

The entire group scrambled to their feet, each taking their allotted ration of water and a spear before trudging rapidly, trying to close the distance between Ventras and themselves.

Ventras set a rapid pace. He took long strides with a fluid gait, wasting little energy.

Belvidius staggered under the load of his enormous body and the water vessel, his feet sinking deeper into the sand than anyone else's. Shortly, he was tired and begged the group to wait on him.

The group stopped. Ventras took a large pull of water from his vessel, and all others did the same, mimicking their self-appointed leader.

"Perhaps," Ventras said, "if we carried some of your water and lightened your load, Belividius, you could keep up. We are, for the most part, strong enough."

Belvidius looked at the group with suspicion. "We must measure!"

"Of course. We will count the dippers full and repay you when your water gets low."

By then the sun was already becoming unbearably hot. Each person knew water was gold out here.

Belvidius could not possibly carry all of his water any further. "You all swear I will have water when I run low?"

They all swore it was the truth, like the corrupt politicians they were, and Belvidius counted three dippers into each of his companion's vessels.

After resting, he stood, picked up his vessel, and said, "Much better! Thank you all for helping me. I am forever in your debt!"

Ventras and Derian walked in front, shoulder to shoulder. They glanced at each other out of the corners of their eyes, not turning their heads. Each of them picked up the pace.

Another half hour passed, and Belvidius begged again to stop and rest. Again, he lightened his load: two dippers apiece. As the trek resumed, he exclaimed at how much lighter his load had become. Several more of the group smiled knowingly at one another.

The day dragged on. The sun rose higher, and the day's heat became a blast furnace that baked them all crimson.

Ventras continued. Many begged to stop, to rest until it became cooler. Belvidius was no longer carrying his vessel or spear but dragging them behind him.

Ventras said, "The rock outcropping ahead, the map shows shade there. We must not stop here in the full sun or we will be baked alive; we must reach the protection of shade and then rest."

"I cannot go on! I absolutely can't continue!" It was, of course, Belvidius.

There were others in the group who were obese—several, in fact—but none so bloated as the man who now beseeched them.

"I'm going to the shade!" said Ventras. Most the others nodded assent.

Belvidius whined in a shrill, girlish voice, "I could possibly make it if someone would carry my vessel and spear. Would someone do that for me? I will share my water. I'll give four dippers to the one who helps me."

Ventras was first to speak. "I will carry your water. If you fail to make the outcropping—if you die before—your water ration becomes mine, and the same goes for your water that everyone else carries. Is it agreed?"

"Yes, Ventras!" he said, nodding. "I can make it. I just need to walk without the burden for a short distance."

"It is decided!" Ventras said, taking the second vessel, which was less than half-full, and the second spear. He set a brisk pace for the outcropping of stone.

All the others followed, with Belvidius far behind, slowly bringing up the rear.

\* \* \*

The shade seemed heaven sent. Each person found relief from the blazing sun in the coolness that emanated from the thermal mass stored within the rock from the previous night's chilled air.

All were exhausted and quickly fell asleep—all except Ventras. He waited until he could see sand dust being kicked up from Belvidius's footsteps in the distance, and then he picked up a spear and stole silently away from the sleeping group. He walked briskly through the heat waves towards his quarry.

Belvidius was staggering drunkenly, his stamina gone, drained under his enormous weight. "My old friend Ventras," he cried. "I am so happy to see you! You have come to assist me! How gracious of you!"

Ventras said nothing while he took in the pitiful sight. There was no way the massively overweight, staggering man could walk through this desert another four to five days, Ventras thought mercilessly. Even if it were possible, he was alone with no witnesses. If Ventras chose to spear him, who would ever know?

Belvidius saw the thoughts in the tall man's eyes. "You wouldn't! I have been a *friend* to you, a counselor in times of distress!"

"You, *dear* Belvidius, have *always* been a royal pain in my ass!"

With those words, Ventras thrust the spear savagely into the fat man's stomach.

Belvidius screamed.

"I would leave you here wounded, to suffer while the vultures pluck your eyes, yet I see you will make *way* too much noise!" Ventras plunged the spear again, this time into Belvidius's throat.

The screams subsided to a gurgle.

Ventras knelt before his victim and used Belvidius' clothing to wipe the spear clean of blood. The vile, bloated man, soon to be a corpse, twitched in his death throes.

Striding back towards the outcropping of rock, Ventras had a spring in his step. With this simple, enjoyable task complete, he was richer than any other person in the group.

Not far along the way back, a figure could be seen standing, looking towards Ventras. Ventras turned, looking to see if Belvidius' corpse was noticeable. The body stood out like a sore thumb on the barren desert.

Approaching the figure, he soon recognized Derian.

Derian was smiling.

"My complements, Ventras! Disposing of the excess baggage along our trek has been foremost on my mind. Surely you realize there are others who stand no chance out here?"

"Surely," was all the reply Ventras offered.

"Perhaps you and I could form a partnership of sorts?"

"And what sort of partnership do you have in mind?" asked Ventras, his eyes narrowing.

"You have taken care of one. I will take care of the next. At the same time, we watch each other's back. The need for sleep will be great and the fun has just begun. Do you think that when the water runs low we will all be cordial as we are now?"

"I am not a child nor do I act or play as a child. Few, if any of us, will make it out of here. TayGor has planned this to the letter: he's plotted the distance and analyzed the personalities. I guarantee you, this very instant he is out there, gloating and wondering how many of us are dead or murdered!"

"All the more reason for you and me to form a secret alliance," Derian said. "There is no need for the hopeless cases to consume water we could have for ourselves."

"I will agree to a partnership if one more is dead before we set out this evening; they are already consuming more water than a sensible ration allows! Do you agree to my terms?"

"Rest assured, Ventras, it *will* be done. We cannot have the ghosts of people we once knew consuming water that will be our very salvation."

"I wouldn't have put it quite like that, but you always were the one with the words."

"So we have an agreement?"

"Yes!"

They shook hands, each suspiciously eyeing the other.

They began walking back. Derian said, "I have been thinking, maybe it would make sense to stay in the safety and shade of the rocks until nightfall, and then walk by moonlight, when it is cool."

"First off, Derian, we do not know if this planet even has a moon. Surely TayGor thought of that! Do you think he would afford us that luxury?"

Derian looked perplexed, so Ventras continued.

"I guarantee he has calculated every last detail. If there is a moon, we will have been dropped during its dark period. He would see to that! No! We must set off as soon as the sun lowers in the sky but still affords light to travel four hours more. I have done the calculations.

If we can keep a good pace for eight hours per day, we could be to the mountains in as little as three and a half days. Theoretically, we carry enough water to last us for five days, but today has been the easiest by far."

"What do you mean?" asked Derian."

"I mean that TayGor picked this drop zone so that we would have shade halfway through our first day. It was a luxury."

Derian looked at Ventras with widening eyes as the true brutality of their predicament dawned on him. They were both sweating profusely.

"We have, in theory, five days worth of water; but the way we are perspiring right now is the rate we will be losing water for the rest of the trek. Do not think of the moon. I guarantee the bastard TayGor has had years to plan our demise; he has left nothing out of his blueprint!"

The two walked back in silence. Ventras considered how he could protect himself from his new partner.

Derian looked forward to dispatching his least favorite person in the group.

Along the way, a small snake with black, red, and brown diamond patterns upon its back crossed their path. Derian immediately stepped lightly on the snake behind the head. Picking the reptile up with fingers just behind the head, he inspected the writhing creature.

The reptile was not happy and made his anger well known by opening his jaws wide and snapping. Venom squirted from the hollow incisors.

"It is poisonous, I guarantee you! These young snakes are the worst!" Derian giggled and said, "What a bed partner this will make for Fervorous!"

"You have chosen him?" Ventras asked in disbelief.

"Yes! I have had a problem with him for a long time. You see, we have never met eye to eye. Fervorous always negotiates behind my back, never showing his cards, always currying favor with the Fifteen and trying to discredit me."

"So even though he is strong, healthy, and able to carry his burden, you wish to lay waste to him?"

Derian smiled. "Yes, of course! If we are to be trapped together like so many shipwrecked sailors and rats sharing a raft, why not throw the most despised rats overboard?"

Ventras looked at the man again in a new light. "Derian, it is your choice; however, I thought we had agreed to take out the weakest of our group, not just the ones who have frustrated us in the past."

"Oh! And *you* did not have a personal grudge against the late Belvidius?"

"Well, we all knew I cared little for him, but he was also weak," answered Ventras.

"*Cared little for him!* I say when you stick a man in the belly with a sharp spear, you care for that man more than just a little, even if the emotion is not love!" Derian chuckled at his own words.

Ventras fell silent, pondering the situation: Derian was a thinker; always had been. *Beware!* he thought to himself. *Beware of this man who represents himself as your friend.*

They came upon the outcropping, and Derian placed one finger against his closed lips in the ancient signal for silence. They crept along, and then Derian walked directly towards Fervorous.

# THE SEEDING SEVEN'S VISION

Derian had been torturing the little snake, shaking it and taunting it. He walked quietly up to Fervorous, gently lifted the front of the sleeping man's tunic, and dropped the angry reptile upon his chest. He then quickly moved away.

At once there was a commotion: screaming and shouting, and the dismay of Fervorous's voice when he understood he had been bitten multiple times by the viper.

All gathered round to console the afflicted man.

Derian was the most vocal. "My friend, what bad luck! Surely the snake was not poisonous?"

"I can feel the venom working as we speak! What can be done to save me?" asked Fervorous.

The others tore open his tunic to inspect the damage while Derian watched, controlling his happiness and affecting a sincere look of dismay.

"Bitten many times," one said.

"And on the neck—not good!" said another.

"What! What does it mean?" cried Fervorous.

"It means, my dear friend, that you must rest quietly," Derian said, with well-contained delight. "Keep your heart rate low, for if you excite yourself, the venom will only travel more rapidly."

Fervorous quieted himself. "Is that all I can do?"

"We were, unfortunately, left here by TayGor without medical supplies. All we can do is wait."

Fervorous's neck began to swell immediately. His breathing became a restricted rattle, and his face began to bulge and turn a dark shade of blue.

Derian motioned all the onlookers to move away from the fallen man. Silently, they stole to a location out of earshot.

"He is done for! There is nothing we can do, the poor, unfortunate soul," Derian said to the crowd.

Ventras watched as Derian addressed the group and then broke in: "We must set off while we still have light. Every hour we procrastinate means more water consumed. If we do not leave now, we will be forced to stay through the darkness of night, and then we may not have enough water to sustain us through to the spring of water marked on the map."

Ventras had dictated the terms of passage into the promised land. Assent was unanimous.

Derian then said, "We must not leave all his water. The most he can last is a few hours. We should leave him with a few dippers and be on our way."

"And what of Belvidius?" someone asked.

"He is no doubt lost out there or dead. We cannot wait on him either!"

All agreed.

Ventras added, "I carried Belvidius' water and spear. Do not forget that each of you carry five dippers of water that belong to me!"

"It is true, Ventras," Derian said, "yet I do not think you can carry all the weight. I shall help you!"

All were made to reluctantly take five dippers of the treasured water from their vessels and place them into the vessels that would be borne by Ventras and Derian.

Fervorous' remaining water was appropriated from him and divided equally among the group. Ventras and Derian ended up with more water than they had started the journey with, each carrying two vessels that were two thirds full. All others in the party had much less than their original ration.

The trek continued. By the time darkness fell and the group stopped, all were severely sunburned. With no hats to protect their faces from the baking sun, they were suffering greatly. Blisters had already begun to form, and it was only the end of the first day.

Ventras began shaping some dry desert grass he had collected, weaving the blades into a crude helmet. Others in the group had seen him collect the desert grass but had no clue as to how he would put it to use.

"Derian!" Ventras called.

"Yes! I am here."

"Check the water and see how our fellows' rations are holding."

The day had been feverishly hot, even though the group had rested in shade through the worst heat of the desert afternoon.

Derian checked the rations and then reported back. "Most of the vessels are two thirds full, Ventras. Some less."

Ventras stood. "Listen to me, all of you. Tomorrow and every day thereafter, you will be allowed only six dippers per twenty-four hour period! This rule applies until we have replenished our water. Is this clear?"

Some agreed, but others questioned his authority.

"Who are you to control our water?" someone muttered, yet no one wished to challenge openly Ventras' leadership.

The mood was dark; the sun and the grueling trek had taken its toll. With no food to eat, many were suffering from piercing hunger and unstable blood sugar.

Derian agreed with Ventras. "He is right. Those that drink too quickly will perish out here!"

Ventras spoke loudly so that all could hear. "There are over one hundred kilometers yet to travel. Today, with all of us in good shape, we traveled about thirty-two kilometers."

"How do you know how far we have traveled?" someone asked.

"Surely we have covered much more than thirty-two kilometers!" another added.

"I calculated the length of my stride and counted every step. I can assure you the distance is correct."

"If what you say is true, we won't be out of this God-forsaken wasteland in four more days."

"If we keep traveling at our present rate, yes, we will make it out."

"How can we last four more days in this heat?" another beet-red, blistered, and sunburned person asked. Then he broke down into gut-wrenching sobs. Tears would not come because dehydration was beginning to set in.

"Some of us may not," Ventras answered.

The obese Telthin could be heard snoring already. He had wasted no time in getting to sleep among the bickering, sunburned travelers.

"Telthin has the right idea. We should all get some rest," said Ventras.

"We must start walking in the morning, as soon as we can see," Derian added.

Another asked, "Why don't we travel at night? It is so much cooler."

"You are welcome to go on if you have the energy," Ventras answered, "but can you see the range of mountains we are heading towards?"

"No."

"Then how do you propose to find your way? We have only one compass, and right now it is too dark for me to read the needle."

"Surely the moon will come up, we could walk some more by moonlight."

Ventras responded, "If there is a moon and it does become light enough to make our way, I would gladly walk when it is cooler."

The deep of night came briskly, and along with it a bitter cold and a chill wind that reached into their bones and wrung any remaining heat from them. Those who had been suffering from the heat during daylight now shivered and shook, teeth chattering.

The bitter wind raked the unprotected landscape. Ventras rose and began to dig in the sand with his hands and spear.

"What are you doing, Ventras?" asked Telthin.

"I am digging a sleeping hole. I intend to cover myself with sand in an attempt to stay warm."

"A good idea!" said Telthin.

Others began the same process, and soon ten shallow impressions in the soft sand were made.

Climbing into his pit, Ventras began raking sand back over himself. He laughed mirthlessly. "The sand is still warm and feels wonderful. I never thought I would find joy sleeping with sand in my various crevices."

The weary trekkers began laughing—a sound that had escaped the group since the grueling journey began.

Others could be heard marveling and sighing happily in the new-found warmth of their burrows. Telthin was the last to dig a hole large enough for his massive body.

Before long, the silence of sleep came upon them. It was only broken by Telthin's intermittent snoring.

Ventras was awake before false dawn. He waited for the first slivers of light so that he could begin walking for the second day. *Today we will see what this group is made of and who will be contenders for the finish,* he thought.

The day before them would be the worst so far; they were all weary and skin burned, and many had been complaining of blisters on their feet.

Ventras spied the disheveled Derian, sand in his hair and dried crust in the corners of his eyes.

"Morning, Derian."

"A good morn to you, Ventras."

The blackened sky began to turn a lightened gray, and Ventras loudly ordered the group awake. They moaned and groaned, but all rose. A more ragged, sorry-looking lot would be difficult to imagine, thought Ventras, as he dusted the sand from his hair and tunic.

Looking for his hat, he saw that it was missing and remembered the wind. "Blast! And damnation!"

"What?" asked Derian.

"My hat has been blown to who knows where!"

"More is the pity. You looked so fashionable in your desert creation. We were all jealous!"

Laughs emitted from the gritty group.

Ventras instructed them to make sure no sand remained in their shoes, for it would rub their feet raw within a few kilometers.

Telthin began to dump the sand out of one shoe. Along with the cascading sand came a small green scorpion. The creature fell to the desert floor and scurried away.

"Holy mother!" Telthin exclaimed. "Those little green guys are the *most* poisonous!"

Furtive looks passed through the group of ten, and then they began trudging wearily towards the distant mountains, which still slept in a blanket of white-grey mist and fog.

Another torturous day passed.

# SEVENTEEN

Tay, Alex, and their trusted few woke each group as the ship drew near their respective drop zones. Full consciousness was not allowed so they could ensure that the many dangerous criminals would be easy to handle. The groups of former life prisoners, still in a state of half-sleep, were left with clothing, bedding, proper footwear, and rations to carry them a few days. There was plenty of edible vegetable matter on the planet, as well as fish in the streams, berries in the forests, and grain ripening in the savannas. No weapons were allowed, but there was an abundance of wood available that they could use to fashion primitive weapons. For a man or woman who had been sentenced to life in prison, it should be considered a heavenly reprieve.

Upon awakening, not one of them was happy. "Where is the ship? Where are our weapons? Where the hell are we?" the groups asked. Each of the different groups waking in drastically varying climates asked similar questions, and when no answers were forthcoming, they all swore revenge—revenge upon the men who had set them free. The evil ones did not see this place as freedom but simply another sort of prison. There were no innocents to rob, murder, rape, or swindle. Most everyone was unhappy.

They built crude shelters and found caves and fashioned weapons in the ancient style. They settled into suffering their lot as food gatherers and pitiful farmers until the day TayGor would be found.

Over time, those who had been dropped in the hot southern climes migrated northward to more moderate areas, and those who had been dropped into the cold northern climes migrated southward, brandishing unhealthy sunburns. Foremost in every group's mind was the dream of finding steel, gold, or precious gems—and of revenge. The only person to blame was TayGor. The false legends began to grow. The vendetta to find TayGor and act out their hate and frustration became the driving force amongst them.

Their ruthless determination and dissatisfaction with what could have been a wonderful new beginning became instead a canker, an ambition to move on to find the place TayGor called home.

Only one of the groups would be successful in the quest to find Tay: the northerners, the meat eaters. With blood on their clothes and rotting teeth, they came, moving further south each year until one day they saw smoke from fire. In their wayward travels, fire had been elusive. There had been only rain and more rain: wet, soaking land, and no flint. No steel. Sometimes in the summer months, a fire could be made from rubbing sticks, or by catching the burn from lightning. Mostly, meat was eaten raw. Fish were caught from the rivers with sharp wooden spears or by hand and eaten raw. Animals were plentiful, the group easily killed as many as they needed. Still, they cursed the lack of fire. No one was suffering and no stomach was empty; their hunger came from the sense of entitlement born within the criminal mentality.

Here, they all had to *work* to survive. They could not just take from another because each was as ruthless as the next. Ancient primeval laws came into being on their own; no one stole from another or someone died.

These were not the mostly innocent caught up in archaic laws that imprisoned a starving person for stealing something to eat; they had been culled from a highly sophisticated and tolerant society. They were the worst of humankind—skulking, murdering, venomous creatures who had previously made their sordid way in life, taking from others.

They could not afford to lose members of their tribe. The tribe must grow in numbers, multiply into a force that would inspire fear. So within a culture born of man's base nature, a set of rules were spawned: primitive, redundantly primeval, and brutally real at the same time.

They bred like rats and dragged their dirty, disheveled children along behind them.

Before many years passed, hundreds of children accompanied the groups. The children were all engrained with a hatred that had been painted into their young, impressionable minds by their ruthless parents. Mostly it was hate for the one who had left them stranded in the stone age. The thankless parents told the children embroidered tales of a past life of luxury and of power and wonder stolen from their families.

A planet is a small globe, seeming large when walking on foot, yet the northern people built crude boats.

They traversed the vast north sloping lands in only a few years and found, further south, horses: vast herds that could transport the tribe over eighty kilometers a day.

A tribal meeting was called once they had mastered the wild horse. The culture was divided in two, and they spread, agreeing to send a group of messengers back once a year for a council in which they would report any new lands found.

One group headed southwest, finding lands rich and expansively beautiful. The southwestern group was a selfish lot who did not want to share paradise. They decided not to send messengers to the annual meeting, fearing they would have to share this new land where the sun shone warm and the game was plentiful.


Andarean's group would land on the Virgin only a short eighteen months before being discovered by the wild ones. Their family consisted of a close-knit group of less than forty persons who all believed they were the only humans inhabiting the Virgin.

Their numbers were much less than the horde from the north.


Tay landed with his small party and first organized the camp, directing the construction of earth shelters that they should easily be able to complete before winter set in. Each shelter would be comfortably heated with a small fire and be defensible from wild animals.

He chose a level site that faced southwest and rested above a steep slope. The spot had a crystal-clear, ice-cold stream that sprang from a rock promontory higher on the ridge above. The shelf upon which they would build their settlement was high above the valley floor. The soil had evidently been washed down from higher on the hill over eons and was deep and rich. There were few trees. It seemed that grazing animals had kept this spot clear of brush and forest. Tay was concerned about the great numbers of elk. Elk loved to roll in fresh earth and could destroy a subsistence garden in a minute or two, and they could easily jump an eight-foot fence if they set their mind to it. However, the strategy to have the small settlement up off the valley floor should protect their gardens somewhat, as the elk tended to roam only the lower valley.

He planned the placement of the homes: they would be built against the upward shoulder of the shelf, backed into the hillside. This would afford each home a large flat area in front for a small garden. The site also meant the structures could not be seen from the valley below. A big bonus was that with little effort, the cold stream could be diverted to run along the back of each home and thus be used not only for household water but also to chill perishables. The site was perfect. It reminded Tay of the place in his dreams where he had encountered and had a stand-off with the large, dark stallion.

His group did not need a huge pasture as yet. They had no horses or meat animals. They would hunt protein for the table and grow their vegetables in small plots next to their shelters. The ship had carried seed and other stock in its holds as emergency staples in case of a forced landing, so they had plenty to work with.

Everyone was busy, some planting, others building or hunting. Everything considered, life was good. The group got along well, and every person carried their part of the load. There was still much needing completion before winter set in.

Alex walked up to where Denali was digging. She was excavating into the hillside and, although she had been working for only a few hours, she had moved a surprising amount of earth.

"Hey, Denali. How's it going?"

She looked up from her work and noticed that Alex had a shovel in his hand. "Good, Alex. How are you?"

"Great, I was thinking that we could work together on a place. It's going to be a long winter...and I thought... well...maybe we could try living together, keep each other company maybe?" Alex's smile was warm and hopeful.

Denali paused from her work and took him in. She thought, *I truly do like him. He's sweet and gentle...but he deserves something better than me.*

"Alex, I'm not very good company," she said, "and I like being alone. Don't you ever give up?"

"I've never thought of being without you as a friend. Give up? I mean, it's not like I'm attempting to scale an unclimbable mountain." Alex looked into her eyes and smiled again, attempting to make her smile or laugh in response.

"You are, Alex. I've told you the same thing countless times. I can't be with you."

"What's wrong with me then? I adore you! I would never mistreat you! I will be faithful and honest. I'll work hard on this new beginning we're all facing, so you never have to go hungry. Can't you see, Denali...? I would do anything for you."

"I know you would, Alex," she said, shaking her head. "There is nothing wrong with you. The wrong is with *me*!"

"Denali, please, just let go of all that...the darkness you've spoken of. Just let it freaking go!"

"I can't, Alex. I've tried. It will always haunt me. Sometimes, I shut myself up and don't go out for days. The memories come. I'm a prisoner to them. I can't turn the vid off! It keeps running until I'm so exhausted I crash into sleep. And it keeps playing...even then! I've explained this to you before. You don't want to be around me when I get like that!"

"Yes, I do!"

"NO! You don't! I dream of executing people in my sleep. I'm a modern grim reaper, taking people's lives. When I'm overcome, all I can do is shut myself in like a vampire so I don't hurt someone! I could, in one of my fits, hurt you, and not even know it *was* you!"

"That's crazy! You would know me. You've sworn to be my guardian, my protector. Would you break a sacred oath? No! I don't think so. You see, you are worrying about something that can't possibly happen, so just give it up! Let's move in together. Let's builds a cabin and a life here...together."

She looked at him in silence. He smiled his warmest, most heartfelt smile. Her face was blank.

"Alex, we can build together...but two separate cabins. I'll help you and you help me. We'll both have our own places. I can offer you that much, nothing more."

"It's a lot more work, Denali. We could just build one. It would be so much easier!"

"I have never cared about 'easy' before, and I won't start now. It can only be the way I said, nothing more. I don't want you getting your hopes up…when there are none possible."

"Okay, Denali," he said. "We'll do it your way."

Alex began shoveling alongside the woman of his dreams.

# EIGHTEEN

VENTRAS set a grueling pace with his long strides, and soon most of the followers were a quarter mile behind. They could be heard pleading and wailing in loud voices, crying for him to wait.

Ventras stopped and turned around, taking in the group, which he assumed would not last the day. All were obese except for Derian, but some were more so than others. Derian was quickly beside him and breathing heavily. He was a small, wiry man, yet Ventras' long legs made the task of keeping up difficult.

"We should leave the lot of them!" Ventras said in disgust.

"Do not forget, Ventras, if we leave them, we would be ditching a great treasure in these barren lands. The most valuable thing any of us carry is our burden of water. Surely, if it were gold, you would not be considering leaving it behind but contriving of some way to part it from its owner." Derian smiled knowingly, appraising the tall man's reaction.

"Before abandoning the stragglers, let us focus our creative juices on the quandary, not on the despicable traveling companions we have been burdened with.

What do you say? We have some time before they catch up; we can talk privately. I have my next victim selected. It is only a matter of time."

Derian took a small piece of cloth from his pocket and untied the string that bound the ends together. The makeshift satchel opened to reveal a small, green scorpion. Derian quickly wrapped the package back up and returned it to his pocket.

"You picked up the scorpion that fell from Telthin's shoe?"

"Of course, my dear Ventras," Derian said, smiling. "We do not have many tools here. I did not desire one so valuable to escape without it ever being put to use."

"What do you have planned?" Ventras asked.

"Surely we must dispatch at least two more of these weary travelers and put them to rest so that they suffer no more. Just look at them: some cannot even walk in a straight line; they will never make it out of here. Why have them suffering for days, consuming our precious resources? We should be commended for being so full of mercy. It is our duty, Ventras. Do not shirk."

"I do not. I am only thinking of options."

"Good! Good! I love options." The sunburned little man giggled like a young girl, clearly enjoying the situation.

Ventras looked Derian in the eyes, thinking that the two of them would be alone soon, and then the most dangerous portion of the journey would begin. Derian, the great orator, was a deviate—not just corrupt. Ventras realized that Derian was gaining personal enjoyment from this sick situation. He would bear watching closely. Ventras would not sleep, he decided, when only the two of them remained.

Ventras' mind went back to the problems at hand. He watched the wayward group who were still trudging toward him and Derian. "The fat ones who make it through the day, we leave behind tomorrow. They are drinking way too fast," Ventras spat in disgust.

"Even at our present pace, we ourselves will run out of water before we reach the spring. Our next victims must be those who have the largest reserves of water remaining. However, you and I cannot carry their burden through the heat today. Better to pick it up in the morning, and leave the others behind while they still sleep."

"A good plan, Ventras, yet I was hoping to have a little fun tonight." Derian patted the pocket that held the scorpion, still grinning.

"Do as you wish. Some will not make it through the day anyway. Look at the way they stagger under their burden of lard. Their lack of self-control and their voracious appetites will be the death of them. They won't die by our hands, rest assured of that."

"Aye, Ventras, and just as you speak, one has fallen."

The group of stragglers stopped and gathered around the prone man. After a short while, they picked up the unmoving figure's water vessel and continued.

Derian said, "Three down and seven to go. How many more do you think will drop before this day closes, Ventras?"

"You see the three bringing up the rear?"

"Yes," Derian answered, watching the group through slitted eyes.

"They know they are doomed. They are so fat, they are drinking way too much trying to keep cool. Their water is nearly depleted, and they know they cannot continue much longer. It shows in their countenance. Soon, they will simply give up. Look at the sky above them."

Derian's eyes roamed the platinum-blue above. A host of condors waited, circling effortlessly, soaring upon invisible air currents, watching the scene below.

"The vultures know as do I that those pitiful creatures will not last much longer. They wait patiently, knowing their bellies will soon be full."

Before Ventras had finished speaking, the great birds began to glide downward, one after another. Derian counted seventeen in all. "That bloated corpse who was once a man should feed them quite well. Soon they will be so fat they may not be able to take flight," Ventras said.

Derian began laughing uncontrollably, and then he began hacking. He bent at the waist, coughing in a prolonged fit, and then expelled a nasty gob of greenish phlegm.

Finally straightening up, his face a dark red and purple color, Derian exclaimed, "Ah! This desert air and the three-day fast is doing me a great service: cleaning the city air from my lungs and the poisons from my body. I should be thanking TayGor right now for my all-expense paid visit to this magnificent dry sauna!" Derian's eyes filled with humor. "I shall walk out and see who has fallen," he said.

Derian met the stragglers about fifty meters from where Ventras stood. Ventras could hear them pleading to rest and saying that the great orator and chair of the Twelve, Gentrelle, had fallen, apparently dead from heat stroke or heart attack.

Ventras estimated the group had taken over ten minutes to catch up. In that time, he would have been over a kilometer closer to the spring. He made a decision in that instant, one that he had been considering for the past two days.

The weary group finally came together, some sobbing, others gasping, all gulping water. The more weary of the bunch spilled some of the precious fluid in their careless attempts to quell a thirst that was inevitably going to kill them.

Ventras spoke in a loud and commanding voice: "I waited here for over ten minutes for you to catch up. In that time, the sun has grown more severe and the heat more unbearable. I should by all rights be another kilometer closer to the spring, yet I waited here for a bunch of pitiful, obese whiners who are zigzagging to their deaths. I can only feel disgust, not sympathy or compassion. Destiny and fate is falling upon every head here!"

Frerand broke in, interrupting the tirade: "Our feet are raw from the sand. We are weary and sunburned. We must rest, for surely we cannot continue at this moment."

"You are welcome to stay with your friend Gentrelle and the new acquaintances he has made." Ventras gestured toward the bloated body in the near distance behind the sniveling group. All turned and took in the seventeen voracious scavengers, fighting with each other for position and ripping shreds of meat from the fallen man.

"I'm going now! We are heading for that rock pinnacle in the distance. There is a valley to the left of that landmark, and within the valley is a spring that flows from a rock face about three kilometers up the valley. Stay on the right side of the valley and you will find the spring easily. All those that can keep my pace, follow me! We must not be slowed by these stragglers or all will perish out here!"

Ventras turned and began walking. His long strides seemed effortless to those who could not possibly continue.

Those who could walk followed Ventras towards the mountains. Heat waves rose from the desert floor in front of him. Ventras appeared to be walking into an oven, and none in the group relished following him, yet they had no choice: they could follow, or be eaten half-alive by the buzzards. A few of the more exhausted ones, whose water was nearly depleted, collapsed in fits of crying, yet no tears came; dehydration had stolen them. Even the spine-tingling shrieks and hideous squawks from the revolting creatures that dominated the desert floor behind them did nothing to spur them into moving.

Seeing Gentrelle's fate, and knowing they could go no further, they turned three pairs of bleary eyes away from the gruesome scene and towards their former companions, who were shrinking into the horizon with each passing minute. Shortly, the figures in the distance seemed to be only ghosts or wisps of dust vanishing into the shimmering mirages of the desert.


For those who continued The merciless sun pounded their already tortured and deeply burned skin. Throbbing blisters formed, then burst and scabbed over on the feet, lips, and faces of all. Each man truly believed they had entered hell. All remaining wondered whether they would make it out of this blast furnace alive.

Still, Ventras would not let up. As though possessed by some supernatural demon, he continued his long, seemingly effortless gait, without a backwards glance.

The afternoon sun began to wane. Just as the temperature began to drop slightly, another man collapsed, evidently from heat stroke, for upon examination he was still breathing.

Ventras continued. The others followed. He was a powerful magnet, pulling them along. Everyone knew that to stop meant certain death, while continuing meant excruciating pain, unbearable yet endured for lack of any other reasonable option. The sand scoured and drew blood from their feet.

The five sun-scorched trekkers finally collapsed into the sand just as the sun set behind the western mountains. Drinking the store of water remaining, each man pondered what was to come on the following day. Most wondered how they could possibly continue, and two knew that most would not be traveling farther. The weak would rest here...indefinitely.

There was very little water remaining, and they were only three days into the journey. Ventras had calculated the distance to be five days' walk, meaning the last two days they would have little to no water to sustain them. The thoughts of the group were grim. Some considered the remaining distance. Others calculated nightfall and the despicable deeds that would soon be done.


Ventras and Derian feigned sleep as the other exhausted men fell into slumber, not knowing it was their last. Derian was the first to move, silently crawling towards one of the sleeping men. He opened the cloth package and shook out the scorpion above the face of the unsuspecting victim. Upon landing, the scorpion began viciously stabbing his stinger into the man's forehead.

A ruckus ensued. Everyone woke to find Arraz swatting and pulling at his hair.

Derian and Ventras backed away from the others who had been drawn by the commotion and came to help the stricken man, unaware of the evil intent brewing in the two men standing behind them.

Ventras and Derian had planned the distraction to a tee: as the men were engrossed in disentangling the scorpion from Arraz' hair, they struck from behind: swift spear strikes in the kidneys. The men never screamed, only fell to their knees, and then onto their faces, which were frozen in a look of pain and surprise. Arraz was left standing alone.

Derian smiled most wickedly and simply said, "I have nothing against you personally, old friend; I just need your water."

With that, Derian proceeded to run his spear point through the heart of the afflicted man. Arraz, eyes wide in disbelief, died well, without a sound. He was doubtless happy to be free from the torturous events that had consumed them all for the past three days.

Ventras and Derian set off at daybreak with their store of water increased. Ventras set a pace so grueling that the much smaller Derian had an impossible time keeping up. It was as if Ventras was made of well-tempered spring steel, never tiring, rarely drinking, and completely oblivious to the elements Derian felt shredding his once spry body.

Derian stopped often to drink the life-giving fluid. He would stop and be extremely careful not to spill a drop, and each time Ventras drew farther ahead.

"Ventras!" Derian yelled.

Ventras never even looked back.

Derian began to plot, seething in anger. He dreamed of drinking Ventras' water—and then his blood! The thought of having the blood of Ventras on his hands kept Derian trudging along, placing one blistered, raw, and bleeding foot after the other.

Hate grew like a fungus, consuming Derian's brain. It spoke to his enfeebled mind like an old and trusted friend. It said that the man who had driven him on so relentlessly—and who had made him walk so quickly that he had to consume all his precious water—that man must die!

When nightfall came, Derian pledged silently to himself that he would be the only one standing when dawn's light fell upon this God-forsaken land. Somewhere within the twisted, heat-baked fabric of his mind, he justified the crime of killing one whom, just a few short hours ago, he had counted as his friend.

Ventras pretended to sleep, snoring lightly. He could feel Derian watching him. The only remaining water lay beside Ventras, and Derian's thirst was burning, not only in his throat, which was so dry he swore that sand had filled it, but also his tongue, which was so hard it was beginning to crack and bleed. Derian could taste the blood; it burned into his throat. The burning reached into the depths of his mind, a fever raging, subduing rational thought.

*I must have water!* Derian thought. He could hear Ventras snoring and silently crept towards the vessel. The life-saving fluid was his only desire. His was depleted, but he must have some; and Ventras had made it clear he would not share.

Derian crept on his hands and knees closer to the sleeping man: the hoarder, the bastard who had driven him so hard Derian had consumed his water far too rapidly. It was only fair that Ventras should share.

Ventras, hiding the position of his spear, calculated the other man's movements and continued to fake a rhythmic snore. Regardless of whether Derian meant to harm him physically or just steal some water in the blackness of night, Ventras planned to kill him. He could not take the chance of leaving the desperate man alive; one slip, one drop of the guard, and Derian would do the same to him, thought Ventras. Of that, he was certain.

Ventras could hear Derian's quiet breath, the sand moving beneath his hands and feet. Adrenalin flooded his body. His heartbeat drummed in his ears, and he could literally feel the blood racing through his vessels.

He opened his eyes, and found Derian kneeling at his feet, his eyes gleaming like a feral animal's in the meager starlight.

"I am sorry, old friend. It must be you, for there is not enough water for the two of us!"

A spear point glistened, shuddering and turning wickedly in the dimly lit night sky. Derian dropped the point quickly, aiming for Ventras' solar plexus.

Ventras was ready. He kicked the point to the side and brought his own sand-covered weapon to bear. Derian let out a shrill shriek, like a girl, as the point took him directly in the liver. Ventras twisted the shaft and plunged it deeper. Derian let out a moan that could almost have been mistaken for a young woman climaxing in euphoria.

Ventras gained his feet and then looked down at his quarry.

Derian's eyes were not so bright as they had been a moment before. "You knew," he gasped.

Ventras nodded, pulled the spear point clear and then wiping the blood off on Derian's tattered clothing. "I guess our partnership has been dissolved," he said.

Derian trembled, then expelled his last breath with a gurgling sigh, which Ventras understood to be agreement.

In the morning, Ventras woke as the first grey light etched across the forbidding lunar scape. He noticed that his water vessel had been toppled over in the skirmish. He had been so satisfied with himself after killing Derian, he had fallen into a deep and restful slumber and had not thought to check the position of the vessel. It had been capped tightly, but evidently some sand had kept it from sealing perfectly. A wet spot in the sand made Ventras' heart jolt. "No!" he screamed, righting his overturned treasure chest.

The water within was nearly gone. Only a small amount remained. Ventras felt sick in the heart. What remained was less than a liter, and he knew it would not last till midday.

Ventras was unsure of the distance left as his course had led him to wander a bit, and he had lost count of the steps in a heat-induced fatigue. Surely, he thought, he could make it to the spring by that evening.

He set off, his pace not as brisk the few days past. His heart was filled with dread. Before him lay the last stretch of heat-baked sand, which stood between his burning thirst and the promised pool of water. He looked to the compass, and to the blue-green hills, so near. The desert offered its tricks to a man dying of thirst, yet Ventras would not be fooled by the apparitions.

In this part of the desert, the sand had drifted into dunes. No longer was the walking surface flat and fairly easy to traverse. Each step sapped more of his waning strength as his feet sank deep into the soft sand. With every step, he silently cursed the one who had abandoned him here.

"TayGor!" Ventras shouted, swearing revenge. If he made it out of there, his one goal in life would be to kill that bastard TayGor! Ventras trudged along painfully, his mind filled with hate and delirium. Eventually, a trancelike state encompassed him. He was driven by thoughts of the despised TayGor. He vowed to seek retribution, no matter the cost, and he gained strength from thoughts of torturing TayGor—getting even for his personal suffering.

# NINETEEN

When the morning sun broke the horizon, the warmth soaked through Ventras' body. He lay where he had collapsed, his breath ragged and throat parched. It felt good, he thought, lying there, the suffering nearly over, his life at its premature close.

Reflecting on the many years of his promising life, he found it odd that he lay here friendless and alone, with no one to witness his last hours. It was fitting, he thought. He had always been a lone wolf, and so alone he would die.

A shadow passed over him, breaking the sun's rays for an instant, then another shadow and another. In his dehydrated stupor, it took a few moments for the shadows to penetrate the fog that had enveloped his mind, but finally he thought, *Vultures!*

Ventras rolled onto his back and opened his scabby eyes. The sun hurt them and pounded into his brain like a sledgehammer. The sky above him was full of winged creatures with ragged feathers. They circled silently, effortlessly, lower and lower. Ventras counted thirty of the scavengers before giving up; there were too many to count.

*So this is it,* he thought. Eaten alive by some stinking birds who did not even care who he was or how *powerful* he had been. He was just something to fill their bellies. "So be it," he said, in a croaking voice.

One of the boldest condors slid silently down from the sky and landed a few meters from the fallen man, sizing him up with beady eyes. The bird could see that this creature was still breathing and remembered being challenged by a similar dying animal once before. But in the end, the flock always won. The vulture hopped forward three times. The man did not seem to move.

Exhausted and crippled by lack of water, Ventras braced himself for the inevitable. He would give himself to the flying creatures, he thought. Because he had no strength left. He knew that once this bird began feeding, the hoard would descend and finish him quickly. He had no desire to prolong his suffering; he could endure it no more, so he was happy knowing his end was at hand.

The condor struck. It bit his left forearm and jerked violently, attempting to strip a chunk of flesh from Ventras' bones.

Ventras, to his own amazement, grabbed his spear, sprung to his feet, and struck the giant bird a fatal blow.

More of the creatures had already come down from the sky, greed pulling them. They had not wanted to be left out of the feeding frenzy about to begin. Ventras swung his spear in an arc over his head and then low to the ground, like a farmer cutting tall grass. Three of the condors' heads came off, and blood pumped from their thrashing, flailing bodies. He had caught them by surprise, before they could alight and escape to the sky.

The birds were clumsy on the ground, and the man moved quickly, jabbing them with his long, sharp weapon, some while they were still beating their wings, frantically trying to break gravities forceful suction. He quickly skewered five more.

He was exhilarated: Ventras had thought he was done for, but he had found energy in reserve. Springing into action gave him hope, determination, and the willingness to set off once more towards the mountains and the spring of cool water of which he dreamed.

Ventras had known exhaustion. As a young man, he had worked bucking hay in the fields. Bales weighing over fifty kilos were tossed for twelve hours a day. He recalled how, on the first few days of that job, he had felt as though he would collapse, but he had rested for a few minutes and then began slinging bales again.

Perhaps, he thought, he had pushed himself too hard. From now on, he would walk for ten minutes and rest for three. In this manner, he made his way over the last dune. Then he saw what lay before him, some kilometers in the distance: a valley so green and lush he felt as though he could taste the crystal cold spring water.

He staggered like a blind man, puss oozing from the many cracks in his sun-damaged skin. His eyes were scabbed slits, barely open enough to see. Still he went on, feet raw and bleeding from the sand, lips cracked deeply like sunbaked mud. They, too, bled, and the oozing blood had blackened and dried, so that his face became an unmovable mask of disfigurement, an unrecognizable horror. On he trudged, dragging his feet through the soft sand.

Finally, with nothing more to give to the hostile land, no reserves left, he tumbled to the earth, croaking through his cracked and bleeding mask. "Noooo!"

He could move no more. Every muscle in his body screamed for mercy. His mind spoke words of comfort: *Just lay still. It will not be long now. Your suffering will be over. Soon you will suffer no more.* But the other voice spoke, too: the one that reminded him of his hatred for TayGor. Ventras did not know which voice to believe; the one that spoke of hatred or the one that told him to lie still and assured him, he would hurt no more.

Ventras knew he was finished. The spring of water was so close, a mere two kilometers away, yet he could travel no more without water. Without nourishment, he was dead. A haze came over his mind like a fog drifting in over the ocean. A bright light shone through the fog, beckoning to him. *Come,* it said. *Leave that crippled body behind and be free. Suffer no more.*

Ventras begrudgingly held on; he was not yet ready to let go of his hate.

Ventras thought of TayGor's unwillingness to die, his unwillingness to rot in prison. Ventras admitted to himself, even within his delirious mind, that he had underestimated a foe, and *that* was why he was here. Not because of Karma and not because of past deeds, but because he had underestimated a foe. He had miscalculated his opponent's creative resilience, so he had lost the game. *I have lost, and TayGor has won*, his mind screamed, as he prepared himself for his inevitable death.

Thoughts of his childhood raced through the fog, and then there was nothing: no thoughts, no emotions, only resignation to the fact he had slowly accepted over the past few hours.

Ventras had no energy left to even keep his crusted, cracking eyelids open. He closed them at last, bringing himself some peace and tranquility, and felt the happiest he had been in a long, long time. *Take me! Take me!* he thought.

A thump resounded on his chest. He waited for the inevitable pain, which would come from the flesh being ripped from his breast, yet all he felt was another thump, this time on his waist. Still, there was no pain. Ventras' curiosity was piqued. Struggling, he painfully opened one eye and saw something brilliant red shining on his chest. Ventras thought, *Surely I am not so far gone that I would not feel the vultures plucking flesh from my bones.*

There were no squawks or screeches—and no giant birds fighting over his flesh. Ventras pondered for a few minutes, and then a cactus fruit fell directly onto his face. Breathing in the fragrance, he was immediately hungry. He moved his arm, which was stiff from the broken sun-scabbed skin and that, moments before, he had thought he would never move again. He shoved the heavenly manna through his broken, bleeding lips. He chewed. The fruit was dry, with little moisture, yet some saliva came from an unexplained place, and soon his tongue worked again. The sugar from the fruit gave him energy enough to grope the ground for more.

Soon, exhausted from the effort, he rested, not knowing what lay in store yet happy that his empty belly was full. At least he would die satisfied with memories of his last meal.

A degree of clarity returned to his enfeebled mind, and he wondered whether his ragged, sun-wracked body could crawl the last few kilometers to the spring. With that thought, he went to sleep, the ancient cactus shading him from the sun.

Ventras awoke to the stars overhead. The moon was not a sliver that night but a thin crescent that glistened, casting its silver bounty upon the land. Ventras moved an arm, and an ice pick seemed to jab deep into his muscle tissue. He moved the other arm, and the same debilitating pain came, immobilizing him.

Ventras lay thinking of TayGor and the hate he held so dear. The desire to find TayGor and make him suffer brought Ventras to his scabby knees. He screamed, a blood-curdling, primeval sound that echoed down the valley. Ventras attempted to stand and fell on his face. He tried again, and fell, tumbling face first into the sand. He had the will, but his body would not obey.

*Two kilometers!* Ventras thought. *Surely I can crawl that far.* And so he began. Knees already raw, hands burned and cracked by the sun, he crawled. Soon the pain was relegated to the subconscious; it was replaced by hate and the desire to find TayGor and punish him as Ventras had been punished. He had found the will to live.

Slowly he made his way into the bed of the valley. The slopes above the valley floor were lush and verdant, but the valley floor was still barren. It sloped gently upward.

Ventras spied, through bleary eyes, a rock face in the distance. It was covered in lush greenery and seemed to be the one on TayGor's map. The cliff was so near, yet now, bleeding from his hands, knees, and feet, he doubted he could make it. Nonetheless, determination to reach the water and to find the man who had done this to him drove him forward, one painful foot at a time.

The condors came, shadow after shadow, passing between Ventras and the sun. He began crawling faster, not caring how much skin or muscle tissue he left behind. At last, the water could be seen: rivulets sliding over the smooth stone. Heaven could be no more beautiful, he thought. The sound was a symphony. He saw, through swollen and blurry eyes, lush green plants that crept down the sheer rock face, their tendrils dipping into the pool below.

He had made it! Unable to crawl now that the flesh was completely gone from his knees, he slithered like a snake through tall grass towards his salvation, pulling himself along with his hands and arms.

*Just a little more,* he kept telling himself. Then he was at the pool, submerging his overheated face into the cool, clear water; drinking the never-ending flow; thanking he knew not whom for this salvation.

Ventras slowly drank his fill. His numb limbs came back to life and throbbed. His mind began to clear. After some time passed, Ventras began speaking, the first words in the past day he could actually speak: "Yes! Yes! I am Ventras!" Ventras laughed, and it hurt. He laughed more to prove that pain had no hold on him. He laughed like the madman he was.

Ventras rolled onto his back, splashing water over his battered body, continuing to laugh madly while the coolness revived him.

Lying on his back, he looked across the pool at the cliff and admired the upside-down rock face. The vision was surreal in the most exaggerated sense. Enjoying the beauty of the cliff, he began exploring every moss-filled crack and crevice above him. The back of his head lay in a few inches of the crystal cool water. Wildflowers grew amongst the green moss and grey stone. The pool of water reflected the image, mirroring the beauty of the cliff. Surely, Ventras thought, he would sojourn here on a yearly basis and give thanks for the gift of water that had been his ultimate salvation.

It was then that he saw her: the female, the super predator, staring down upon him, her crouch exposing the sinew beneath her beautiful coat. Her huge, frightening eyes watched him for any movement. She remained still, surveying his evident weakness. Above her on a ledge were four kits, which appeared to be half-grown. The mother mountain lion's mesmerizing eyes gleamed with curiosity and hunger combined.

Ventras shuddered, not from the cold water but from the thought of being torn to pieces by this fearsome creature before he would have the strength to put up any fight at all.

She crept silently, stealthily, down the sheer rock face. Ventras, too weak to resist, watched her come. Her movements were as fluid as the water. Her silence was absolute. She came with one thing clearly on her mind: food for her hungry family, and Ventras was the necessary nourishment.

Holding his spear tightly and considering his odds, he closed his eyes, waiting for her strike. He thought it odd that this spot, which had renewed his life, would also take it from him.

The sound of her padded feet touching down on the rock-strewn bank of the pool started him into something: the will to fight, to *survive,* streamed into him along with the newly found moisture being absorbed by his tissue. He felt adrenaline surge through him, yet he lay as though dead, luring the predator in.

She came cautiously, never having seen or scented a human before. She was curious and a bit unsure; this being did not smell like anything she had ever killed. Was it food, or an illusion created by her piercing hunger and the need to feed her babies? She hesitated, crouched, as if frozen in place—as was Ventras.

# TWENTY

VOLTRANS had arrived at his office at first light. He planned to leave work early and take the autocar to the prominent hill, where the new Dome of Wisdom was being built.

Mick had readily accepted the monumental task of reconstruction. The work had steadily progressed and was near completion. It had taken six years. The planet had been hammered by the asteroid strike. Most of the reconstruction effort and budget had been focused to that end. Funds and equipment to re-build the dome had to be squeezed out wherever Voltrans could wring the turnip.

Walking down the stairs to the garage, Voltrans thought back to the day he had proposed the project to Mick, while he sat in his wheelchair. He thought of how fantastic Mick's progress had been since then. He thought of the man who had brought Mick freedom from the dangerous depression into which he had sunk after his terrible injury. He thought of Duhcat and the gift he had given Mick.

The autocar raced over Sevenia. She had always been a beautiful city, he thought. She was once again the centerpiece—the most magnificent city in all of Seven Galaxies. Of course, Voltrans realized he might be a bit impartial as a judge; he had been born here and loved his home.

To see it now, risen from the destruction and gleaming, gave him immense satisfaction. The reconstruction and improvement of the city had been his baby. He had nurtured it through its feeble beginnings.

Sliding down from the bluest sky he could remember, he admired the Dome of Wisdom. The seven falls were cascading and merging their flow into the small lake below. Prior to the Dome's destruction, it had been a pool of water. It had been enlarged now, and in a few days, it would be dedicated to Admiral Gor, in remembrance. Beneath the shimmering water, at the bottom of the lake, could be seen thousands of sapphire blue sparkles that caught the sunlight.

Voltrans slid the autocar out of the sky and onto the ground. The door opened, and as he stepped out, he saw Mick running to meet him, smiling like a kid with a brand new bicycle.

The door auto-closed. He stood face to face with his best friend and thought that Mick had never looked better.

"Mick, all looks great! I see you're wrapping it up. Will everything be ready for the dedication on Friday? The clean-up, and everything else?" Voltrans asked.

"Yeah, boss! We'll be ready. Everything will be shinning as bright as your smile is right now!"

They laughed together good-naturedly for a few moments, and then Mick turned serious. "Volt, there are a couple of things bothering me though."

# THE SEEDING SEVEN'S VISION

"Tell me."

"The crystal columns. Or should I say, the lack of them. The Dome is just not the same without them. I mean, you could see them from almost anywhere in the city. They were the showpiece of Seven Galaxies. It set Sevenia apart from all our best cities." He shook his head.

"It breaks my heart that we haven't been able to grow crystals anything like them—not in shape, size, or perfection. It is baffling."

"Well, incorporating the thousands of broken pieces that were left into the lake's bottom was a great idea," Voltrans said. "From the sky, the water in the lake glistens with all the colors of the columns. I guess we'll have to be satisfied that they *are* still here, and still beautiful, just not as imposing as when they stood across from the seven falls, and before the Dome of Wisdom."

"I know, Volt, but with all our technology, you would think we could have reproduced them. Really, it is too bad."

"Yes. But you've done an extraordinary job with the Dome! It looks the same. Don't fret over the crystal columns. After all, we aren't miracle workers."

"Gentlemen, if you would please humor me for a few moments, I have a solution to the dilemma you were just speaking of."

The voice came from behind Voltrans and Mick. It struck them as familiar, and yet it couldn't be…could it? They both turned at the same time and looked in the direction of the voice—and then both of their mouths dropped open.

"Great job, Mick!" Duhcat said. "Voltrans, Sevenia looks even better than before the tragedy; my compliments! You two have exceeded my highest hopes!"

Duhcat shook both men's hands warmly, graciously. They closed their mouths and managed to say, "The pleasure is all ours," at the same time. They traded baffled looks and broke out laughing.

"Enricco!" Voltrans said. "What a splendid surprise! We are thrilled beyond words to see you after all these years!"

Mick just nodded in silent amazement.

"As I was saying," Duhcat continued, "I have something to add to the conversation you two were having when I arrived. Please, if you will follow me?" He didn't wait for an answer; he simply started up the Dome's seven steps and made his way through the entry hall. Voltrans and Mick followed him. To their utter surprise, all the doors auto opened before him as they walked down the great corridor to its end.

Once there, another door, which was unadorned, opened, and beyond it both men could see vast gardens stretching down to a blue-green body of water. The water was back-dropped by the sheer slopes of mountains that were topped by the pristine white of fresh snowfall.

The two men shared glances of disbelief as they followed behind Duhcat, hurrying to keep up. His stride spent nothing on wasted movement and covered the ground quickly.

They walked downslope toward the water and then turned a corner on the path that skirted a grove of very tall avocado trees. Duhcat stopped and turned to see their reactions.

"Magnificent, aren't they?" he said, smiling.

Below them on the edge of the blue water stood seven massive translucent sapphire-blue crystal columns. They dwarfed two other columns that appeared to be carved out of pink granite.

Mick was speechless, but Voltrans said, "Enricco.... Magnificent is too *weak* a word. But how?"

"Do you mean how did they get here?"

"Yes!"

"I brought them with me. They are my gift to the people of Seven Galaxies, and to the Dome of Wisdom. It just wouldn't do *not* to have them here."

Mick and Voltrans looked back the way they had come and expected to see the Dome commanding the gardens on the hill above. All that was before them was a vast and varied landscape.

"Where...is the Dome?" asked Mick. It was Voltrans' turn to fall speechless.

"It is where we left it," said Duhcat, as if it were common knowledge.

"How in the world will we get the columns from here to their place before the Dome of Wisdom?" asked Mick.

"Oh! That's the easy part. Bringing them this far, however, was no picnic, I assure you!"

Mick and Voltrans traded looks of confusion.

Suddenly, the seven columns lifted slowly off the ground and turned from their vertical positions to horizontal, as if they were weightless. They began moving in a long, orderly line up the hill, back the way the men had come.

Mick and Voltrans watched with unbelieving eyes as the first column began to slowly shrink in length. The far end disappeared, and then the nearest end was gone, too. It reminded Mick of sticking a straw into a milkshake: a person can't see the end of the straw but knows it is there.

The last of the seven columns passed by, and Duhcat said, "Come. I want to see them when they are set in place."

The three men walked back up the hill with Duhcat in the lead.

The last column disappeared, and Duhcat, who was right behind it, vanished also. Voltrans and Mick walked a few more steps and suddenly found themselves inside the great corridor of the Dome of Wisdom.

The last column was just exiting through the entrance, with Duhcat still right behind it. Mick and Voltrans trotted to keep up.

When they got outside, all seven columns were hovering vertically above the pedestals that had been prepared for the columns Seven had been attempting to grow. As if the floating columns had minds of their own, all at once, they slowly descended and lit upon the pedestals, each one perfectly aligned.

The three men heard the sound of one set of hands clapping thunderously and someone saying, "Bravo! Bravo!"

Looking away from the columns and towards the voice, they saw Leandra standing nearby.

"Enricco, what a wonderful surprise. I mean, the pillars are exquisite, but I was actually speaking of you. How have you been, dearest?"

"Leandra! As always, I am extraordinary; however, setting eyes upon you has taken a wondrous day and whisked it into the heavens! You are well, I trust?"

"Yes, yes…what a wonderful gift! Will you miss them terribly?"

Duhcat looked at the sparkling blue columns for a few moments, in obvious introspection. "I would say, yes…but perhaps now that they reside here, I will be pleasantly forced to come and visit you more often. Which, I must say, would be a very fine trade."

"Will you be staying a while…at least for the dedication?" she asked, looking at Duhcat as though her heart would literally break if he said no.

"Alas, Leandra…you know well that while I appreciate the invitation, such gatherings, although most definitely important, are not for me; I am not much of one for crowds, lone wolf that I have come to be."

"The fourteen of us were truly hoping you would take your rightful seat at the crescent table. Since the admiral's tragic passing, we are one short."

Leandra paused for a moment, allowing a short silence in remembrance of one so dear to Seven Galaxies—one who walked with them no more. Then, after the heartfelt silence, she continued her persuasion: "A *truly* qualified replacement is a rare jewel indeed!"

"I am flattered in the highest degree, Leandra…but…no."

Leandra was not so easily put off. "All these years, the centuries that have passed…you have avoided your seat here in the Dome like a child who doesn't want to eat his vegetables." She spoke in a motherly fashion, but her frustration was evident.

Duhcat looked carefully at the old woman, letting her know he had taken her words to heart. Then he gazed up into the sky, not looking at anyone in the group. He began to speak softly, with a faraway look in his eyes.

"Perhaps...perhaps, when I find what I've been searching for...possibly then I'll settle down, Leandra. For now, I must keep searching. I *know* that missing piece of myself is out there...somewhere..." His voice trailed off: it became a thin wisp, filled with longing and sadness.

Then, as if a switch had been flicked, he changed the tempo and smiled widely at Voltrans, who had been speechless while attempting to take everything in stride. With the happy flair of camaraderie, he said, "General Voltrans, would you be interested in doing me a *very* grand favor?"

"Of course! What is your wish?"

"Would you sit in for me: take my place and fill the fifteenth seat?"

Voltrans could not conceal his shock. "As...as...one of the Fifteen?" he stammered.

"Yes, my friend, as a special favor to me?"

"I...I would be truly honored!" He thought for a moment and said, "But who would fill my position?"

Duhcat stepped up beside Mick so the four of them were standing facing each other in a loose circle. Placing one arm around Mick's shoulders, he said, "Many times, the answer we search for is standing right in front of us, if we only open our eyes to the wondrous possibilities." Duhcat looked from Mick to Voltrans and back again.

"A splendid idea, Enricco! Splendid indeed!" Leandra added jubilantly.

The four of them broke out laughing. Joy and wonder took hold, and the fit of laughter grew, as humor sometimes will.

After a few minutes, when they had calmed themselves and seriousness had taken hold once again, Mick looked at Duhcat and said, "Mr. Duhcat, where in the universe did you find the seven azure columns? And, pray, tell me, how did you just manage to set them in place?"

Duhcat looked deeply at Mick for a time, and when the silence had reached its crescendo, he said, "Mr. Mullowney, if I were to share all my secrets with you, I would cease to be the mystery and *Legend* that Seven Galaxies believes I am. I prefer to keep things as they are."

Duhcat's dark eyes sparkled. "Until next we meet," he said, then turned and walked away, gliding towards the portal doors and disappearing into the gardens.

# TWENTY-ONE

Ventras lay bleeding, flashes of memories struck like lightning in an evening sky. His body, wracked with pain, twitched with each stabbing glimpse into the past. As his life seeped out, drip by drip onto the soil from the many shreds and punctures in his sun-ravaged skin, he reflected, sorting the mists of fantasy from the realities that had brought him to this end.

The lanky frame of the mother mountain lion lay still beside him, her blood comingling with his own. The fight had been a test of wills. Ventras had never given in: thrust after thrust of his spear had not taken down the hunger-crazed mother. She had slashed him and raked her claws over his wrecked body, but he had held on. He had not given in.

Then, just as his efforts had seemed for naught, he had managed a fatal spear strike; her eyes had shot wide open, as if stimulated by a massive electrical shock. She screamed. Then her voice was muffled by gurgling blood pouring into her lungs. She looked at him in her last moments, a forlorn, almost human sadness in her eyes, as if to say: *What of my children?*

She had died quietly beside him.

It was now Ventras' turn. The flashes continued. He reviewed the course of events that had inevitably placed him here, and he soaked in the exhilaration of having beaten the desert, and then the cougar with eyes like Satan's. Through the haze that flooded his mind, he could see a tunnel. Something—a force—was persuading him to give in, to quit the struggle, to come away from the shredded wreck that had once been his hardened and virile body.

Ventras attempted to see what lay at the end of the tunnel yet he could not; there were only shadows and darkness, mists that swirled in eerie and foreboding patterns, and a whisper that came from he knew not where, saying, *Come away from that broken body, feel pain no more.*

Ventras squinted, trying with all his might to see through the darkness, to understand where the shadowed passage would take him. A shiver came over him, cold and dreadful. He had read of many near death experiences before. Most of them spoke of tunnels with a bright light shining from the other end, but his was unlit, damp, slippery, and so frightening. Ventras shuddered involuntarily.

The whisper came again, and Ventras wondered whether the series of past events that kept flashing through his mind had brought him here: to this dark, slippery tunnel that was apparently his only choice for exiting a life he had previously thought of as charmed.

The marauding male wolf's ears prickled. In the distance, he heard the unmistakable scream of a female cougar, then the primeval and guttural sounds of a struggle. *The super predator was killing!*

The wolf smiled inwardly. There would be nourishment tonight.

The big cats ate with abandon. A frugal animal such as the wolf would surely find some tasty morsels: if not meat, then at least blood spilled by the giant cat that could be licked carefully from the ground.

Saliva worked its way, first from the sensory impulses sent to the animal's brain, then from the glands themselves. A ring of drool formed inside the beasts hairy lips. The wolf picked up his pace, cautiously placing each paw so that no sound was made.


Ventras heard breathing. At first, thinking it was his own, he paid little attention. A dawning finally came to his dying mind that the breathing was too rapid to be coming from him. Struggling to open his eyes, he attempted to see what was making the strange sound.


The wolf stood frozen, mesmerized by the sight and smell of the scene. Two carcasses lay side by side, and the scent of lifeblood lingered heavy in the air. The big cat was still, apparently dead, for there was no breath left in her. The other creature, a strange thing the wolf had never before seen, began to move. *It lived!*

The unknown thing opened its eyes. The wolf was extremely wary. The creature was injured severely, yet it had killed the super predator. The wolf crouched in wonder, pondering the power this being must possess to have killed a mountain lion single handedly. Hunger gnawed at his empty guts, yet primeval survival instincts kept him at safe distance, despite his desire to feast.

Ventras' blurred vision saw something. He squinted, rubbing his puss-filled eyes with a ragged hand. Ventras then scented the pungent odor of wild dog. His hair bristled. He wondered how many there might be.

A moment of desperate humor came over him and he said, "It figures: first the scorching sun, then the thirst, the hoard of filthy vultures, and the cougar, and now you." He laughed mirthlessly at this turn of events, "Just right, TayGor!" he screamed. "Just right!"

The wolf had never heard the voice of man before. Jumping back quickly, he withdrew to a safer distance, waiting to see what this strange new creature would do.

Blood scent, thick in the air, caused a string of drool to run steadily from his mouth.

Ventras saw the form move and came to his senses. The animal was obviously hungry. With monumental effort, Ventras took his spear and began sawing pieces of flesh and fur from the dead cat's body. Between winces of pain, he spoke to the wolf in a friendly voice. "You're hungry, boy? Like something to eat?" He cast the first morsel towards the curious onlooker.

The wild dog took no time: one sniff, and then the chunk was gone. Hungry eyes looked upon this frightening and curious new animal that had voluntarily shared meat after tearing it off the dead cat, using teeth on the end of a stick.

The quizzical wolf knew the creature was severely injured. Blood oozed from many wounds, yet it continued to rip meat from the carcass and cast it out to where he was crouched.

After a while, Ventras ate some of the bloody meat, which came free of the cat's carcass easier once the fur was trimmed off. The food seemed to thicken Ventras' blood. His bleeding slowed. The oozing wounds dried. The raw meat sent waves of tingles over and through his starved body. He continued to carve, each time giving the wolf two pieces to his one.

Soon he was finished. He could feed the wolf no more. In a delirious and carefree state, he fell fast asleep.


Dawn's first light sent thin fingers of color through the morning sky. Golden light shone through the vegetation, casting shadow patterns on the ground. The reflection shimmering off the pool of water created a shining play of shifting golden and azure light upon the rock face.

The wolf watched the sleeping man: the strange one who shared meat. He felt a deep-seated emotion that he did not understand. Wanting to show thanks to this wondrous new being, the wolf came closer, inch by inch, attempting not to wake the creature.

The creature's wounds were filthy with dirt and hair. The grateful wolf began licking and cleaning Ventras' afflictions.


Ventras was in dream-state: he was back on Seven's Seven, in bed with one of the courtesan's he frequented.

The woman was kissing him lasciviously all over his body. Ventras moaned in appreciation of the woman's talent. Her tongue slid fluidly, causing some of his pain to diminish. *Pain*, he thought, and the dream evaporated with the flick of his eyelids.

What replaced the subconscious and wonderfully sensual vision was a hairy beast. *The wolf!* His brain screamed, yet Ventras lay perfectly still, fearing to move lest the beast become aggressive. The animal's tongue continued its work.

Ventras relaxed slightly, realizing the wolf was cleaning him and not nibbling or tearing at his broken flesh. Once Ventras' mind had accepted the wolf's actions, he relaxed more and began to enjoy the attention. He had received no affection for so long; the dog was a welcome change from the course of events that had torn, scraped, slashed, burned, bitten, and withered his once-strong frame.

The wolf finally stopped the licking, and Ventras opened his eyes. The wild dog had moved back and was looking anxiously between the man and the dead cougar. Saliva streamed from his long mouth. He licked his lips now and then. Ventras understood. He picked up his spear and used the handle to push himself into a sitting position, grimacing with the pain and, at one point, screaming in anguish.

The wolf cocked his beautiful silver-blonde head at the sound and the sight of this mysterious thing righting itself. The animal also understood pain and torment.

Ventras situated himself and began slicing away at the carcass, this time in a more artful fashion. His clothes were in shreds and his sandals were gone. He needed covering for his body. With that in mind, his cuts into the dead animal became more precise. He took care not to damage the valuable hide more than it already was.

He skinned the cat expertly while he fed the ravished wolf, dreaming of a headdress and cape that would be unlike any other on this planet. The wolf watched curiously, expertly catching the pieces thrown before they hit the ground. Ventras ate as well. The nourishment and his new partner both gave him necessary hope and the will to survive.

When Ventras had the animal skinned, he was past fatigue. A thread of strength deep within his tenacious being drove him on. Dragging himself and the hide down to the pool, near the outflow of water, he laid the hide in the stream below the pool and then lay his battered body in the cool water, too. He rested while the wolf watched.

The healing would be slow.

Ventras had the presence of mind to slice thin strips of meat from the dead cougar before it spoiled. He laid them in full sun on a very hot rock to dry and preserve. They would need this store, for it would be a long while before he would be capable of hunting.

The Sun lowering in the evening sky became cool. Ventras, remembering the bitter nights in the desert, began a small fire with an ancient tool he had learned about in his youth. Using the cat's intestines, he cut threads and made a small bow. Then he began twirling one dry stick against another. Soon, he saw the glow of heat. He placed dry grass upon it and blew. The grass began smoking, and then the pop of a flame danced. Ventras gathered some small pieces of wood, each step a painful remembrance of the six days of suffering he had just passed through.

The wolf's eyes opened wide in amazement as the flames grew. He backed away, obviously fearful of the bright, dancing light. Ventras coaxed the voracious animal in closer with small pieces of scrap meat, which the animal ate with quick inhales of breath. Ventras backed closer to the fire with each piece, and soon the wild dog could feel the fire's heat.

The wolf's intelligent eyes took it all in. This strange new creature had created fire, a fearful force in the wild. Deep-seated instincts spoke to the wild animal of fire's devastating force, yet the man seemed unafraid. In fact, he sat close, seeming to enjoy his powerful creation. Perhaps the strange two-legged creature gained strength from the dancing light, the wolf thought. Insatiable hunger forced the fearful beast to remain close, and before long, the heat felt good.

Ventras searched painfully for wood to feed his creation while the wolf watched. Much firewood was needed to keep the flames going over the long evening, and so Ventras worked. Just as he was near collapse, the animal came with a stick in his mouth. Ventras took the stick and gave the wolf a tidbit, and soon the beast was back with another piece of wood, only this time the piece was larger.

Ventras admired the animal's intellect and gave him two tidbits, a fair trade in measure. The wolf returned shortly with two sticks in his teeth, and Ventras laughed. "You are a quick learner. I think we are destined to become very good friends."

He gave the crafty animal three tidbits for the effort. The wolf spun and disappeared into the darkness.

Ventras thought, *You, wolf, will need a name: one that is powerful and has a bit of mystery imbedded as well.*

The wild dog came back dragging a monstrous piece of fallen limb, and Ventras laughed harder. "You are looking for a bigger portion I see."

The wolf looked curious and cocked his silver-blonde head from side to side, looking at the talking creature as if to say, *Yes, and where is my reward?*

A good-sized piece of liver flew, and the intelligent creature caught and devoured it in a second.

Ventras said, "I shall name you Smoke, for where there is smoke, there is fire; and the name matches the color of your beautiful coat."


Soon the meat from the cougar was gone. Ventras was healing but unable to run. He had suffered several deep slashes to his calves and hamstrings. Eight days had passed since the cat confronted him. He knew it would be several more weeks until he was ready to travel.

The wolf went out regularly to hunt and was sometimes successful, bringing back small game, rabbits and lizards, which they shared. Ventras was amazed that the wild dog shared his game with him. The animal obviously felt loyalty to the partnership, and Ventras appreciated the wolf's contributions.

Days earlier, Ventras had gathered wild nettle and placed them into a depression he'd made in the rocky gravel near the spring. He had read extensively in his youth of survival tactics in the wild. Once the low spot had filled with water, he beat the wild herbs with a stick, pulverizing them and releasing the formic acid. He then placed the big cat's hide in with the herbs to let it soak for a few days and allow the nettle acid time to preserve the raw hide.

After this time, he pulled the hide from the pool, scraped it with the edge of his spear point, and then pounded it lightly with a smooth stone to break down the fibers a bit more. He then stretched the hide between two poles and placed it in the sun to dry.

The next day, the skin was ready. He painstakingly cut some lacelike threads from the leather and then cut two large pieces that would be big enough for heavy moccasins. He poked small holes in the leather with the point of his spear, and then used the threads to sew the edges together. The end result was a sturdy shoe, comfortably lined with the cougar's soft fur.

Ventras had been venturing out barefoot. During his mending, any sharp rock poking into his feet sent reverberations of tension echoing throughout his entire body. The moccasins were like a taste of heaven upon his feet. He reveled in the mobility they afforded him.

The next morning at dawn, Ventras rose and said, "Smoke, let's hunt."

His faithful friend rose, stretched, and then followed.

Smoke trailed after the strange creature who had become the only other member of his pack. He had never seen a creature without wings walk on two legs before meeting this man. The wolf thought, *Two Legs, where are you going?*

Ventras walked a ways until he found a trail that had been well used by deer and other animals. He followed it to a fork and concealed himself between two bushes, where he could strike well into both paths.

The wolf looked at him quizzically.

Ventras said, "Hunt, Smoke," and thrust his spear several times quickly into the path.

The wolf's eyes sparkled with acknowledgement, and he trotted off through dense brush.

Moments later, Ventras heard the pounding of hooves. He braced himself, readying his thrust. A young deer, fear in his eyes, bolted down the trail. Ventras lunged, thrusting the spear with all his might. It hit home. The animal reeled and fell. Ventras plunged the weapon deeper, not chancing that his quarry might slip away.

Smoke appeared, and Ventras could swear the wolf smiled when he took in the scene.

"Good job, Smoke. We make a good team, eh?" He patted the dog on the head. They would eat well tonight.

Each day that passed, Ventras became stronger. The hunting went well, as did the drying and tanning of hides. Ventras eventually made two sets of hide clothes for himself. He also dried plenty of meat, and he fashioned the cat's head hide into a mask that sent the wolf running anytime Ventras donned it. No matter how many times he showed the wild dog that he was just putting on a fearsome mask, the wolf still seemed to think Ventras had become a cougar and turned tail and ran. In the end, Ventras had to hide the mask from the wolf so as not to disturb him.

The cougar's front paws were fashioned into coverings for his ravaged hands. The cat's long, sharp claws rested over Ventras' fingers, creating the appearance that he possessed them himself. The teeth he placed into a leather bag. The tail was skinned and used as a waist wrapping.

When the wolf was asleep, napping in the hot afternoons, Ventras would don his fearsome new costume and gaze at his image in the waters of the clear, calm pool at the bottom of the rock face.

This was the only way Ventras could stand seeing himself. He had been disfigured by the brutal days in the baking sun and from the many lacerations dealt by the dying cat. His appearance was frightening. But with his newly found identity in the cougar's skin, he felt empowered. No longer did he see himself as disfigured; instead, he saw a powerful being: a being who had conquered the desert, the vultures, and the giant cat, and tamed a wolf.

Ventras felt ready: ready to set out and settle an old score. He was ready to find TayGor, the one responsible for all of his suffering. He was ready to see TayGor on his knees, begging for mercy.

In that moment, Ventras thought he would be healed. In the moment before TayGor's death, Ventras believed he would once again be a whole man.

# TWENTY-TWO

After breakfast, Tay went to the small lean-to where he kept his scythe. Picking up the tool, he walked down the trail to the large field that bordered the river. He had been cutting the tall grass for a week and had it stacked in teepee-shaped piles to dry in the sun. Some of the party thought he had lost his mind, but Tay had taken their jokes with a smile.

They had no animals, so he knew his cutting and drying of hay seemed odd.

He had also cut poles and peeled them early in the spring when the sap was running and the bark slipped off easily. He had cross-stacked these poles and covered them with cut grass to dry.

If both plans came together, he would have a small barn built soon after the poles had dried sufficiently. The dry hay would then be put into the barn for winter storage.

"Why?" they had all asked.

Tay only smiled and said, "You'll see." Then he kept working every day on the two projects.

He would be done with the hay that day, and then he could quickly erect the poles to form the skeleton of a barn. He had already hauled enough rock from the river to stack for the barn's foundations.

In the woods nearby was a massive cedar tree that had blown down in a storm. The tree had been hollow, and when it fell, it had broken in giant slabs. The cedar would be cut to lengths and then split into siding and roofing. Materials for the entire project were coming from the woods surrounding the field.

Tay had seen the unmistakable signs of horses here. There were many hoof-prints in the dried mud along the river and other trails. The tracks appeared to have been made by a large herd in the rainy season. Tay hadn't actually seen any of the animals, only the prints and their droppings.

The weather was turning cooler. Fall was coming. He thought that the horses must be in the higher country where it was not so stifling hot and where there would be plenty of rich, fresh grass during summer months.

The valley he had chosen was well sheltered from the cold northern winds, which he expected to rake the surrounding areas in the dead of winter. The ridges surrounding this valley would block the north wind, and the close proximity to the sea would keep the area warm.

He felt sure that this was the herd's winter feeding grounds. He intended to cut the grass and place it in storage so that he would have something valuable to the horses when they appeared in the winter, perhaps near starving due to the snow-buried grass. This would help him make friends with the wild animals. However, the task was monumental.

Tay enjoyed thinking of the horses while he worked. He sometimes dreamed of them coming. Most of all he thought of the charcoal-grey stallion that came in his dreams: the one he had named Eclipse—the one that was Shadow's mirror.

If he were to tell anyone in the group his plan, he feared they would think him un-settled. Attempting to tame the stallion of your dreams? He could almost hear the responses, and so he kept his mouth shut.

Sometimes Alex would come and help him. Most the time, Alex was hopelessly wrapped up in trying to pursue Denali. Tay saw Alex's enraptured glances at the woman who rarely acknowledged him and felt pity for him. Alex was trying to win a heart that darkness had possessed for too long.

Denali often came and worked. She was actually more of a physical help than some of the men. Somehow, she understood his plan without asking. When she wasn't tending her garden, she would come and bundle, pack, and stack hay. She had also helped him peel the poles and pack river rock for the foundations. Sometimes, he let her take a turn at the scythe.

He had never imagined he and Denali would work together for a common goal.

Once he asked her, "Are you doing penance here? You don't have to. I forgave you long ago, aboard *Intrepid One*."

She answered without looking up: "I know. Not a day goes by that I am not in awe that you *could* after what I did."

"So then, why are you here sweating on my non-sensible project?"

"I think it makes perfect sense. I need a horse myself. Do you think I'm so unselfish as to not have a primary motive? I know what you're up to, TayGor, and I approve." She looked up from tying a bundle of hay and smiled.

She smiled so rarely, it seemed a treasure just for him. Tay felt he would never forget how she looked that moment: sweating in the hot sun, pieces of hay caught hopelessly in her red-blonde hair, her blue-green eyes with that hint of dry humor showing at the corners. She was truly mesmerizing when she smiled. He wondered why she did so only rarely.

She stood, throwing the bundle over her shoulder, and then carried it to where they had stacked the river rock for the foundations. It was the last one; the cutting was finished.

Tay was tired. He had been working since just after breakfast, and now the sun was dropping rapidly in the western sky. He walked to the river's edge and sat down on a large rock.

Insects were flying low over the moving water, and the trout were jumping. Every once in a while, an extra-large one would break the surface, its silver body speckled with black, gold, and green spots. Some had a sunset-colored stripe running the length of their flashing bodies, while others were the color of true coin: untarnished silver, glistening purple in the sun's waning light.

The river's voice, soft from little rainfall, soothed his aching body. A slight breeze stirred the leaves that hung over the water, filtering the sun's golden light, creating an ever-changing painting of light and shadow upon the water. Up and down the valley, the leaves rustled as they brushed and rubbed against one another. He loved this time of night at the river and enjoyed the drama the fish put on without a fee.

Tay heard soft steps. Denali sat down next to him without a word.

She seemed to be contemplating the river, but there was no joy in her eyes. It was as if, he thought, her past life had somehow stolen the beauty of her soul. Often, her eyes showed no emotion at all. He had never heard her laugh.

"It's beautiful here this time of evening," Tay said. "I love to sit here after work and watch the trout breaking from the water. The swirling green and blue water...it reminds me of your eyes." He stopped talking and looked to her, expecting some sort of response.

Denali sat still, staring blankly into the water, saying nothing.

"Don't you think so?"

"Tay..." She paused, as if trying to find words that were not quick or harsh. "There was a time—long ago—when I reveled in nature's grace and beauty. It was a time I shared for a brief period with...someone...a friend I loved dearly. Life stole that person—the little girl I loved and the little girl I was. In one instant, they were taken from me. What you are talking to is only the shell that remains. Nothing else."

She looked back to the river without saying more.

"You could tell me about her sometime."

"I have just told you more than I have told anyone. *Ever.*"

"But there is *more*. Perhaps if you talked about it...?"

"Don't! Don't ask...! I can't...! I won't!" The look she cast closed the subject indefinitely.

Tay understood. She had opened a crevasse of pain and shared it with him. Then, as if she were a machine, the shutter closed again. The moment passed. Tay let it go and changed the subject.

"Denali, Alex...he...he's my best friend. He would like a chance with you. He is truly a wonderful young man: honest, intelligent, sincere. I think he loves you, though he's never said so. Is it possible? Could you...consider giving him that chance?"

"Tay, I *can't* love. I would only hurt him, and I like Alex too much to do that."

With that, she stood and walked away without another word, leaving Tay beside the river, alone with his thoughts.

# TWENTY-THREE

Fall came, and the colors on the surrounding hillsides melded from vibrant greens into the paling yellows of dying leaves. Then at last, the reds, oranges, and browns draped the forest in patches wherever deciduous trees pushed back the predominant conifer canopy.

The weather changed quickly, from brisk evenings that whispered of winter's approach to the full-fledged chill that ran the length of days lived here. Soon, the horses came. Tay was awakened by a sound that shook the ground: the sound of hundreds of pounding hooves coming closer.

He catapulted himself from bed and ran, throwing a towel around his naked body. Not taking the time to don shoes, he opened the door and leapt out in one fluid motion. He landed in snow, knee deep. He was surprised, but not daunted. He longed to see their arrival, as he had countless times in his dreams.

A wedge of multicolored and undulating hair, sinew, and muscle swept towards the valley like a tsunami: scores of steam plumes shot out of muzzles raised high as they ran, bucking, nipping, lunging, kicking, their hooves thundering. Fleet and graceful bodies came, throwing snow upon one another in flight, dappling their many colors with abstract blotches of white.

The wave of the pulsating equine herd was led by a stallion: the stallion of Tay's dreams. The massive beast's color contrasted with the pearl-white of fresh snow. He was black at first glimpse against the backdrop of white, but as he drew near Tay saw he was a deep charcoal-grey, *almost* black. He led, running the wedge like the point of a flying arrow.

Tay was awestruck. *They are here! He is here!* His heart leapt. He tingled all over and goose bumps popped out all over his skin—not from the cold, but from the electricity cast towards him when the big male horse finally brought the herd to a stop and looked over the change in his valley. Then, as if feeling Tay watching, he looked up to the ridge: to the place Tay stood on the shelf.

They stood frozen, the man and horse, for a moment, appraising one another. Then the charcoal-grey stallion let out a shrill, short squeak and reared, dancing on his hind legs. The flash of his front hooves pawing at the air caught Tay's enraptured eyes: the hooves were striped in vertical bands of creamy white and charcoal black. Tay spoke. He could not be sure, but still the name came: "Eclipse!"

He felt something warm beside him. Turning his head, he noticed Denali standing close to his side. He had not heard her approach. She said nothing, but in the corner of his eye, Tay thought he saw the look of satisfaction coupled with a rarity for her: enjoyment.

She smiled and said, "They *are* truly magnificent! I can see the one you have your eye set on, Tay. He looks a true and rough handful!"

Tay said nothing yet his mind spoke, saying, *Yes, he always was.*

Then Denali's look broke from the horses to him and what he *wasn't* wearing. "Nice outfit. You better get dressed if you plan on tackling *that* beast. Frostbitten feet won't be much good for anything. What if you have to run from him?" Her humor shone once again, not in a smile but in her eyes, which betrayed deeper feelings than those she let float to the surface.

Tay turned and quickstepped to the house. Upon entering, he found Zuzahna wide-eyed with excitement. "They are here!" she said. "Let's get dressed and go out. You will want to feed them this morning, I'm sure."

Tay looked to the woman he loved. He had never told her he loved her because of another: a phantom enchantress, a woman who came only in dream sleep and who tore at his haunted heart.

Zuzahna pulled his heart one way in conscious hours, and then, in the subconscious of darkness and sleep, the other came to him and pulled him in the opposite direction. The struggle was constant.

Only in grueling physical labor could he, at times, forget them both.

The two loves baffled him.

"Yes, let's," he said, smiling at her.

They dressed quickly without eating. Tay's excitement permeated every part of his being.

Zuzahna laughed lightheartedly at his feet, which were blue and red. "What were you thinking, running out there without dressing?"

"I wasn't thinking about anything other than seeing them running. To *see* them arrive was what I wanted, Zuzahna. It was a sight I will never forget. Their rushing bodies churning up the snow...it was everything I had hoped for and more. And he's here!"

"Who, Tay?"

Tay, caught in the excitement, had let slip a secret, one he had not intended to divulge: the feeling that Shadow was here, reborn. If he spoke of his thoughts, she would probably think he had gone off the deep end. He recovered, saying only, "The stallion. He's led the herd here!"

They left the house and walked to the shelf edge. Looking over the abrupt drop, Zuzahna gasped. "Oh my! Tay, there are so many. And oh! Look at the big black one. He's magnificent, isn't he?"

"Yes, *very!* Would you mind so much, Zuzahna, if I went down alone? It could be dangerous, and I don't want to spook them into running if I can help it."

"I don't mind. Whatever you think is best."

"Thanks, it means a lot to me." He leaned towards her. Zuzahna's eyes sparkled, mirroring the joy she saw in his. Tay pulled her close. She felt his warmth through the thick clothing as he pressed her tight against himself and kissed her long and hard.

His lips left hers just as her lungs felt like they were about to explode. Her heart raced and she said breathlessly, "I'll make something hot to eat. It will be waiting for you when you get back. As will I." She gave him a look that told the story of her desire.

Tay said, "I'll be thinking of you."

"Liar! I know when you are with them"—she gestured at the herd—"I will be the farthest from your mind."

"You are probably right, but when I return, I will be *all* yours."

"Somehow, I think that big black horse will be there, too!" She smiled knowingly. She had lived with his dream of taming the horses long enough to *truly* know his mind.

"Thanks," was all he said before he turned and made his way down the trail towards the valley below.

Tay came out from the trees that enveloped the trail and stopped on the edge of the field. The stallion pawed the snow until the stubble of short grass was exposed. He looked up and shook his huge head as if in disbelief when he saw Tay watching. The shrill squeak came again, an exclamation point to the question running through the horse's mind. Eclipse stood again on his hind legs and pawed the air, whinnying wildly. He then set out, bolting towards the river and the new barn.

He ended up near the strange box, a large foreign thing in this valley where he had so long ago been born and where he had grown up, being bullied by the older lead stallion.

He had eventually challenged the older stallion in order to become the herd's leader. Now they were *his* responsibility.

He drew in a long pull of air, scenting the sweet hay within the box. Then he turned towards the strange creature standing on two legs, the creature who had evidently locked the sweet grass away, secreting it behind the wood that now stood between his appetite and the necessary food to feed his family. Eclipse's temper flared. Rearing on his back legs, he began hammering on the barn with both front feet. *This thing was the enemy. It was starving his people. He must defeat it!*

The siding boards began to splinter and break. Eclipse kept pounding. Finally, one gave way completely. The dark horse reached in cautiously and dragged a bundle of hay out through the opening and into the field.

The other horses came and ate. Eclipse stood and glared at the two-legged creature now running across the field toward them.

Eclipse bolted towards the two-legged creature, cutting between him and the prison of grass.

Sliding to a stop in front of the thing, he breathed in hard, taking in its scent. The smell was new, and yet from somewhere deep within came a familiarity. A voice spoke within the horse's mind that said not to fear; the two-legged creature was his friend, his…

Tay spoke in soft tones, just as he had as a boy to Shadow, back on Seven. Eclipse's ears were forward, and he watched as Tay slowly skirted him and made his way toward the barn. Eclipse kept his distance yet followed.

Tay said out loud, "You always were a curious bugger!"

Once inside the barn, he threw open the loft doors and began chucking a measured amount of the sweet dry grass down on the ground. The horses, fear in their eyes at first, would not come, yet their empty bellies soon softened their resolve to keep a distance and before long they slowly started to move forward, heads low to the ground, sniffing long pulls of air.

Some of the braver ones, Eclipse being the first, grabbed a bundle and then ran farther out into the field where they obviously felt safer.

Tay did a rough count. There were at least sixty animals. He threw down thirty bundles and watched them eat until they were licking the remnants from the snow.

Before long, the group made its way to the river. Tay, in their absence, took some spare boards he had left in the barn and shoved them across the hole the stallion had made in the siding. He thought, *That one will take some watching!*

Soon the animals sauntered up from the river and milled about quietly, as if satisfied by the meal. The mares were nursing healthy, striking foals that were fat from last summer's grass and from their mother's rich milk. The stallion had fathered many of the foals. Tay could see his color and conformation in the young ones.

Many of the horses pawed the ground and continued eating the short grass, which had grown slightly after Tay had cut the field and before the frost had come. They came up with mouths full of dark-green, frozen grass. From the way they reacted, Tay could tell that it was a far cry from the sweet grass stored in the barn.

Just before mid-day, Eclipse screamed loudly and bolted down the field, away from the barn and Tay. In a second, the entire herd was following. They were soon out of sight. The thunder of their hooves reverberated through the air, and Tay's heart pounded in his ears just as loud.

*What a sight,* he thought. Never in all his days had he seen so magnificent a group of horses in one place. His stomach growled, reminding him he had not eaten, even though it was after morning. Tay shut the loft doors and trudged towards the house, through the snow that showed thousands of score marks from the horse's hooves.

# TWENTY-FOUR

SPRING came at last. The snow melted, and the rainy season began. The cold and brutal downpours drove everyone indoors, but Tay was itching for a ride. He had spent the winter becoming a friend of the herd. They allowed him to walk among them without spooking. After all, his scent had been on every bundle of hay they had eaten over the past three months. They were accustomed to seeing him. It was as though they had accepted him.

Every morning, as he threw the loft doors open, he saw their hungry, beseeching eyes searching his and trying to look within the barn to see how much of the sweet grass remained under his control. As the barn emptied of hay, he built some stalls.

The new grass had not yet broken free of the cold ground, and there was little for the horses to eat but ferns. Tay had kept some hay in reserve for just this purpose. He knew it was now or never. He set out to lure a few of the animals into the barn before spring's fresh green sprouted, for when that spring came, they would not need him anymore. He didn't want to go through another summer without a horse to ride, but the herd would do nothing without the stallion's consent, and so Tay set out to lure him in.

After three days with not feeding them, he woke in the morning before daybreak, fearing the big beast would attempt to break and enter once again.

As Tay walked out from the trail and into the field, he saw Eclipse standing by the barn in the meager light. The big horse was pawing the ground and pacing back and forth in front of the loft doors, waiting.

Instead of opening the loft doors, as he normally did, Tay opened the double barn doors on the ground level and waited inside. Eclipse was like a child testing the water before jumping in to swim. He would stick his head in the door a moment, then pull it out, let out a shrill, short squeak as if in complaint, and then tear around the field.

Before long, he would be back.

Tay had come prepared to stay as long as necessary. He had brought sandwiches and water: enough to keep him well into the night. I didn't take near that long. Eclipse, driven by his empty belly, made three or four forays of protest before entering the barn completely.

Tay had raked up all the loose hay days before and fed it out. The only hay on the ground floor was inside a very sturdy stall with solid wood walls eight feet high. Eclipse could see the lush, dry grass piled high in the feeder and made his way towards it. Tay sat in the loft with a rope attached to counter weights. Once the big horse was eating in the stall, he pulled the rope. The stall door closed, and the locking bar pivoted into place.

Eclipse went ballistic in the small space, but Tay had designed it to minimize the horse's ability to turn. He reared and kicked, but after a while, he gave up and settled into eating, forgetting about who was *now* in control and filling his belly instead.

Tay pulled out some carrots he had taken from the root cellar that morning and rubbed his hands over them one at a time. He dropped them into the feeder when the big horse had finished the hay. Eclipse sniffed the first one with cautious disdain but soon weakened. Tay listened to him crunching the treat, chewing rapidly. The second carrot went down without a sniff.

*Candy for a baby,* thought Tay, as a beautiful tricolored mare, a paint, inquisitively stuck her head in the barn doors. He swung another stall door open and exposed the treat of hay inside. She and her foal were soon in the stall next to Eclipse, happily eating hay and then the carrot treat that followed.

By lunch time, Tay had filled the seven stalls he had built. There were five gorgeous mares, all with foals, and one very young mare that Eclipse seemed to favor. They all seemed content in their confined surroundings. When the rain began to pour down and they remained dry and warm inside, Tay's shelter and prison seemed to the beasts a soft touch of control not to be feared. Tay then threw open the loft doors and fed the rest of the herd.

Tay left the field and started up the trail. He did not notice Denali sitting on a fallen log at first, even though her clothes were a different color to her surroundings. When she sat so still, it was as if she were a chameleon; she could blend into her surroundings even though her shape was easy to see once focused upon. He didn't understand the phenomena and never pretended to.

"So you have twelve, including the stallion," she stated without emotion.

"Yes," he said, slightly taken aback by her presence on the trail.

"I know the black one is yours. Which one do I get to train?"

"Any of the others."

"Have you forgotten your bedmate? She will want to choose one for herself. Don't you think it would be wise to allow her pick one before me?"

"You are right," he said. "I should allow Zuzahna the first choice, after my own."

Denali smiled, although it was barely perceptible. "But Zuzahna hasn't lifted a finger to help build the barn or to cut and dry the hay. Why should she have preference over me?"

Tay stammered something incomprehensible in response.

While he stumbled, she said, "And if I allowed you to share bed with *me?* Would *that* give me first choice?" Her smile dropped, and she looked at Tay with her usual seriousness.

"D-Denali...Alex.... He is my best friend...I could never... Even though I find you enigmatically, physically, and gorgeously appealing, I could never..."

Her rare smile came again. "I was just testing you, Commander, to see what kind of man you *really* are. I'm happy to choose *after* Zuzahna."

With that, she turned and moved up the hill like a smooth, dark wind.

Tay chuckled to himself. That woman had a way of unsettling him that he had never before experienced.

Shrugging his shoulders, he thought of a hot meal, Zuzahna, and the warmth of the bed they shared together.

Zuzahna met Tay at the door. She had been waiting for him, excited, knowing he had been at the barn all morning with the intent of capturing some of the wild herd he had been feeding for the past few months.

He came in the door, and she asked, "Well?"

He smiled like a young boy bringing home a trophy-sized fish. "You wouldn't believe the stallion. He kept ducking his head in the door and then tearing around the field like a wild beast. But he always came back, a little closer each time. It went on for a couple of hours, but he finally caved. I guess his empty belly finally changed his mind. He ate the carrots like they were candy after the first one. It was hard to keep from laughing. So now I've got him! What do you say we have a bite to eat, and then we can go down and *you* can choose one."

Zuzahna's eyes lit up. "You've got more than one?" she asked.

Tay chuckled and explained how all seven stalls were filled with the stallion's favored mares. "Once one went in, the others had almost broken down the barn door crowding in. It was like they didn't want to be kept away from him, so it became kind of competitive. You should see the mares, Zuzahna; they are truly exceptional!"

"Did the multicolored one, the one that looks painted, did she come in?"

"She was the first! I was shocked, because in the field she treats him kind of like Denali treats Alex. She stays so aloof, but the big guy is crazy about her."

"Well, Tay, women need to keep their mystery. Without mystique and playing a little hard to get, you men would just take us for granted."

"Oh really! Is that how it truly works?"

"Well, most of the time anyway." Zuzahna's mind flashed back to when she had met Tay. She pondered whether she had failed in that respect. "Did I come to you more rapidly than I should have, Tay? Are you feeling tired of me?"

Zuzahna posed and gave him a look that led Tay to believe lunch might have to wait. Tay stumbled over his words: "Your beauty is so enchanting, I'll never tire of you."

She said, "Come to me, love," just as she had the first time they'd shared each other. Zuzahna let her house robe drop silently to the floor. Standing with one leg slightly forward, she turned a little to the side, raised her hands over her head, and clasped them together so that all the dimensions of her form were displayed. She looked into him with her wide, dark eyes, the golden flecks sparkling. "Is this what you want?"

Tay went to her, placed his hands on the graceful sweep of her waist from behind, and whispered in her ear, "Always, darling. Always."

# TWENTY-FIVE

Zuzahna woke in the morning while Tay was still sleeping. She rose, slipped quietly into her clothes, and then took a bowl from off the drain board. She went out of the small dwelling, which was nestled into the hillside. Birdsong filled the air. Swallows swooped and dived for flying insects and showed golden bellies and blue-green backs that glistened in the early morning sunlight.

She walked across the flat area in front of the structure towards the shoulder of the hill below. Dew drops licked at the toes of her shoes, changing their color from light brown to dark. When she reached the place where the hill dropped away steeply, she stopped and took in the view.

The river, rustling un-seen, was hidden beneath low-lying mist that held a last breath of early summer's coolness, which would shortly give way to searing heat. The air was brisk, and she shuddered lightly as the sun dipped behind a passing cloud.

Zuzahna had seen some wild strawberries growing just over the edge of the hill a few days before, yet they had not been ripe. She had waited patiently and hoped she could pick enough this morning to dress up the bland pancakes she so often made Tay for breakfast.

The ripe berries were plentiful, and she soon had a bowl full.

Walking back to their little cozy house, she thought about how happy she was. Here in this primitive rustic world, scratching the ground for a living, she was *truly* happy. She allowed her thoughts to drift backwards in time, to a place in the past where all she had thought about was wealth and power, things she had worked feverishly to accumulate, although having them never left her truly at ease or fulfilled. There had been a form of tension driving her belief that material things and power over others would bring her joy, even though they had not. The longing had become a sort of addiction: the more she got, the more she craved.

As a young girl, she had been trained as a Duhcat: she learned to shape the soft clay of men, to mold them towards her desires and, in her old life, to sacrifice them if necessary to consolidate her power and wealth. She laughed lightheartedly about the absurdity and the change she had experienced since falling into Tay's loving arms. She shivered again, this time not from the cold but from the thought of the way he made her feel in those intimate moments when her body was intertwined with his.

It was all a first for her, she thought, and it had lasted over six years aboard the ship where there was little else to do but all those private, intimate things never spoken of outside of the closed door to their quarters.

Zuzahna smiled to herself as she opened the door softly and saw the sun glinting through their one small window, illuminating Tay's face lying peacefully on the pillow. She quickly set to work cleaning the berries. She would wait until he awakened to make the cakes, she thought.

All of a sudden, she heard him speaking. She thought he was awake, yet when she looked, she saw his eyes were not open. He called out the words softly, the unmistakable words: "Don't go!"

Zuzahna walked to him and sat on the edge of the bed. "I'll never leave you, dearest," she said.

At once, with the sound of her voice, the dream ended and his eyes flashed open. Instead of the joy she expected to see in them, she saw disappointment—and the look cut her painfully.

"What is it dear? The dream again?" she asked.

Tay avoided her eyes and looked past her, saying, as he always did, "Oh it was nothing, just a dream. You know how they can be."

"Tell me about it?" she asked sincerely. "Maybe if you talk about them, they won't come as often."

"I can't…I don't want to talk about it, Zuzahna. It would make no sense to you."

"Try me, dear. I might surprise you." She smiled warmly, stroking his hair. It was wet from perspiration. "Do the dreams…are they frightening, like nightmares?"

"I said I don't want to talk about them. I've told you that before."

"I know, Tay, but since coming here, they have been occurring more frequently, and lately much more. Perhaps if you shared with me…?"

"I can't. I have to sort them on my own. Okay?" he said, in a tone that suggested she should drop the subject.

"Sure." Zuzahna felt uneasy about the dreams. Every time Tay had one, it blew a chill through their normally affectionate relationship. She was baffled and wanted to understand what they were about, and what their meaning could be.

She shrugged, caressed his hand, and let it pass. Changing the subject, she said, "I got up early and picked wild strawberries for pancakes. Shall I fix them now, or would you rather get your morning exercise first?"

She jumped on the bed, straddling him, and then leaned over, brushing his face with her chest while kissing his forehead and the top of his head. Zuzahna squeezed her legs between his.

"What do you think, big boy. You want to come out and play?"

Tay rolled her on her back and asked, humorously, "Do you think we should before breakfast? You may get weak without food."

"I'll take my chances." She tickled him lightly and then melded into him.

Tay was as consummate at love as ever, yet she noticed a far-away look in his eyes at times, as though he were drifting to a place a great distance from her.

# TWENTY-SIX

Tiny fawns with dappled coats losing their spots were seen in the fields and at the river. They never strayed far from their mothers. The fragrance of wild berries blooming and beginning to ripen mixed with the fresh growth of the conifer forest. Warm western winds brought in the salt of the inland sea, combining with the other scents and flowing on breezes warmed by a strong golden sun, granting all who were weary of winter's icy grasp a brilliant and fresh outlook.

Everyone in Tay's village had been bored and antsy. Trapped indoors much of the cold months did little for morale. However, all had been busy; there was always something to do. Some had fashioned crude clothing and footwear from hides. The group had jokingly started a fashion show to encourage new and interesting ways to wear the simple furs and hides that piled up after the hunts. The game began as a joke to keep the villagers chuckling, yet, as time passed, some very utilitarian designs were incorporated.

Tay had scouted for tool-making material and found a deposit of iron ore a few days' ride down river. Whenever he left for his surveillance, he came back dragging a travois made in the ancient native-American style from Earth. The travois would be bent and loaded to capacity with the rich red ore.

They had an assortment of basic homesteading tools from the survival gear aboard the ship but would need many more implements. A forge was constructed, and a kiln for pottery.

Eclipse's well-muscled frame became a bulging, rippling sight to behold. Not only was the horse Tay's favorite but he could also outwork any of the other animals hands down.

The work was never-ending. Slowly, the settlement was no longer just a haphazard group of shelters thrown up to protect them through the winter; it had taken the shape of a well-thought-out village. Everyone referred to it as home. As it grew, discussions were held to find an appropriate name for the settlement. A thousand ideas were thrown around in casual times by the cooking fires and indoors at night with the flickering candles and fireplaces illuminating the small shelters in which they lived. Finally, someone came up with the name "River's Bend." They all agreed it was fitting, because just downriver from the barn the channel made a wide sweeping bend that doubled back upon itself, meaning each section of the river was only a hundred meters or so apart, flowing in parallel lines but opposite directions. "River's Bend," stuck.

One big problem was that ever since Tay had mastered and trained Eclipse, the herd stayed near River's Bend most of the time. This put a press on the grass that would be needed for the following winter, and so the monumental task of fencing an area that could provide enough hay began.

Downed virgin cedar slabs were lying everywhere in the primeval forest. A crew began cutting slabs to length for a split rail "stacked fence," while others yarded the wood in the field, split the necessary pieces, and constructed the fence. Blisters were common yet no one complained about the grueling project.

Everyone wanted a horse, and there would be need to supplement the wild herd during the frozen months, so that they would grow accustomed to wintering nearby. The plan afforded the village a large inventory of magnificent animals to choose from without needing to care for a large herd. Everyone agreed and threw themselves into the tasks at hand.

Tay began making swords in the ancient laminated style taught to him by his Chinese master Sifu. He also made tools. Blacksmithing had interested him since his boyhood, but now necessity drove him to learn the art at a rapid pace.

Finally, in late spring, Tay felt comfortable leaving the many projects to the others and decided to set out and spend some time alone on the trail, scouting out new areas and, secretly, visiting the crescent-shaped cliff where he knew at some point in the not too distant future Andarean's settling party from Seven would arrive.

He said goodbye privately to Zuzahna and then to the others before setting off on Eclipse, relishing a week of adventuring alone. Zuzahna had begged to go, too, but he had refused her, explaining that he would be keeping a brutal pace, sleeping on the trail, and riding long hours. She had accepted the explanation reluctantly.

Tay's actual reason for not allowing her to come was because, when the perfect ones arrived with Andarean, he wanted no one in his group to know they existed. His grandfather's instructions were clear: the mandate was that he should not mix nor interfere, unless Andarean's settlement was threatened.

After four hard days' ride west along the river, Tay arrived in the valley of the crescent cliff. The place was extraordinary. The lush grass was thick and blue-green due to the rich, mineral-filled soil. The inland saltwater sea was only a few kilometers from Andarean's future settlement. Fish were plentiful in the river, and in the bay. At low tide, shellfish of many varieties could be plucked from the beach. Sealife of all descriptions made the water boil with movement. Great whales blew stacks of water into the air. The plumes looked like the grey smoke from thousands of campfires curling skyward. Dense and innumerable swarms of seabirds filled the sky and dotted the water as far as one could see.

Tay set up camp on a rock promontory above the sea, and then walked the beach just before sunset. He gathered a variety of things that looked edible. The clouds, large blotches of undulating darkness ringed in irregular halos of silver and gold, slid across the grey-blue sky. The setting sun etched fanning shafts of multi-colored light across the fading azure horizon.

As evening fell, Tay built a fire and roasted half of a large-shelled creature he had pried off the rocks when the tide was out. The meat was tough and chewy yet had a wonderful flavor. He set his mind to the problem of cooking the remainder of the meat to be tender.

He sliced the meat at an angle into strips and then beat each piece flat with the handle of his large hunting knife. He then rolled each piece in some flour and quickly fried it on both sides in a little bear grease. The result was fantastic: tender and flavorful meat that didn't wear out his jaw muscles from chewing.

Tay lay down for the night at complete ease, his belly full. He was satisfied in the mind and stomach and ready to go home. Andarean had not yet arrived. He wondered how far his ship was from here, and how many people were aboard.

# TWENTY-SEVEN

VENTRAS understood from the moment he began to travel that he could never complete a quest of such scope and distance unless he could find and tame some type of beast to carry his burden. He had no idea what the planet had to offer in the way of four-legged creatures, so he minimized his provisions of dried meat, berries, and hides and tried to fashion a pack for the wolf to share the load between them.

However, when he tried to coax the wolf into carrying the pack, the wolf fought his attempts and refused. Ventras was frustrated, but he came upon what he thought of as an ingenious inspiration. He filled the pack with dried and smoked meat.

The wolf watched Ventras' hands as they handled meat. Smoke was always hungry and seemed to keep an eye on the provisions. It was as though he were assessing Ventras' honesty in divvying up their stores.

Smoke was wary of the odd thing Ventras had kept trying to put on his back, but when he saw it being filled with meat, his eyes brightened. This time when Ventras attempted to tie it onto his back, he did not fight it.

Ventras smiled to himself. "I see. You don't mind having this thing on your back as long as it is full with meat!"

Smoke looked up, and Ventras believed he saw the dog smile.


Ventras could have chosen a solitary existence: he could have built a shelter in one of the many pristine areas they had found and simply settled down, just him and the wolf. However, he had itching feet; they would not stay in one place. He longed for the power that could be wrung from associating with large bodies of people who were less driven than he was.

They walked northwards for weeks that ran into months. They found water easily amongst the intermittent green patches of vegetation. The days were warm but not scorching hot, as they had been farther south.

With no idea of this planet's geography and no map, they wandered. Their travels one day brought them to the largest creek Ventras had yet seen. Most of the trickles they had found in the early months of their journey dissipated over the great, flat plain or vanished underground. They had not found any flowing waterways that *grew* in size.

They followed the water as it meandered west. Many animal trails crisscrossed their path, but Ventras could determine by the host of tracks that they were mostly deer and smaller animals. What he desperately needed was a horse or some other beast of burden. He felt sure that attempting to tame a deer for carrying a pack would be an effort in futility.

One day, after following the river for a couple of weeks, they came upon a great mountain range that stretched from north to south as far as the eyes could see. Despite the heat, the vast line of peaks was topped with snow.

The lands they had traversed had been barren of grass for the most part, except for the pockets of green around the many artesian springs that bubbled up from the porous ground only to be swallowed a short distance away from the earth that had birthed them.

Ventras at once understood from where the water had originated. The melting snowpack seeping into the earth at high altitudes was creating the green pockets that had sustained them in their wandering.

To the west, on the far side of the range, Ventras could see the giant grey-white forms of cumulous clouds, heavy with future rainfall. They had backed up on the west side of the mountains and were squeezing through the high passes in spots. The clouds that made it over the range were no longer dark and billowing but light and wispy.

It dawned on Ventras that this range was what kept the area through which they had travelled from being the verdant place he had so desperately hoped to find. He figured that the other side of the mountain range would be cooler, with more rainfall. There would no doubt be herds of animals that might be captured and trained.

As he searched the horizon with eager eyes, a rumbling rattle from the distance sounded. He looked towards the emanation of sound and saw small and faint flashes of light sparkling within sections of the peaks. *Lightning and thunder*, he thought, and no doubt with it a deluge of rainfall.

They followed the river west, and within three days, Ventras noticed that the river was meandering more and becoming deeper and sluggish. On the fifth day, they came upon a large lake, into which the river fed. The water's color shone a deep, clear blue, but the shores were rocky and steep. Very little grass grew except right next to the water.

After another three days of skirting the edge of the lake, Ventras heard another rumbling sound. He thought at first it was more thunder, but the sound continued unbroken and grew louder as they walked west. Finally, he realized that the only thing it could be was a waterfall.

Ventras picked up the pace. Even his twisted brain appreciated natural beauty. He longed to see the cascade of water.

The sun dropped lower in the sky, changing its brilliance into subdued shades that heralded nightfall. By this time, the rumble had grown into a deafening roar. Ventras could see plumes of mist swirling upward and then being caught by a strong updraft and whisked briskly into the darkening sky. He realized he must be near the top of the waterfall.

As the sun dropped from view beyond the horizon, Ventras began to trot. He was near the cataract and wanted to witness the setting sunlight play upon the falls. The ground was wet from the waterfall's mist, and the rocks were slippery, so he slowed to be more cautious. Soon he could see a vast green and blue landscape opening wider as he came nearer to the sheer drop.

Reaching the fall's shoulder, he watched the water rolling from a flat, swirling blue into a broken curve of white laced with grey. Picking his way carefully as he moved a little higher upslope, he skirted the slippery danger of the precipice. He then traversed the steep, boulder-strewn slope and made it around to where he could actually see the cascade of liquid crashing into the blue-green pool nearly a hundred meters below.

The setting sun, a half-circle of crimson light, moved quickly into the vast ocean that stretched over the curve of the planet until at last there was no water on the horizon, only a purple and blood-red sky streaked with shades of darkening blue, grey, and charcoal.

In the fading light, Ventras could see a land so green it seemed to glow. He could literally taste its lushness on the warm breeze that blew over the precipice.

*The land of horses!* Ventras smiled at the thought.

When first light came the next morning, Ventras rose and ate quickly. The wolf looked at his bustling form and stretched languidly, as if to say, *What is the hurry?*

Ventras threw the wolf's morning meal down in front of his nose. "Let's go, Smoke! We will be down there today, if we start early."

Ventras motioned with his hand to the land, which lay like a crumpled piece of paper directly below them. The valleys and ridges were sharply cut from the base of the mountain range. At lower altitudes, the steep broken ridges melded into rolling foot hills and seemed to flee from the falls. Light and dark greens contrasted with golden meadows he could see meandering along a myriad of rivers running a web of valley floors.

Scattered islands dotted the river mouths and channels that formed an intricate web of waterways. Protected inlets and canals reflected the early morning sun. Surely, somewhere down there, there must be people, and horses, thought Ventras.

Ventras noticed a grey-blue haze far to the north that feathered out of one of the lacelike valleys. He could not help but wonder whether it was a forest fire, or perhaps the cooking fires of a settlement. He began walking in a brisk, careful stride, picking his way laterally across the rough, steep slope.

*There will be an animal trail here somewhere,* he thought. *I just have to find it.* Before long, he saw the unmistakable pattern of a switch-back trail on the slope ahead. Once he was on the trail, walking was easy. The path was well used and seemed to be the most efficient way to get down the mountain.

Ventras began whistling a song he had almost forgotten: a tune from his childhood, a time when things had been simple, as they were now. *It is simple,* he thought. *First a horse, then I will find people.*

After several days of hard walking along well-worn animal trails, Ventras left the foothills and emerged in an area that showed the distinct signs of having been visited by many herd animals. Deer and elk prints were abundant, and every now and then in the dried mud he could make out the prints of horses. His heart beat loudly in anticipation of seeing them.

On the afternoon of the following day, Ventras came around a sweeping bend of the river and saw, in the distance, the prize he sought: a group of horses grazing the tall, verdant grass. Most of the horses had their heads down, eating, but one or two were simply standing, watchful eyes constantly scanning the horizon for anything that might endanger the herd.

Ventras quickly stepped into the tree line at the river's edge and looked out from behind the trunk of a massive cedar tree.

A breeze blew from the west, and Ventras could smell the unmistakable scent of horses: a mix of sweat, young nursing foals, prolific droppings, and sweet grass being cropped.

Ventras scanned the area, looking for a good place to camp—somewhere he could watch the herd's patterns without being seen or scented. Right now, the wind was in his favor. However, it could change in a moment, and in the evenings, it tended to blow from the east. If he stayed in the valley, he ran the risk of spooking the flighty animals. If he did, they could run a distance in minutes that would take him a full day to walk.

He spied a rock face upon the hill that had a trickle of water running down it. It appeared to be a good vantage point. He decided in an instant to camp up there, high on the ledge, where he had water and an unobstructed view of the valley below.

He backtracked through the trees and along the curving course of the river, and then crossed the field, remaining out of the animals' line of sight. Ventras found a deer trail that ran diagonally up the steep slope and made way to his chosen vantage point.

Before long, he could hear the unmistakable trickle of water threading its path over stone. The dark forest around him was filled with brown, silver, and rust-colored tree trunks and limbs. The trees seemed to cling to the unforgiving ground. In places, massive rocks stabbed up through the thin layer of soil.

Stepping quietly out upon the abrupt stone ledge, the view was everything he had hoped for. Below, the coats of the horses seemed to glisten in the sunlight. Ventras counted over thirty fully grown animals. There were many young as well. He had found them. Now he needed a workable plan to capture at least one, although two would be better, he thought. The task before him was daunting. He immediately put his mind, which was well trained in scheming, to work on the problem. First, he would need rope.

As he made a small fire, Ventras contemplated the next day and those to follow. He resigned himself happily to this place. He decided he would travel no farther until he had captured and tamed one of the horses.

Ventras awakened to a dark sky lit on the horizon by first light. Rising, he first rolled his bedding and then took a bit of venison jerky. He walked out to the cliff edge and took in the sunrise.

While sleeping, he had experienced a dream. In it, he had found a plant that seemed vaguely familiar from his childhood days on the farm. He had taken the plant's long stems, stripped off the outer shell, and braided it into rope. He thought for a moment and then remembered: the plant was hemp. He had seen it growing on this planet in many places, yet, until the dream, he had not remembered that it was an excellent source of strong strands of fiber.

When the day was light enough, Ventras went in search of the plant that he could use to fashion a lasso.

He remembered a field of hemp from his travels a few days earlier. He made his way to the spot, found the field easily, and then cut and stripped the plant's fine threadlike outer shell. He then bundled enough for his needs into two packs before beginning the trek back to his camp above the valley. Smoke followed at his side. Along the way, he spied a patch of mature wild corn. He stopped and spent some time husking and cutting it from the cob until he had filled all the extra space in his packs with the sweet, juicy treat.

The weaving of fiber went well. Ventras actually enjoyed the rhythm of braiding the fiber into a useful tool. He laid the corn out in the sun on a large flat boulder to dry. A few days passed, and in that time, he made several stout lassos. The first was stiff and didn't cinch well, so on his second attempt, Ventras took the rope he had woven to the trickle of water and soaked it for a few hours. Then, he beat it against a rock until he had worked the stiffness out of the line. He laid it out in the sun to dry but continued to pick it up often and whip and beat it again so it didn't re-stiffen as it dried. When the last of the moisture had left the hemp, it was supple and easy to fashion into a loop.

He rubbed some deer fat onto the looped end of the lasso, and soon it slid easily into a working noose.

He had noticed a small grotto at the base of the rock outcropping and decided to use it to construct a stout stall that would hold a horse or two. To do this, he used some of the small poles that were abundant in the woods to fashion a gate.

He had observed the horse herd and noticed they preferred to drink from a sweeping bend in the river where the slope was not sheer, as it was in many other places along the banks. A monstrous maple tree grew above the spot. It had very large lateral limbs that reached out over the water and shaded the area.

Ventras had also noticed that during the dark hours, the horses disappeared up a canyon that ran perpendicularly away from the river. *They must sleep up there,* he thought, *where it is less exposed and warmer.*

Early the next morning, as soon as Ventras could see his way, he instructed Smoke to stay and guard the camp. The wolf was naturally protective of their food and had been easily taught to remain at camp, guarding their stores.

Ventras picked careful footfalls down into the valley floor. He made his way quietly to the big maple tree along the river. Before climbing the tree, he picked up some horse dung and smeared it on the rope and onto himself to mask his scent, which would no doubt alert the horses to his presence.

He laid the lasso in a big loop in the water, between two large rocks, and weighted it down underwater with a few small stones so that it would stay in place and not float. After covering the visible portion of the line with large fallen maple leaves, he climbed the tree and tied off the rope.

He waited.

Ventras had snuck down at times when the wind was in his favor. He had observed the animals previously as they drank at the water hole. He knew that one gorgeous mare with excellent conformation preferred to drink from the spot where he had placed his snare. The mare also had a young nursing colt. Ventras chose her for two reasons: she had a sturdy build, and because of the baby by her side. Where she went, the colt would surely follow. Ventras planned on capturing two animals but could not possibly handle two full-grown wild beasts.

The morning breeze blew in his favor and away from the herd. He could hear them coming; his heart pounded from the excitement.

Soon the animals arrived at the river. The one he had picked waited patiently for her favorite spot to open, and then gracefully stepped to the water's edge and lowered her head to drink.

Ventras, sensing the timing and position of her head was right, jerked the lasso in a quick, strong motion. The line flew from the water perfectly on the first try and closed about the mare's well-muscled neck. She went ballistic in fright, and the herd broke in frantic, primal flight.

She reared and bucked and fought until, eyes bugging from exertion, fear, and lack of air, she finally collapsed onto the beach in a foaming sweat. Ventras pulled a quick release knot and gave the line some slack before retying it. He was ecstatic. He had believed his strategy might take many tries to get right, if it worked at all. She was his.

The colt had bolted with the herd but soon realized his mother was not among them. The little guy whinnied, and she answered in a breathless shrill sound; soon the colt was by her side.

Ventras climbed down from the tree, talking in the smooth, soothing tones he had learned as a boy. Taking some of the dry corn from his pack, he laid it on the ground. He then moved near the worn-out beast. He wanted her tired and not too full of energy. When he touched her back, she rose wearily and ran to the end of her tether. When she realized she was trapped, she began the fight all over again. Her eyes looked upon him as if he were a demon, and she fought until she once again collapsed.

Ventras repeated his attempt to stroke her, and this time she was too spent to do anything but protest his touch by snorting and throwing her head.

The colt watched from a short distance. His intelligent eyes were filled with curiosity and concern. He managed, however, to eat the sweet corn, while observing his mother and the strange new creature.

Soon she stood again. This time when Ventras approached, she didn't flee or fight. Trembling legs revealed the mare's fatigue. The colt came to nurse, and the mother calmed a bit until Ventras was able to touch them both.

He had brought enough food to stay the day. During that time, he fashioned a crude halter to fit her head and attempted to fasten it about her neck. She protested stubbornly at first, but eventually he was able to fit the makeshift halter on her, affording him the control he so desperately needed.

The hours passed, and at last the mare ate some of the sweet, dry corn. Soon, she was dribbling saliva from the treat, and the look in her eyes had changed from one of fear into something that appeared to Ventras to contain a hint of trust.

As evening came, Ventras was able to lead her up, away from the river and towards the stall in the rock face.

# TWENTY-EIGHT

NEARLY four years after Tay's ship had landed on the Virgin, Andarean's ship arrived.

Soon, a series of events that had been set in motion long before Tay and Alex escaped the penal moon would unfold. These events would be called destiny by some, misfortune by others, and, by a few, good fortune. Each person involved had a part in the play and a choice in how to play that part.

I Am That I Am watched with earnest, eager interest. In the chorus of minds, one thought was predominant when it came to watching the Virgin: *Humans are a complicated species.*

# TWENTY-NINE

Landfall for Andarean and Estellene's family came after the almost twelve-year voyage. The ship was pre-programed to automatically return the vast distance to Seven Galaxies after first particle accelerating the settling party of thirty-seven persons, and all provisions. The ship, controlled by preordained flight programs, then blasted out of the Virgin's gravity pull, destined for Seven Galaxies.

On board the unmanned vessel, a complicated series of programs ran a complete check of all on-board data banks, sensor memories, and flight plans, swiping the ship completely clean.

Upon return of the vessel, it would appear that the ship had been in hibernation mode for twenty-four years. All laboratory and research material was auto-jettisoned into a sun's gravitational pull as she passed. The mystery ship would arrive at Seven, to the wonder of all, retaining no clues as to where it had been or of the journey's intent or direction.

The location for the drop had been careful chosen to provide instantaneous shelter in the form of a large, crescent-shape cliff, which faced due south, catching

## THE SEEDING SEVEN'S VISION

full solar gain. The cliff consisted of ancient limestone formations with pure spring water and airy caves, which provided the settlers with ample room for the family. The caves would give immediate shelter from the elements while a burgeoning village grew.

Andarean and Estelline were ecstatic. Never had they dreamed that the site would be so comfortable and easy to live in. The children who had never been anywhere but the ship, were awestruck by the beauty. They wanted to run wild.

Andarean immediately set boundaries for the family. "Please listen, everyone! We must first work to organize our gear and food. We don't know what kind of wild animals are present here, but surely there will be predators. We know the planet contains a variety of bears and other feral animals that can be quite dangerous. You have all been schooled in the necessary survival and outdoor skills. This is no longer the classroom. What you have been taught must not be forgotten. Abide the rules, and do not become distracted by daydreams regarding this amazing new world. Let us work quickly to stow our gear. We will set out on an exploratory hike this afternoon."

"Yeah! Hoo hoo!" screamed all the children, large and small.

The excited group made short work of their chores. Rooms in the caves were chosen quickly, with some of the oldest children pairing off with members of the opposite sex. Genetics within the group had been carefully engineered by Andarean to minimize DNA similarities. The future would bring the normal problems associated with small isolated communities, yet the young people were well versed in genetic theory, so Andarean was confident that the family would have little trouble in that respect.

Once all the necessary work was done, the older children picked up long brush-cutting blades and the group set off, intending to cut a trail to the saltwater sea that lay a few kilometers to the west. To the surprise of all, a well-worn trail was already present, apparently formed by some sort of herd animals.

Estellene had taken the children's natural history education seriously and had taught them the types of wild animals to be expected, what they ate, and how to identify their tracks. She had also taught them how to protect themselves from possible aggressive actions, such as obeying the age-old wisdom of avoiding female animals with their young. Such information was drilled into the growing children during their education and development aboard the ship. The children identified the tracks as from an elk herd, and they were anxious to see one, having only heard of them during their studies.

The hike, which Andarean had estimated would take several hours cutting their way through the brush, was instead an easy walk. It also afforded the group time to study the animal tracks as well as the flora and fauna. Other tracks were evident on the trail, including the tracks of deer; wild dogs, probably of the wolf genus; bears; and one print they could not identify right away. It was ghostly in its impression, as if the animal had walked so carefully and quietly while stalking that it left hardly anything in the way of tracks.

Andarean gathered the children, and Estellene asked them what animal had made the track. "Puma," "Cougar," "Mountain lion," many of the youngsters said in unison.

"So you see, we are fortunate enough to share this world with both the most fearsome and gentlest creatures you have learned about," schooled Estellene.

They walked on and came out of the woods upon a bluff that overlooked a vast saltwater estuary. The estuary appeared to be a few kilometers wide, and not one of them could see its full length. On the other side of the water were mountains, which the youngsters had only seen in books and electronic archives. To see them for real was completely different. Most of the family stared with their mouths hanging open.

Sunlight filtering through the distant rain clouds cast light rays that spread in grey-gold shafts downward to encompass the mountain range in an ever-changing play of color.

The glaciers boasted iridescent aquamarine and azure. The snow-capped peaks jutted into the sky, and many cliff faces dropped sharply to a shore lapped by blue-green waves.

Silence ensued, which was a rare thing among the family. As the awestruck group attempted to take it all in, one of the smaller children, named Adelle, said, "Daddy, can I name that big blue glacier? The one coming off that mother of all mountains in the middle?"

"Dearest, what would you like to name it?" Andarean asked. "Perhaps we should put it up for vote."

"I would like to name it in honor of our ship, for bringing us all safely to this wonderful place!"

"You would like to name it Eden Glacier?" The family had decided to name their vessel Eden, because harmony, safety, and love were all possible within the confines of her bulkheads.

"No, Papa, I think we should call it Eden's Glacier in honor of her that was our home, so all who come here in the future and enjoy this view will remember the one who delivered us safely."

Andarean looked at Estellene and could see the hint of a tear. Taking in the rest of the group, he saw all their heads nodding in consent.

"Today," Andarean said, as formally as possible, "we christen the glacier that comes from the mother of all mountains Eden's Glacier!"

"I would like to name the estuary," someone said. "And the other mountains," another said. "And that point which sticks out into the water so far!" They all began speaking at the same time, all anxious to place a name on Mother Nature's designs.

"I think, children, that we should not act too quickly to name all that is Nature's splendor, all that has taken eons to materialize. How about we choose just one name per day? That way we can give our new home and all her treasures and wonderful landmarks the most careful consideration?"

Everyone was in agreement. They were all mesmerized by the view, paying tribute where it was due. Many said the glacier's name over and over, so that it became like an echo: "Eden's Glacier, Eden's Glacier, Eden's Glacier."

Just then, a double rainbow broke over Eden's Glacier, and all who had never seen a rainbow other than in archived photos gasped in awe.

# THIRTY

Ventras and the wolf, two lone marauders of different species, had lived and worked as a team for over a year and a half. The partnership had suited each beast well.

A solo existence can wear on a person, and freedom unhindered, after weeks and months, can turn to a devastating loneliness. The wolf and man were good company for each other in an otherwise companionless land.

All animals have their social groupings, life rhythms, and cycles. The marauder is one who has been altered—changed by destiny, fate, or as some would believe, divine cause and effect—and who, in essence, becomes a reclusive, hermit-like being. Ventras was not naturally so. His dark talents shone in social arenas where a manipulative and fast-working intellect could feed on the inherent weaknesses, desires, and perversions in others, and thus become stronger.

The wolf named Smoke was not weak. He had been the alpha of his pack and sometimes dreamed of going back, defeating the one responsible for his loss and regaining his position. Yet he knew that eventually another would challenge, and another.

The thought of the constant struggle was tiring, so he stayed with Two Legs, and they moved farther north into lands he had not roamed before, until one day he no longer knew for certain which way *was* back.

With the horse and the yearling foal, Ventras and the wolf made good time in their wanderings. They moved constantly, never stopping for more than a few days. Ventras was searching for something, and although the wolf did not know for certain what it was, he faithfully followed his partner. Together they made a fearsome hunting team and never went hungry. During the cold winter nights, Two Legs' fire felt good to the wolf.

Day after day ran into months, and they continued their trek. Ventras finally spied part of what he was searching for. The fresh carcass of an elk lay along the path. Ventras could see without dismounting that the animal had been butchered by man and not some fearsome, fur-covered predator. The hacking marks where the haunches had been separated showed without question that the hunter had used some sort of very sharp and brutally effective butchering tool. His heart raced. They were near, but who were they?

Ventras' sharp mind tuned into every sound emanating from the forest. As they moved cautiously, he remained focused, scenting the air as they went, listening, stalking.

At mid-day, he smelled the unmistakable odor of a cooking fire. He stopped by a still pool along the small river he had been following and checked his appearance in the water's unbroken mirror. *Fearsome*, he thought. He reveled in the look with which he had come to identify himself. The cougar's hide and head cast the picture upon the water of a man who had killed the most feared of super predators. Smoke stood beside him. The wolf had finally gotten used to Ventras donning the headdress and no longer fled. The pair formed an image that demanded respect and admiration.

Ventras was sure that if those near were escaped prisoners from the penal moon, he would have no trouble working his way into their tribe. If it was TayGor's group, however, he would fall back to watch and wait, searching for the moment when he could have TayGor in his merciless grasp.

Ventras walked his horses quietly along a trail that became more well-used with each mile travelled. Soon he could see shelters and many people. He moved off the trail and stopped, well hidden by the trees. He listened.

He heard rowdy drunken laughter and much rough, very foul language. Men shoved the women around. Dirty, half-naked children with no shoes ran around like savages. They, too, were swearing like drunken sailors. *A perfect kind of rabble,* Ventras thought, as his mind ran a gauntlet of possibilities.

Finally, after much contemplation and observation, he mounted his horse and called the wolf. Then he rode fearlessly into the wild people's camp, with Smoke by his side.

Someone noticed the fearsome stranger approaching and announced the surprise. The shabby settlement became quiet, except for the sound of dogs barking. Two of the male dogs approached Smoke, hackles raised and teeth bared, challenging this newcomer.

The wolf was nonplussed. He waited for the inevitable attack, and when it came, he quickly dodged the ferocious lunge of the lead dog and grabbed it just behind the head. With a vicious crunch of his jaws and a powerful snap of his neck, the attacker was flung and landed in a twitching heap.

Murmurs ran through the disheveled crowd. Children pushed their way through the grown-ups and took in the spectacle.

Ventras spoke with authority: "I am a shaman. I have visions. In my dreams, I see the one called TayGor defeated. I see these people before me formed into a powerful army! A force that will find and destroy TayGor! We will take his women and kill his men! We will rule this planet! This is the dream I've had countless times in the past two years."

The crowd around him came alive with talk, hoots, and rowdy cheers.

One man stepped forward. He was very large, almost as tall as Ventras but much more stout. His hair was shoulder length, thick, wavy and black streaked lightly with grey. He was a handsome specimen, except for a disfiguring scar that ran from his forehead down over the left eye and onto the cheek. The damaged eye was opaque.

"I am Dazar!" he announced. "I lead these people. Where do you come from, stranger?"

"From the same ship that dropped you. The one called TayGor dropped my party in the middle of a vast furnace of a desert. There were twelve of us. Only I survived. TayGor is fearful of my powers, so he left me to a certain and torturous death. But you see that now I am here!"

Many cheered. Dazar studied Ventras quietly. His eye missed nothing. He knew he could not turn this one away.

The tribe had spoken its approval, and they had no other spiritual leader. Better, Dazar thought, to have a shaman who hated TayGor as much as he did than to risk another rising at some point in the future. He knew though that this one would bear watching closely. He sensed he could not trust the stranger too quickly.

Dazar did not show his thoughts; his face was a mask. "Come, Shaman! Sit by our fire and tell us of your great adventures!"

The crowd roared in approval.

# THIRTY-ONE

Tay had become the secret and self-appointed guardian of the perfect ones. One thing had been made clear by his grandfather's notes: he was not to intervene in their society unless they were threatened.

Tay watched them secretly, making sure that no threat from the wild tribe intruded upon their settlement.

One day, not many years after landing the Virgin, everything changed. It became clear that the wild tribe was soon to find Andarean's family. Andarean and Estellene's family had been on planet for a year and a half. They had no idea others roamed its surface.

Tay had scouted a perimeter of roughly a hundred ten kilometers around Andarean's village. The wide, crescent-shaped arc took a week to traverse, starting at the saltwater estuary south of Andarean's village and ending back at the saltwater estuary north of the village.

Once a month, Tay broke away from his group's settlement and made the solitary trek under the premise of needing time alone. He had spoken to no one among his group—not even Alex—about the existence of Andarean's village.

That day, he rode his usual route along a series of ridges that offered stunning views of the many valleys and waterways below. The scene from above was hard to believe. The altitude gave him such surreal vistas that sometimes he questioned their reality. He wondered how so much beauty and splendor could be found in one small area.

Across the complicated series of inland waterways, the snow-packed mountains stood, reflecting the early morning sunlight. Golden amber and white mixed with violet purple and red, contributing to a scene that filled him with wonder. Tay stopped Eclipse to take in the view. The shifting sun changed the mountain's coat of color. Soon, the varied hues disappeared, leaving the brilliant blinding white of fresh snowfall. Shadows showed only where there were deep crevasses and canyons—places where the sunlight's force was diminished.

The conifer forest that blanketed the ridge rustled and whispered in the breeze. The spicy needles were constantly stirred by the thermal layers that moved upward in the new day's warmth. Scents of cedar, fir, and the pungent spicy perfume of myrtle were carried upon the swirl of air currents.

Tay breathed in deeply and thought back to the prison, and the war, and his grandfather's gift to him: this place. For that moment, taking in the view once more, he felt completely at peace, despite all the rolling seas that had rocked his life. Here on this breathtaking planet, he happily took on the simple existence of being a farmer, horse breeder and trainer, hunter and food gatherer. He was fulfilled and happy with the simplicity offered here.

Tay might have taken on the role of a simple settler, but most often his past training and experience as a leader overpowered any casual enjoyment. He left his reverie and returned to his role as a commander in search of the enemy. These trips were a chance for him to be alone, but more importantly, they were part of his constant search for signs of other humans—anyone besides his group and Andarean's. He focused again on his organized scanning of the land below him and was immediately struck by something unusual: in a small valley to the north rose what might look like a foggy wisp of mist to the untrained eye; however, he knew instantly what it was. The color of the vapor had a light-blue tint. It was not fog or a low-lying wisp of cloud but smoke! Tay was sure of it.

The question arose in his mind of whether it could be a hunting party from Andarean's village, yet in a nano he knew that their camp had no need to move so far in search of food; game was plentiful, even close to the settlement. On previous occasions, he had seen their ongoing struggle to keep the devastating elk herd from thrashing their gardens.

*No, this is some other group,* he thought. Without hesitation, Tay signaled with his seat for a fast walk. Eclipse responded and began moving briskly—not a silent walk but one that would allow him to come upon the valley of smoke before dusk so that he could gain an idea of the people's origin and strength.

He thought back, remembering the many times in his life when he had been thoroughly enjoying a peaceful moment or the fruits of hard-won labors, only to have his peacefulness suddenly interrupted by imminent danger or tragedy. He realized that he was relishing this new mystery. As he made haste towards the valley, he wondered whether he had actually become bored these past few months. He knew this contradicted the thoughts he had just had while enjoying the view, but he no longer trusted those thoughts. "The human mind is a complicated piece of equipment," he said to himself.

When they arrived at the last ridge before the valley, Tay brought Eclipse to a halt and dismounted. They were on the edge of another tiny valley that abounded with tall, lush grass. He un-tacked the huge horse and brushed out the saddle marks from his coat.

Eclipse was unshod, and anyone seeing him would think he was part of the wild herd that often roamed through the area.

Gently stroking Eclipse's neck, he spoke softly: "I will return shortly. Do not follow; stay here and eat this wonderful grass—and stay out of trouble."

He stowed all his gear beneath a monstrous fallen tree and covered everything with leaves to make sure the stash was invisible to a scrutinizing glance. Then he set off at a brisk pace, turning only once to look at the scene behind him and ensure nothing was out of place or forgotten. Satisfied, he moved on up the ridge, an intense curiosity gnawing at him.

Soon, he had gained the ridge top. He walked parallel to the crest rather than over it, so that his body remained obscured from the valley of smoke and also to avoid knocking down any stones or gravel whose sound might give away his position. He could just see over the crest when he craned his neck. The forest on the higher elevations of the ridge was sparser than it was farther down the slope. He could see some breaks in the tree line where rock outcroppings shot upwards and afforded vantage points, but he kept searching for the right spot: somewhere he could lie undetected and watch whoever was camping in the valley below. Perhaps it was only a small hunting party who were staying here temporarily before returning to their main camp in some distant location, he thought.

Suddenly, in front of him, was a sheer rock face with a ledge a couple meters wide running the length of the face, which was over eighty meters.

Belly crawling out on the ledge yet keeping close to the vertical face of the rock wall above, so as not to be seen from below, he soon came upon the site for which he had been searching. Several small trees grew on a widened area on the flat stone ledge, enough to offer him cover and afford an unobstructed view at the same time. Crawling forward, he soon reached the small trees and nestled in amongst them. Cutting some small branches from the miniature forest, he made his way to the edge of the rock face.

Virtually invisible to anyone in the little valley below, he watched. It was no small hunting camp. It appeared to be a full-fledged settlement with shelters for numerous people. More than thirty horses were confined in a crude corral constructed from what appeared to be fallen tree limbs. People milled about the open cook fires, and children were plentiful. Young boys were diligently practicing the art of bow and arrow, and fighting with wooden swords and shields. Older boys rode horses and practiced with lances against straw dummies that had been attached to posts in the field.

Tay could see many horses nearby. They had clearly mastered the wild horses. He started a headcount and counted around seventy people, in the open. He presumed there to be many more inside the shelters.

Just as the sun began to sink beneath the horizon, what appeared to be a hunting party came riding briskly into camp, hooting and hollering, brandishing bows, arrows, spears, and staffs as they rode through the primitive village. Several horses were in tow, carrying slain wild game. The hunting party consisted of more than fifty men and women. Tay calculated the number of people in the village to be nearly two hundred.

Tay belly-crawled back the way he had come and walked quickly back down the ridge towards Eclipse, knowing darkness would fall momentarily. He concentrated not on what he had seen but upon his footing and the overhanging branches of trees that were attempting to stab him in the face.

Upon reaching the miniscule valley's level floor, he whistled once, mimicking a whippoorwill. Eclipse let out a quick short squeak, and Tay heard the brute's hooves pounding. Eclipse came flying out of darkness. Tay let the call out again so as not to be run over in the non-existent light. The big stallion slowed his headlong rush. The hoof beats sounded time, a rhythm that made Tay's heart pound in excitement and happiness; Eclipse's gait, along with so many other traits, were identical to his old friend Shadow's. Tay truly believed that Eclipse was Shadow, born upon this planet years before Tay's arrival.

The two of them, by some unexplainable miracle, had been reunited.

The big horse snorted, took in a deep breath, and sidled up to where Tay was standing. Tay grabbed a handful of dark mane and swung up easily, saying, "Quiet walk, boy. Tack up."

Eclipse knew what the command meant and immediately walked softly, each step high and careful, towards the hidden cache of gear, which Tay would have had difficulty locating in the blackness that now enveloped them. They walked with nary a sound other than the tall grass brushing Eclipse's legs.

When Eclipse stopped, Tay said, "Thanks, my old friend." Stopping in the exact place Tay had un-tacked was something Shadow had been taught on Seven Galaxy Seven with no small amount of trouble. Once Tay had begun riding Eclipse, he gave the old command and found that the new horse needed no education. Knowing the order as though learned in another life, it was followed impeccably.

Finding the fallen tree, Tay brought his gear out into the field and began tacking up by feel. On a dark night, if light could not be cast on the position for reasons of security or secrecy, there was no other way. Studying the ancient equestrian training methods of Genghis Khan and Alexander the Great as a boy had given Tay the strategy. Some people might have laughed in disbelief, seeing him practicing tacking the horse blindfolded. Here in the dark and in danger, the task was performed flawlessly.

Ready to ride, he patted his old companion on the neck and blew hot breath into Eclipse's nostrils. "You and I have our work cut out for us here. No easy life as a pasture potato; a challenge is before us!"

Eclipse let a short, low squeak, as if to say, *"I know! That is why I met you here!"*

The moon broke over the eastern ridge, casting a silver light upon the valley, man, and horse. Tay swung into the saddle of the gentle beast he loved like no one else and the two, appearing as one, galloped out away from the enemy and towards the village of Andarean's family.

When they reached the tree line and entered the forest again, he gave Eclipse enough rein to let the horse know he could not see the trail; he was giving the animal lead enough to carefully pick his footing through the darkness. They walked under a canopy of timber so thick that no moonlight wound its way through to the forest floor.

Tay felt an urgent need to distance himself from the enemy camp so that he could make fire and have a hot meal without the slightest chance of someone seeing the blaze or scenting its smoke. He knew of a small clearing in the forest where a lightning strike had recently ignited a fire and burned a few acres of forest before being extinguished by the spring rains. Tay had discovered the spot a couple years before and had returned there with a sack of seed to plant feed for Eclipse. When they camped here, the horse was ever-thankful to have an evening meal, while he and Tay were safely under cover of the thick timber.

Tay was pondering a dilemma. The settlement he had discovered contained an element of society that was undesirable at best. The gene pool of the group was a concentrated mix, and nasty in many respects—cut-throat murderers, vicious thieves—their moral fiber was lacking, and greed ran through the group like wildfire.

The wild ones were training their young in the ways of war. Surely, there could be only one reason: they possessed no steel. They would need more than wooden swords to become a daunting force.

Knowing Andarean's village sat on top of rich deposits of steel and other metal ores and minerals, while the northern tribe had none, made Tay realize it would only be a matter of time before the northern tribe found Andarean's village and considered a conquest for the necessary elements to create weapons.

Tay was completely surprised to find that the northern tribe had traveled so far in only a few short years. They had horses, and they must also have built boats, for there was no other way the rugged terrain to the north could have been traversed in so little time.

Building a small fire, he fried several eggs, heated some smoked venison, and made strong coffee. He would not sleep this night; instead, he would plan his words carefully and form a presentation that would be received by Andarean in the most favorable light.

Conflict with the wild northern tribe was a forgone conclusion. They were driven, as were all violent criminals, by the desire to possess power and wealth. Without steel, they were at a distinct disadvantage. It would only be a matter of time before they realized Andarean had the things they wanted, and the base nature of the group would justify any atrocity to gain what they desired.

Staring into the fire, a plan formed in Tay's mind. He would go to Andarean, offer his protection, and train his family in the virtues and art of war; there was no other way. A society or culture that was weak or passive would be unprepared to meet the wild tribe. The northern hoard would quickly evaluate Andarean's group, realize they were in no way prepared to fight, and then strike while the advantage of surprise was on their side.

If the northern tribe displaced or conquered Andarean's group, the strategic materials in the area would be controlled by the evil ones. There was no choice: Tay must warn them to prepare, to train and fashion weapons and build defensible positions just in case the wild ones came to conquer.

The problem of convincing Andarean of the necessary course would be no small task. Andarean had always been a man of peace. Striving to create a utopian culture had been his life's work. Now his dreams and the carefree existence of his family were at risk.

# THIRTY-TWO

Early the next morning, Tay rode Eclipse into the valley of the crescent cliff: Andarean and Estellene's valley.

"Quiet walk, boy," he said. Eclipse responded by stepping high and softly.

The sun had risen not long before, and a cool wind blew off the river, bringing with it the briny scent of the estuary at low tide. A pair of coal-black ravens flew up from the tall grass when he startled them. They flew high enough to catch the warm updraft above the cliff, and then circled effortlessly, watching him.

The village was quiet. Tay had chosen to come early as a courtesy. Most of the children would still be in bed or eating breakfast. He wished to arrive at a time when his appearance would go mostly unnoticed should Andarean wish to keep his visit secret.

Having been out of diplomatic circles since leaving Seven Galaxies, Tay was unnaturally nervous. The news he brought was not good, and his appearance would be a shock to the village and primarily to Andarean, who, of course, believed that his family were the only humans on this planet.

Life was never simple, thought Tay, reflecting on his own: it always seemed that just when everything was lined up and there appeared to be smooth sailing ahead, the spinning curve ball slammed in. It never seemed to fail.

Imparting the news he brought would be the simple part. Convincing Andarean that he needed Tay and his skills would be a tough sell. Andarean was a scientist. He had been sheltered from the brutal realities of life by spending all his years working in a lab.

Eclipse walked so softly his hooves could scarcely be heard. Tay scanned the cliff for signs of activity. A young boy was coming out of a pole building that was configured as a barn. He was followed by two massive dogs covered in dense, long coats of blonde and black hair. He was carrying a basket loaded with eggs. The boy turned, as if sensing the presence of another, and stumbled lightly, catching himself before dropping the basket.

"Careful," Tay said. "You won't be getting breakfast if you drop them all."

The boy stopped in his tracks.

"What's your name, young man?" Tay asked.

"Josy."

"Well, Josy, I've never seen such magnificent dogs. What breed are they?"

"Tibetan mastiffs. Their genes come from Ancient Earth. Who are you, mister? And where did you come from?"

"My name is Tay, and I came from..." Tay gestured, pointing to the sky.

"Sounds like you are telling a tall tale, mister Tay, because horses can't fly!"

"I did not say I rode this beast here, did I?" Tay said, following the boy's obvious humor.

"Well, you sure are a surprise. We haven't met anyone else in the time we've lived here. I thought just *our* family lived on the Virgin."

"Well, you can see I'm here. I live on this planet, too. Can I speak with your father? Will you tell him quietly so that not everyone hears?"

"Sure, I'll run and fetch him. Maybe your horse would like some oats. I can get him some in the barn if you tie him in there."

"Okay, Josy. His name is Eclipse, and he'll be forever your friend if you feed him."

"Boy, he *sure* is a beautiful...giant of horse. I love horses. I take care of ours. We just have a few, but I'm breeding them and soon we'll have a whole herd. But none of them are like this one."

Tay dismounted and held out Eclipse's reins. "Would you like to lead him in? I can hold the eggs."

"Would you let me!"

"Of course. Go get him some oats and then run tell your father I'm waiting here."

Josy took the reins and handed Tay the eggs. The boy leaned in close to Eclipse's nose, almost touching it with his own. "He smells good," he said, and stroked Eclipse on the forehead. The horse bobbed his head up and down, magnifying the strokes. "He likes that, doesn't he?"

"Surely he does. I can see you two are becoming good friends already."

"I simply love horses. Ever since I first saw pictures of them when I was little, I wanted one of my own. I can't remember ever wanting anything else so much. And now we have them!"

Tay reflected on his early years of childhood, and remembered how he had longed for a horse. "When I was a little boy, I wanted nothing more than a horse, too. So you see, you and I have something in common." Tay winked at Josy, as if he had just let go a precious secret. The boy winked back knowingly.

Josy led Eclipse into the barn and was shortly back outside. He grabbed the egg basket and said, "I'll go get my dad. You sure have a beautiful animal, mister—I mean, Tay. I think he's a very special one."

"I agree with you. He's more special than you'll ever know."

Josy trotted smoothly towards one of the caves in the cliff and disappeared inside.

Andarean saw his son come running with the egg basket. The boy was flushed with excitement. "Now, Josy, slow down. I don't want you running around with the eggs, especially when I'm hungry and need them for breakfast." Andarean hugged his son to show him he wasn't cross.

"I know, Dad. I didn't mean to, it just...it's just that I need to speak to you about something private, and it can't wait."

"Okay, take the eggs to your mother and we'll go and talk."

Josy was back like a flash and tugged at Andarean's hand. "Come, Dad...this way."

"I want all of you to stay here for a bit," Andarean said to the others. "Josy needs some private time."

A chorus of nearly forty voices sang in acknowledgement. They understood the boundary of "private time." Raising as many children as Andarean and Estellene had was no small chore. Boundaries had become an absolute necessity, as was private time.

As they broke from the cave to the outside, Josy said quietly, "There's a man at the barn named Tay. He wants to talk with you. He rides a big dark horse, and they both seem very nice."

Andarean knew Josy had a vivid imagination, but he was still shocked he could come up with such a story. He began his usual speech regarding the acceptability of having imaginary friends. Josy merely pointed towards the barn where Tay was waiting.

Andarean glanced in the direction Josy was pointing and visibly started.

"Go back inside, son," he said immediately. "I'll go and speak with him. What did you say his name was?"

"Tay, Father."

"Very good. Go on inside and, for the moment, please don't talk about this to anyone, okay?"

"Yes, Father," Josy said, obviously disappointed at being left out.

Estellene saw Josy come back inside and immediately knew something was up. He sauntered into the kitchen with a sense of importance that spoke volumes: He knew something the others did not. She began her usual soft-touch fact-finding. "That was sure a short talk you and your dad had."

"Yeah, I really didn't need alone time." He glanced away, as if looking for something expected, like the arrival of someone.

"Where's your dad, Josy?"

"Down at the barn."

"What's he doing down there? I thought you already took care of the chores?"

At this point, the boy became a little flustered. He stammered a bit and then said, "Honestly, he asked me not to tell, so I can't. If you want to know, you'll have to go to the barn yourself."

Estellene's curiosity was piqued. She had been having dreams lately, some of them unsettling. This particular sequence of events gave her a feeling of déjà vu. She quickly wiped her hands dry on a towel and made way to the door of the cave.

What she saw made her gasp. The two men hadn't seen her yet, so she approached quietly, skirting their line of sight. She wanted to hear the conversation without being seen. Estellene had been trained since she was a young girl in the art of walking softly and silently.

As she approached the barn from the far side, she heard Andarean saying clearly, "Absolutely not! I won't have it! We will be fine here. We will make peace with these marauders...these 'wild ones' as you call them. I will certainly not have my family trained in the art of war."

"Andarean, please, let me speak," Tay said. "I know this all comes as a terrible surprise to you, but these men will not be stopped with a negotiated peace. You cannot trust their word; they have no honor. They are the worst of sorts."

"I've heard enough! I want you to leave! We cannot mix with inferiors, don't you see? The Fifteen's vision would be ruined. The perfect race of people, the Virgin planet—this cannot change. I don't believe for a minute we would be drawn into fighting these, these...these wild ones!"

"Andarean, I have come to help your family. I have come as a friend, yet right now you are speaking as if I am attempting to take something from you. What I have offered is given in the hopes of future friendship."

"We don't need your friendship!"

"The ones I speak of have many horses. I have spied upon them and witnessed them training for combat. They are even training the children. The site of your settlement is the only place on this planet where iron, silver, gold, and other necessary minerals exist near the surface, where they can be collected without deep mining. These ones I speak of have primitive wooden and stone weapons. They have found agates and obsidian for arrow and spear points, yet they cannot make swords, plows, or shovels. They will never move forward and out of the stone-age without these materials. Do you honestly believe they will let you live here in peace and not come in force to take the things they need? They are also short of women."

"Enough! Enough.... If they come, I will make peace with them. We will give them what they need and keep the separation. We cannot live with those who are not perfect! Don't you see? The whole reason for traveling twelve years through Deep Space to this planet was to fulfill the Fifteen's vision. I will not allow that vision to be broken! I was appointed Guardian and Steward of the Virgin by the Fifteen. I will not go against their dream."

"Dreams evolve by necessity, Andarean. Change has come here. I want to help you adapt and protect the

Fifteen's vision. It is dear to me as well. I must add, however, that at times, a guardian must be prepared to fight if necessary, to protect what he or she guards. This is one of those times. We can be friends. We can hold onto the Fifteens' plan for this planet—but not by making peace with the impossible likes of the wild ones."

"No! I have decided! I will resolve this quandary not by fighting but by negotiating. I will offer them what they want and in turn have them give their word that they will leave us alone. I will make sure in the agreement that they will stay a great distance from my family."

"Andarean, they cannot be trusted," Tay said, shaking his head in frustration. "If you give them the materials for the very weapons they need to conquer us, they will not be satisfied. Instead, they will be empowered to take what they desire. Don't you see?"

"Leave now! You must never come back! Go!"

"Andarean...wait, I—"

"Leave!"

The barn door opened and out came Eclipse led by Josy. The boy looked sheepish and defiant at the same time. He walked up to Tay, handed him the reins, and said, "You sure have a magnificent horse, Tay."

He looked Tay straight in the eyes, and Tay felt the message...that the boy thought his father was wrong and wished Tay were staying among them.

The boy turned, ran back to the cave's mouth, and disappeared inside.

Andarean glared.

Tay placed a foot in the stirrup and swung into the saddle in the same motion. "If you change your mind, my camp is about a four day ride upriver."

With that, he signaled Eclipse, and the dark beast broke into a gallop that sent chunks of sod skyward.

Andarean was in shock. He walked around the corner of the barn and almost bumped into Estellene, who was watching Tay and Eclipse pounding across the field towards the river trail.

# THIRTY-THREE

Estellene tried talking sense into Andarean after Tay left. The wild ones had appeared just a few hours after his departure. They were out in the field before the village. Andarean would not listen to reason.

"If they want food, we will give what we have," said Andarean.

"And weapons, my love?"

"Weapons? Of course not! We have no weapons!"

"Andarean, my dear and sheltered husband, steel, nickel and brass in a shovel or a hoe is a tool for growing food, yet within a violent one's hand it is a weapon to kill. It can be smelted and reconfigured as armor and the sword."

"What and where have you learned this?" Andarean asked.

"I am not just a navigator and starship pilot. I am also fluent in the arts of war. The Ancient schooled me."

"Leandra saw to your education?"

"Yes. She personally was my only formal teacher. Leandra taught me of art, in nature, in paintings, in poetry, and in the human entity, yet some humans are not art; they are trash. You know this to be true!"

"I will not have it! I will speak to the barbarians from the north. We cannot let this one and his followers mingle within our group! Don't you see? Inevitably, the genealogy of the perfect ones would be adulterated and smeared, darkened by imperfect blood."

"Do you know who this man is?" she asked.

"No. He did not offer a last name."

"He is Admiral Gor's grandson. The admiral is an honorable and just man, and his grandson seems the same. I know Leandra loved them both. How he arrived here I do not know, but be sure that if he offers us protection, then he would sacrifice his own life and those of his followers to that end."

"I did not accept his offer of protection!"

"I know, my love, but my sixth sense speaks loudly, telling me that we need his help!"

"He is very handsome, strong, and no doubt virile. Do you, *young* Estellene, desire him?"

"Do not be foolish!" she said, surprised. "We have never had jealousy enter our thoughts. At this moment, do you entertain thoughts that question my love and dedication to you?"

"I cannot help myself!" he cried out in frustration. "In one short hour, our perfect life here has been tainted by something I don't understand!"

"Darling, darling, I only want what is best for our family. If these barbarians threaten us, it would be wise to associate our society with one who is honest, true, and knows the ways of war. He has also tamed many of the wild horses."

"We will not speak of war," Andarean said, making up his mind. "The dream of the Fifteen has been fulfilled here. Peace, harmony, love. All these things have been ours. I cannot comprehend the change. We were to live here: only the perfect ones. Now the barbarian hoard approaches, and a potential savior, a knight in shining armor, comes to our rescue. Yet all that these two forces have to offer is conflict. I shall not take part in this madness. The northern tribe flies the white banner of peace. I will ride out and speak to them!"

"Do not!" Estellene said, shaking her head in a panic. "I forbid you! I do not trust them...their energy. I felt it before we actually saw them. I have felt it for the past year, becoming stronger month by month. Soon they will arrive on our doorstep. My dearest Andarean, they are not to be trusted. Do not go, I beg you!"

"I have no other choice! I will speak to them under the banner of truce and come to a peaceful resolution."

"Don't go! In my dreams, I have seen your death by their hand. I have seen it in nightmares that come more frequently these past few months. Do not go! I beg you!"

"You have never once mentioned this! Is this some trick by which you attempt to control me?"

"My love, I have never attempted to control you. There has never been a need to. Do you not see? The evil ones, their energy, is reaching into our family already. It is supercharging our emotions. We are not thinking rationally."

"Speak for yourself, Estellene! I am always rational. Do you hear me? I am *always rational*!"

The man standing before her was one she had never before seen. Gone was the gentle, loving Andarean; before her was a person who would not listen to reason or common sense.

She said only, "I beg you, don't go! I fear if you leave I will not see you again."

"Quiet, Estellene! I command you to be quiet. I will return soon enough."


Andarean rode out into the field, intending to speak with the northern tribe. He was riding towards his fate, feeling sure that he was to be a primitive diplomat. The men on horseback smiled. They seemed friendly, and the white flag waved. Surely Estellene was being unreasonable, he thought.

Andarean stopped ten meters in front of the group and said, "I bid you good day! Welcome!"

There were twelve men. All were smiling, when suddenly a sound drew Andarean's attention. It sounded like the wings of a hawk in steep dive.

The men gave him even larger smiles when, suddenly, he felt a sharp, searing pain wrack his body. Confused, Andarean looked down to see what appeared to be an ancient weapon: a thin rod of wood, feathers attached, protruding from his chest. He looked up in disbelief, saying only, "We have met under the white flag of peace!"

The group spurred their horses wildly, sweeping by him. He had enough breath left to turn in the saddle and see them riding toward his village in a frenzied gallop. They were all screaming, hair flying. Behind them, a huge cloud of dust obscured his home, and his family.

Andarean could only think, *Estellene was right*, before toppling from his horse.

# THIRTY-FOUR

Taygor was motionless, as though rooted deeply into and growing from the cleft of grey-blue limestone. He wore the colors of earth, ones that melded with and seemed birthed from the stone—smeared clay, charcoal, and ash. He could feel the warmth of summer sun, yet from the foundation of his perch within a grey-black sky, the day was dark, as was his mood.

The morning had held such promise.

Now, as afternoon waned and he reflected upon the earlier hours of the day, his mind pondered a dilemma, and he wished the events that had just unfolded could somehow be changed. He wished that he could have foreseen the future, and that he could have forestalled the disaster.

He felt responsible. He felt he could have said something that would have altered the events of the morning, and perhaps changed history. He knew his desire for the tragedy to be erased was impossible, yet his reeling mind could not help but wonder.

Andarean, the one he had sworn to protect, lay still. Golden green grass brushed and rubbed. The day's breeze caressed nature's golden bed, into which Andarean bled no more.

Tay's heart was filled with sorrow. The consummate diplomat had failed, and because of that failure, Andarean's family was in jeopardy.

The wild tribe had arrived.

They had hoisted a ruse into the sky: the trick of an amoral clan. The lie, which Andarean had believed, was white on the surface, but black with malevolent intent beneath. The white flag of truce and negotiation had drawn Andarean into the golden grass.

The twelve marauding northerners had come.

Andarean's village was quiet.

Everyone in the village had been directed into the caves by a woman, and they had all obeyed. The woman, who wore a straw hat that hid her face and whose fluid gait seemed vaguely familiar, had orchestrated the movements of the family. She was a mystery to Tay, a presence that drew unexplainable feelings from within him.

Within the limestone cleft, Tay watched the surreal scene. His mind ran through all options. He considered intervening, taking these men armed with bows, arrows, and long spears himself. However, from a military standpoint, he knew valor in this instance would do nothing but ensure his certain death.

He waited, scanning, thinking of an ambush point, planning his stealth approach, visualizing a location and set of circumstances that would allow him to prevail, outnumbered as he was.

The filthy men on horseback came into the deserted village and quickly dismounted. They hastily tied their horses to anything convenient, left the animals, and walked briskly up the main path to the central cave mouths. Shortly they disappeared inside the dark openings of the stone face.

Tay's heart raced in concern.

His feeling of impotence grew into anger. *I should do something*, he thought, feeling that he should race down the trail and into the village, even if armed only with a sword and his wits; yet he knew, instinctively, that the attempt would be futile.

He needed a plan of attack that would have a good chance of success, not some harebrained plan quickly thrown together and easily defeated. He was the village's hope: their designated protector. Calming himself, he breathed deeply, waiting, listening.


Estellene, from a safe vantage point, watched after gathering the children and hiding them within the complex system of caves. The passageways wandered, labyrinth-like, deep below ground from the opening.

Andarean had been resolute and unmovable. All her pleading had not dissuaded him from meeting the strange ones on the open field. Her heart had shrieked within her breast when she saw her beloved topple from his mount, and the wild ones come.

Estellene was unworried for her family, who were hiding safely behind the shield of her ingenuity. Swearing an oath to herself, she prepared mentally. She would give these base marauders something to remember.

Sudden painful death forces honest spiritual reckoning into the fading consciousness of even the most gruesome and violent beasts, she thought. *None must escape.*

The loathsome excuses for human beings, searching, drooling, desiring, longing for tender plunder, would find in the shadows their miserable and violent ends.

As Estellene's heart mourned the loss of Andarean, her logic and superior intellect overpowered her grief. She must meet the evil force that had killed Andarean beneath the white flag of truce with a brutality that matched their own.

Surrounding Estellene in a tightly knit group stood the families' protective pack, their hackles raised. Her dogs needed no command to unleash savage vengeance upon those responsible for slaying their master.

Moving swiftly, she led the dogs to three cave mouths that all opened into one large cavern and told them to hold, ready in the shadows, waiting to launch.

Estellene herself took up position in a well-hidden place behind a rock outcropping. She wore leather gloves made from thick hide that had been beaten and softened into suppleness. She crouched low and opened a small wooden case she carried over her shoulder on a leather strap. Sunlight, faint within the cave, lit hundreds of shining points protruding from the star-shaped discs all packed carefully into the case. She slipped her hands into a small cleft on each side of the case and withdrew two shurikan stars—ones that did not carry lethal poison.

The Tibetan mastiffs crouched, ready to attack. She heard the men dismount, and then their footsteps nearing. She readied herself. Estellene had never taken human life yet felt no compunction about doing so now to avenge her lover's death and protect her children.

The interlopers were fearless; they believed there were only adolescent boys and girls in the village, and had figured it would be easy pickings now that Andarean was dead, so they were feeling bold.

At first, they felt no warning of impending danger, only the slightest prickle of skin, and then a light snarl that could have been the snore of a small child. However, with that slight sound, the hair rose on the backs of their necks.

Greed, and a lust for young women and steel, pushed each man forward.

Estellene had run the ambush through her mind a hundred times in the preceding months.

Two of the mature Tibetan Mastiffs could kill a full-grown mountain lion with their short, powerful jaws filled with serrated teeth and lightning quick speed and agility. They also had thick, three-layered coats that protected them from serious damage. The malicious enemies of the village were in for a very short-lived and rude awakening within the dim light of the limestone cavern.

The wild ones heard a softly spoken word, which was nearly inaudible to them.

The voice unleashed a flurry of fur, muscled sinew, bone, and flashing teeth. Bright glints of whirling, razor-sharp stars flew into startled faces and made a brutal impact on the previously overconfident intruders. A few who remained on their feet attempted a hasty retreat, but they were run down within a few steps by the brute force of eighty-kilo male Tibetans.


No more than a few seconds after the men entered the caves, two came racing back into the light of day. Not more than a step or two from the limestone, flashing hulks of fur leapt upon the retreating men from behind, savagely taking the evil ones to the ground and ripping them into screaming, blood-oozing shreds.

Shortly, all was once again silent.

The dogs searched intently for other malevolent trespassers to dispatch. Two of the fearsome animals stood sentry at the cave mouth. They reminded Tay of lions: ancient guardian statues, exuding power and restraint. Several others of the beasts scoured the village, evidently seeking remnants of the wild northern clan.

Within minutes, the search obviously concluded, the dogs congregated at the cave mouth and then disappeared inside.

# THIRTY-FIVE

The woman in the straw hat came out into the light of day. She bent down over the bloodied, shredded corpses and appeared to pull something from one of the men.

She then stood erect, and Tay saw a momentary flash. She held a small, glinting object in her gloved hand. It appeared to be a small metal disc stained with crimson.

The dogs were about her in protective circle, and Tay watched, unseen, as she took a moment to caress and speak to each of her fur-covered guardians, one at a time. *Who is she?* he thought. How fearless she appeared. Tay wondered what the woman would do next.

Estellene looked upon the limestone cliff and directly at Tay, who, with smeared clay, ash, and charcoal camouflaging his appearance, was virtually invisible against the backdrop of grey-blue stone. She then searched the crescent bluffs, scanning the cliff intently. Her eyes sought the source of whatever was tickling her sixth sense: the reasons she felt observed.

Tay, in his niche, remained unmoving. The woman's eyes and face were masked in shadows cast by the wide straw brim. Try as he might, he could not discern her features, only her obvious sensitivity to his presence.

Who was she? His mind screamed the question again, as he leaned against the coolness of cliff, frozen in place. His yearning grew stronger: the desire to know more of her. His primal instincts pulsed, keeping him from showing himself, guarding the secret of his presence from the mysterious warrior woman below.

The woman turned at last. She appeared unsatisfied, as if she knew something were out there, some force she was unsure of, an emanation that had left her on edge. Reluctantly, she turned from her search of the cliff's face and walked towards a wooden, barn-like building. Her steps were light upon the ground. Where had he seen the woman before? Tay asked himself in frustration, yet no answer made itself known.

A few minutes later, she returned with a two-wheeled wagon drawn by a pair of horses. She drove it near the caves and then backed it to a ledge that was nearly the same height as the wagon's bed—just a few inches taller. Tay noticed fresh hay spread loosely in the back of the wagon.

He watched, transfixed, as the woman disappeared into the cave again.

Shortly, two of the massive dogs appeared from the opening. They were dragging something. The thing turned out to be a lifeless body: one of the twelve northern marauders. Soon, another pair of dogs appeared. Estellene led them to the wagon and into its bed. The dogs followed with their burden.

The wagon was soon loaded with twelve filthy corpses. The task had taken less than ten minutes. The woman jumped lightly into the driver's seat and set the horses into a trot, heading towards the salt water a couple kilometers away.

The dogs stayed, some guarding the cave mouths, others waiting inside.

After the woman left, Tay climbed higher up the cliff to a vantage point that afforded a more distant view. He could see a trail of dust near the sheer rock face that fell to salt water far below.

Shortly, the wagon returned, empty. Tay continued watching as the woman washed the wagon out and scraped up bloodied soil. She appeared to be covering all traces of the violently concluded visit of the wild northern tribe. They had come seeking plunder. They had found only death.

Tay's feelings for this mysterious woman were rising. He found the ingeniously conceived and fearlessly concluded ambush remarkable. He knew, through some unexplainable instinct, that he was to become her friend and ally; that together, they would hold the northern tribe at bay and protect her family, along with its material and moral worth.

Tay's mind ran quickly into the future, wondering how they would meet, anticipating the moment. He longed to know her name, to see her face, to hear the lilt of her voice and the laugh that he was certain would bring joy into his soul.

She came from the cave with the children. The shoulders in the group were slumped, heavy with sorrow. Many in the group stopped and began sobbing, while others fell to their knees in anguish. A few lay upon the earth, unmoving, except for the trembles that wracked their bodies; hopeless tragedy, and unexpected loss, stabbed at their tender loving souls.

Tay knew the feeling. It was an old friend to him, an acquaintance grown vaguely distant with passing years yet one that visited in quiet, contemplative moments when some small cue brought the desperately painful memories of love lost close to the surface again.

Tay cried with the group. Tears fell for Andarean, and for the loss of his grandfather. Compassion and understanding sprouting and growing, he cried with and for the children below.

The woman, along with three of the older boys, took the wagon from the village out into the grass, which no longer swayed and danced. For a time, the wind quieted, and nature calmed, as the wagon tread a path through the green and golden field. Everything seemed to move in slow motion as the wagon made its way to where Andarean, in stillness, lay.

# THIRTY-SIX

Tay watched the pain-filled scene of Andarean's family retrieving the body of their father, then he walked away, head held low, looking to the ground and feeling ashamed. He had failed in the duty he had sworn: to protect Andarean from the wild northern tribe.

All the promises, all the months spent in preparation scouting the perimeter of Andarean's village, and his visit to warn Andarean of the wild one's presence had yielded nothing but disaster.

As Tay neared Eclipse, the horse nickered. His beloved mount brought him out of circumspection and the past and into the present, startling him.

"Hey, big fella. How ya doin?" They were the same words he had spoken countless times to Shadow in his childhood. The words were so familiar—words spoken to a timeless companion. Suddenly, his dark thoughts lifted.

The horse's nose nudged him, and Tay rubbed the flat spot between the huge beast's eyes. Eclipse bounced his head up and down, magnifying the friction, enjoying the warmth Tay's hand created. Then he looked upon the man as though he were concerned: concerned for the quiet approach, and for the time tethered alone in the forest while Tay had been gone.

Eclipse was the man's guardian, this the horse knew with certainty. Now, with Tay so melancholy, the horse felt inspired to stir him from the dark mood. Eclipse squeaked: that absurd sound that Tay had heard no other horse in his life make—except Shadow.

"What?" he asked.

The charcoal-grey beast scampered, hooves stutter stepping in anticipation of taking Tay down the ridge trail to the valley below, which was filled with lush green grass and cool water.

"You want to hit the trail?" Tay asked, laughing softly.

The dark beast's eyes flashed with emotion, attempting to say things that could not be conveyed with words but only by the rush of anxious breath, the tapping, stuttering, pawing hooves and the emotion-filled squeak used as an exclamation point at the end of a primeval sentence.

"Settle, Eclipse. If you want me to put this saddle on, settle."

The big horse calmed himself.

Tay moved fluidly, not wasting a single action. A minute later, he swung effortlessly into the saddle and the two beings, appearing melded one into another, broke down the ridge trail in a graceful canter.

Sunlight's slanting rays shattered into pieces, flickering through open places in the forest canopy and illuminating the horse and rider in momentary flashes of moving color.

## THE SEEDING SEVEN'S VISION

Soon, glints of brilliant golden green could be seen between the massive trees.

The scents drifting on the warmth of summer air had changed. No longer was the spicy aroma of the conifer forest predominant; instead, the fragrance of grass growing, wildflowers, and the briny flavor of the river meeting tidewater filled the air.

Reaching the river trail, Tay gave up a little more rein, signaling Eclipse, and they broke into a gallop of pounding hearts and hooves, of rushing, steaming hot breath, and sweat. The horse and man startled many wild creatures along their path as they flashed by.

A few miles upriver, Tay shortened the reins and brought Eclipse down to a walk, allowing his horse to cool while he attempted to collect his thoughts and feelings.

Tay was unsure of where he was going. His permanent settlement and group were farther up river. Four days' ride, and he would be home, and in Zuzahna's warm embrace. However, he was also being pulled back in the other direction, as if some magnetic quality of Andarean's village had attached to his physical and mental being and was drawing him back.

He stopped, dismounted, and led Eclipse down to the river, where he unsaddled him. Tay then took off the hackamore and let the big animal drink.

He knelt beside the singing, swirling river that ran without end like the tide of his emotions and drank as well.

Once watered, Eclipse snorted lightly and looked to his charge with eyes that said, "What now?"

Tay signaled with a long sweep of his hand, and the horse understood instantly: this was camp, and he was free to seek out that sweetest patch of grass, the one he had scented while testing the air as Tay un-tacked him.

Eclipse squeaked softly, trotted up the river bank, and disappeared over the crest.

Tay found himself sitting upon a large rock outcropping, which the river swept around in a shimmering arc. Contemplation set in. His thoughts ran the gamut of sorrow, excitement, and intrigue. He thought of the woman in the straw hat, of the mourning children, of the wild ones yet to come, and in that instant he knew: Andarean's village could not survive an organized attack by a force that so vastly outnumbered them.

He knew the only solution was to return to Andarean's village and help them prepare for the inevitable. The village of the crescent cliff sat atop the only deposits of strategic minerals and metallic ores, which were easily extractable with the simple tools available in this primitive way of life. The wild ones needed steel.

Tay knew instinctively they would come. It was only a matter of time.


The horse's dark color changed in the waning evening light. Eclipse became a muted shadow, the ghost of a horse in darkness. Soon, the only proof of his presence was the sound of green grass being cropped, and once in a while the rush of breath sighed from deep within.

Tay banked the fire he had made before turning wearily to his bedroll. Hunger ran from him, driven by his racing mind. His thoughts returned incessantly to the woman in the straw hat. He must convince her that she needed his craft: the Art of War.

The night's passing, proved only by a sliver of silver-white moon slipping slowly through the sky, dragged on.

As a thin grey line formed on the eastern horizon, false dawn lighting the meadow and Eclipse's silhouette, Tay fell asleep. His sleep was dream filled. The enchantress came once again—out of reach, mysterious. Her eyes drew something deep within him closer to the surface: a longing, a need carefully kept secret. He felt it rising from where, consciously, it was always kept subdued and in check.

She was his private obsession taking him on an odyssey running more than nine years into his past. Once again, she slid gracefully towards him out of mist that lay in the low areas in the valley and the river's channel.

Her eyes were somehow different this time: still hauntingly surreal, but there was something unsettled in them. They spoke of uncertainty, or of fear.

She came nearer, and the dark horse appeared magically by her side. The horse was identical to Shadow and to Eclipse. They walked in sync, closer to him.

This time perhaps, he wondered, would she speak? In that moment when he asked the question, just as she was nearly close enough to touch, the vision evaporated.

# THIRTY-SEVEN

The village was in mourning. The day before, they had buried Andarean high above the valley, atop the limestone cliffs in which they lived. Estellene had been pondering the dilemma of protecting her family from future attacks ever since Andarean's death. Tay's visit kept coming into her mind. He was trained in the art of war and in the ancient style of fighting on horseback. He had also been successful in taming and training many of the wild horses—something her family had had little success in doing. They had managed to acquire a few work horses, and now they had the wild interloper's horses, but they had nothing that would allow them the battle mounts necessary to protect the village from a well-organized offensive by a much larger force.

The morning after Andarean was laid to rest, she instructed the children in defensive positions and in the use of the dogs for protection. All the boys and some of the girls were quite good with lances and spears. They could easily defend from safe positions in the cavern mouths without her help.

She saddled one of the new horses they had taken as spoil from the dead interlopers and set off up river toward the location Tay had described as his camp.

She had prepared to be gone a week or more. As she rode, she worried. A constant flurry of unanswered questions clouded her mind and stole the beauty before her, locking it into a place she could not see.

Her thoughts while on the trail were focused on the man she believed to be Admiral Gor's grandson.

Tay woke to early morning sunlight falling through the trees, creating angular patterns of dark and light greens and browns.

Rising, he rubbed his face, then straightened and rolled his bedding. He stirred some glowing coals up from deep within the ashes of the fire. There were no more flames, just a thick, dark smoke that drifted so heavily he could taste its familiar flavor. He placed some small, dry broken branches on the coals, and the wood crackled and sparked, assuring him that the fire could be re-kindled.

Tay rose from his crouch and looked around for Eclipse. The horse was no place to be seen. *Probably down at the river for a drink,* he thought.

Walking down-slope, he noticed sunshine illuminating a stream of mist that clung to the river's course. The water spoke, unseen, beneath the blanket of white. In places where the air was warmed by sunlight, wisps climbed in swirls, rising into the azure sky above before vanishing. A scene from a dream, he thought, and stopped for a moment to enjoy the picturesque sight.

Eclipse nickered, unseen. The sound reminded him of how Shadow had once greeted him. Eclipse was speaking, but he could not see him. *Somewhere down-river,* Tay thought. The sound seemed muffled by the heavy mist, and Tay could not tell with certainty how far away his horse was.

Preferring not to call out, he made his way slowly, enjoying the morning's ever-changing moods. As he neared the river's sweep and the rock he had sat upon in deep contemplation the evening before, Tay heard the unmistakable sound of hoof-falls on stone. Then, above the music of water, he also heard the soft sound of a woman's voice.

*Surely I'm still dreaming,* he thought. *There could be no one here.*

Eclipse always announced visitors, either by a silent nudge to grab Tay's attention or a quick stamp. *It's just a bird singing in the distance*, he thought, yet all the logical explanations didn't remove the feeling that someone was here…with Eclipse.

Tay stole silently along, wondering whether the sound had substance, or whether he was imagining things. He felt a dreamlike sensation pass through him. He was still unsure, so he moved cautiously forward towards the sounds, wondering whether it *could* have been a bird. Again the unmistakable voice: soft, like the water, and full of affection, as if talking to a beloved child.

In that moment, a curl of the heavy fog broke away from the river, exposing sections of water that resembled large fragments of broken glass sparkling brilliantly in the morning sun. In an unlit place between two of the jagged shining plates stood two silhouettes: one of a charcoal-grey horse and the other of a woman with long hair, which the muted sunlight highlighted into varying shades of ebony and redwood.

The woman's back was towards Tay. She was stroking the horse on the flat spots of his cheeks and speaking in soft tones. Eclipse stood frozen, ears forward, entranced.

Sitting down in overwhelmed disbelief, Tay picked up a small pebble and tossed it back and forth, feeling it softly between his hands. *A dream?* he thought.

She turned, as if sensing his silent, querulous presence, and looked directly at him without searching.

Eclipse started slowly towards him and she moved as well, appearing to glide beside the beast.

The two of them came as he had seen them move countless times in his sleep.

They came.

Her eyes were the same.

He waited for the inevitable, the vanishing; the loss upon awakening—the loss of something so longed for, something so wanted, and dear.

They came closer, and the horse stopped.

*So close*, thought Tay. He could almost reach her, if he tried…but not quite.

She took another step nearer, and Eclipse gave her a soft, unexpected nudge from behind.

Caught off-guard, she stumbled lightly against a rough ridge protruding from the rock. Tay sprang up to catch her, and she fell lightly into his arms. Her scent drove deep—so familiar. Her form in his arms felt as though she had been created by some miracle to fit him perfectly.

Tay's heart leapt. He could not let loose, for fear of losing her once more. Disbelief in the moment's reality, and hope that she *was* real, pervaded every fiber of his being.

Eclipse squeaked.

Estellene clung to him. The slightest tremor ran through her. It grew into trembling, increasing until she shuddered involuntarily, her heart mourning the loss of her beloved, and her mind attempting to understand the overwhelming bliss engulfing her senses. She sobbed uncontrollably in his arms.

Estellene had never before felt the tumult of emotions running through her. A wild range of overwhelming feelings: love, sorrow-filled loss, shock at her brutality towards the wild ones in the cave, joy at finding this new friend, fear for the future and for her children's welfare, and loneliness. The past day had brought her heart into a dark, unknown place—a place unvisited on any other days of her previously joy-filled life.

Tay knew now that she was no apparition. He could feel her hot tears soaking his shirt. He could see the moisture of her breath rising to steam in the brisk morning air. Her heart pounded against his, her hair tickled his nose, her scent filled his lungs as he breathed deeply of her essence.

Tay held onto her tightly, not uttering a word. He longed, as he had for nearly a decade, to know her name. He felt that if he let loose, she would evaporate as the mist rising and disappearing into the azure realm above.

# THIRTY-EIGHT

Estellene at last composed herself and said simply, "I'm happy to find you. Please, forgive me. I could never have imagined this moment or how I would feel, even though I have seen today many times in my dreams. I have seen it, yet I never understood. I never understood what tragedy would befall my family before meeting you. When you came to warn us, when you spoke with my husband Andarean, I saw you. I knew you were the one who came in my dreams, yet I could not have understood this meeting. Everything that has transpired since your visit...I must tell you..."

"I know," said Tay.

"What do you know?"

Tay's eyes filled. He felt her loss. He saw, in his mind's eye, Andarean falling into the golden green grass.

She knew somehow and said, "You were watching. You saw my husband meet the ones you warned us about. You saw him fall?"

"Yes."

"My husband never told me your full name. I would like to hear you speak it."

"Tay. My name is TayGor."

"Somehow," she began, "somehow I knew. I had seen pictures of Admiral Gor when he was young and you have his look, and his stature...yet I wonder how I knew when I saw you...without your family name. The mind has powers that are a mystery, powers that even the most advanced intellect could never understand. My mind told me who you were, even though you never spoke your name."

Tay longed to know her name as well.

As if reading his thoughts, she said, "I am Estellene."

"*Estellene.*" He said her name as if the word were a priceless jewel he held in his hands. "Estellene."

Her eyes sparkled with happiness when he said her name, and he saw the colors that he had seen flashing countless times before in his dreams: colors that long ago, had bought his soul.

# THIRTY-NINE

Tay and Estellene rested in his camp by the river. Estellene was still puzzled about something. "Tay, when you spoke with Andarean, you said we could find you up river, a four-day ride," she said. "Why then are you here? So near?"

"I began to ride away from here, to return to my village, but when I got to this spot on the river I could make myself go no further. It was like some form of magnetic energy was holding me fast. I could not escape its pull. So I stayed, and you came. Now we are here, speaking for the first time. You will never know how much this means to me. What happened was a tragedy to me, although I can't explain the circumstances. However, as terrible as it was, I can only feel the result. I'm more than happy you came. I will not apologize for that."

"TayGor, I too feel the same. Before finding you, my heart was drenched in sorrow. When I had the good fortune of finding you so easily, so quickly, it was as if I had been given an elixir to cure my broken self. You are that medicine, Tay. Don't ask me to explain it further."

"I won't."

Estellene had brought a bedroll. She was packed for the trail. Tay asked, "Will you stay here tonight? If you're not comfortable, I understand. I can come to your settlement in the morning if you choose to leave this afternoon. We could talk more then, but I feel a need to stay here this evening. I want to wake here, just as I did this morning. I want to etch this place into my memory: the spot where *we finally* met."

She looked thoughtful. After a while, she said, "I would enjoy being here with you. I need some time away from my village, and from the memories of the past two days."

The two of them said little. Basking in their newly found friendship seemed to be enough. They stared into the campfire, the silence broken only by the crackle of the burning wood, the river's rustle, and the sweep of the evening swifts as they flew by once in a while. When their legs grew tired from sitting, they walked the woods, picking huckleberries. They fished the river together and caught the evening meal.

Every once in a while, Tay would glance at Estellene, and she would return the look. In the silence of camp, their eyes spoke words that were safer left unsaid.

Finally, when drowsiness claimed them, they each rolled out their bedding close together so that they could lie within arm's reach of one another.

After lying down, Tay took her hand. It felt so familiar: the shape, the size, the softness; it was like he had held it countless times before.

Soon, they were both sleeping peacefully, completely comfortable beside one another.

The next morning, as they broke camp, Estellene looked searchingly into Tay's eyes and asked, "Will you accompany me to my village? I would like you to stay there with us for a time. I want to introduce my children. There are many."

"I was hoping you would ask. I would be honored.

# FORTY

TAY had been in Estellene's village nearly a week and had enjoyed the stay beyond belief. Estellene had given him a spot in the loft of the barn. Every morning, he woke with hay in his bedroll and various other places he would normally find irritating, yet irritation never crossed his mind. However, Zuzahna often times did. He knew she would be worrying and that he was being unfair by not returning and quelling her fears.

He could not tear himself away from Estellene. She was everything he had seen in a decade of dreams and more. In the dreams, she had never spoken, but during the past week they had talked incessantly. He was experiencing what his subconscious had already seen, although in his mind the scenes had had fewer dimensions...less depth.

Estellene had swept him away. He wanted nothing but to be with her, to work for her, to train her family, to be their protector. At times, often, he thought of being her lover. Tay knew she was mourning the loss of Andarean and that it was absurd to think those kinds of thoughts... yet.... Tay knew he must take his leave. He must return to Zuzahna. He could not hope to press himself upon Estellene so soon after the loss of her husband, no matter what he hoped for the future.

He pondered the decade of dreams and relived the feeling in conscious state, while he was near her. Upon waking from the thousand dreams, as he had begun to think of them, she always vanished. Surely there had been a thousand dreams and more. He felt as if, when he left Estellene's village—as surely he must—the time spent with her might feel the same way: surreal and unbelievable.

But now she was flesh and blood, not a fleeting apparition that came and went in the flutter of eyelashes.

Tay's time spent in the valley of the crescent cliff opened his eyes to the many daunting issues facing Estellene after losing Andarean. The children were suffering from grief. Although many of the young children seemed to adapt well, Tay could see sadness in their eyes. The adolescent children experienced obvious moments of mourning. Tears came easily to them all. Andarean's memory haunted everyone—Tay included.

On waking one morning, he developed a plan. He found some twine, wove a net, and strung it up between two poles. He was ready to teach the ancient game of volleyball to the kids, and to Estellene.

The children's minds, transported from sorrow by the distraction, flew into happiness with the comical struggles inherent in learning to play. None of them had played before, and the game was a huge success.

The next day, Tay awoke before light and walked to the river, just as the rising sunlight made seeing possible. He cut down some small willow saplings and made a dozen fishing poles by tying a strong thread to the poles and attaching the hooks he always kept in his saddlebag.

Tools crafted at his forge were large and small. Fishhooks and needles for sewing had been a most difficult challenge to make. After many unsuccessful attempts, he had finally mastered the art.

After breakfast, he asked the children if any of them wanted to go fishing. Of course, they thought he meant with a net, which was the way the village had caught fish for the table in the past.

When Tay brought out a pole, many of the older children laughed.

Josy asked, "Why would we want to catch one fish at a time when we could cast a net and have many?"

Tay smiled and said simply, "Fishing this way is a challenge. What if you were in the mountains and had no net?"

Many of the children begged to go, and Josy was one of them.

For the next day, Estellene and Tay decided on having a picnic at the saltwater beach. Tay had calculated by the moon that there would be a very low tide, and he planned on teaching the children about Abalone and Goeducks.

As he packed shovels into the wagons, one girl, a blonde of twelve years named Serrenda, approached and asked what he was going to do with the shovels. Tay responded with a sly smile that they would be doing some duck hunting, and that's why he was packing the shovels.

Serrenda laughed at him. "How in the world do you expect to catch ducks with shovels?"

Tay smiled back knowingly and answered only, "You'll see!"

He could hear Serrenda telling many of the children what he had said, and they broke out laughing over and over. "Duck hunting with shovels!" was echoed time and again as they trekked to the beach.

Once on the sand, they walked way out to where the tide had exposed long spits reaching out into the receding water. Tay carried out a piece of a hollow cedar log that was about a meter in diameter, and the same in length. The kids laughed more uproariously when they asked him why he was lugging the piece of log out onto the beach. Smiling enigmatically, he said simply that it was his duck trap. Of course, more laughing ensued.

After reaching a spot on a spit that had many holes concentrated in one area in the sand, he stood the hollow cedar upright and began digging. Tay was removing sand from the inside of the wooden tube. Soon, he had made a hole deep enough to slide the cedar log into vertically. Then, he continued digging, sloughing wet sand from inside the wood. Every so often, he would shove the wooden tube deeper into the hole and then dig more.

The children all gathered around to see Tay, sweating and creating a hole that was a meter in depth in the wet sand. They all laughed at his appearance. Inevitably, he had become well covered in wet sand. Still, he worked with frenzy.

At last, they heard the shovel bang something hard at the bottom of the hole. Tay then used a flat steel bar and a hammer to chip away at the hard pan, while he leaned over the edge and lowered his upper body into the hole he had made.

Soon his head appeared. His smile boasted something magnificent, and all at once he withdrew his arm from the wooden tube. In his sand-drenched hand was the biggest clam the children had ever seen. The goeduck had a neck larger than many of the children's arms.

Exclamations ran over top of each other: "Gigantic!" "Monster clam!" "Wow!" "Unbelievable!"

Tay, enjoying the children's exuberant reactions, was silent. He wanted to keep the kids in the throes of amazement for a bit. Then he said, "This is the duck I was after. A Goeduck!"

Many of the children wanted to hold it, others to pull more specimens from the deep hole. The group was abuzz with excitement.

Estellene looked at Tay with adoration. When the children became preoccupied with digging for their own clams, she said quietly, "Thanks, Tay. You've been wonderful for them. I'm so happy you are here. The children have begun to love you. I see it in their eyes, and in their voices when they speak of you amongst themselves."

He looked at her with an intensity she could not ignore, and said, "And you, Estellene?"

Her eyes said the words, but her voice remained silent.

After the children had dug a mass of the giant clams, Tay took them up the beach to a rocky area where they pried some very large Abalone from the rocks. Later in the day, when the tide had come in over the sun-warmed sand, Tay took the kids down to the beach to a place where sea grass grew from the bottom. They waded into water about knee depth and spotted many large crabs that had come in from the deeper water and into the warmth of the shallows. Tay picked the crab up carefully, teaching the children how to hold them and not get pinched.

They built two fires on the beach: one for cooking and the other for warmth and to dry out the many wet children and their clothes before the coolness of evening came.

Tay instructed the group on cleaning preparation and on how to cook the delicacies they had gathered during the day. Then they all ate until they could fit no more into their bellies.

At last, with the sun gone from the sky and its remnants of waning light displaying a rainbow of colors, they loaded the wagons, dowsed the fires, and happily headed home.

It had been a gorgeous day, full of frolicking fun, good adventures, learning, and the marvelous food that nature offered in plenty.

# FORTY-ONE

Tay was awakened by the creak of a stair. Opening his eyes, he noticed a faint grey light showing through cracks between the barn's cedar siding. It was early...false dawn, he thought.

Then he heard another stair complain against a footfall. He wondered...

The faint glow of candle light moved, flickering on the rafters above the stairwell.

Shortly, he saw her unmistakable hair. Even in the dim light, its contrasts could be seen. Her eyes mirrored the candle's light as she said, "I couldn't sleep. I brought you some tea. Do you feel like talking a bit?"

Overwhelmed, as usual, by her presence, Tay could only utter, "Sure."

Here in the barn among the sweet-smelling bales, her fragrance drifted to him; in the dreams, he had not been afforded the undeniable pleasure of her scent.

Estellene sat on a hay bale next to him. He sat up, and she handed him the cup.

Just before their hands touched, a small bolt of static electricity jumped between them. Startled by the charge, she accidentally spilled some of the tea down the front of him.

Tay jumped and began to rub the hot liquid off his chest and stomach. When he had finished, he looked up and noticed a look he had never seen in her eyes before: it might have been a spark of desire, but he wasn't sure.

Estellene continued looking at him, her eyes flashed varying colors in the fluctuating, flickering candle light.

"I dreamed you were leaving, Tay. Are you?"

"I've been thinking I should go home…for a while. My people will be worrying. I am normally gone no more than a week, but it's been ten days already—ten wonderful days. I love being here with you, Estellene…I really don't want to leave, but…"

"I know. You must. Thank you for your help. I've needed you here. Without your friendship…"

"I know, Estellene. I feel the same."

"Do you?" Her eyes questioned much deeper than the words. The look he saw was that of an innocent young girl, a young woman wondering…

Tay took a long drink of the tea, sorting his thoughts into words. "Estellene, in other circumstances, I would not hesitate…. I long to feel you alongside of me. I have dreamed so many times of that moment, but I—"

Estellene placed one finger to her lips and uttered a soft shush, then she took the same finger and placed it to his lips. Her hand slid behind his neck and, by some miracle he did not comprehend, she was next to him. Her softness, her form, her scent, her eyes…he could think of nothing else.

His arms trembled holding her and his heart pounded, beating a chorus with hers.

"All you were trying to say, we have both thought many times. Now is not a time for words." She fell silent and looked up into his eyes.

She then turned and blew out the candle's flame. With that breath, Tay fell weightless, as though he had been carried off to some mystical place of enchantment.

Without her heart pulsing against his chest, he would have believed it all a dream.

# FORTY-TWO

Zuzahna waited excitedly for Tay's return. He was late by a few days, and she wondered what was keeping him. She hoped he was not in trouble, lying injured out in the wilds. She knew from the past that he was a survivor. She also knew he needed this time away to be alone, to think and adjust.

Tay was no longer commander of a Deep Space vessel. Here on this planet, he was a farmer and food gatherer, and the leader of the people in their settling party. It had been a difficult beginning, scratching out an existence in primitive fashion. In all, however, they were happy, and she hoped to carry his child soon. She had broached the subject on many occasions, but he had never answered her and chose to be away from her when her time was right.

She felt sure he would consent before long, and then he would be tied to her by an unbreakable bond. With a child they would, in essence, be married: it was the thing Zuzahna had desired for years, and the thing Tay had tactfully avoided.

Never in her life had she found a man so compelling. Tay was at times the consummate warrior: training horses, practicing his fighting art, and making weapons. At other times, he was the most sensitive and loving man she had ever known. Thinking of him often gave her a small spike of adrenalin and a feeling upon her skin as if feathers were brushing her lightly.

In her distant past, *she* had been the one in control.

Tay, she had to admit, took her places she had never before visited emotionally. In those moments, which were unlike anything she had ever experienced, she gladly relinquished herself to him.

Being brought up a Duhcat and trained since a young girl as courtesan to the wealthy and powerful, Zuzahna had practiced her art without mercy. Now, after six years together aboard *Intrepid One* and several years on planet since then, Tay had sewn Zuzahna's heart hopelessly into himself. She, for once in her life, felt need of a man, a need she could not satisfy completely.

When he was away, her heart yearned for him. Upon waking without him next to her, she would be cast down into momentary disappointment. Then she would consciously bring herself out of this childish emotion by the thought of his return.

Zuzahna smiled involuntarily. They had been meant for each other from the beginning, she thought; and he had been drawn into her without reserve…at first.

Zuzahna's smile faded quickly when she thought of the dreams—and of the look on his face when he woke. When he woke and she questioned him, he would be elusive, as if the dreams held some secret, something he did not want her to know. Then the moment would pass, and he would be himself. The man she had grown to crave, and to love, would return.

She walked from camp up the ridge trail to the rock promontory that afforded a view of their valley and the length of the river. Often times, when she expected him back from one of his trips, she would watch until she could see the dust from his movement in the distance. Then she would race down the trail, mount her horse, Paint, bare-back, and gallop full tilt towards him.

She would meet him at their special and private place along the river. The place where they could greet one another in ways that must be kept from listening ears, for their love was sometimes—often times—vocal with passion.

Sometimes her curiosity drove her to attempt to follow him and to see where his trail led. Normally, she would tire of tracking him, or lose his trail among tracks of the elk herds that were so plentiful.

Zuzahna sat upon the rock, waiting…watching.

She did this each afternoon, until the setting sun sent crisp slanting shadows through the trees, and the river's sparkling water changed from blue-green to violet, and then she would walk back down the trail, thinking, tomorrow…*tomorrow* he will come.

A week passed since the day she had expected him, and Zuzahna worried without end. Every evening she would return from her vantage point a little more downcast than the day before… when the sun set into a darkening horizon, a horizon that sometimes reminded her of blood.

# FORTY-THREE

THE next morning Tay awoke and turned to see Estellene, but she was gone. For a moment he thought the dream had once again come to haunt his sleep, but when he drew a sharp breath he could still smell her, and the candle rested in a pottery bowl where she had set it down the evening before and then....

The sequence of events that had unfolded flashed through his mind. He relaxed, laid back on his bedroll, and sighed deeply. It had been no dream. She had come to him in the first light of morning, and as the sun drew nearer the horizon and its light seeped through the spaces between the siding, her features had dawned as well. Her multi-colored hair had cascaded down upon him, its silky feel on his skin, its scent flowing as she moved. Her smile swallowed him.

She had been a powerful warm and sensual wave washing over him, sweeping his body and mind into a place where, in the throes of their passion, he prayed hopelessly that he could stay forever.

She had been a fleeting glimpse of heaven.

She was gone.

He looked at the sky through the siding's cracks and realized the sun had been up for hours. Rising and dressing, he swiped his hands through his hair and then slipped down the stairs and outside.

The settlement was busy, and she was nowhere to be seen, so he walked up to the main cave entrance and said, "Estellene," softly.

She came out wiping her hands on a towel. They were covered in flour.

"Well! Good morning! I trust you slept well. You must have been worn out."

Her words, to anyone else listening, would have been taken for casual talk, but her eyes spoke a different language. She was smirking. Tay found it arrestingly compelling and felt himself flush.

"Yes…I had trouble getting to sleep last night. I had a lot on my mind and…I didn't actually fall off to sleep until after sunrise."

She motioned to him with her hand to follow as she turned and walked back inside. Tay willingly trailed behind.

A few young girls were helping Estellene make bread.

"What could possibly have occupied your mind and kept you awake for the entire night?" she asked, teasing him.

Tay said offhandedly, attempting a forced nonchalance, "Oh, a lot of things actually."

She smiled. "Are you ready for some breakfast?"

"Actually, I'm famished!"

"I thought you would be."

She busied herself making eggs while humming a tune he had heard before yet couldn't immediately place.

Tay turned to the three young girls. "Ladies, how are you this morning?"

The three chimed in at once: "Very good, Tay." "Fine, Mr. TayGor." "Wonderful. Mommy is *really* happy this morning!"

Tay looked to Estellene, and it was her turn to pinken slightly. She smiled softly, avoiding his eyes, and kept busy with the food.

"Young ladies, I wish you could all just call me Tay. I think we will all become very good friends, and I just like being called Tay best."

The three chimed in sync, "Yes, Tay," and giggled.

After eating, and with the bread baking in the oven, Estellene directed the girls to begin tidying up the kitchen.

"Let's take a walk to the cliffs, Tay," she said. "The girls know when to pull the bread."

"Yes, Mr....I mean, Tay," one of the girls said, and all three giggled together again.

Tay smiled at the children and their evident happiness before walking with Estellene out into the sunlight. He could hear the girls talking in whispered voices between fits of laughter. The whole episode made him smile deep down.

"What's gotten into those three this morning?" he asked in good humor.

Estellene smiled knowingly as they walked towards the cliff-top trail. "Some of the children are telepathic—those three particularly. They have never told me so, but I believe they often communicate between themselves without speech. You see, they are triplets, but not identical. They are our only ones. All others were single births. I think they know."

"But how could they?" he asked. "You were so discreet."

Estellene shrugged her shoulders as an answer and continued up the steep trail without saying more.

Tay always kept in excellent shape. He was, by his figuring, five years younger than Estellene, although he couldn't be sure and knew better than to ask a woman's age before she offered it willingly, without being prodded. And so he should have had no trouble at all keeping pace with a woman much smaller than himself as she walked up the grueling climb of over six hundred vertical feet. However, Estellene didn't walk; she seemed to glide.

Tay's ego drove him to keep up, but it was not easy. Her strides in many of the steeper places outstripped his own.

By the time they reached the top, he was winded. She turned and looked at him. He tried to act as though he wasn't out of breath.

He couldn't hear her breathing at all.

His show was difficult to pull off. Estellene watched him and smiled inwardly.

As they turned from each other, and gazed out over the valley, and the inland sea beyond, she said, "Tay...I know you must leave. I would never be so presumptuous as to think I could keep you here.... I only need to ask if I might know when to expect you again? I don't want to be looking at the river trail constantly, expecting you when I should not."

"I wish I did not have to go away, Estellene," he said. "I will leave my heart here and will be thinking of you constantly."

She smiled demurely. "You flatter me, TayGor. I would *never* expect—after the briefness of our time together—to have *won* you. You speak as though I am an enchantress who has beguiled your soul."

He looked to her, and in that moment almost spilled the longing that had grown from his dreams for the decade past. He said, "*You* ..." and then stopped.

Finally, he said only, "You are truly dreamlike... I could think for years on what the woman of my dreams would look like, how she would act, what she would smell like... and never come close to the way you have impressed me with your beauty, grace, and warmth. Your friendship is an extraordinary pleasure." Feeling he had said more than he should, he added quickly before looking back to the view, "Thank you, Estellene."

She moved toward him. One moment she was a few paces away, and then, before Tay had heard a step, she had closed the distance between them. There was no air separating him from her touch. He felt electricity, just as he had before she had spilled the tea upon him. As her breasts touched his back, the bolt struck. Like an electric jolt, it stimulated his heart, his adrenalin, and...

"I know you must go," she said. "I want to know when you plan to return. Tell me this, and then if your answer pleases me... I have a very special place I want to share with you."

Tay's mind leapt forward, hoping she meant they could revisit the intimacy she had shared with him in the loft, amongst the hay.

Tay answered quickly. "A week's ride round trip, if I push Eclipse hard and spend a couple days in my village. I will return in nine days if everything goes perfectly, but you should look for me in twelve days. That is more realistic."

"Twelve days was earlier than I had hoped, although nine suits me *even* better.... Come."

She took his hand and led him along the cliff's edge. They walked the smooth, flat limestone, following its crescent arc for few hundred meters. Then, as they began descending, Estellene stopped.

"Here is where the going is a bit tricky," she said. "Follow my movements. Place your hands and feet exactly as I do, and you will have no trouble."

Tay's mind raced backwards. He had been here before. He had found this ledge long before Estellene and Andarean had landed. He had watched from a place nearby...had watched the wild ones come.

Tay followed in silence, not wishing to break the spell of the moment. He chose instead to consciously bury the past—to follow and watch, mesmerized by the woman before him.

After a time, they came upon an opening where a fissure had been cut through the stone by the force of eons of flowing water. The fissure ran deep into a cleft in the cliff. Estellene worked her way through the narrow opening and squeezed through easily. Tay had to expel all his air to clear the narrow throat of rock.

Once through the fissure, an open area appeared: a tiny, green valley with tall limestone walls. The sun's high path cast shadows across the vertical blue-grey stone. It was draped in moss, lichen, and, in pockets of soil, even wildflowers. A flat grassy spot lay next to a small blue pool, which was fed by a rivulet of water cascading down from above.

"Magical..." Tay said. "How did you ever find this place, Estellene?"

"I have a talent for discovering the remarkable."

She looked right through him. Her eyes pulled his soul into what felt like a knot that only she could untie.

"Until today, I have never shown this place to anyone. If we are to be here together...you must keep it sacred between us. You must not bring anyone else here. This place is my sanctuary, my peace, my tranquility. It is where I come when I need to be away from the press of my large and loving family. I come here to think, to reflect, to plan, and to dream. I have dreamed of you here. When I first found this spot, I was tired. I lay down to rest and fell asleep without realizing it, and you came... you came riding through a field of lush, tall, blue-green and golden grass. You were riding Eclipse. I glimpsed you and felt as though it were a premonition, a vision of the future that I could not possibly have understood at that time. And then...you were gone. I saw you again, the day you rode in and warned my beloved Andarean of the wild ones. The day my love was slain..." Estellene's voice caught. Her face turned towards the ground and her shoulders slumped.

Tay said only, "Thank you for bringing me here...to this very special place."

He held her until her sobs subsided.

Tay thought of all the children. There were at least thirty five of them, although he had not actually counted. *That's a lot for one woman to handle,* he thought. Then he thought of Serene. She was so lonely, so distant. He wondered if Estellene might welcome some help with the children and thought it would do Serene a world of good.

"Estellene, there is an older woman who lives in my settlement...she is alone, with no mate, and she is very sweet. I wondered whether you might welcome some assistance with the children. I'm sure Serene would be much happier here."

Estellene turned toward him, a look of shock upon her face. "Did you say her name is Serene?"

"Yes."

"Does she have big, wide-set eyes the color of aquamarine?"

"Yes. Do you know her?"

"Did she work in the Dome of Wisdom?"

"Yes."

"She's here?"

"Yes," Tay said, a bit perplexed by Estellene's questions.

"My dearest Serene? Here? That is absolutely fantastic! Can you bring her when you return? If you tell her I'm here, she will come. Please, Tay? I need her here!"

"Yes. Of course. If you want her help, I'm sure she would be happy to come."

"I am in need of her friendship first. Her help will, of course, be wonderful. Oh! Tay, what news!"

Estellene was suddenly filled with light. Her smile radiated happiness that brought out Tay's smile as well.

\* \* \*

In the morning, Tay saddled an anxious Eclipse and rode east along the river trail.

Riding in silence punctuated by the river rushing over stones worn smooth by time, he thought of Zuzahna and the nine years they had spent together.

She was a woman who, in waking hours, had consumed him...yet in his dreams, she could not own him.

Tay reflected, pondering the situation: the two women possessed his heart completely. One grew powerful with the rising moon, the other with the rising sun. They were both utterly irreplaceable. How could one man be so torn? No clear answer came, only that he wanted—needed—both of them and could not continue without either one.

Now he was journeying to cut one loose for another, to cast the one adrift, the one who had bewitched his willing heart for nine mesmerizing years. He was about to cast her off for the one he had just met a few days before but who had haunted him in his sleep for a decade.

And so Tay rode forward, to fulfill his destiny. He longed for children, children he could never have with Zuzahna because she was Nesdian—the sworn enemy of Seven Galaxies. Every time Zuzahna's monthly window opened during the past nine years, she had attempted to weaken him. She had done many things, attempting to drive his needs so that he would be desperate for her tender affections when she might catch within her open days.

Tay had mounted Eclipse and taken to the trail each time. He could not weaken; he would not, he repeated to himself countless times. So their relationship had been forged into something of a game. *Her* game. Tay tired of it.

Now he had shared Estellene's bed, a bed that would welcome children of Earth into this pristine new world without cross-pollinating with the backward Nesdian gene pool.

His mind was made up. He would ride to Zuzahna and tell her. He would tell her...he would say...that he could not sleep with her any more, that he was Estellene's *only*, and that he and Zuzahna...as *lovers*, were finished. Eclipse's even stride became exclamation marks.

He thought of Zuzahna's bed, where the two of them had shared vast and varied pleasures; her deep, dark, golden-flecked eyes; her hair—a black, flowing mass, pooled upon the pillow beneath him and draping her form when she was above; her scent.... He had to reposition himself in the saddle, because any thought of her aroused him. She aroused and entrapped him. He felt as though she owned him and that he was setting out towards her plantation to beg her mercy...to beg for his release from her grasp, even though it was a grasp he undeniably craved.

# FORTY-FOUR

Tay met Zuzahna on the open field, ten days after their normal monthly meeting day. She rode at a full gallop towards him on her beautiful Paint. Fluid grace encompassed both rider and horse. They appeared to be one, not two separate beings.

Tay considered each of the animals approaching; together, they were both so beautiful that they startled the heart. The surreal sight pulled an unexplained and primeval yearning from a place all too familiar. It left Tay wondering whether he was really watching her flamboyant arrival or whether he was simply in deep sleep, witnessing fantasy.

Tay resolved to himself that he had no desire to own either of these spectacular creatures. He had vowed to set them free, to speak to Zuzahna of the need to separate himself from her hold, her power over him. He knew she would not take the surprise well.

Zuzahna and the horse came flying at him, her black hair streaming behind, her stunning features flushed with exertion and excitement.

Reining the animal to an abrupt halt, she used the horse's momentum and catapulted from her seat into a spiraling dismount. She landed in his outstretched arms.

Tay had prepared to catch her, yet she was completely in balance and his strength was not necessary. It was as though she had just completed an intricate ballet movement, flawlessly.

"Dearest Tay," she said, breathless, "I have missed you more than I care to admit!"

"And I you, Zuzahna! As always, when I am away, you come to my dreams. When I wake with longing, I ponder the feeling I am left with. It is, for loss of better words, an emptiness." Tay could not believe he had just spoken these words; they had tumbled out involuntarily. His resolve to part with Zuzahna had crumbled with the first brush of her warmth. Puzzled, he felt her power, her magnetism.

She gave him her most wistful look, turning to reveal a profile Zuzahna knew he adored, and glanced sideways out of the corner of her eye to see his reaction.

Tay was impressed. This woman had talent and the power to melt resolve and bend a man to her will. He had made up his mind to be with Estellene, yet he felt himself wondering of the possibilities of both. Surely, if he loved them both equally, and if he did not favor one over the other, if he was willing to sacrifice his life to protect each of them, they could not find it within their hearts to be jealous of one another.

Tay realized without question that he loved them both dearly, though he had spoken words of love to Estellene only, and never to Zuzahna.

"I have made camp in our special place, in the trees by the river. I long for you. Let us go now and not waste time in small talk," she said.

Tay felt himself aroused and beneath her undeniable spell. Zuzahna took his hand and led him forward without the least bit of resistance from him. With her touch, he found himself following and wanting to be led towards her bed. The bed of so many pleasures, the bed he had planned to tell Estellene he needed no more.

Tay awoke to the river's voice, soothing, caressing, and hypnotizing. He was happy here in her arms. *What more could a man ask for?* he thought. Glancing at Zuzahna's sleeping form, he admired the rise and fall of her breath. Her dark lashes quivered as she dreamed. Her feminine body, which was covered only in a thin sheet that accentuated her curves, pulled at something deep within him. He sighed deeply, wishing life could be less complicated while remembering the promise he had made to himself: that he would be true to Estellene, even though she had never broached the subject.

Zuzahna stirred. Her sleep-filled eyes opened, taking in her surroundings, the tent, the river, and at last him. She smiled and wiped a bit of drool from the corner of her mouth. "Have you been awake long?" she asked.

"Not very long," he answered, not wanting to give away thoughts that had been all-consuming a moment ago.

"Shall we eat? I packed a bit of smoked redfish, some flat bread, and cheese made from our goats. I even brought a small vessel that contains my first attempt at wild berry wine. Would you care to try some?"

"Zuzahna, you offer such wondrous choices. If am to pick one, I would say yes happily to all."

Zuzahna smiled in a genuine show of happiness she rarely let surface. "How about we eat and then walk the winding path that threads the river's edge?"

"That would be wonderful," he said, smiling and taking in the look she had upon awakening: the mussed hair, the pillow wrinkles on the side of her face. He found her compellingly, hauntingly beautiful when she looked at him with her sleepy, longing eyes.

The salmon was scrumptious, the cheese and bread were delicious, and the berry wine was surprisingly good.

He asked, "Did you really make this nectar?"

Zuzahna blushed. "Do you not like it?"

"No, I do! I just wondered what part you had in its construction."

"Well," she said, smiling the genuine article for a second time, "I conceived the idea while walking in the woods and thinking of you, and at once there appeared an abundance of small black berries growing on wind-felled trees. I immediately thought of your appreciation of fine wine and set to picking a profuse amount of those pesky, very tiny berries. I really had no idea as to how I should proceed from that point, so I enlisted the help of a few others who taught me that the berries needed to ferment in something airtight. Not a small undertaking, considering the primitive nature of our existence here. We had found a bee hive previously, so we used some honey in the wine, poured it into a hide bag, and used the beeswax to seal it. What you are sampling is my own concoction. I must tell you, my fingers and nails were completely stained purple for over a week!" Zuzahna threw her head back and broke out laughing, honestly enjoying the memory of her work and suffering. "So what do you think?"

"I think that if you began making this wine commercially, you would soon have the whole planet bowing at your feet begging for a glass!"

"You kid me?"

"No, I do not," he said. "You are to be commended for your first attempt. It *is* wonderful!"

"I always dreamed of being a queen as a young girl. Perhaps I shall become known on this primitive world as the Berry Wine Queen!" She laughed, an honest sound, which Tay completely adored. He had never seen her so relaxed and at ease.

Zuzahna became serious in an instant. She looked deep into Tay's eyes, and he felt as though she were seeing right through him.

"How long do we have together, Tay? Why have you been gone so long?"

"I must leave in the morning."

"But why so soon?!" she asked. "Do I not please you?"

He had known this woman intimately for over nine years, and had never dared tell her how he really felt. She was, of course, from another race, a race that swore death to all those of the Seven Galaxies. Yet they were no longer in the Seven Galaxies.

"Zuzahna, I have duties I must not disregard," he said. "They take me away from you—not my feelings."

"Normally only for a week though! What kind of duties?"

"I must ride to inspect the perimeter of our small area and make sure the northern tribe has not made it so far south. I have seen their sign, and I cannot afford to be caught off guard."

"Let me ride with you then and spend a few more days together. I long to share a bed with you!"

Her eyes pleaded with him. Tay had never seen Zuzahna beseech him, but she did so now.

"My route is known to no one but myself and must remain so. I cannot take you with me." This was true, yet he had failed to explain to Zuzahna about the enchantress of his dreams and the fact that she shared this planet with them. Tay had also not shared his plan to move permanently to Estellene's village, to train her family and make preparations for war.

"Where will you spend the remainder of your time? Surely you will not be on patrol twenty-eight of the moon's days?"

"No, I must tell you honestly that I am not. I will be making my home away from you with another group."

Zuzahna's face dropped in anguished disbelief. "What! Surely it is not another woman? Tell me! Look me in the eyes! Is there another?"

"Zuzahna, I apologize for my terseness, but I can tell you no more."

"Always so discreet, so secretive...I have come to accept your ways even though I do not admit to understanding them. Please Tay...what would I do without you here? I can't believe what I'm hearing. I deserve a better explanation that this!"

"For now I have told you all I can," he said. "There are obligations, necessary preparations that I must make for our safety. These things take up my time when I am away from you." Tay felt guilt creeping into his conscience; he had not told Zuzahna the entirety of his attachments to Estellene and her people.

"Where does this other group camp? Surely you have not befriended the wild ones?"

"No, I have not."

"So that's it? All that you will tell me?"

"Yes," he said, nodding. "Thank you, Zuzahna, for understanding. I appreciate your acceptance of what is necessary."


Yet Zuzahna did not understand, and in the past she had sometimes tracked Tay's trail backward after their meetings. She had spent as many as three days on his trail and had not yet found where he spent his days away from her. She vowed now to do so, when he left her in the morning. She would find this new home and explore what was drawing him away from her.


Each time she had followed Tay's backtrail in the past, she had lost it. Today her resolve pushed her on. She vowed not to give up when the tracks were nearly impossible to follow. Many things made the task the worst sort of difficult to her untrained eyes, but she learned. Zuzahna learned to follow them through the mud and the wild animal trails and to pick them up on the other side of a creek or down its stream. Zuzahna was fierce in her dedication. She quickly learned the art of tracking. Time passed as she waited and learned his trail. *Soon,* Zuzahna thought, *soon I will find where he stays when not in my bed!*

A settlement lay before her. It was not a grouping of some backward hovels but a well-organized village built against and into the cliffs. Terraces and fields were being worked. Many people ran and toiled—all appearing to love their task and those about them. Zuzahna was aghast, not so much due to the size of the settlement but that everyone worked in unison and harmony. As if that were not enough, they actually seemed to be enjoying their chores.

Zuzahna would not have imagined that so many people could be living within four days' ride of her home. It was a society from which she had obviously been banned. The repercussions rammed their way into her heart.

Tay was obviously embarrassed of her; why else had she not been presented to his people? It was true that she was not of Seven Galaxy birth and was, therefore, an outsider, an embarrassing secret, although he spent passionate days and nights in her bed and willingly came to her time and again.

Her, Zuzahna Duhcat, an imperial courtesan, left in the mud, waiting for his gracious and inordinately short visits. She had to reconcile this with the fate that now stared her directly in the face.

"No! No!" she screamed. She would not!

*Nine years!* she thought. *More than nine years!* They had spent them in perfect harmony aboard *Intrepid One* and here on-planet. All that time, Tay had never once uttered those three words that every woman from every place in the universe dreams of hearing. He had stood mute, enjoying her talents, her company, her warmth on so many otherwise lonely nights. He had avoided her on those brief days when she could become with child.

The simple truth remained: he was embarrassed by her. Hence, he had not brought her to this beautiful place.

Zuzahna had been chewing hides for clothing, gathering berries for his wine, rooting and grubbing the earth for food when game did not offer itself, and all the while, TayGor had been visiting here without inviting her.

"OOHH! OOHH!" she said, her blood boiling. "We shall see. WE SHALL SEE!" she repeated, not exactly knowing what she intended to do.

Zuzahna was crushed. She had been trained and raised with a hardened heart, yet now she cried. Tears ran down her face as she bent at the waist, heaving with grief and disbelief. Finally, she collapsed onto the earth, beating it with her fists. Her tears created a pool that quickly became mud: soft, soothing mud that covered her stricken face, leaving it a mask of aboriginal color. She sobbed until there was little energy left in her and then drifted into sleep without realizing it.

She woke, exhausted, disheveled, dirty, and mud-caked. She rose from the earth. The woman who stood was night and day from the pitiful creature who had weakened in the knees and fallen to the ground not long ago. She stood erect, resolve permeating her being. She became the goddess of surveillance and vowed to watch the settlement in the future and determine which of the women Tay called his own.

# FORTY-FIVE

ESTELLENE waited. She knew he was near. She knew also that he had come from seeing the foreign woman Zuzahna.

Estellene was not familiar with the emotion of jealousy. The only time she had witnessed it was in her beloved husband, Andarean, moments before his death. She vowed silently never to allow jealousy into her world.

Estellene had grown up learning many talents, ancient and modern, including telepathy, martial arts, creative arts, and those of science and literature. She was by no means sheltered and understood very well the craft some beautiful and talented women throughout history had plied.

Estellene knew Zuzahna to be one well trained in the arts of love. Tay had spoken her full name in his sleep, and Estellene knew of Zuzahna from her days in the Dome of Wisdom. She was breathtaking. *No wonder,* she thought, *that Tay is attached to her.* After all, they had spent more than nine long years on the vessel and in their time together on the Virgin. Within that space of time, many attachments could cement themselves into a person. Things could root so deeply that they became part and parcel with a being.

Estellene had experienced similar feelings with Andarean and still missed him. She grieved regularly for her inability to convince him to stay in the village that day.

As long as Tay was happy, Estellene had no cares. She knew no jealousy, and Tay's absence from her bed was easily coped with, for she was sure he would return, full of smiles and energy. Compliments abounded from his lips, and she felt completely safe and fulfilled in his arms.

TayGor, riding Eclipse, galloped towards the cliffs as Estellene watched from a part in the window covering. He was a man of many beauties, she thought. He possessed strength, kindness, and a fine mind for strategy in all respects. He was, for her, the perfect one. She felt her heart beat faster as he neared the settlement.

She walked out to meet him. He reined Eclipse into a circular sweep of the village's edge, waving to some of the family as he came closer to where she stood. When he halted, Josy ran up and asked to groom and tend to Eclipse's needs. TayGor thanked the boy and took in Estellene with eyes that missed nothing.

"You wish to talk, Estellene? Let us walk somewhere, shall we?"

"Where would you desire to go, Tay?"

"Let's hike to the top of the cliff. Sunset will be soon. It would be wonderful to share it with you."

She took his hand and led him until they broke the edge of the settlement and started up the steep trail.

Tay walked behind her and marveled again: her movements appeared effortless and her footfalls were silent, as though she were a spirit gliding up the trail.

When they reached the top, Tay was breathing hard. Keeping up with this woman was no easy task, he thought. Estellene was not even breathing heavily. She stepped close to him and placed her right hand on his chest. "I have missed you, TayGor."

"And I you, Estellene!"

"I believe you have. How is that possible, when you have been with Zuzahna?"

Tay had believed she was a telepath, and now he found no doubt remaining. "Seeing her and sharing our old friendship is necessary, for I must be sure she is okay. I brought her here with my party. I enjoy seeing her prosper. I will be seeing very little of her in the future."

"And do you also enjoy her bed?" Estellene had a humorous look in her eyes showing she was not upset but at the same time was searching for honest answers.

"Must we speak of her, dearest Estellene?" asked Tay.

"I desire understanding. You have said you love me. Do you speak in kind to her?"

"No," he said, shaking his head. "She is not of our race, as you well know. My future and destiny lies here with your family."

"I am happy to hear you speak these things. I do not pretend to own you, TayGor, and would never be so presumptuous. I am fulfilled when you are near and thankful you have chosen this place and my people as your home, yet I must say, I miss you when you are away."

Tay held her tightly in his arms. "My longing for you when I am away is constant."

"Even when you are in her arms, TayGor?" She smiled again.

"She is not comparable to you. I think of you always."

"You, my dear man, are very skilled at avoiding my questions while appearing to answer them. Am I to presume that you do not wish to divulge the answers to my questions?"

"I am truly only putting them off until such time as I may answer them readily with the assurance of truth."

Laughing, Estellene threw back her head, revealing a throat that Tay always desired to kiss. She threw her arms up above her head, exposing the softness beneath them, and swayed back and forth in a motion that sent primeval urges racing through his body. Estellene noticed the effect and said, "My, my, I thought you would be worn out from your journey."

Looking at the woman who was his destiny crystallized in human form, admiring her, he said, "Do you wish to stay up on this cliff edge bantering, or shall we walk down and turn in early?"

"By all means, let's go down. This sunset pales in comparison to you, my dearest."

# FORTY-SIX

Zuzahna waited, well hidden, lying in ambush for the woman—Tay's woman. Zuzahna seethed, grinding her teeth in anger. She had planned this day a thousand times in her imagination.

Feeling the bulky knife beneath her deerskin vest brought forward the primeval desire for revenge. She waited silently. *Appropriate,* she thought. The *very* knife Tay had given her eight years ago would now be used to kill *his* woman.

Zuzahna's heart beat loudly, drumming in her ears. The woman came daily to the river and bathed, but not once had Zuzahna seen her bring a companion in all her months of surveillance and preparation. The woman evidently took this time as her own private moment. It would work out well, Zuzahna thought. There would be no witnesses to the despicable deed that jealousy and hatred had forced upon her. It would be between the two of them and no other person.

Zuzahna plotted, in a self-induced frenzy. The body would be carried far down river, she thought. Searchers might never find it, and would suppose that Tay's other woman had been carried off by wild animals, with no one near to hear her scream.

Footfalls sounded on the path to the bathing pool. Zuzahna's blood raced. Her mouth was dry, and her hands trembled. She had never taken a life by the knife before. She had made slaves of men—controlled them, extracted her desires from their dependence on her and from their addictions to her talents, yet she had never struck the death knell personally.

Today, all the past would change; she was prepared to sink lower than ever before into the dark side, to travel the road from which few return. The blackness beckoned her, drawing her like a powerful magnet that she felt utterly unable to resist.

Through the broken cover of leaf and branch where she was hiding, Zuzahna could see the unsuspecting victim approach the river. She watched as Estellene shed her simple clothes and took to the water, swimming as though she had been born in the swirling element.

Zuzahna crept closer, taking her largest steps when the woman was turned away or when her ears were beneath the water's surface. A large boulder of granite protruded from the beach. Estellene had draped her clothing upon it to keep them from the sand. Zuzahna crept behind the massive rock and waited.

Estellene swam and washed herself. She loved the feeling of the river coursing against her naked body. She swam on her back, her breasts protruding from the water, gazing skyward through the leafy green canopy. Sunlight filtered down and cast a pale green and golden light upon her. Zuzahna watched, surprised by the fluidity of Estellene's movements and by her beauty, which Zuzahna thought unparalleled.

*Who is she?* Zuzahna found herself asking. Surely not some common strumpet. Tay had chosen well. Feeling evil intent rising, the bitter taste biting at the back her throat, the wonder of the moment passed. With the blinking of Zuzahna's eyes, the black monster took her once more.

Estellene stepped out of the water and walked to the boulder to retrieve her clothing. As she bent, slipping on her skirt, she saw a shadow. An uneasy feeling had come upon her this morning, and her well-developed, finely tuned sixth sense began speaking loudly. Here was the shadow, an arm attached to a body, with the hand holding some form of knife.

The dark shape blurred with speed, and Estellene spun in a half-circle while launching herself away from the attacker in one giant leap. She landed, standing low to the ground, and appraised her assailant, who was over five meters away.

Estellene held her ground, not moving, judging, with an expert eye, the assailant's length of stride and the position of the knife. Zuzahna moved closer and spoke in a shrill, anxious voice: "You have stolen the one thing dear to me! You have left me in desolation of the heart, mind, and body. I am miserable because of you! You have ruined me, and I shall be the ruin of you!" Zuzahna surged forward, wielding the weapon. She thrust with the knife, and Estellene, anticipating the movement, sidestepped easily. The crazed woman's momentum carried her through her intended victim's previous position and into thin air. Zuzahna spun around.

Estellene registered the tearful and crazed countenance and thought, *Zuzahna! This is Zuzahna!* She had seen her in archived photos, had imagined her, and now she was facing her, murder in her heart as well as in her eyes. Her intent was clearly to kill.

"Who are you? And what have I done to deserve this aggression?" Estellene asked, in an attempt to buy time.

Zuzahna said nothing, she just moved in closer.

Estellene said, "Zuzahna! We must speak!"

Zuzahna lunged forward, saying, "How do you know my name?"

Estellene took four leaping half-circle spins backward and set herself lightly into a low defensive stance once more, over twenty meters away from Zuzahna.

Zuzahna looked perplexed, obviously wondering how this slip of a woman could so quickly move such a distance away.

Walking slyly and slowly towards Estellene, attempting to distract her, she asked again, "How do you know my name?"

"He speaks it in his dreams," Estellene said calmly, without emotion.

"In his dreams? He speaks my name while he sleeps?"

"Yes, often. He obviously cares for you greatly."

"He should! I have been his woman for more than nine years, on the ship coming here and on this planet, yet he keeps me in seclusion! I will have it no more!"

Zuzahna had come close enough for her intended strike. She had attempted to make the woman emotional, to stir her jealousy and create an opening or a mistake. She swung in an arc towards Estellene's throat.

Estellene swayed back out of reach without moving her feet. She timed the movement perfectly and followed it through by striking a lightning-quick blow to the back side of Zuzahna's hand as it went by. The knife flew through thin air. Both women watching its path as it splashed far out into the river, into the deep, swift current.

The women turned, facing each other, estimating, calculating, thinking. They took each other in: Zuzahna full of hate, and Estellene filled with love for this beautiful, distraught woman before her.

"Zuzahna! Come to your senses and talk with me. I mean you no harm, please! I beseech you, carry this evil no further. I do not wish this madness to escalate."

"Escalate? Escalate! You! You! Man stealer! You soft little vixen, I will show you pain! I have dreamed of this moment. I will have my vengeance."

Zuzahna leaped, a frenzied cat flying at Estellene. She landed in the sand with no one beneath her. Estellene was like a mirage, visible and yet farther away whenever Zuzahna got close.

Zuzahna screamed in frustration. "Stand still! I want my hands upon your throat, my nails in your skin, and your screams in my memories!"

"I do not wish to harm you, Zuzahna, but if we engage, I will have no choice."

"Engage me, you simpering coward! You fear me and run! You talk of sweetness yet you steal my man! He sleeps in your bed nightly instead of mine. He relegates me to the wilderness while allowing you the comfort of a settlement I had not even dreamed could exist on this planet until a few months ago. Stand, I say. I want to feel your blood on my hands. Only then will I be satisfied."

"As you wish," said Estellene.

Zuzahna looked surprised that her intended victim had agreed to stand still. She ran at her, attempting to grab her and take her down to the ground, to maul her like the angry predator she was. What Zuzahna got instead was a brief touch of skin, and then she felt two strikes upon her flesh, delivered with force and precision into the soft ribs just below her right armpit. She screamed in agony and crumpled to the ground.

"Do not come at me again, Zuzahna; there is only worse waiting for you if you demand it of me."

"I demand it!" Zuzahna launched herself from a crouch, grimacing, pain etched into her face.

Estellene simply twisted her body out of the way, leaving one leg in Zuzahna's path. She tripped the ferocious woman, grabbed a handful of her hair, and whipped her around in a half-circle, catapulting her onto her back on the sand. Estellene landed atop Zuzahna with one knee square in the middle of her chest, knocking the wind completely out of her.

"Do you yield?" Estellene asked.

Zuzahna could not speak. She tried repeatedly to take a breath, yet it would not come. She heaved and convulsed until at last her cramped chest muscles allowed the intake of much-needed air.

She stared up at Estellene in amazement, her eyes watering and her vision blurred. Her mind was filled with only one thing: her desire to triumph over this woman.

Estellene offered a hand to the fallen woman. "Come," she said, "let us be friends and fight no more."

Zuzahna lay still for a few moments, regaining her strength after her loss of oxygen. Raising her right arm, she grasped Estellene by her wrist, and Estellene pulled back to right the fallen woman. At that instant, Zuzahna sprang like a cat, intending to surprise Estellene and take her down.

Estellene, who had expected the worst, simply dropped to her knees and let Zuzahna's momentum carry her overhead as Estellene rolled into a backwards summersault, still holding on to Zuzahna's wrist. She landed upon the crazed woman again, straddling her and pinning her arms to the ground beneath her knees.

Zuzahna screamed and fought to no avail. Estellene had struck the woman twice and did not want to again, but Zuzahna was hysterical, ranting and frothing at the mouth. She had completely lost her senses. Estellene understood well the physics of the knock-out punch, although, in all the years of her previous life, she had never had reason to use it before.

Estellene attempted reason once more.

"Come! Come with me to my camp. We will meet him together as sisters who love him equally. What could be wrong with that?"

"He is embarrassed of me! I am not of your kind. He has hidden me away, a mistress—not part of the family. No! No! I will only come when he asks me. He has not shown me in public, only enjoyed me secretly."

"Come with me, Zuzahna. I will introduce you to my people."

"You have attacked me out of jealousy and hate," Estellene said. "Do you deny it?"

Zuzahna did not answer.

"I do not judge you for your actions. I am one of the fortunate few who cannot know the feelings you are now experiencing. I need not forgive something that is an integral part of your genetic makeup. Of that, I have been spared. I offer my hand as your sister. I know Tay loves and cares for you, as he does me. Let us live together and share his life and his beauty without jealousy for one another."

"What do you know of his love for me? You have him in your bed all month, and I a day or two. How could you understand my torment? I wait every day for the close of the next, which brings him closer to the fleeting moments I may spend with him. I must satisfy myself, knowing that the rest of his days are spent in your arms, leaving me longing to be held." Zuzahna sobbed uncontrollably, her countenance breaking, her shoulders slumping. She would not look upon Estellene. "He leaves me alone. This is not life. It is agony!"

Estellene let loose with a punch that landed squarely on Zuzahna's jaw bone, just below her ear.

Zuzahna's eyes fluttered in disbelief for a second and then she slumped and lay like a disheveled ragdoll, fast asleep.

Estellene had trained since a young girl in martial arts, while Zuzahna had trained in the arts of love and its manipulations: one of the women was master of the bedchamber, the other a master of the killing ground. Zuzahna had been dominant in her field. Yet the day's events had been adeptly controlled by Estellene.

When Zuzahna awoke, she was alone and found it difficult to believe she had lost the contest that day.

# FORTY-SEVEN

Tay longed for some exercise and headed to the river for a swim. He also wanted some uninterrupted time to think.

He swam laps across the expanse of the river, enjoying being home and pondering the new information he had gained on his monthly reconnaissance journey and how he would put it to use. Sunshine reflected off the river bottom, shining upon the many hues that made up the river bed. He began searching for a beautiful stone.

Tay enjoyed bringing home interesting rocks, and he had created a small flower garden in which he displayed them all. While diving and searching for one, something odd caught his attention. A flash of light glimmered in the deep, swift water. Whatever it was, it appeared to be metallic. Taking a deep breath, he dove into the deepest part of the river and swam towards the object.

Coming closer, he realized it was a knife. How careless, he thought, that someone could lose such a valuable tool in the river. He figured it must have been one of the children, for all the adults would certainly have retrieved it, if possible.

Underwater, without a dive mask, Tay's vision had no clarity, so it wasn't until he reached the shore, climbed out, and inspected his find that he realized he had seen the knife before. He had given it to Zuzahna aboard *Intrepid One*, after they had escaped the penal moon on the prison transport ship. His mind began to reel in the possibilities. How had the knife come to be in the river?

Perhaps, he thought, Zuzahna had been here without his knowledge—or maybe she'd lost it far up river and it had been washed downstream into this deep hole by the current. He should talk with Estellene and find out what she knew of this mystery, he thought. Surely Zuzahna had not found the settlement?

Tay felt uneasy. He couldn't help believing that Zuzahna had been here, but why? Unable to enjoy the moment, his enquiring mind searching for answers, he climbed out of the water, dried himself, and got dressed. He picked up the knife and slid it into the waist of his leather pants.

Tay walked up the woodland trail towards the settlement. Entering the cave he shared with Estellene, he wasted no time. Approaching the subject like an inspector instead of a beloved partner, he showed the weapon to her and asked if she had seen it before.

Estellene's eyes flickered. "I am not entirely sure. Could I see it more closely?"

Tay handed the knife to her, and she inspected it with care. "I have seen many knives, but I cannot be sure I have seen this one. Many look so similar."

"Well, Estellene, this knife is a very special one."

"Why would that be, dearest Tay?" Estellene asked, yet the humor in her eyes told Tay that she already knew the answer to his question and was simply trying to make him squirm a bit, having a bit of fun at his expense.

Tay ignored her play and drove to the point. "I gave this knife to Zuzahna while we were aboard *Intrepid One* on our journey here. Has she been here? Have you seen her?"

"Tay, I would never lie to you. I want no trouble from Zuzahna and wish to be left completely out of your issues with her. If Zuzahna has lost a gift that you presented to her, you would be best taking it up with her, on your next trip. I have no more to say on the matter."

"You refuse to answer my questions?"

"I have not refused, my dear, only given you a more direct path towards the answers you seek."

Tay looked at Estellene. She was resolute, and when Estellene had decided something that affected her person, she was stubborn as a mule. Tay looked perplexed. He had thought there would be some simple explanation, yet the mystery had become more complicated.

"Very well then, I will ask Zuzahna!"

"A very good choice, TayGor," Estellene said, giving him her warmest look and moving towards him. "You understand, Tay, I am not trying to be difficult, only sensible in these matters of the heart. Perhaps we should invite Zuzahna to join our group? It must be a very rough existence for her out there."

Tay could hardly believe what he was hearing. Estellene was serious, he knew.

"You love Zuzahna, do you not?" Estellene had never asked him the question before. Now Tay's eyes flickered, and his speech faltered. He was at a loss for words.

Estellene laughed lovingly and said, "My dear man, I don't believe I have ever seen you so tongue tied. Are you unsure of your answer or simply hesitant to share it with me?"

"Both!" he shot back.

"TayGor, my love, do not forget my origin, my genetic makeup. Jealousy is not within me. Love for you and love for that poor heartsick woman are foremost on my mind."

"Why would you think Zuzahna is love sick?" he asked, looking completely perplexed.

"My dear, you are a man of many depths: kind, strong, intelligent, soft at times hard at others, extremely attractive, and a most consummate lover. Any woman who has been fortunate enough to share your company and your many talents for a time would pine as I do when you are away. I have the benefit of you in my bed most nights, while Zuzahna is fortunate if she has a few per moon. Certainly she is lovesick not knowing your intentions—living in limbo, if you will."

"I have never said I share a bed with Zuzahna."

"You didn't have to, Tay. You call her name out in your sleep, and on those evenings you toss and turn restlessly. When you come back from your monthly journey, you sleep well for a time, yet the closer to your next departure, the more often you dream of her."

TayGor asked sheepishly, "How long has this this cycle you've described been going on?"

"Since I first shared your bed. It was worse in the beginning. I thought then that there was no hope for us, that she held your heart in some form of bondage you could not break, even if you wanted to. She is a very powerful woman, Tay. She should not be allowed to move towards the dark side. We would be well to have her in our camp."

TayGor considered all Estellene had just said, thinking for a few moments while she watched.

"You mean to tell me that you would have Zuzahna here, sharing our life, the children, and becoming one of us, even though she is Nesdian?"

"Tay, whether she was Nesdian or not, I would; however, there are things you do not understand about her."

"What things?"

"Wait, I must explain my beliefs in this matter to you. Then, if you wish or insist, I will tell you what I know."

"I'm listening. Go on, Estellene."

"I sense her heart. Even in her stricken state, I feel the goodness, the love that drives her torment, the loss she feels when you are away. Anyone who cares for you like she does is welcome here, provided they possess qualities that can be directed towards the right path: the path of light, the path of love."

Tay took in all she had said. Zuzahna could be an asset to the family, and even though she was Nesdian, he finally had to admit that he loved her. But how could Estellene have such an understanding of Zuzahna's present mental state? he asked himself.

"What of this other information you said you had? And how could you possibly know so much about her? Her feelings, Estellene? Are you absolutely sure she hasn't been here?"

Estellene ignored Tay's most pressing concerns and continued on her own track.

"Tay, even though Zuzahna was born on Nesdia One, she is not truly a Nesdian."

"What on earth do you mean?"

"She is a Duhcat, is she not?"

"Yes, how did you know that?"

"Two reasons: one, you sometimes speak her full name."

"And the other?" he asked, attempting to brush by the obvious: that Zuzahna held a special place in his heart.

"I believe that no woman other than one accepted and trained within the Duhcat Foundations program could hold your attention so dramatically while you are with me. Of this, I am sure."

"Do you have some information on Zuzahna's genetic makeup, Estellene?"

"There are many things I have never shared with you, TayGor. For want of a simple life, I have been satisfied to live as I do here, not as I did on Seven's Seven. However, our life here is becoming more complicated. The wild tribes are near, and Zuzahna is involved with you, so she is involved with my family.

"There is more, but what I have just imparted is enough for now. We must prepare ourselves. We must be ready for a conflict. It is only a matter of time, I feel this very strongly."

"I agree," Tay said.

"Zuzahna is an asset. We will need all the adults we can muster to prepare for whatever is afoot. We will also need the rest of her group, if you feel they have the morals that are necessary to live amongst us." Estellene had given him the final say on who would join their group.

"I will consider all that you have said. I wish to know more of Zuzahna's history and genetics. Do you possess this?" he asked again.

"I possess certain knowledge because of my position at the Dome before I was chosen to migrate with Andarean."

"You were living in the Dome?" Tay said, his voice registering shock at the revelation.

"In the Dome, I worked. I lived in the gardens."

"What were your responsibilities there?"

"I was special assistant to the Ancient," she said. "For all intents and purposes, she was, and is my mother."

Tay was flabbergasted. First, he had never known that Estellene had been chosen by the Dome, or that she had known the Ancient, Leandra, personally. "My grandfather spoke of Leandra sometimes," he said.

"What would the admiral say of her?"

"That a finer person could not be found. That her personal sacrifices during the Twenty-Seven Years War with Nesdia enabled him to manipulate Xeries of Nesdia into the battle front, which was inevitably his downfall. Also that she trusted my grandfather's judgment implicitly and gave him carte blanche to finish Nesdia, even though the war had stressed our society to its breaking point. The politicians and the populace were screaming, blaming the entire war's length on fictitious mismanagement. Leandra was the scapegoat they wanted to sacrifice. Through all the hot speak, she held to her guns, stayed the course, and trusted Admiral Gor to finish the Nesdians.

"He spoke of her as his mentor, the one he looked up to in the darkest moments, the one who inspired him to succeed when the naysayers wanted a treaty with Nesdia—a treaty that would have left us with a very limited future. Now, looking at what the Seven Galaxies became in the two hundred years that followed, Leandra was correct. She lost many old friends in the war, yet she never let her personal tragedies surface or show. That is the extent of my knowledge of her."

Estellene paused, remembering Leandra, her beloved mentor, the woman who for all intents and purposes was her mother. She felt the loss intensely.

"Each time I watch you leave and wonder if I'll see you again, my heart pines in your absence." Estellene spoke of fear—fear that Zuzahna held unexplainable power over him, a power he was unable to control, a force that could remove another one whom she loved.

# FORTY-EIGHT

SERENE came with Estellene. She had intentionally kept her distance from Tay. He was her lost love's grandson. Normally she would have embraced him, yet in her mourning she saw only the similarities to the older Ty. It had been more than her weakened heart could bear. The tragedy of the admiral's death still weighed heavily upon her.

It was time, she thought...time to place the distress behind her, to embrace this young man and become an integral part of this family, leaving behind the solitary existence she had led since the death.

She followed Estellene, admiring the statuesque woman who had emerged from the gangly young girl. Time passed, she thought, and life changes, yet within every day were beauties that could be seen and appreciated or missed and ignored.

She took stock and decided that the past eight years had not been life but rather a cloistered existence: she had been trapped within her sorrow.

Walking into the home Estellene and Tay shared, she was taken by the young man. He was tall and lean, and his handsome face showed strength and kindness.

"Tay! Good morning. I am happy to see you have returned."

"Serene. As always, it is a great pleasure."

Tay moved forward to embrace her. He noticed her give, softening in his arms. She had always been reserved and rigid around him, but this morning she was different.

"Tay has need of information regarding Zuzahna Duhcat's genetics," Estellene said.

"All that you know, Serene, please impart."

"I am encouraging Tay to bring Zuzahna to our camp," Estellene added. "She has been living in the wilds long enough. It is time we united all our friends here. We must increase our strength and meld as one family. We must include those who have love for our members in their hearts and prepare for what is inevitably coming."

Serene looked at Tay. He was searching for answers. In that moment, Serene knew she had much to share with him. She would start with his grandfather.

"Please understand, Tay, I have kept away from you as much as possible over the years, both aboard *Intrepid One* and then here. Losing your grandfather was a devastation I thought I may never wade through. It was a dark current sucking the very breath from me. Whenever I saw the similarities in you, my heart plunged deeper in despair.

"Today, with Estellene's visit and your request, I realize that I have not been living, only suffering in seclusion. Please forgive me. I am truly sorry."

"Sweet Serene, I can say that we share the same loss. Ty was my grandfather, yet when my father left us as a small boy and did not return, Ty also became my father, filling the void in my life. I thought no one loved him as I, yet here today I meet your true self and realize we have a common bond. You are welcome here always. In fact, we have much extra space. Will you join us here? Live with us?"

The idea had occurred to Tay spontaneously. He looked to Estellene, and she nodded in approval.

"I...I think it is a lovely idea. You two must talk about it first. This is such a surprise!" As Serene spoke, some of the tension in her body seemed to ease.

"Tay has offered our home, Serene. It would make me happy as well if you would consent to stay," Estellene said, pleased by Tay's surprising invitation.

"It's very sudden. Are you two sure?" Serene's eyes brightened at the prospect. Years lifted from her face, and that vibrancy Tay had seen when she hung on the admiral's arm seemed to return. Tay and Estellene nodded, smiling.

"Okay. I will! This is so exciting. I never thought when I rose this morning that such a wonderful new world would be opened to me."

The three sat in silence for a few moments, allowing the change to settle in.

"Tay, the knowledge I have of Zuzahna comes primarily from her medical records," Serene said. "While she was aboard *Independence* after her capture, she was given a comprehensive physical by the ship's medical center."

"Yes. I am aware that took place."

"One of the required tests was DNA identification. The Dome has long been interested in genetic correlations within our vast society; hence, her records were forwarded to the database archive within the Dome.

When reviewed by experts, some very surprising things popped up."

"Such as?"

"Where shall I start?" Serene was silent for a few moments, obviously organizing her thoughts. "One very interesting fact is that even though Zuzahna was born on Nesdia, she is not, genetically speaking, Nesdian. Oh, she has a smattering of Nesdian characteristics, such as the body hair: the percentage of hair coverage on her body is similar to the Nesdian characteristics, although, in her case it is so fine it can hardly be seen. Typically Nesdian body hair is much coarser and longer. However, within her DNA, the actual gene ratio is less than five percent Nesdian."

"What other genes does she possess? From where does the rest of her genetic makeup originate?"

"Ancient Earth, just like us." Serene paused for effect.

Tay was silent, absorbing like a sponge, attempting to comprehend what had just been imparted. "But how is this possible?"

"As you know, genetics are not an exact science. There are rules that normally follow true, but none hard and fast. From what we understand, Zuzahna's makeup holds recessive genes that surfaced when she was conceived. She has a preponderance of DNA that is quite enlightening when understood. Shall I continue?" Serene asked. "I assure you, her story gets more interesting the more deeply it is told."

"Please, by all means," answered Tay. He was astounded by this new information.

"To put it simply, she is the genetic progeny of *Enricco Duhcat*. She also has traces of other DNA in her makeup, and these slice across a broad band of astonishing people and many brilliant minds from our past. None of this becomes very surprising once we realize she is Enricco's blood daughter. As you know, he is arguably the most brilliant mind in our history."

"Duhcat's daughter! This is truly the fabric of fantasy. The odds of meeting her, upon capture of Xrisen's yacht—because of Grandfather and me. This is so intertwined it is unbelievable."

"Tay, you can believe it. I have reviewed the reports with my own eyes. Anything found that has to do with Duhcat—his whereabouts, movements, quest, our search for possible children—it is all of the utmost secrecy, but the Dome attempts to keep abreast of his work. The man astounds the mind. I have met him personally."

"Okay, Serene, I don't know if I can take any more."

"I was going to share the content of one of my meetings with him, but if it's too much, I won't."

Tay's mouth was literally hanging open. "Wait…! I want to hear. All this is so incredible…I just need time to absorb it. I'm processing right now. Could we eat or something? I would like to think on what you've shared before you lay more on me!"

Serene and Estellene laughed, got up, and walked into the kitchen to prepare some snacks.

Estellene began talking to Serene in a low voice, almost a whisper, so that Tay couldn't hear.

"Serene, I don't think I have ever seen Tay speechless before, yet today he's been stuttering and stammering several times. When I told him I thought Zuzahna should come and live with us, he about passed out. All this time, he didn't think I knew about them being romantically entwined."

Serene smiled knowingly and said, "Well, they were quite the unit for the entire voyage here, although it was none of my business. Honestly, I thought they were very good for each other. She is quite the female foil. My goodness, that woman *exudes* sexuality!"

"All I saw when I met her was craziness and hostility."

"When did you ever meet Zuzahna?"

"At the swimming hole the other day. She actually tried to kill me. She came at me with a knife. I had to get pretty brutal; she wouldn't give up even after I wailed on her. It was epic! I finally had to knock her out. I left her lying on the beach, unconscious. But I haven't told Tay, so please don't let on. She's heartbroken. I guess she followed his trail back here or something. He's pretty much abandoned her since coming to live with us."

"You're kidding me? She attacked you?" Serene asked in disbelief.

"She was hiding when I came out of the water to get dressed. I had been a little edgy all morning, and then I saw the shadow. Luckily my antenna was up."

"Estellene, we have to bring her in," Serene said. "Zuzahna's intellect, if channeled properly, could be a monumental asset to our group here. She loves Tay as you do. I've seen it in her eyes many times."

"I know. We have to convince him that she's absolutely welcome here. I want her on our side, not against us, but the state she's in right now, anything is possible. Let's go talk to him. How could he resist us both?"

The two of them giggled quietly, finding the idea of ganging up on him a bit of a treat. Walking back into the main chamber with the tray of food, they found Tay looking as if he'd seen a ghost.

"Tay? Are you all right?" Estellene called him out of his contemplation.

"I'm fine. I think. It's just that all this time, I've been keeping her away from here because, well…I'm not quite sure. Estellene, you are so important. I don't know what would happen if I lost you. I guess that's what I feared."

"Darling, I'm not the jealous type. Do you think you could put up with us both in the same house?"

"My wildest imagination could not have dreamt such a thing."

"Try and put it in perspective. You love her, you love me, we both love you. What could be simpler than that?"

"You call it simple. I would like to think it could be. Honestly it seems unlikely."

Serene chimed in, "Hey, don't forget, I live here, too. And I love Tay, too! If Zuzahna comes, there will be three of us and one of him."

"What do you think about those odds, buster?" Estellene asked, while she plopped into his lap. "See, Serene. He's speechless again. I think it's a world record!"

The women laughed while Tay just nodded.


They ate in silence, all absorbing the day's events. When finished, Serene asked, "Do you want me to finish my story about Duhcat?"

"Well, why not, Serene? I could use some excitement; it's been pretty boring around here today."

Serene smiled, enjoying the fact that Tay was taking it all in stride. "He came one afternoon when I was in the garden of melody," she began. "Summer was in full swing. It was very warm…no, it was hot, more so than I like. I was lying on the stone terrace beneath the arbors because the rock was cool. It felt so good. I was almost dozing when I heard a voice say, 'Excuse me, but I think you are in my spot.' I opened my eyes and he was looking down at me with those eyes, eyes just like Zuzahna's: big and brown with that incredible golden flecking. I had never seen a picture of him and didn't know who he could be at that point. He was, of course, teasing about being in his spot.

"Well, we sat and talked for a long time. The sun was going down when I finally asked his name. It was the most natural thing, to be talking with him, and asking his name had completely slipped my mind. Well, I remember his answer like it happened last week. He said, 'Just call me traveler. I visit here often. In the distant past, a dear friend and I stumbled onto the many wonders of this place, so there is special meaning for me here….' His voice trailed off, and he had a far-away look in his eyes, as if he had left me for a moment. Then he picked up where he had left off. He said, 'Often, I am compelled to return and remember with mixed emotions those days…'

"He paused and had a wistful look in his eyes, as though he had lost something dear and was reliving the memories when he visited the gardens. Then he said, 'You see, I've been visiting here since long before the Dome protected the portal. In those days, there was no guardian of the gateway. So for me to be here, to stay awhile, is a journey back in time to simpler days when I was much younger, when carefree adventuring took most my time. Alas, I am now burdened with many responsibilities, but this place still brings those old days flooding back to me. Serene, I have enjoyed visiting with you. Perhaps we shall see each other again sometime in the future.'

"And I said something like, 'I enjoyed your company and *do* wish you would come back soon.'

"With that, he stood, gazed between the pillars to the view beyond for a few silent moments, and then walked away. It then dawned on me that I had never given him my name, yet *somehow* he had known it. Also, I had completely forgotten to ask his name again! I had no idea who he was. I was so perplexed. I went and talked with Leandra. She told me who he was.

"I was speechless…my heart was racing. I had been talking with *Enricco Duhcat!* I hadn't even known it! Afterwards, I thought there had been something about him, but I could never quite put my finger on it. It was like he was an ancient soul traveling through time and that the loves and losses of his life had threaded a bit of melancholy into his persona. Not that he was sad at all. He was funny, charming, extremely handsome, and alluring; I've never met anyone who affected me the way Enricco did…except possibly your grandfather, Tay." Serene smiled with a far-away look in her eyes, a slight bit of sadness creeping in.

"Serene, do you think perhaps he chose to meet you?" asked Estellene.

"I'm not sure. I just was awestruck. He was so…so calm, yet filled with electricity. You could feel it. His energy literally reached out and touched me. I think from that day on I have been a slightly different person. I still think of him often."

"He said that he would perhaps see you again. Did you…did you ever meet him again?" asked Estellene.

"A few times over the years that I resided at the Dome, always in the garden of melody, always in the late afternoon, and always in the summer when it was very hot. That's when he came."

Silence engulfed the three, as if they were all picturing the mystery, and the legend of a man thought by many to be a fable.

Coming out of the haze that had enveloped them, Estellene spoke: "Tay, you have to go to Zuzahna and convince her to come. Make her understand I want her here…that we *all* want her, right, Serene?"

"By all means! She is one of us. We need her here, Tay. I feel that her mind and energy focused on the right path will bring us good fortune in the days to come."

# FORTY-NINE

Zuzahna pushed the paint horse's endurance to the limit, till the gorgeous beast's sweat ran and foamed and her blood vessels bulged with each beat of her heart. Paint began to blow and falter, staggering at times, heaving her exhausted body forward, bending to Zuzahna's will. Paint was spent and stumbling when Zuzahna finally came out of her self-induced frenzy and realized she had been punishing the animal cruelly. She reined Paint to a halt and dismounted, and then walked her loyal friend, allowing the horse time to cool down.

Zuzahna's mind began to cool as well. From the heat of jealousy and heartbreak that had bruised and scraped her self-worth, logic began to work. Instead of the wild rolling surf of emotions she had been riding, something completely different grew. Resolve broke through the many feelings that welled within her intensely powerful mind, and her extraordinary potential for deviousness took hold anew. Old roots, long buried, brought dark nourishment from deep down within the shadowed side of her being. Thoughts of personal desire, power, and selfishness began organizing, searching for plots, playing out a multitude of scenes, running through take after take of cause and effect.

Before she had met Tay, Zuzahna's mind had been constantly consumed with thoughts of dark gain, but she had relegated them to her past since having him. In her new perspective, a future without the man she had come to love, black thoughts sprouted fresh and as powerful as ever. She reveled in them, crafting a different sort of revenge.

Certainly, if Tay did not want her mixing with his people, the loyalty she had felt for him in the past was immediately erased. Zuzahna's mind began to work in a way it had many years ago, before she had been imprisoned, before she had been rescued by Tay, and before she had fallen, tumble-down, head-spinning, heart-stopping, breath-panting and idyllically in love with him.

Zuzahna felt that Tay had betrayed her. For his betrayal, she swore he would suffer. She would unite the three tribes and make war. If she could not conquer his heart, then she would come like a wildfire, like an uncontrolled tsunami, and she would roll over top of him, his people, and especially Estellene.

As in Zuzahna's old dreams, she believed in that moment, in her deluded and heart-broken state, that she could prevail. The negative electrical pulse cast into the ether by her powerful mind raced, broadcasting toward any being sensitive enough to receive, listen, and understand. Estellene felt it first, and then Tay. A few hours later, Duhcat himself understood the volatile storm brewing within Zuzahna.

I Am That I Am watched, intrigued.

Zuzahna walked, leading the horse for hours, untiring. Her hatred helped her formulate a plan, one that would bring TayGor to his knees and that, if successful, would in essence make Tay her chattel. Oh, seeing him on his knees before her would bring such sweet sorrow, such satisfaction, such, such...

On the trail before Zuzahna stood a man she had never before seen on this planet. His dress was simple, as a farmer's might be, yet something was not right; he seemed, to her intuitive spirit, to be a foreigner, yet there was nothing she could put a finger on visually that made her think this. The man's head was turned down as he leaned back against a tree, the hat of a frontiersman covering his eyes.

Zuzahna, for some reason, felt no fear as she walked towards the silent figure. "Can I help you?" she asked. "Are you lost?"

The stranger looked up and stared into her eyes. Zuzahna stopped. He was no longer a foreigner but someone familiar...someone she had met before. *So familiar,* she thought. Yet where had she seen him?

Zuzahna moved closer. His eyes were beautiful, extra-large and very deep brown. Somehow, the eyes struck her with a sense of déjà vu. *How is this possible?* she thought. A few steps closer and her question was instantly answered. The stranger's eyes were her own: the same color, same shape, same straw-colored flecks. She was startled and faltered, stepping backward slightly.

"Do not be afraid, Zuzahna. I am here to assist you in this black hour. I promise, no harm will come to you. Please visit with me for a while." His voice was filled with compassion.

"It is not fear you see, Enricco. It is disbelief, amazement, shock, and happiness all at the same time, but not fear."

"It is good then?" he asked.

"Very good," Zuzahna answered, with a long, heartfelt sigh.

"How is it you recognize me after all the time that has passed?" he asked. "You were a very young girl when we met so many years ago."

"It is your eyes," she answered, not believing he was before her. "I have never in my life seen the likes of them since that day so long ago, except when I look at myself in a mirror. Can you explain this mystery to me?"

"Today, no," he said, shaking his head. "There are many important matters before us. The explanation you ask for is a very long journey in the telling, a journey, into the distant past. I give you my word I will share the story with you, if your future life's path deserves to know the truth of this mystery, as you call it."

"The path of my life, I do not control. I was born an outcast of Nesdian society. I was groomed as a young girl to be courtesan to the rich and powerful, for I had no other path of choice. As an adult, I was kidnapped by the Nesdian regent, rescued, and then imprisoned against my will. Now the one I love, the man of my dreams, has shunned me as though I have leprosy. How can you speak to me of life's path as though I have any choice in the matter?" Zuzahna faltered, her composure shattered.

She looked only at the ground, for that was where her self-worth lay at that moment.

He said, "I know all of this. I have witnessed your tragedy. It is important, Zuzahna, that you listen with an open mind to what I will share with you. It is imperative. Within my words will be many answers. If you fail to pay attention, or if the emotional state that encompasses your being right now is not pacified, silenced, and controlled, then much of what I am about to say will be lost. That would be a great shame to me—and to you as well."

"I do not understand!" Zuzahna replied, tears welling in her eyes.

"I know." Enricco Duhcat took his daughter in his arms, holding her tightly. He felt the trembling, the anguish, the hate and desire for revenge. He also felt love and compassion kindling in the depths of his ancient heart and soul. Most of all, he felt the bond of fatherhood with this beautiful creature who was suffering so painfully, a bond that left him in awe because for him, remarkably, it was the first time he'd felt it.

Finally, after a long while, Zuzahna's sobs subsided.

"There is a spring behind that boulder over there," he said, pointing to a massive piece of granite the ancient glaciers had left behind upon retreating. "Tie the horse up to that tree limb so that she can drink and graze a bit. Then you and I shall take a walk to a very special place that I chose specifically with our meeting in mind."

Zuzahna obeyed without thinking, the natural reaction of a young girl minding instructions that had been spoken in a fatherly manner, yet Zuzahna had never known a father. When she finished with the horse and returned to him, his back was to her. He was gazing downhill into the woods, evidently eyeing a well-worn trail Zuzahna had never before noticed.

The thought occurred to Zuzahna that he was amazingly handsome, not to mention the most powerful human in the known Universe. Normally her mind would be calculating the odds of seducing him, yet nothing remotely close to those emotions entered the path of her thoughts. The paternal bond made it impossible.

"Are you ready?" he asked.

"Yes," she said, sighing. The relief of having someone to talk with soothed her frazzled nerves.

Enricco Duhcat took Zuzahna's hand and led her down the wide, meandering trail. She could hear rushing water in the distance, and the air became cool, filled with mist. Zuzahna stayed quiet, not wishing to quell the feeling of peace that had pervaded her being since Duhcat had held her and reassured her with his presence. In the face of disaster, the problems that had moments ago filled her thoughts now settled. How odd, she thought, that this man could appear and erase all the suffering that had been weighing upon her for the past few months. Zuzahna resolved to listen calmly to everything Enricco had to impart. They walked, him leading and her following.

The forest trail opened upon the most amazing play of water Zuzahna had ever seen. A waterfall with four separate drops, like a cascading staircase, stood before her. The falls were a hundred and fifty meters high. Looking up the canyon, Zuzahna could see a series of caves in the sheer rock walls. Some of the caves had steaming water flowing out into pools at their mouths. The mist from the falls curled skyward and disintegrated into vast azure.

Zuzahna was awestruck. "Enricco, this is truly one of the most beautiful places I have ever seen. How in this world did you find it?"

"Well, my dear, I have a few secrets up my sleeve—and more than a few surprises. Shall we take a hot soak while we talk?"

"That would be lovely," she answered, sincerely dumbfounded by the events of the past few minutes.

They undressed and lowered themselves into the hot mineral water. Immediately, Zuzahna felt the stress disappear.

Enricco said something to her but she could not hear him because of the roaring water. However, the words sounded in her mind, She heard, "Nice...ever so nice," and she wondered whether he was communicating telepathically.

His answer came back instantly. *Yes.*

The steaming water was a magical elixir that soothed the soul, relaxed knotted muscles, and cleared the lungs. Neither of the two talked much; they spent the time unwinding and looking closely at one another, studying the similarities in each other's features, movements, and mannerisms.

After some time, Enricco said, "Okay, you win. I must get out for a bit."

Running like a school boy, he jumped in at the bottom of the lower falls. Zuzahna was amazed. The water in this mountain river was ice cold and she wondered how he had not suffered a heart attack or stroke.

He laughed at her shock and motioned for her to jump in as well. Zuzahna was compelled by a force she did not understand to obey Duhcat's requests. She ran with abandon and leaped into the icy water. The brisk water sent waves of rippling tingles all over her body. A rush of blood pumped through her veins, and she felt elation at being here, doing something she had never done before, with this man, with whom she had some unexplained and deep connection.

They spent time going back and forth between the two pools, laughing and playing. Zuzahna realized that for the first time in months, she was truly happy. Looking into Enricco's eyes, she saw the same feelings mirrored.

When at last the water had sapped their strength, when it had stolen the stress and anxiety away, they climbed from the water and dressed.

Zuzahna followed Enricco up the sheer rock canyon to the second stair in the falls. The wide mouth of a cave yawned at them. When Enricco walked through the opening, she followed.

The cave's interior was roomy and wide, well lit, and comfortable. Zuzahna was sure they would sit down, but Duhcat kept walking. A set of steps appeared around an unlit alcove. They were carved from the stone and wound upward through the solid rock. Higher and higher they climbed. Zuzahna counted more than four hundred steps.

At the top was a small landing that boasted a massive hardwood door, complete with forged steel hinges and a lock that looked custom made. Enricco took out a key and opened the massive door by pushing lightly with one fingertip. It swung in without a sound, and he motioned her forward.

The first room was extremely well lit by huge south-facing windows. The afternoon sun shone in, yet the space was comfortable, not hot as would be expected. Mist curling upward from the falls ebbed and flowed with the air currents, creating a beautiful, moving portrait.

She followed Duhcat to the next room and was awestruck to find state-of-the-art appliances in a modern kitchen. He was showing her something that *did not* exist on this planet. *This must all be a dream,* she thought. *I have fallen from my horse and hit my head.* Zuzahna pinched herself. It hurt. Duhcat took in her little test and smiled, that smile she herself used on rare occasions when she truly cared for a person and wanted them to know her innermost feelings.

"The best part is this way," he said softly.

Zuzahna followed him down a wide corridor that was lit from above through window-lights in the roof. He opened the door and, to her utter disbelief, a large master suite unfolded. It had a huge sunken tub, windows galore, and a bed any pioneer would give their right arm for.

"How is all this possible?" she asked.

Duhcat simply put one finger to his lips in the ancient signal of silence, took her by the hand, and led her to a glass wall, which immediately slid open as they stopped before it. Enricco motioned her through while he stood, waiting beside the threshold.

Zuzahna walked out into a wonder of gardens perched high above the falls. Terraces boasted beautiful flowers and edible landscaping, all of which staggered her mind. She wandered in awe, stopping and bending to enjoy the many fragrant flowers, picking ripe berries and fruit, stuffing them like a hungry child into her mouth.

Duhcat sat upon a rock wall, enjoying a handful of purple huckleberries he had picked. Watching her joy filled him with happiness.

Zuzahna ate her fill, dulling the cravings she had experienced on this planet. In truth, she was not well nourished. The primitive fashion in which she had been forced to live and the never-ending search for food was, at best, a grueling quest.

Duhcat felt all that Zuzahna experienced, but he also felt shamed for having left her to the crude and wanting life she had been forced to live.

Duhcat also understood TayGor's quandary in not bringing Zuzahna to the settlement of the so-called perfect race. So here he was, about to give a daughter, his only offspring, a slice of perfection: a reward for her perseverance, a thank you for understanding and for not resenting his previously callous handling of her strategically important life. So they were here together, and he spent no little time admiring her glow, her similarities to him, and her unwillingness to hold any sort of grudge against him. She was happy to share a friend. His heart saddened when he thought of leaving.

Walking up to Zuzahna, Duhcat touched her lightly on the arm and motioned with his eyes for her to follow. He walked down a meandering path, which eventually began ascending a steep pinnacle. In places along the severely steep path, steps had been cut into the sheer rock face. Breathless, they reached the top and stood panting, gazing out over a countryside view that was unobstructed for as far as their vision allowed.

Zuzahna turned towards Duhcat and away from the spectacular scene. His profile matched her own, only in masculine form.

"What is this place, Enricco?" she asked.

Answering without taking his eyes off the horizon, he said simply, "It is a place I created, and my favorite place of all: a haven that is sacred to me. I come here to rest, to think, to plan, and to be alone. I have never brought anyone here before. You are the first and only person other than myself to visit here, or even to be aware that it exists."

"But surely workers had to build this? I cannot imagine that you would have the time. This accomplishment would take several lifetimes."

Duhcat looked Zuzahna squarely in the eyes and said, "That would depend entirely on the length of a person's lifetime. Some of us live but a few short years; for others, it is not the same."

"Are you saying that you alone created this? You built this place with your own two hands?"

"Not exactly. To be entirely truthful, most of the heavy work was done by robotic drones. Even to this day, they maintain the gardens and security and keep the house in order. You will see them if you choose to stay."

Zuzahna looked at Duhcat as if he were joking. Did he possess some dark sense of humor, to tease her with such fantasy only to dash her hopes? "You cannot be serious?" she said, glancing quickly away so that he could not read her facial expressions, forgetting in that instant that he was a telepath.

"I am completely serious and plan to give you—and only you—free access to my home, provided you understand certain conditions and abide by them. An understanding must come between you and me."

"What sort of understanding?" Zuzahna asked.

"That is what I have come to talk with you about. Are you up for such a talk? The conditions amount to a set of, shall we say, for lack of better words, rules to live by."

"I believe I am ready to consider what you say with an open mind," she said. "I will listen."

"Good. That is all I wished for when I undertook the journey here. First, I ask that you take no offence to any of the things I say, and that you do not deny, admit, or debate anything. I wish to have the floor; there will be no negotiation. Truth in all you do in the future will determine your path."

She nodded her understanding.

"I have followed your entire life, Zuzahna," he continued, "as with all persons accepted into the Duhcat foundation's plan. However, I have a special interest in you; therefore, I have spent more time following the path of your life than any of the others. I know everything about you: who you have been with; your schemes and plots; the love you share with TayGor; and the demise of Xeries and the influence you exerted with regard to his involvement in the brutal attacks on the Seven's settlements. I also know about your involvement with the late Xrisen, your subsequent capture and imprisonment, your rescue from the prison transport ship by TayGor, your very long and intimate relationship with him, and the fact that he has virtually abandoned you recently. Finally, I know about the attempt you made on Estellene's life, and the dark preparations you have planned since then. I know much more about you, my dear: your talents and weaknesses, your desires, your cravings, your light side and your dark."

Zuzahna looked at the man before her in utter disbelief.

"Do believe, Zuzahna, for everything I have just shared is true. Your adult life up till meeting TayGor has been for the most part a very dark and selfish existence. Look at where it has brought you before our meeting. Hate, greed, and lust for dominance and power over others has been the focus of your path. Is all I have just said true?"

Zuzahna broke down for the second time since meeting Duhcat. Involuntary shudders wracked her body. Tears flowed, and her face reddened with shame. She could not look him in the eyes and felt caught within the whirlpool of misery her life had become. She looked in retrospect at her chosen path with new, wide-open eyes. She could only weakly nod her head, acknowledging the truth in all he had just said.

Duhcat sat in silence, watching Zuzahna's turmoil, her agony in accepting that he knew everything about her.

She thought, *Instead of despising me, he has come and taken time from his life to console, to cheer, and to offer me support.*

She felt undeserving of his attentions. She felt she was a very small and insignificant piece of filth. She begged his forgiveness.

"Enricco, I'm...I'm...*so* sorry!" The words came out broken into bits, shattered by the tumult of emotions.

Duhcat took her head to his shoulder and held Zuzahna for the second time. He loved this wayward child like no other. He could feel Zuzahna's questioning mind wonder what he saw in her.

Answering her unspoken question, he said, "Dearest Zuzahna, let us speak no more of the past but of your future: one that is bright and beautiful as the summer sky. Let us speak of a life's change for you, of redirecting your power and energy towards a path that, once followed, will bring everything you have wished for, desired, and craved all these years. The things I speak of can come to you without extracting from others. How does that sound?" He grasped her chin lightly, bringing it up from the embarrassed and shameful downward tilt it had taken. Gazing into her mesmerizing eyes, which were bloodshot and swollen from the tears, he kissed her with intense affection on the forehead.

A wide, bright smile broke over her face, and her dark mood passed. She looked at him in true amazement. He had come, she now realized, to rescue her from herself. In that moment, she loved him, and it was a love unlike anything she had ever experienced in her life.

"We will share this place in the future," he said. "I am rarely here, so most of the time it will be yours alone. You are to bring no one here, not even pet animals, with the exception of your horse. I have cleared her. Anything else must be security scanned by me and me alone. I have learned in my travels that all things are not always what they seem, and I have reasons for the rules I am laying down. They must not be broken. If they are, you can stay here no longer. Do you understand?"

Zuzahna nodded.

"This place is essentially a fortress to anyone living on this planet. The cliffs are unscaleable with the technology readily available here. The caves mouth closes with an alloy door that auto cloaks when shut, forming a rocklike surface on the outside. It is undetectable to anyone searching for the opening from the outside. The house is self-maintaining. All the work is done by the robotic drones who helped me build it. The stairwell up from the cave entrance has three separate, automatically closing alloy doors. If you were ever pursued closely from behind and something managed to get through the large cave mouth before the door closed, it would be stopped—lethally—in the stairwell. The entire place is tuned and programmed to your movements. Detailed explanations of all the systems are on record in the library, which you have yet to see. You can learn anything you need there—anything.

"Now, we must talk of your future. You must first make peace with Estellene." Duhcat sensed jealousy and hostility bristle inside of Zuzahna. "It is not an easy thing to think of, yet it's the only way. Both of you love TayGor, and rightfully so; he is a man worth both of your love. But he cannot be yours alone."

Zuzahna's eyes showed her pain. She asked, "How could it be possible? Estellene? After what I did…"

"You will find that Estellene harbors no jealousy or hatred for you. That has been solely your emotion, and you must now cast it away. You must subdue your pride and realize that when Estellene offered the hand of friendship to you, she offered a gift of great value; however, you, in your anger, did not see the jewel. She is as exceptional a person, just as you are. You complement each other. Ally yourself with her, and Tay will be yours."

"To share him?" she asked.

"No woman owns a man, contrary to beliefs you have held in the past; it is only with a man's consent that it is possible."

"I will do as you say," she answered humbly.

"I did not say that what I am asking of you will be easy. Your next task is fraught with danger and intrigue. You must go to the camp of the wild tribe to gather information. They have united. A man called Ventras from Seven's Seven is here, and he has become shaman to the tribes. He foments anger among them and is planning to attack the settlement of TayGor and Estellene, to settle an old score and to take the ground, which is the only pocket of diverse minerals and metallic ores on this planet. This cannot happen. You, Zuzahna, will be TayGor's eyes and ears. You will warn him of Ventras' plan and the timing of the planned attack. Do you understand?"

"Yes."

"I appoint you as protector of Estellene and TayGor's family and of the land where they reside. Do you accept?"

"Yes."

"If anything goes wrong, if you are found out by the tribes or by Ventras, you will flee here. Walk your horse up the river bottom and through the small stream that enters the cave mouth. The water will cloak your tracks and scent, and the house will automatically take care of anything else. Do you understand?"

"Yes."

"Again, I repeat: this is my sanctuary; I am allowing you to use it as long as you abide by my conditions and carry through my instructions. Everything I have spoken to you in our time together is recorded in the library archives. You are cleared for access. If you need to review our agreement, or if any of my instructions are unclear, refer to the recorded document. Do you understand?"

"Yes."

"Do you agree to my terms?"

"Yes."

"Then under this meeting of our minds and the stipulations presented and agreed to by you this day, my house is your house. Welcome, Zuzahna."

Duhcat had been all business, but now he broke into a disarming smile. She wondered what he had up his sleeve.

"Come," he said. "I have something more to show you."

He trotted down the many stone steps and down the path that meandered through the gardens. They arrived back at the glass wall leading into the master suite. The tall glass slid open, and Zuzahna followed him inside, wondering what he was up to.

Duhcat walked up to a wooden wall and stopped in front of a raised panel, which then slid open. He stepped through and motioned for her to follow. A small, comfortable room with closets and a dressing table presented itself. Duhcat opened a few of the closet doors, exposing clothes of all sorts, mostly very utilitarian and some quite fancy. Abundant footwear rested on shelves.

"All of this is yours," he said. "A small gift of affection. You will find that all fits you perfectly."

Zuzahna was speechless for a moment. She had spent much of her time crafting coverings of the crudest kind, and here was a wardrobe that any woman on this planet would long to possess. "Enricco, you are truly breathtaking; you've thought of all my needs, and I have done nothing for you—I am embarrassed. I thank you. The time you have spent with me today is the most meaningful in my life. These gifts, your sanctuary, I am breathlessly overwhelmed. How could I ever repay such thoughtfulness, such kindness?"

"Through the fresh path you have chosen, by the truth of your words, and through your future deeds, I will be repaid a thousand fold. When I see you prospering and truly happy, my happiness will be multiplied as well."

# FIFTY

Tay slipped silently from bed at daybreak, leaving Estellene undisturbed.

He intended on visiting River's Bend and bringing Zuzahna back to the crescent cliffs. He would invite the rest of the group at River's Bend as well. The former crew members and ex-prisoners prisoners who lived there would unite with Estellene's group. The ride to the small encampment would take a good four days.

When he walked into the barn, Eclipse nickered good morning.

"You ready for a trip boy?" Tay always talked to the horse as if he were a person. Some people would think the habit crazy, but Eclipse had a personality that craved attention, and when he got enough, he cooperated much more readily than if he were ignored.

Taking a few short minutes to saddle and ready the beast, Tay said, "Quiet walk."

The two left the village without waking anyone. It had been decided that Zuzahna would be offered her rightful place with Estellene's people. He hoped fervently that she would accept.

Estellene had never actually answered his questions about Zuzahna's knife. He pondered finding it in the river. He was convinced that Zuzahna had visited the village.

Tay knew that Zuzahna was possessive and could be jealous. If she knew about his relationship with Estellene, he would not put it past her to become violent.

He directed Eclipse with his seat towards the trail following the river. Sea-run trout coming upriver to spawn were rising in the early morning light. Flying insects near the water's surface were their prey. Fleeting, sleek bodies flashed bright silver, reflecting the sun's low angle of light before they disappeared beneath the surface, leaving ripples moving all directions.

Oh, for more carefree days, he thought, when a line could be cast from under a shady tree and a portion of the day could be spent languidly attempting to catch dinner. His sixth sense told him of changes to come, moving excitement and danger towards him. He rode on, thinking of the land and how it could be defended against a force much larger than his own.

Tay knew the area well. In his mind, he could easily picture any ground within miles of the village. He would choose a strategic location where they would stand and fight.

Knowing the wild ones numerical advantage, Tay searched for a strategy that would prevail. Many commanders would look upon the sheer numbers of each force and call his disadvantaged, but Tay always took the psychology of the enemy into consideration and believed his small numbers to be a distinct advantage if utilized wisely. As he rode away from the village, a plan formed, which was not his own but a compilation of battle strategies taken from historic military conflicts. *All is well,* he thought, enjoying the ride and changing his thoughts, focusing on speaking with Zuzahna.

He would persuade her to come. Normally showing in the morning, he had decided to arrive the evening before. Zuzahna normally made camp the afternoon before they met. He would meet her then. They could talk while he helped her set up camp.

They would go and meet the others in their group. Everyone would hopefully agree to join the force opposing the wild tribe from the north, and return with Tay and Zuzahna to Estellene's village. He could see no objections that would preclude them from wanting to join the village; life would be easier for them as one large group.

They were at risk living in small numbers. From his surveillance, Tay realized that the wild northern tribe appeared to be short of women. If so, they would think nothing of overpowering their small, unfortified encampment, killing the men, and taking the women by force. They had become the barbarians from the north, and Tay felt compelled to diminish their numbers before they grew exponentially into a force overwhelming in size.

Tay had felt heavy of heart lately but did not truly understand its cause. He breathed deeply, exercising his abdomen, willing the heaviness to depart bit by bit with each outward breath. He wondered what it was that oppressed him. The answer soon came.

He had spent six years aboard *Intrepid One* and nearly three years on the Virgin with Zuzahna. He had more than enjoyed her company. She had loved him and, as a young man, Zuzahna had been his first.

All the while, in the back of his mind, he had known Zuzahna's background. He had known she was no innocent waif, but in his need he had overlooked the mysteries of her past.

Then, upon meeting the enchantress who had been haunting his dreams, he had immediately placed Zuzahna on hold. Tay had only seen her briefly—still enjoying her talents but relegating her to a position of closeted mistress. She had been gracious, not understanding his distance yet resolving to have his company when she could. Their relationship had continued as a fractional facet of what it once was. He had focused the force of his attention on Estellene, feeling that she was destiny embodied, yet the nagging in the back of his mind became increasingly louder as time went on.

Finally, he realized his conscience was speaking to him, voicing the wrong done to Zuzahna and warning him that such a powerful persona would not do well as second best. Guilt for his actions swept over him as he rode, and the sound of Eclipse's hoof-strikes punctuated the revelation. He realized what a *jerk* he had been, wanting Estellene and yet keeping Zuzahna on a veritable string. It had been a bad choice of direction. Tay hoped and prayed that Zuzahna would forgive him and that she had not done something rash in her distraught mental state.

# FIFTY-ONE

Zuzahna rode her trusted Paint towards the camp held by the wild tribe. Fear etched itself into the deepest recesses of her heart. Duhcat had said she need not worry, that she had been trained for just this sort of situation. Trepidation and doubt still clawed their way into her resolute mind. What if she were found out? What if she were detained or—worse—killed. How would she warn Estellene and Tay?

The rhythm of her horse's stride, over time, soothed her anxious thoughts. Zuzahna relaxed a bit and pledged her best performance towards the end Duhcat had said was necessary.

On the sixth day of riding, she saw smoke and smelled meat roasting over a fire. Her mouth watered. She had been eating pack staples for the past three days and had consumed her fresh fruit in the earlier part of the trek.

Reining the horse to a halt, she tuned in her well-trained ears, searching all directions for any sound that would give a clue as to where the settlement might be. She nudged Paint to face the wind and continued in that direction, knowing she was following the path of the smoke.

She was expecting at any time to be confronted by the evil for which Duhcat had prepared her.

She had no intention of wandering into the wild tribe's settlement without first spending some time in cursory surveillance.

A ridge presented itself, and she dismounted. Tay had worked with Zuzahna and taught her how to train an animal as large as an equine to choose footfalls as carefully as she chose her own. They picked their way carefully up the ridge, placing the valley floor farther beneath them with each step.

Zuzahna's tactic was to find a vantage point where she could clearly see the comings and goings of the settlement, the number of persons, and to possibly have a chance of gazing upon Ventras. She wanted, if possible to observe his relationship and power within the group.

Soon her goal was in sight. Ahead lay a rock promontory with a few small conifer trees growing on the ledges that ran along its length. She belly crawled out onto the promontory of rock, threading her way between the small trees like a snake in tall grass.

Zuzahna was astounded: before her lay a vast settlement of over one hundred shelters, many of them crudely built and covered with hides but some more permanent-looking and made of timbers and stone. She could see at least fifty adults, most of them women. Zuzahna wondered what the actual numbers of people here were. She was in awe of the overwhelming sprawl of the camp. Surely she thought there must be many more people than she could see. She had studied Tay and Estellene's settlement carefully and had determined that there were few adults residing there.

How could Tay and his group possibly deflect or defend an attack brought by a force that outnumbered them so drastically? All these things raced through Zuzahna's mind: her loyalty to Tay and Estellene, for she had promised Duhcat that; her own skin, and how she would preserve it; and the battle Duhcat had told her was imminent. She was overwhelmed with data. Zuzahna decided to simply observe, instead of thinking too much.

Laughter and much rough language drifted up towards her perch in the sky. One thing she felt certain of: the men must be out of the camp, for there were only a few elderly ones and the rest of the people were women and children.

A few hours passed. Zuzahna nearly dozed off, until suddenly she heard the pounding hooves of many horses. A dust cloud rose in the distance, moving towards the encampment.

The roar of hooves became louder, and before long a great number of men on horseback cantered into camp on a variety of fine-looking mounts. Game animals were stretched over the backs of the pack horses, and many of the men carried bows and arrows or spears. Zuzahna counted over sixty riders. All seemed fit and appeared to be accomplished horsemen. She waited, attempting to see whether she could discern the leader, Ventras.

As the riders reined in their mounts and came to a halt, a tall lean figure in some kind of a headdress came from one of the larger, more permanent-looking shelters. A tingle ran down Zuzahna's spine. She instinctively knew the man. She had seen him once aboard *Intrepid One*, and another time outside her cell when he had arrested Tay.

The height and carriage were the same but somehow the man was different. Ventras turned and, even from her great distance, she could see the headdress was fashioned from a cougar's skull and his gloves were made of paws with long curved claws. He swaggered as though he thought himself overly important.

Ventras turned and began scanning the ridge. Zuzahna shrank back into the shadows of a small cedar tree. The lean man's gaze fell upon the rock promontory, as if he knew she were there.

Zuzahna had plucked a fern and held it front of her face to further camouflage her presence. Looking through the frond, she saw his eyes linger on the small trees that hid her. He was obviously searching for something he could feel but not see.

A large wolf came alongside Ventras and followed the man's gaze. The wolf's ears pricked, and the wild dog began to sway ever so lightly back and forth.

Zuzahna, in that moment, knew this was no place to err. Any of the simplest mistakes could be her unraveling. She watched undetected until just before dark and then made her way back to her horse. She led Paint back down the ridge, on the opposite side from the wild tribe's camp, and settled herself in for the night.

Zuzahna dared a small fire, long after dark, and contemplated her plan for the next day. She thought of stories to tell: ways to break into the confidence of the tribe she was about to infiltrate.

## THE SEEDING SEVEN'S VISION

\* \* \*

Smoke knew something was upon the ridge. He had been following the nearly undetectable sounds that gave away the presence to him only, and not to the humans of Two Leg's pack. Ventras seemed to feel something, yet the wolf *knew*. The creature upon the rock above was curious, not evil or threatening, as most of the camp were. Some instinct spoke to Smoke, telling him the creature was a friend, an ally that he had not yet met—a being that was gracious at heart and not like the group here in camp.

The wolf's curiosity was piqued. He decided to slip away and explore later, when Ventras was not watching and when the camp was becoming drowsy.

Two Leg's pack built up the fires, and the dance began as the meat cooked, dripping and sizzling over the fearful heat. Many of Two Leg's people pushed and shoved, bickering and vying for position. In many ways they were similar to the pack Smoke had deserted in order to survive. Smoke saw the similarities in this wild pack, of which Two Legs was alpha.

The wolf tired of watching the competition and wondered how long it would be before Two Legs would be driven from his pack by another rising alpha stronger than he.

After the feast, Two Leg's people became drowsy and began to file away to their dens. The wild dog waited until he was sure none of the camp would see him, and then he slipped away into the early evening shades that blended so well with his colors.

The forest floor smelled of the many travelers whose paths he crossed: the wood mouse and squirrel, the deer and raccoon. These animals held no interest for him this evening.

His mind was entirely focused high above, upon the ridge. His ears moved constantly, flicking this way and that. His breath forced quick pants through his hypersensitive nose. His eyes, which could see well even in the dim light dusk allowed, flashed back and forth between the innumerable sensory perceptions pounding into his brain.

All his senses were trained towards the unknown being who lay ahead.

Silently picking his footfalls to avoid small twigs or dry leaves that would give away his presence, the marauder stalked towards the mystery before him. He scented smoke drifting down the ridge and then heard the crackle of a fire. He knew that there must be another of the two-legged creatures ahead, for no other animal created fire for enjoyment.

Crouching and listening, he could hear none of the loud language that was in constant use among the camp's people. Perhaps this two-legged creature was alone, he thought.

This intrigued the wolf, for ever since he had met Two Leg's pack, he had found that most of the pack paired and kept families—even Two Legs himself had taken a mate and slept every night in her bed. This creature was alone, a solitary enigma to the wolf's curiosity. He rose and crept, half footfall by half, waiting between each step as he had seen the cougar do when silently stalking quarry.

Soon he saw a bright flicker through the trees and underbrush. Moving cautiously forward, he crept low to the ground, taking care to use the shadows of trees and fallen logs to conceal his approach.

Finally, Smoke saw a figure. He wanted to be closer so that the two-legged creature could be more readily observed, but he held back, primeval caution allowing him to proceed no further.

It was a female two-legged creature, and she appeared to be alone. Her scent drifted to him, sweet and entrancing. She sat on her haunches before the fire, its dancing light flickering in her enormous eyes. The wolf watched, frozen by the apparition before him, wondering why she was stalking Two Leg's pack.

Zuzahna felt something near. Surely in the wilderness there were always animals of some sort around, she thought. Yet this was something else, her sixth sense told her it was a being that possessed great intelligence.

"Who is there?" she asked.

The wolf, startled by the voice, involuntarily began to bolt, like a horse when something unknown streaks into its lateral vision. Smoke took an unplanned step upon a dry leaf, and then froze. The sound of the leaf crushing beneath his foot rushed out into the night.

The skin on the back of Zuzahna's neck prickled. Something was out there, very close, and watching her, she thought.

"Who are you? Show yourself," she said in a friendly tone, grasping the wooden knife she had made.

Smoke was broadside to Zuzahna, frozen between a primeval instinct to flee and the voice that spoke kind and soothing tones. The fire's light danced through the trees and reflected off the highlights of Smoke's coat.

"Oh my!" Zuzahna exclaimed. "You are beautiful wolf. Are you the one I saw in the camp below? Come nearer so that I may see you fully."

The voice was soft and reassuring. The wolf, instead of fleeing, turned and sat, looking anxiously at the enchantress who was pleading in a language he did not understand.

"Come, I say." Zuzahna used her most alluring voice. Surely, she thought, if it worked with men, it should be just as useful to coax a wolf into her confidence.

Something in the woman's gaze, in the voice, in her eyes, melted any fear the wolf felt, and he cautiously approached the fire, half-step by half-step.

Zuzahna had a small piece of dried venison she had been saving for her meal. She carefully and slowly unwrapped it so as not to frighten her newly found friend, and then broke it in half and laid a piece of it upon a stone, halfway between the animal and herself.

Smoke took in the offering and the countenance of the woman before him. *No bad*, he thought, *only good*. Even though Smoke was completely full after the tribe's feast, he came forward and took the gift, knowing it was right.

The woman smiled wide. Her eyes sucked in his wild soul. In that moment, Smoke switched allegiance from Ventras to the woman he had found upon the ridge.

She took the other half of the venison jerky and began to chew upon it.

Smoke realized that this creature had no fresh meat, for no two leg ate dried meat when fresh was available.

## THE SEEDING SEVEN'S VISION

The wolf spun and disappeared into the blackness from whence he came.

Breezes cooled the ridge, carrying the fragrances of cedar, fir, wild honeysuckle, and the verdant growth of innumerable species of wildflowers.

She sighed deeply, taking in the fragrance, and wondered where the wolf had gone. She questioned whether something she had done had frightened the animal.

What a wonderful experience, Zuzahna thought. Surely sharing food with the wolf was a good omen.

Zuzahna settled by the fire, rolled out her bedding, and began to ready herself for sleep.

The wolf's gait, like water running unobstructed downhill, carried him quickly back to the camp of Two Legs and his pack.

Silently approaching the smoking racks, he took it all in. The guard of the meat was sleeping in a stupor, as usual. Smoke had never stolen from the pack of Two Legs, and tonight he felt he was only sharing the bounty of his people with the woman on the ridge.

Stealthily grasping the hind quarter of a yearling deer from the rack, he spun silently, unnoticed by anyone, and made his way back to the woman's fire.

Approaching Zuzahna's campsite, Smoke was not cautious as before. Holding his head high to keep the leg of venison from the dirt, he nobly sauntered towards Zuzahna, who was resting on bedding.

She, seeing the wolf and his gift, was astonished. "I hope you won't be in trouble for this, wolf. Thank you for understanding my hunger."

Smoke watched the strange woman devour his gift of meat. The wolf felt nurturing emotions—the type a wild animal feels when success in the hunt brings much needed food to their young.

Zuzahna, hunger satiated and bone-weary from her grueling travel, soon fell asleep on her bedding.

The wolf watched over the sleeping woman, knowing she was alone. He became, in that evening, her self-appointed protector.

Zuzahna woke at first light when the sun's low position in the new day's sky caused a myriad of rainbow's hues to flicker through the mists that lay low in the valley.

The wolf appeared to be gone. Rubbing sleep from her eyes, she called out to the animal in the soothing voice that had made him her friend.

There was no sound of his footsteps, only the birdsong and the morning's breeze drifting through the glistening canopy of leaf and needle. Zuzahna made breakfast of the haunch the wolf had presented. She was grateful for the meal.

Walking along an animal path, she again visited the rock outcropping that offered her a clear view of the valley below. Obscured in the small fir and cedar trees as before, she watched.

The men and boys were training, as were a few of the women. She counted over sixty people. There were many more. All practiced the arts of bow and arrow, lance, wooden sword, and shield. They took turns on horses dressed in the semblance of ancient armor. The ones practicing were dressed in similar fashion. The armor was made of sticks bound together by rawhide laces. They charged dummies attached to posts with long lances. Cheers rose among the onlookers when a mortal strike was shown.

Surely, as Duhcat had explained, the wild tribe was preparing for conflict. It was Zuzahna's mission to find out all she could about the preparations, the numbers of warriors to be dedicated to the engagement of arms, and when the planned attack was to take place. It was no small task, she thought, since she had never been introduced to any of the wild tribe but the wolf.

Zuzahna watched for a few hours until her back and stomach ached from lying upon the hard rock. She wondered how she could infiltrate the wild tribe. If any fault were found in her story, their ruthlessness would be her demise. Duhcat had made very clear to her that she was perfectly suited for the task, and he knew more about her than she probably knew herself.

Rather than overthinking the dilemma, she decided to ride into the camp and play the scene, extemporaneously, without a plan. Devising not to devise, she would fall upon her instincts and training.

Choosing the time of her entrance would be of monumental importance. Zuzahna decided to approach from the west, as the sun set. She would be a shadow, a silhouette, a mystery entering camp with the sun at her back at the hour of evening, when the senses of the tribe would be dulled by food, drink, and the desire to sleep.

Zuzahna made her way toward the camp, shivering with excitement and anticipation of the meeting she had feared for the past two weeks. The wolf heard Zuzahna coming down the ridge, leading her horse. Six distinct sets of footfalls were taken in and understood by his acute hearing. Darting quick glances in all directions to see whether Ventras or others were watching, he stole out of camp unnoticed.

Smoke wished to see where the woman was going. He had bonded to her, and if she were leaving, he would join her. The politics of camp and Ventras' mercurial moods were wearing on his faithfulness.

Slinking towards the sound of the footfalls, he came upon the woman leading her horse.

Zuzahna noticed the wolf peeking from a clump of brush at once.

"Hello, wolf. Thank you again for your gift of meat."

Zuzahna stopped, willing the wild animal forward with her eyes and sweet words. There was a scent about her, unlike that of the other two-legged creatures: a scent that drew at his very being.

Coming forward slowly, enjoying her coaxing, he finally stopped a few feet in front of her, forcing her to make the final step of greeting. Zuzahna knelt to be on the wolf's level, extending her hand in a gesture of friendship.

Smoke sniffed lightly and then licked her hand. Zuzahna knew then that he had accepted her.

Standing up, Zuzahna said, "I must meet the tribe. Will you come?"

She began once again leading Paint towards the settlement of the wild tribe. Smoke followed and wondered whether she would go into the camp or just look upon it before leaving the valley. Torn between his waning loyalty to Ventras and the affection he felt for this new friend, the wolf dropped in step with her stride, scouting the perimeter before her.

Soon Zuzahna broke out of the tree line. Her already pounding heart danced inside her chest; never before had she felt the exhilaration of risking herself in an attempt to protect ones she loved. With this thought, her heart quieted, her chest quit throbbing, and the pounding in her ears subsided.

She mounted Paint, broke into a canter, and drove straight towards the evil ones with the wolf leading. He would glance back at her now and then, his nose low to the ground to enlarge the periphery of his vision, and Zuzahna swore in her heart that he was smiling.

Smoke had thought that his new friend would only watch Ventras' pack from the tree line, and that she would lack the courage to confront an unknown force and a potentially hostile enemy with such fearlessness. This two-legged creature drew at his heart. Picking up his stride and holding his head high, he escorted Zuzahna towards Ventras' camp and her uncertain fate.

Soon she was noticed. Calls began to sound, as well as warnings and gasps of disbelief. She was but a silhouette, a dark shadow, an imposing stranger coming straight out of the setting sun. A woman escorted by Ventras' wolf. A sorceress perhaps. Some saw her as a protector, others simply a stranger. The single men all found themselves hoping that she would be beautiful. Each one wished for a mate.

Ventras saw his wolf escorting a complete stranger into camp like some form of honor guard. When she came near, the woman looked familiar. She was no stranger but one he had condemned to life in the penal planet's cells. Ventras checked his headdress. He did not need an enemy, so he did not want Zuzahna recognizing him.

Fearless, Zuzahna rode in amongst the on-looking strangers, straight to their leader who stood masked beneath the skull and hide of a full-grown mountain lion.

Reining Paint to a halt in front of the tall, lean man, she said simply, "I have come to join your tribe, to defeat the one named TayGor. He has wronged me, as he has all of you."

Ventras took Zuzahna in. She hadn't changed much: a bit leaner, but her indescribable beauty shone through her rustic coverings. "How has TayGor wronged you?" he asked.

"He pretended to love me aboard the ship coming here, but once here, he abandoned me for the one called Estellene. I seek revenge. I wish him to suffer greatly."

"As do we all," replied Ventras.

Murmurs and grunts of ascent rippled through the shabby crowd.

"Why should we take you in? What can you offer us?"

"Because I know things about TayGor that you do not. Knowledge that will give you the advantage, and enable you to defeat him as surely as I stand before all of you!"

"We will hold council and discuss your request to join us. How is it that the wolf comes leading you?" asked Ventras suspiciously.

"He met me when I came from the tree line. I know nothing more."

"There is food at the fire. Eat if you are hungry. We will talk."

A group of eight, including Ventras, went from the crowd and entered one of the many shelters.

Zuzahna sat by the fire waiting. She ate the roasted meat with relish, still weary from the trail. Time passed slowly as she pondered what might be said in the meeting.

\* \* \*

Ventras spoke first, as the group gathered in the small, smoky room. "I, for one, am not sure we can trust her. Where has she been since landing, and what has she to offer us? Surely we don't need her. We outnumber TayGor's group greatly."

Others shook their heads. Dazar, a large man with a scar across one eye and a bush of a dark beard, spoke while all the others listened intently. "We should take her in. We have need of more women, and perhaps she *does* have information, which would gain us a larger advantage. She knows TayGor. He is not to be taken lightly, even though we outnumber his tribe. Besides, she is beautiful, and the wolf escorts her. That wild beast is close to no one but you, Shaman. Is this not an omen of good?"

Others spoke agreement.

Ventras did not wish her to know his true identity. If it weren't for Gor saving her from prison, she would be rotting there now because of his scheming while he was still in power on Seven. Most of all, Ventras was playing the devil's advocate; if something went wrong, if she was bad medicine, he did not want anyone saying that he had promoted her within the council.

"If you all feel as though we should shelter this woman, I will consent, for the sake of a unified agreement. Does anyone object?

All were silent.

"Then she will become one of us!"

All rose and went back to the fire where Zuzahna rested.

The wild tribe was curious. Everyone gathered around the central fire to hear the council's decision.

"What do you call yourself, woman?" Ventras asked.

"I am known as Zuzahna," she said.

"Well then, Zuzahna, we have decided to allow you to stay. Our rules here are simple. Wrong no one. Take nothing that is not offered to you. Stay away from men who have women mates, and swear allegiance to the tribe."

"I swear, I will do as you ask."

A cheer went up. The newcomer was slapped on the back by many of the women. The men held back, admiring this new one and wondering who she would take up with.

All but Ventras wished to share bed with her.


The weeks passed slowly, and Zuzahna learned. Walking constantly on a razor's edge, she forced herself to be calm and carefree on the outside. Inside, her quick mind was constantly alert for any trouble.

Ventras gave her the shivers, but she didn't let it show. His eyes, steely blue and hard, seemed as cold as ice and much more dangerous. She walked softly and did nothing to enhance the jealousy she could feel emanating from the other women in camp. The men watched her with longing eyes, and many came to her with manners learned in the gutter, attempting to woo her. She kept her distance and shunned all advances.

The children were her only joy. Their dirty little faces were so innocent, yet they had been trained by their culture to grow from everyday children into mirrors of the wild tribe. Her heart went out to them; if only it were another place in time, she thought, they would have had a chance to grow up normal.

She swam in the river with them and gave lessons to the ones who could not swim. She helped them bathe and quietly taught a few who were more interested in learning about true manners and decency.

Before long, she would leave them. She hoped that her brief time here would help some of them to see another path...a path that would whisk them, mentally, away from the negative environment in which they grew every day.

# FIFTY-TWO

Zuzahna woke early, grabbed a change of clothes, and left her small shelter. She walked towards the river, intending to bathe and swim while the camp was, for the most part, still sleeping. The morning was cool. Mist clung to low areas, signaling the approach of fall.

The forest covering the surrounding hills had changed of late. The dry hot days of summer's waning breath had sucked moisture from anything willing to give it. The deciduous leaves had paled from the vibrant green of new lush growth, and clues that striking red and yellow would soon carpet the hills were evident in the pale complexions and age spots on the leaves.

The river's soothing music played softly in her ears as her feet scrunched along the trail. She thought of her time here, of the things she had learned, which she would soon be taking away. Her departure neared; it was almost time. She felt relief, thinking of returning to her home and to the valley of Estellene's people.

As she walked around a bend that opened on the trail's view of the river, Smoke startled her by poking his head out of the brush right in front of her. His eyes were bright and wide, saying he was happy to meet her.

"Hello, boy, how are you this morning?"

The wolf sidled up to her, prancing in a playfulness that made Zuzahna laugh softly. "Oh, you want to play?" She rubbed his back and head and pushed him around a bit as he danced, dodging and feinting. Smoke brushed against her in a show of affection she had never seen him give to others in the camp.

She continued around the bend with the wolf at her side and walked towards the sandy spit, which made a good entry point into the water. A figure was swimming, and she thought it must be Ventras. She had not seen him here without his headdress before. She sat in a spot where she blended in with the large boulders strewn along the shore. She was curious about this man and was drawn into silent observation. Smoke sat beside her, watching as well.

Here was the man responsible for imprisoning her, Tay and Alex. Her life had been changed drastically by his dark actions, and Zuzahna wanted only to look upon him in his naked state, to see him without his costume, as a figure unadorned by symbolism and the legends of his making here on planet. Smoke sat next to her, so close she could feel his warmth and the brush of his fur.

Ventras, finished in the water, walked up onto the sand towards his garments. He glanced up the small beach, as if wondering where the wolf was. In the bright angle of the morning sun, his eyes shone that icy grey blue she remembered from the first time she had met him—when Tay had been taken from her cell and arrested. A web of scars patterned his body, and his face had been disfigured from what looked like massive claw marks. Whatever it was had torn deeply through the flesh.

Ventras' roving eyes settled on her sitting among the rocks and he started. He grabbed up his garments and dressed hastily, placing the cougar's preserved face upon his own. Once adorned in regalia, the man looked intimidating again, yet Zuzahna had seen his lean body, weakened by the injuries, and the limp he masked well when he knew others were observing him. The hunched posture of an aging man had been hidden again as he pulled his shoulders back and up, forcefully kept straight to increase his height and stature.

Ventras said nothing, yet he was seething internally; this woman had seen him without the mask. If she had recognized him, he was in jeopardy. Many of the wild ones had been sent to prison when he had gutted organized crime upon Seven and taken over the black-market trade himself in the vacuum created by their absence. If they knew his real identity, his life would no doubt be taken.

In that instant, he knew Zuzahna had to go. She was a threat, a wild card; he could not allow her to play. He began plotting to kill her.

The wolf remained sitting next to her while Ventras dressed. Others in the tribe had commented on the wolf's affection for Zuzahna, some saying she was an enchantress and others that she was a witch. Regardless, she was stealing some of his power as the shaman in the tribe. His killing of the cougar and taming the wolf had been strong medicine among the superstitious lot. He could not have this woman taking drops of his magic, bleeding him ever so slightly, day by day, of the mythical force and influence he carried here. His magic was the only thing that gave him power over the unruly and ruthless tribe.

He spoke, not in a friendly tone, to the wolf. "Smoke, come!"

The wolf sat for a moment, unmoving. Ventras shouted again in obvious frustration. "Smoke! Come!"

The animal glanced up at Zuzahna. She saw the flash of reluctance in his intelligent eyes as he broke from her side and walked slowly towards his master.

"Good!" Ventras exclaimed, but the dog did not wag his tail or prance as he had done for Zuzahna. It was as if, by going from her to the tall lean figure, he was being locked away in unhappiness.

Ventra finished straightening his garments and then walked towards Zuzahna. "You should announce yourself, woman," he said brusquely. He considered strangling her in that instant. No one was near to see. He could throw her body in the river.

Smoke leapt from beside Ventras, moving in front of Zuzahna and snarling ever so slightly. The sound came from deep in his throat.

Ventras looked down at the wolf. Disbelief etched itself into his face as he realized where Smoke's loyalty *now* rested. Saying nothing more, he moved quickly away.

Smoke nuzzled Zuzahna's hand for a second and then dropped in step behind Ventras.


Zuzahna was silent. Feeling the chilling breeze of his passing presence, she sat in the warmth of morning sunlight. It filtered down through a gorgeously brilliant azure sky.

Still, she shivered involuntarily.

# FIFTY-THREE

Ventras left the river sweating profusely. The woman Zuzahna seeing him unadorned and naked had brought an otherwise wonderful morning to a close.

The skeleton of a plan formed: he would tell the elders in council that he had seen her talking with a stranger at the river early this morning—she was a spy. Ventras would tell the council that they could not trust her and that she had been sent to gather information on their preparations for war. Therefore, she must be killed immediately before she could escape and give away their plan.

Surprise was the wild tribe's advantage in the attack against TayGor. Without surprise, they could suffer extreme casualties, and these losses could set back their plans to take TayGor's settlement and the precious land found there.

With the precious natural resources of iron and gold, the tribe could become the ruling force on the planet, and Ventras would be its leader, hailed by all in orchestrating the attack, training the tribe, and making weapons from the primitive material available, all to enable them to prevail.

In actuality, Ventras did suspect Zuzahna of spying. He had no proof; however, when watching the camp, as was his habit, he'd witnessed Zuzahna often skirting around the camp as well. She was apparently listening to conversations. Ventras had seen her do this on many different occasions. The camp was rife with gossip and speculation; all in the camp knew they were about to make war. So Zuzahna surely knew as well.

Zuzahna had said TayGor abandoned her in the wild, leaving her to scrape for food, and—as she said—to barely survive. In her favor, she had spoken vocally against him, and she had appeared thin and strained when she arrived. She appeared to be on their side, yet, Ventras reminded himself, what appeared on the surface was not normally what swam the unseen currents below.

# FIFTY-FOUR

SMOKE was dreaming fitfully. The hunt had been challenging and had demanded every bit of his leadership and skill. Being an alpha male meant responsibility for the pack, and the search for food was never ending. They had come upon an elk, a massive bull late in years and slow enough to run down yet dangerous in a standing fight.

The wolf had chosen the quarry well and had orchestrated the attack. He had been in the most dangerous position: head to head with the antlered beast. All had gone well, and the massive male was eventually worn out. The feast would begin soon. The alpha had only to keep the antlers away from the attacking pack. He challenged, dodged the charges, feinted and weaved, giving the others safety to do their bloody work.

Towards the end of the struggle, a younger wolf, one who had constantly challenged him, darted behind the alpha, timing his movement for when the bull was in a last charge and blocking the alpha's lunge backward.

In that instant, trapped between a devious challenging male and the oncoming rush of the massive antlers, he misstepped. The antlers came sweeping in, causing a sickening crack of bone and flinging the alpha backwards.

Adrenalin masked the seriousness of the injury for the moment. The massive bull was finished. The pack feasted.

The next morning upon rising and attempting to stretch, his injuries became evident. Ribs had been broken, and the breath of life came painfully. Glancing to see which others in the pack might have noticed his disability, he saw the one who had caused the accident looking on knowingly. The lead wolf's days as the alpha had ended.

The younger male challenged, and a brutal contest began. The alpha attempted to meet the instigator on even ground, but it was no use; he was weakened. Without the injuries, the fight would have been easy for him, but with only half of his normal endurance, the alpha failed.

Upon losing, he was avoided. Furtive glances in his direction were prevalent: his women, driven by primeval instincts, left one by one, until there were none to comfort him.

The situation became worse. Instead of allowing him to heal, the new alpha dogged him, lunging and knocking him down, tearing at his throat, determined to harass him until the bones would have no chance of knitting. It was clear the younger wolf still felt threatened by the former alpha; if the former alpha were to heal, his rightful place would be regained.

Then other males in the pack began the same type of aggressive behavior. The tide of jealousy and competition grew stronger. The other males gained stature with the females by dominating the former alpha.

Late one night, in the pouring rain, the wolf who would one day be given the name Smoke, slid silently from the pack's camp and left without a trace. He left in the rain so it would wash away his scent. None could follow.

On that windswept pouring night, he became the marauder, a solo male who endured a lonely existence.


Smoke was awakened from his dreaming by the two-legged pack. They were bickering. Listening intently, Smoke could sense the verbal struggle, the vying for position. Some challenged his partner. The mood, even though embodied in the form of these two-legged creatures, was familiar to the wolf. In time, all alphas lost their position, some slowly, bit by bit, and others in the blink of an eye, as had happened to the attentive wolf.

Upon listening more, he realized the strange new woman he had befriended was being talked of; he heard her name incessantly. The two legs were angry. Ventras kept using the name Zuzahna in bad tone, but the others argued and spoke of her in kind tones.

*What is afoot?* Smoke thought. *Surely they mean her no harm, for she is good.* Yet as he listened, the tone and energy in the late night meeting away from camp boded bad feelings. Smoke's instincts prickled. He felt danger for his new friend. The wolf thought, *They ready for a hunt. Zuzahna is the quarry!*

The wolf slipped away, disappearing in the dark.

# FIFTY-FIVE

The wolf came to Zuzahna's shelter, whining and scratching at the door. He had never come like this before and concern immediately flooded her mind. She wondered what could be wrong.

The moment she opened the makeshift door, Smoke entered the small dwelling and looked up at her, thinking, *Don't you understand? You need leave. Danger! Danger is coming!*

His voice spoke inside her head, short and to the point. Zuzahna could barely believe what she was hearing.

The wolf ran to her horse tack, pulled out the deerskin saddle blanket she had made for Paint, and brought it to her. He dropped it at her feet, whined again, and then spun in a half-circle towards the door. He lowered his nose and looked back at her.

She heard his thoughts again, so clearly they sounded like a voice inside her head: *Go we must. Go.* He returned to her, grabbed the sleeve of her sleeping garment, and tugged her powerfully towards the door. He whined again.

"What's up, boy? You think I should leave this place? Am I in danger?" Three questions, and his right front

# THE SEEDING SEVEN'S VISION

leg came up and pawed the air once, twice, three times. He grabbed her sleeve again and pulled, only this time harder, making her stumble towards the door.

"Okay, Smoke, I get it. We'll go." She changed quickly into her outdoor garments: deer skin and fur to ward off the evening chill and colors that would blend well into the natural surroundings.

She had never felt comfortable here. Constantly on edge, she had never completely unpacked. She was always ready to fly. Quickly she gathered her things and stole silently towards the lean-to where she kept Paint in the evenings.

Only minutes after she had the horse tacked and was in the saddle, making her way down one of the trails leading out of the village, she heard pounding hooves. Many horses and riders were thundering into camp.

*Unusual*, she thought.

She had never seen them ride in this late at night before. She saw the outlines of a dozen or more men on horseback moving past the waning embers of the cooking fires, towards the hut in which she had been sleeping minutes before. They had not yet seen her.

The darkness, while not absolute, made visibility difficult. Smoke appeared in front of her and led the way down the trail. She walked the horse slowly. Her hair prickled, and she wanted to gallop away, but she knew the sound would bring the storm upon her.

Shouts suddenly echoed down the valley: calls announcing she was missing and that her horse was gone.

Soon, others could be heard being roused from their sleep. The whole village seemed to be waking.

It was the beginning frenzy of a hunt.

Zuzahna was the quarry.

As Smoke broke from open ground into the forest, Zuzahna saw torches: a mass of mounted riders had divided into groups to cover the four trails leading out of the village. The sound shook her to the core.

Shortly, Smoke stood up on his hind legs next to her, wanting her attention. He then turned off the main trail onto some form of animal path that led perpendicularly away from the well-used trail they had just left. She followed him.

Branches, unseen in the darkness, scratched at her face. She dismounted, walking the horse slowly behind the wolf. The trail followed a small ravine uphill, and gradually it opened onto a narrow sloping meadow that, in the meager moonlight, she could see continued on for a distance.

A group of horses, barely discernible except for the torches carried by the riders, passed through the trees on the main trail less than two hundred yards from where she, Paint, and her new trusted partner Smoke stood silently.

Zuzahna crouched low to the ground alongside the wolf. He brushed up close, leaning into her with his weight. "Thank you," she whispered. "You are a very smart one, coming and waking me." She reached around him and pulled him tight towards her, then stood and began making her way up the meadow.

She thought of Tay and Estellene. The wild tribe was nearly ready for war; she had heard the elders' plans when she had been moving around in the late-night shadows, listening. She must not be caught. With Smoke's help, she must slip through the net and warn them. She had promised Duhcat.

The small meadow meandered up the slope, and they continued walking, not chancing to make more sound than absolutely necessary. She understood that in the brisk evening air, sound from above would travel quickly to any listening ears.

When they reached the ridge top, an open trail without any overhanging limbs appeared, perhaps the path of some herd animals. Smoke looked up at her, as if to say, "Which way, friend?"

She searched the sky for any sign of morning's light and could see none. Without knowing east from west, she was unsure. She tied Paint to an overhanging tree limb and found a comfortable place beneath a fir tree where fallen needles cushioned the ground. Leaning back against the tree, with Smoke curled beside her, she felt safe; she knew her new friend had senses superior to her own, and she felt sure that together as a team, they could stay clear of the searching tribe. The three of them waited in the quiet of night for first light.

The ride to Tay and Estellene's village was six days in the best of circumstances. Being hunted and travelling cautiously would add a couple days to that, at least. She decided to make her way to Duhcat's fortress, her new home, to rest there a day before continuing on. It was on the way and would give her time to resupply and change clothing.

Slivers of light crept into the sky as false dawn came. In the woods, it was still too dark for making any kind of decent headway; she decided to wait until the trail would be easy to keep. Smoke barely stirred, only twitching now and then in dream sleep.

Zuzahna's mind wandered, traveling back a couple of months. She thought of Estellene and the day she had tried to kill her. She was appalled that her own selfish desires could have driven her so crazy, but since meeting Enricco Duhcat, her thought processes had altered. She was no longer the most important thing. The world did not revolve around her wishes. If Estellene's offer still stood, she would become part of a real family for once in her life. The idea inspired her, changing her more, bringing love for a group purpose closer.

She reveled in the newly found feeling of joy. Being alone, and at risk, would have driven her to despair before. Now she had a meaningful purpose. She felt energized and full of life. Her mind raced, thinking of her path home and of the dangers she would face bringing the information Duhcat stressed as being so strategic to Tay.

Before long, the sky turned morning-grey, and she rubbed the wolf awake.

"Let's go, Smoke." She rose, stretching, as did the wolf. Looking down the ridge, she saw that the trail was clear, with no low-hanging limbs. She mounted Paint and made her way west, to her new home.

Before long, she found an overlook that provided a great vantage of the surrounding area. Down the ridge, slightly below the crest, was a site where someone had camped and made fires. If this was Tay's trail, she would know soon by its direction. The trail seemed to keep abreast of the ridge tops, a less direct route than the valley floor but safer. She travelled unseen, high above the valleys, on a path possibly unknown to the tribe, who had been in the area only a short while.

Birds flew in sweeping, graceful arcs through a morning sky that was shaded with amber, violet, and crimson as the new day's sun rose. Smoke pranced up the trail ahead, turning often to make certain she was still close behind.

Sometimes the wolf would bounce and bound, dancing side to side or standing on his back legs, and then hopping up and down, nodding his head, as if to say, "Our new life is going to be much fun." The more Zuzahna laughed, the more of a show he would make. She had never seen a wolf with so much personality and found simple joy in his wonderful quirkiness.

The day was uneventful, and the farther they travelled along the ridge trail, the more she came to believe it was the one Tay used regularly. Each and every promontory, cliff, and peak were groomed, so that whoever had maintained the path could see across vast sections of the surrounding lands without being seen from below.

Towards evening, Zuzahna spied a makeshift pole ladder. It was over ten meters high and was standing against the back side of a monstrous cedar tree, barely noticeable from the path.

It appeared that whoever had constructed the ladder had used it to reach the first limbs on the massive trunk, perhaps to climb the tree and gain a 360-degree view for nearly a hundred miles. The cedar was growing from a cleft where one ridge joined another. Normally cedar trees didn't grow this high in elevation, Zuzahna thought; there must be a spring or underground water source feeding the giant, allowing it to thrive out of its normal lowland environment.

She had brought two hide water bags, yet during the day the three travelers had emptied them both. Zuzahna had hoped to find a spring, but so far they had found no water up on the ridge. She had resisted the urge to thread her way back down to the lowlands where the water would be plentiful, as the danger would abound there. Now, her thirst had climbed from her throat to her tongue.

Zuzahna dismounted and climbed the ladder to the cedar's first limbs and proceeded to scale the massive tree. When she was some hundred and fifty feet above the ladder, the tree forked into two separate trunks. In the space between the two trunks, someone had built a rudimentary platform; the only logical reason would be for observation.

The platform had spars that jutted out laterally and allowed a daring person to walk them, holding a limb, and be able to view the land in all directions. In the distance, she could see the pinnacle of rock that was her new home. Past that, towards the inland salt water sound, she could see the smoke from Estellene and Tay's village. Low down in the valleys below, she saw smoke from fires in three separate valleys. The tribes were heading in the same direction as she was, perhaps thinking she was going to other settlements. She would have to be diligent and careful, she thought.

She sat, taking in the view, as the evening sky changed color. A fresh breeze driven by the sun's waning heat moved up the ridge, bringing scents from the valley floor.

The wild berries were blooming; she could smell their blossoms.

Zuzahna thought of the wine she had for made for Tay and how he had complimented her creation. In that moment, reliving her work and sweat—the thorns in her fingers and her purple-stained hands—she remembered how she had suffered in order to please and make him happy. She found a universal truth: that working selflessly was rewarding. An answer for which she had blindly groped her entire life had revealed itself. As if by magic, the answer came flashing through her. She had wanted to own him, to control him, to drive him for her purposes, as she had done Xeries.

She felt shame. It drilled deep into her core, weakening her knees and bringing with it disgust and all the feelings she had muscled through when Enricco Duhcat had called her previous life for what it was.

*How is it possible,* she thought, *that I could have been such a person? How did I not see what I had become?* Bliss overtook Zuzahna. She had heard the term before yet had never understood the meaning. She was flooded with understanding and felt her eyes filling with tears. She cried not out of grief or loss but out of joy—joy for having been given a chance to know truth in all things: a love so priceless, she would gladly sacrifice herself to save those she treasured in her heart.

Zuzahna climbed down from the lookout. It was near sundown. She needed to find a decent place to spend the night and find, with good fortune, some water for them all. Once upon the ground, she looked around carefully. If Tay had spent time here, he would no doubt have made a camp site.

She found some broken twigs and worn and crumbled needles on the forest floor, and then at once noticed a path so light in footprint that any passerby would surely have missed it. She followed it downhill for a ways and soon heard the wonderful sound of water. An abrupt shelf of stone broke away below, and the path threaded to the right, following the contour of the small rock bluff.

Soon she was below the little cliff and was pleasantly amazed to find a cave and pool of steaming water. A hot spring! The hot water exuded from a fracture in the rock face, just below the cave's entrance.

She at once went in to explore and was surprised to find a bed made from forest ferns and moss, a makeshift table, a stool, and a wooden chest. Opening the big wooden box, she found a cache of provisions that included coffee, dried fruit, and venison as well as rice, oil, and other necessary cooking utensils. There was a small fire pit by the cave's mouth. It was lined with stones and had a grill and a swing arm for hanging pots. *That little bugger!* she thought, laughing to herself. Tay had obviously spent a good deal of his time here, at this comfortable hideaway along his route.

In a corner of the small cavern, she found bundles of hay fully headed up: provisions for Eclipse, she thought. She dipped water for them all. It was hot and smelled lightly of sulfur, but it was wet and wonderful. She stripped out of her dirty clothes and stepped into the hot pool to soak.

Looking up through the trees to the waning day's sky, she breathed deeply, stress and worry draining away. She had found his path and was sure it would carry her safely home.

## THE SEEDING SEVEN'S VISION

\* \* \*

The next morning, the sound of birds flitting through the forest outside the cave's mouth awakened Zuzahna. She had slept dreamlessly, and the morning sun was high above the distant horizon. *It's late,* she thought, surprised that she hadn't woken earlier. She had planned to get an early start. Nonetheless, the rest had done her well.

She felt relieved at having left the northern tribe's camp. The worry she had been trying to mask all the while she had been in danger had taken its toll. This morning, she drew in the fresh, forest-scented air and washed herself in tranquility.

She looked around and noticed that Smoke was gone. In the wooden chest, she found some biscuits, dried fruit, and a withered apple that was still edible. There was also a shirt: Tay's shirt, she thought. She picked up the piece of clothing and brought it close to her face, smelling his scent, which still lingered in the fibers. A wave of excitement passed through her; the thought of seeing him soon—and whenever else she wanted—instead of the two days a month created a rising surge of happiness within her.

She picked up a bundle of cut grass and went to Paint. The horse saw the food and nickered, intelligent eyes thanking her for remembering. Zuzahna wished to call for the wolf but abstained, not wanting to send the sound of her presence throughout the hills.

She ate quickly, planning to fill her water bag, grab a few things to eat from the chest, and be on her way. The luring scent of coffee in the chest pulled at her, yet she feared making even the smallest fire lest one of the tribe smell or see the smoke. She resolved from native intelligence to have only cold camps until she was out of danger.

The hot pool, with its soothing heat, also pulled at her, and she decided to take a quick soak before saddling Paint and heading out. The wolf would come in his own time, she knew. If they left before he returned, he would follow her trail by scent and catch up later.

She accepted the water's hot invitation, waded in, and then stretched out full length, gazing up through a canopy of evergreen and brown into morning's blue above. With her ears under water, she didn't hear Smoke approaching, nor did she see him sneaking up from behind. At once, his face appeared, looking down upon her from the rock bluff above. His eyes were untroubled, and she saw a bit of humor in them as he observed this two-legged creature floating in an element the wolf took in as small doses as possible.

Happy that he was back, Zuzahna said softly, "Where have you been?"

The wolf, understanding, flicked his eyes and head in the direction they would be traveling this morning.

"Oh, you were scouting ahead. Good boy, thank you."

She climbed from the water, dripping. Steam rose from her body in the cool morning air. She went to the wooden chest and dug out two pieces of dried venison. She gave them to Smoke, and he thanked her with a flash of gratitude in his eyes before lying down to quickly devour the treat.

Zuzahna dressed, saddled Paint, and strapped on the water and food. She then led the horse up-hill, away from the wonderful little hideaway.

## THE SEEDING SEVEN'S VISION

When they were back up to the trail, she mounted and looked back to see if any evidence of their visit had been left behind. The forest gave little signal of their footprints. Satisfied, she nudged Paint into a fast walk, and they trekked westward towards her new, cliff-top home.

# FIFTY-SIX

Zuzahna had been in the saddle for over seven days. Sleeping on the trail had taken its toll on her body. *So much for the pampered courtesan's life,* she thought, as she wearily made way closer to safety and away from the wild tribe.

She had seen and heard the wild ones along the way: they were evidenced by the rising spires of smoke and loud obnoxious voices carrying on the warm, soft breezes from the valleys below. Fortunately, they were making no real effort to hide themselves, and she felt sure that slipping through their ever-widening net would not be much trouble.

Her biggest problem, however, was water. Riding the ridge top had afforded few chances to replenish the two small hide bags she carried. Between the wolf, Paint, and herself, thirst had been a continual discomfort.

Taking time to steal quietly down the ridge in order to find water had delayed her escape, so she had never outdistanced the wild ones in their tenacious search. Today, she had to make the trip to lower elevations once again. They could wait no longer for the chance of a spring.

## THE SEEDING SEVEN'S VISION

Zuzahna led Paint down-hill, following a well-worn animal trail. The trail down followed a shallow side ridge that was parallel to a little canyon. Before long, Zuzahna could scent water and hear the faintest trickle sounding far below.

She kept on, keeping the horse as quiet as possible. Her ears scanned the many forest sounds, and her eyes regularly swept the understory between tree trunks, inspecting the many contrasting tree-bark colors.

They rounded a bend in the trail that opened into a wider and shallower place in the ravine, and the sound of water became much louder. A sparkle below suggested there was a creek and pool. There was a rushing sounded, as if there were a waterfall.

Zuzahna sighed in anticipation. She was covered with a sticky layer of perspiration and trail dust, and at once she imagined the water: its cool caress washing over her aching muscles, cleansing away the dirt and weariness.

The wolf led way, his ears forward, head pivoting gracefully. Smoke had scented Two Legs' pack often on the drifting air currents that feathered through the trees along the ridge. Now he scouted ahead, tasting the air through his nose, listening with his hypersensitive ears for any sign of danger. The smells from Two Legs' people were stronger than ever here. They were close, but how close, he wondered. Smoke could not ascertain for certain. Thirst drove him forward, cautiously.

Soon Zuzahna could feel the coolness and the spray drifting from the falls. She was reminded of the day she had met Duhcat on the trail, when they had bathed by the falls: that day seemed forever ago.

She noticed the wolf taking one step at a time, moving as though he were stalking some prey or another, his silver-blonde head sweeping side to side.

She longed for a cool drink. Paint began to nicker softly under her breath, obviously scenting the water that was so near. The three of them made way slowly, quietly to the falls. At last the glistening pool and rushing stream could be seen. The white water fell, dropping over a sheer rock face about twenty meters high.

They stole quietly to the water's edge and drank. Smoke peeled away silently. His scouting help was never underappreciated by Zuzahna.

After drinking and filling her water bags, and then tying them back onto the saddle, she stripped off her clothes and slid carefully from the rocky edge into the cleansing cool. Paint quickly went to work eating tender young ferns.

The water, while not frigid, was very cold, and Zuzahna soon began to feel the creeping numbness in her fingers and toes. She scrubbed her hair quickly with her fingertips, and then made way to the place where the falling water met the pool. The water was waist deep there. She rinsed quickly and then climbed out, stepping from one large rock to another. Sometimes she was forced into a crawl because the footing was so slippery from the spray.

Squatting by the pool, she washed the clothes she had taken off and put them back on, wet. Then she took her other clothes from her saddle bag and washed the filth off them as well. She twisted the fabric, wringing out all the water she could and then laid the articles out on the warm rocks to dry in the sun. She was uneasy. Having travelled so close to the valley floor, the wild tribe could be near. *Smoke is scouting ahead.* The thought allowed her to relax a bit.

Zuzahna sat in the warmth of golden sunlight, listening to the stream and the music made by the falls. She waited for the water to clear so that she could drink more before they headed back up the ridge, drifting in her daydreams and enjoying the hot sun after her chilly swim.

Suddenly, she was startled from her relaxed state by the sound of the wolf's approach. Something was wrong! Zuzahna jumped to her feet and grabbed up her clothes. Just then, Smoke broke into the open. His eyes were wide. He stopped and quickly looked downstream.

Zuzahna took Paint's reins in her hand, moving as fast as possible, and led her horse to the trail. They began climbing. Smoke followed behind, stopping to glance backward every few paces.

Zuzahna was afraid to look behind, fearing she might misstep, wishing she could put some distance between them and whoever might be coming. A crashing of brush sounded, and Zuzahna chanced a backwards glance.

A young buck deer broke into the pool of sunlight before the falls. Bright red ran down his chest from where a shaft of wood with feathers protruded.

Zuzahna was mentally caught by the contrast of sunlight, the blue-green shimmering water, and the brown-blonde color of the deer's coat. She froze for an instant, taking in the startling scene back-dropped by rocks, which were quickly turning red. Droplets of blood splattered.

The young deer dipped its head for a drink and then collapsed beside the pool.

It was then that Zuzahna saw something that sent shivers of fear throughout her body. Lying on a rock, in full sun, was a pair of earthen colored shorts she had missed, or forgotten in her hurried retreat from the pool. Frantically, she wondered whether she should go back down. If she didn't, and the hunter found the deer, he would certainly see the clothing and know she was near. Her mind raced.

In an instant, she made the choice, praying it was correct.

She began moving, picking up the pace, making way as fast as possible uphill, away from whoever was below. Her only hope was to outdistance them.

Certainly, if the hunter found her shorts, he would not come after her alone. He would return and tell the others, and they would concentrate their search. She was in extreme jeopardy.

Panting from exertion, she at last had to stop. She could see the pool below, its reflective surface broken into small slices by the trees between them. She attempted to see the telltale piece of clothing.

By leaning over the edge of the ravine and holding onto a small sapling so as not to lose her footing, she could just see a corner of cloth. In that moment, the shorts disappeared from view. She gasped. *They knew! They had found her!* Zuzahna wasted no time. Her course of action was set. All that remained was headlong flight: no stopping for water and no rest, except for when it was too dark for seeing.

She caught her breath and began a short-stepped run up the hill. She prayed she had enough endurance left in her to stay ahead of the tribe. She knew they would not rest. There were many of them. They could create a web of interference that would be difficult to penetrate.

Zuzahna thought of Duhcat and what he had said: that she had been trained for just this sort of thing. She thought of Tay and Estellene and all the children she had sworn to protect. *I will escape!* she said to herself, as she made the grueling trek to the ridge-top trail. *I will warn Tay! I will make it!*

Repeating the words in her mind, she pushed herself to the point of collapse. Yet somehow she went on, adrenalin giving her the necessary thrust to accomplish the impossible. As soon as they were off the steep trail and onto flatter ground, she mounted Paint and fast-walked the horse upwards towards her only avenue of escape.

They reached the ridge-top trail, and she forwarded rein to Paint. The horse, sensing her panic, took the signal and broke into a run. Zuzahna held on, moving with her mount as never before, anticipating and leaning into the upcoming corners, bent at the waist to keep her weight centered above the animal's pounding hooves.

Smoke ran in front. He moved like a falcon, sweeping the corners, scenting the air in all directions. He was, Zuzahna thought, one of the most beautiful creatures she had ever seen.

The three of them ran without looking back. They ran for their lives.

# FIFTY-SEVEN

Far below, in a valley filled with lush green grass and a river meandering through, Ventras sat in frustration. It had been over seven days, and they had not found the woman some in the tribe called the Sorceress. The woman he had set out to kill. The woman who could identify him to others in the tribe.

Ventras' frustration could be known by the telltale twitch beneath his left eye. The twitch had been present ever since seeing Zuzahna at the river that morning. For eight days, he had suffered with its annoying presence. Now, as Ventras pondered the next move in his game with Zuzahna, he heard in the distance two distinct sets of hooves hammering the ground.

Perking up, he listened. One horse sounded as though it was down in the valley, but the other appeared to emanate from high above, on the ridge perhaps. Ventras stood, his curiosity piqued. Looking down the valley, he could see dust from a rider's approach. He waited.

Something was happening, something that made the twitch depart. The incoming rider must have caught sight of Zuzahna! Ventras thought. The other set of hooves high above must be her, running from them.

Watching the distant rider become larger, Ventras' black heart hoped. He hoped this game would soon close, and he would be the winner. He hoped the rider bore good news.

The man on horseback came flying into the makeshift camp along the river. He was out of breath from exertion. Reining his horse to an abrupt halt, he dismounted and ran up to Ventras. He had a pair of shorts in his hand that appeared to be a woman's.

"The Sorceress...! I mean, the woman...Zuzahna. She must be on the ridge above! I found these by the stream coming down a canyon of that ridge."

He motioned towards the long, steep ridge that ran parallel to the valley in which they camped.

Murmurs and shouts rose from the search party. A commotion began, and Ventras screamed at the top of his lungs, "Quiet!! QUIET!!"

The camp became still, and Ventras turned his head, cocking it slightly and cupping his hands one to each ear, listening. Many in the camp mimicked him.

All could hear the hooves pounding, echoing, diminishing in decibels as the horse and rider rode further away from the men who listened.

Ventras said, "She is heading west! Four of our fastest riders and horses, alert the other two camps. Split into two groups. We will follow that ridge and stop her before she warns TayGor and ruins the surprise of our attack. GO! NOW! All others: FOLLOW ME!"

Ventras strode to his mount and, without packing anything, tacked up the horse and swung into the saddle.

After watching his disheveled group scampering around for provisions, weapons, and clothes, he said,

"Four men stay here. Break camp and bring our supplies on the pack horses. Meet us downriver tonight. We will have fires burning!"

With that, Ventras whipped his mount viciously and galloped west in the direction of his quarry's flight. Fourteen riders soon followed him.

# FIFTY-EIGHT

Zuzahna, in a mad dash to freedom, had run her beloved Paint to the breaking point. The mare's sweat had turned to foam and she blew long, abnormal breaths. Zuzahna reined the horse to a stop and dismounted. Paint's eyes were wild and steam rolled off her coat.

Zuzahna wondered if it were too late. She began to lead the animal, walking fast, hoping and praying that her beloved mare would recover without failing and collapsing on the trail. Paint frothed at the mouth.

The wolf watched them, his long tongue lolling out of his mouth, dripping as he panted. His fur-covered frame heaved, overheated as well. As Zuzahna walked, concern flooded her mind. She was frantic but restrained herself, ensuring a restful pace until her two loyal partners began breathing more normally.

Stopping, she listened and could hear the distant roar of many horses and riders in pursuit. Surely, she thought, they could not keep the pace; surely they would also have to rest their animals. Zuzahna had no idea how far behind the wild tribe was, but she could not afford to stop or to rest any longer; she must keep going.

Her water bags were untouched since being filled at the falls. Zuzahna felt it was safe to water the horse and the wolf lightly, now that they had cooled sufficiently.

Stopping momentarily, she poured some of the precious liquid into a small wooden bowl and let them both drink. She herself did not.

Once the water in the bowl was gone, they immediately set off again. The sound of hoof beats in the valley, which had been growing louder as they neared, suddenly quieted. Her pursuers had obviously over-driven their mounts to the breaking point as well.

# FIFTY-NINE

Ventras led the rush of horseflesh and men pursuing Zuzahna. He thought of nothing but her capture—not even of his horse, which had been overheated from being pushed too hard without being rested or cooled or given water. He was hell-bent on destroying the woman at any cost. She could be his undoing, and she was fleeing toward TayGor, most likely with the intent to expose his plan of attack.

His horse's sweat had turned to foam miles ago. Every blood vessel beneath the beautiful mare's skin bulged sickly. Her eyes were frantic dark orbs surrounded by inordinately large white ovals.

Ventras whipped the horse's flanks in a brutal rhythm; her will ran stronger than her physical body could possibly carry her. She was an extraordinary animal, one to be treasured and not cast off as a filthy piece of rubbish, yet Ventras' all-consuming hatred made him blind to the animal's plight. She began a rocking canter in slow motion. Her exhausted limbs had no strength left. Still, she ran, and in her last staggering movements forward, Ventras beat her harder.

The mare finally threw her head back in her first and last act of defiance. Her spent legs turned to rubber beneath the vicious man who had ridden her into the brutal, unforgiving ground.

*Finally*, like a battle horse speared, she screamed her last breath in agony. Her bulging heart burst. She tumbled to the ground in an ungainly, sprawling heap of overheated flesh.

Ventras tumbled to the ground. He jumped to his feet in an instant and flogged the body that had been, only moments before, a magnificent horse. When she failed to rise, he began kicking the hulk in the ribs and anywhere his uncontrolled temper directed his feet. The body lay still.

When Ventras, in his fit, realized the animal no longer breathed, he threw his fists to the sky and released a primeval, bloodcurdling cry.

Coming to his senses, he saw no other riders on horseback, but throughout the valley behind him, a startling sight befell his bloodshot eyes: the valley was littered with fallen horses, their riders standing beside their lifeless bodies.

# SIXTY

LIGHT began to fade as the setting sun dipped lower. Under the forest canopy, daylight was dimming rapidly. Zuzahna hoped that after darkness fell, a bright moon would allow her to continue into some of the night. The last few evenings had been black, with thick clouds obscuring the moon. She prayed silently that there would be a break in the clouds that night.

Then she remembered the torches. The wild ones had torches and she did not. They could move in darkness. Even if she could find the necessary pitch to make a torch, she would only give away her position by using artificial light. She pushed on. Her only hope was that the wild ones would stop for the night and that she could rest for a time as well.

Instead of worrying, Zuzahna picked up the pace and began running, still leading Paint. The mare had recovered, but Zuzahna feared that if she mounted again, the animal's stamina would quickly degrade. If she pushed too hard, Paint would be useless the next day, when it mattered most. Up till now, she had easily avoided the search, but now the wild ones knew roughly where she was; as soon as it was light, they would likely focus on this particular area. She worried that they would find the ridge trail and lay in ambush farther along it. For now, she had a good head start, and so she must keep going, without stopping to rest. There would be time later, when darkness came, to recover from the grueling afternoon.

Zuzahna had run for a few miles at a medium lope. Not being used to the kind of physical torment she had gone through that day, her legs were feeling like rubber. She stopped, untied a water bag, and dispensed a measured amount out to Paint and Smoke. She took a few swallows herself, tied the bag back on, and then mounted her mare. She set the horse into a light, even trot.

Tay had taught her the ancient Mongol four-step trot, which would allow a horse to outdistance another equal animal, and ride thirty percent farther in a day. She signaled Paint and fell into the stuttering step of the four point trot. She must conserve the horse's energy at all costs, she thought.

Remembering the vast equestrian herd the wild tribe owned, a feeling of dread crept over her. If the wild ones each had two mounts and traded when one was worn out, they could easily catch up to her. Ventras was evil but not stupid; surely he would figure that strategy and use it.

Zuzahna prepared mentally to finish the most grueling two days of her life. She figured with twenty-four more hours travel, she would be near Duhcat's cliff. If she could make it, she could lose the search party there. Duhcat had assured her that no one on this planet had the technical capability to find—let alone force their way into—his house. For all intents, it was an impenetrable fortress.

If only she could keep ahead and elude the searchers. If she could make it, she would be safe. She could easily monitor the movements of the wild ones from the rock pinnacle. Duhcat had shown her his collection of telescopes and looking glasses. From his hideaway, she would know when it would be safe to make the final thrust: the last leg of the journey to warn Tay and Estellene of the upcoming attack.

Darkness came, and Zuzahna's eyes tried to adjust. She slowed Paint first to a walk and then finally dismounted and led her horse again.

Zuzahna had heard no sounds from the long valley below. She wondered what was going on with the searchers. Had they stopped for the night? She hoped against hope that they would wait until morning before continuing on.

The ridge trail made a gentle, arcing sweep to the south from the westward direction in which she had been traveling. Walking along in near darkness, she came to a place along the ridge where storms had hammered the forest. There were many wind-fallen trees and clearings where she could see far into the distance.

In the distance were campfires—many campfires. Zuzahna could just make out the tree-lined river that meandered along the valley floor. Squinting, she tried to judge their distance and guess how many might be in the camp, but she gave up. They must be at least seven or eight miles behind her, she thought tiredly.

Zuzahna stopped and un-tacked Paint. She distributed more water, rationing the precious fluid and not spilling a drop. She then took a piece of cloth from her saddle bag and wiped the horse down, trying to dry the sweat from the worn-out mare before the chill of evening came.

After she finished, she broke out some venison jerky and gave Smoke the same amount as she kept for herself. It was the first they had eaten since morning, and her stomach growled in anticipation of the meager meal.

As she chewed the hard, salty meat, she watched the valley and prayed the wild ones would not continue in darkness.

Before long, she heard a distant rumbling. What could it be? she wondered. In the valley below, she saw a faint, glowing orange light.

The rumble increased in volume, and she saw that the orange light was a series of individually moving torch lights. The group was much larger than before. The sound was horsemen, many horsemen.

Ventras was concentrating his search with the entire party. She would have to evade them all.

Zuzahna watched, feeling helpless and alone. She wondered what would happen next.

Before long, the group of riders bearing torches merged with the camp along the river. No sound came. The still evening air dampened any noise from their camp.

Then, before Zuzahna's eyes, the orange glowing light once again moved, this time towards her. It was accompanied by the pounding of many galloping horses.

She looked around and saw nothing. Darkness had stolen her visual perception and she could not see the trail. She could only wait while her lead over them diminished with each passing minute.

"Please. Oh, please, let the moon show me my way. For all that is good, for all I am trying to do, for the good I have learned, please let me escape and warn Tay!"

Zuzahna wasn't sure to whom she was praying. She was speaking her innermost feelings aloud. Her voice came involuntarily, pleading with that fleeting thing we think upon as providence, karma, or for some of us, God's gracious will.

Zuzahna looked to the dark night sky, hoping for some light to shine through. In that moment, the clouds in one small area of the sky thinned, and a hint of moonlight lit the trail just enough so that she could re-saddle Paint and begin the weary journey once more.

She rode slowly while the rumble of her pursuers grew louder. They were closing the gap, she thought, picking up the pace a bit. The bright spot in the dark sky broke open, and in that instant a nearly full moon shone through, lighting the trail. To her eyes, which had adjusted to the darkness, it suddenly seemed as light as day.

Zuzahna spoke softly: "Okay, girl, let's show them what you can do."

Instead of galloping, she set Paint into the four-point trot again. They made quick progress down the trail. Moonlight left its handprint in the creeping shadows.

Zuzahna, ever wary, set her seat and held tightly with her legs. Owls called out into the night, making her start for a moment.

At one point, the slope dropped straight away and afforded a view through the broken canyon, giving her a glimpse the wild one's progress. They were gaining slowly, and she made a conscious choice to not look backward again. Instead, she dedicated herself to riding this patchwork of black and silver patterns with diligence, like an owl flying through trees, lit only by the moon.

Smoke easily kept up with their diminished pace. However, the gauntlet of night dragged them into weariness, and soon exhaustion overtook them all. *Rest,* Zuzahna thought. *We must rest and save some strength for the final length of the arduous trek.* The home stretch would begin at first light the next morning.

She reined Paint in, and the wonderful little horse blew loudly twice, as if to say, "Thank you, dear!"

Zuzahna distributed water once more and untacked Paint. She then rolled out her bedding and fell into exhausted sleep.

Smoke slept not at all. Instead, he listened as the wild ones came closer. He could hear the weary stride of the horses and knew it would not be long. Their legs were just as tired as his own. When the enemies' horses stopped coming, Smoke fell asleep, nestled alongside Zuzahna for warmth. She stirred as he lay down next to her and then did not move again.


A screech owl sounded, startling Smoke awake. He looked to the horizon and could see the faint grey of false dawn. He nudged Zuzahna to wake her, but she lay without responding. He licked her face. Zuzahna's eyes fluttered open. Smoke looked into them, thinking silently, *Go! We must go!*

Zuzahna rose. Every muscle in her body screamed for mercy. Forcing herself, she struggled with the saddle and painfully gained her seat.

Looking down-valley, she could see the red-yellow embers of the enemy's waning fires; they appeared to be still asleep. She signaled Paint into a quiet walk and they stole away, gaining some small distance before the wild ones' camp bustled awake.

The trail was hard to see. The moon had set, and all that afforded light was the early promise of a new day. As they continued, however, their visibility increased, and after a few kilometers she signaled Paint into the four-point trot.

Morning had brought an easterly wind with the rising sun. Zuzahna hoped it would mask her movement and carry the sound away from Ventras' camp in the east.

# SIXTY-ONE

Zuzahna had run Paint for days, and her beloved friend could carry her no further. She knew if she forced her horse too give more that the loyal beast would give her all, even if it meant her death.

Zuzahna untacked Paint, except for her bridle. She left everything else behind and walked on. They were near the river. Zuzahna could see it glistening between rare open breaks in the dense timber.

She led Paint downhill towards the meadow that meandered along this part of the river. She had been unable to give the horse grass or hay except for the time at Tay's camp, and up on the ridges they had been running there was little for a horse to eat. Paint had been subsisting on ferns and her ribs showed, protruding out in a manner that Zuzahna had not seen before.

As they neared the meadow, Paint nickered softly, scenting the fresh green grass.

"Yes, girl," Zuzahna said softly. "All you want and more." She took off the bridle and swept her left arm in a wide arc. "Go, girl! Go!"

Paint looked to her as if in thanks and then trotted tiredly towards the open sunlight. Zuzahna stayed in the tree-line as she made her way away from the friend who had carried her so faithfully. She wept as she walked away, believing that she would never see her beloved horse again.

Duhcat's fortress was not far, she thought. She could make it on foot if she was careful and stealthy, and if she could avoid Ventras and his men.

Tonight, she thought, she would be in the safety Duhcat had promised.

About an hour later, some of the searching wild tribe came upon the paint horse. The horse was still damp with sweat. They knew Zuzahna had to be near and focused the search, spreading out on the most likely routes she would have taken.

Some of the men were on horseback, but most were on foot, having run their horses into the ground. Three rode along the river. They knew their horses were spent, but they would push them to the end without a thought for the beasts; they only cared about the prize they sought.

Soon, the three caught a glimpse of movement in the tree-line. Their animals were too worn out to continue, so they left them and, in a frenzy, plunged forward on foot into the canopy of green.

# SIXTY-TWO

Smoke had seen the glazed wildness in the eyes of animals many times before. Animals who fought out of desperation and the will to survive, and who fought even though their eyes told the story of their defeat and their bodies trembled with fatigue. The look came when the last remaining adrenalin was gone, when they were left with no reserves to tap, when death's chill brutally forced its way into their startled, unbelieving brains.

Smoke saw the same look in Zuzahna's eyes now. He also saw her trembling limbs and the staggering steps she took, which foretold her future: unless he could intervene and protect her.

The wolf thought of Two Leg's pack and how they hunted. They possessed the long stick with teeth, and the flying stick with feathers: a weapon that carried death and flew faster than the hawk. Two Leg's pack could take a life quickly, and death could come from just one hunter, which was unlike the way the wolf had learned hunting as a young member of his pack.

Zuzahna had become the family of Smoke in the short time they had known one another. As any wild animal will, the wolf was compelled to protect family—even at the risk of his life. Much of this was instinct, yet within the primeval survival desire was a calculated cunning, a thought process that ended in only one choice: *I must protect her from Two Leg's pack!*

Smoke smelled blood from the many deep gashes and scratches Zuzahna had suffered on her unprotected skin. Branches and thorns had torn at her flesh as she fled.

He could hear the three of Two Leg's pack that were close behind. They were rapidly gaining. He could hear their rasping hungry breathing.

Smoke leapt in front of Zuzahna. Standing on his hind legs, he looked quickly into her eyes. *Go! Keep running!* he thought. He spun and swung his head forward, motioning silently for her to continue. Then, he was gone. Zuzahna, in her state of near collapse, understood his meaning. She had heard him speak into her mind, and she knew where he had gone.

The wolf slid silently through the trees, keeping to shadows until he had circled behind the pursuing men. He came from the back, leaping with jaws wide, catching the man's neck in his flying pass. He snapped down with bone-breaking force. One nano the wolf was there, the next he was nowhere to be seen. The devastating strike was only evidenced by the fallen man who writhed, screaming, upon the ground.

"What the devil?" one of the two remaining pursuers exclaimed in shock. Then another flash, and the man in front fell, with similar injuries.

The lone survivor was afraid. He possessed a spear and thought of attempting to fight the phantom that had stricken down the other two, but instead he turned and ran.

A few steps later, the wolf slashed him from behind, and he joined the other two, falling onto the forest floor, death sweeping over him as he bled into the soft, shaded earth.

Sweat ran into Zuzahna's eyes, blurring her vision. She had heard the distant anguished screams and knew the wolf had prevailed. She also knew she could not continue much farther. She had reached her limits.

Smoke appeared magically in front of her. The crimson of fresh blood stained the fur around his mouth.

Zuzahna stumbled towards Smoke and knelt by his side, grasping him in her arms and stroking him in gratitude.

Smoke started and jerked away from her grasp, his ears moving, searching the air for sounds she could not hear. He looked back to her, his eyes flashing the message: *More of Two Leg's hunters come! Many more come!*

Zuzahna's heartbeat spiked, and with it came a feeble shot of adrenalin from some unknown place deep within. In that instant, her hearing became hypersensitive and she heard water: *The rush of the river!*

Struggling to stand upon shaking legs, she grasped a nearby tree limb and pulled herself upright.

"I must make it to the river!" she said softly, thinking that if she could reach the water she could float downstream instead of running; she could let the river take her the rest of the way. It would work, she thought. They could not track her in the water!

Zuzahna made her way toward the rushing sound, which grew louder by the minute. Shortly, she also heard shouts and screams. The search party had obviously found the wolf's handiwork! She moved a little faster.

At last she reached the water's edge. Along the shore, in a small inlet caused by a bend in the river, she saw a piece of broken log floating in the water. Wading in, she grabbed onto the wood and kicked with her feet until she made it out into the swift flow of the river's center. Then she simply hung on to the log as the current swept her quickly downstream.

The water was cold, but to her exhausted, scratched, and battered body, the chill stole away the pain that had been riddling her. Instead of feeling like a hunted animal, as she had for many days, she felt as though she were gliding to her freedom.


Ventras came with his searchers to the place Smoke had killed the three men.

Murmurs and breathless gasps rose. They spoke in hushed tones of the wolf, and their questioning eyes searched Ventras' face for a reaction to the obvious: the wolf named Smoke, Ventras' companion and partner, had now become loyal to the Sorceress Zuzahna.

The omen was bad, all agreed.

Ventras shrugged nonchalantly, as if he didn't care, but within, he felt diminished. The wolf and the conquered cougar had been a mantle of strength for him. The tribe had accepted him as their shaman without questioning because of them, and he had worked that position into something more. He was the wild tribe's leader. There were others who coveted the position, and Ventras knew instinctively that this incident would give the competition a foundation upon which to build.

One of the trackers shouted, "She's headed towards the river!"

Ventras took charge. "Divide! Three parties! Scour the river! She's obviously trying to lose us in the water."

The men broke and moved off, talking among themselves in tones that masked their words. They divided the search and delegated areas to each group.

Zuzahna had been in the water over an hour when she heard the distant roar—a familiar, low-throated rumble that could only be the falls. *I'm almost there!* she thought. Her hands and feet were numb with cold and exhaustion. She let go of the driftwood and swam to shore. Her door to safety was just a little farther. *I must make it to the cave mouth without being caught,* she thought.

Crawling from the water, her body felt extraordinarily heavy. She could barely stand and hold her own weight.

The wolf showed himself. He had followed her down river. She had caught brief glimpses of him as she floated effortlessly along. His eyes had the electric look of danger, and Zuzahna knew at once she was not clear of the searchers.

Smoke swung his head away, looking in a direction that Zuzahna understood was the safest route. However, it was a path that would take her away from Duhcat's fortress. Of course, Smoke didn't know her intended destination.

She shook her head and pointed down-river, whispering, "This way. We must go this way, wolf."

The wolf looked disappointed, but he followed her faithfully.

A steep animal trail led down the canyon and around the falls. She had no choice. She must go; it was the quickest way.

Setting off down the trail, she soon heard voices calling out loudly over the roar of the falls.

"She couldn't have made it over these falls alive. If she heard them, she would have gotten out of the river above this cataract! We need to search up-river."

Quickly, Zuzahna jumped off the trail and found a fallen log to hide behind. She could hear the men talking as they passed her hiding spot. The wolf was nowhere to be seen.

After the men had been gone awhile, she stood up and made her way back to the trail. She then set off downhill. *I'm so close!* she thought. *So close.*

Zuzahna was unaware of any others. She felt home free. Instead of being careful, she walked rapidly, desiring the safety she knew was in reach. She hadn't much farther to go. The trail forked. The turn to freedom was before her! She was a few steps from the trail that led to the lower falls and cave mouth. *Almost there,* she thought.

At that moment, six men brandishing bows and arrows came around a bend farther down the main trail, about eighty meters away. All were startled and froze for an instant.

Zuzahna grabbed Smoke's neck by his mane and quickly pulled, saying, "Come! Run!"

The men strung arrows as they ran. Having seen the wolf's work earlier, they were taking no chances.

Zuzahna fled down the trail with the wolf trailing slightly behind.

Smoke heard the whistle of the arrows. He leapt upon Zuzahna from behind. She, too, heard several hissing projectiles fly by, and the sickening, grizzly thud of others hitting flesh.

The men paused.

Zuzahna got to her knees.

Her companion and protector, the wolf, lay on the ground, blood seeping into his silver-blonde coat. The falls roared in her ears.

The excited faces of the men behind her filled her with rage.

Zuzahna, sobbing in anguish, quickly caressed Smoke gently on his face. Between broken sobs, she said, "I'm sorry. I'm so sorry!" and then she began to run again.

She had risen from the pitiful wretch that nine days in flight had made her. She ran like the wind, and did not look back. With her last ounce of strength, she would try to reach her safe haven.

*I have to make the cave! I have to warn Tay!* she thought. She could only think of them. No longer did she have worth, not unless she could escape and expose the wild tribe's plan of attack.


The six men pursued Zuzahna at a run, jumping over the dying wolf who lay in the trail. They knew she was finished.

Smoke looked down the trail. He looked after the one he loved. In his eyes were tears not for himself, not for his pain, but for what would happen to her. He feared what

Two Leg's pack would do to Zuzahna now that he could no longer protect her.

Watching helplessly as the men pursued Zuzahna, Smoke saw a sparkling and bright light flash, making him blink involuntarily.

When he looked again, all that remained of the hunters were six pairs of smoking, smoldering moccasins.

# SIXTY-THREE

ZUZAHNA, staggering from complete and utter exhaustion, made it to the cave's mouth. She was astounded to see that the door covering the mouth was open. Taking the last few grueling steps, she collapsed well inside the semi-dark cavern that Duhcat had assured her was safe.

At once, the cave mouth became dark. The fortress door had closed. Duhcat's door, she thought.

Lying upon the cool floor of the cavern, she thought back over the past week of flight, remembering her two dedicated friends who had protected her, carried her, and ensured her safe delivery from the wrath of the wild tribe. Zuzahna sobbed. Her mind raced backwards, wishing something could be different, hoping she could somehow change the past. Despite the miniscule happiness she felt at having evaded Ventras' tribe, her heart was void of all joy.

She had lost her beloved horse in the flight, and the wolf had sacrificed himself to protect her. She had lost him as well. *Why?* Her mind screamed the question in agony. No answers came.

# SIXTY-FOUR

*I Am That I Am observed Zuzahna's tears of pain. She is made like the one called Duhcat. She has his metal. She suffers and continues on in anguish. These humans, what drives them?*

What passion could be so unprepossessing? What intense dedication to the World and the word that we gave away to the great beyond…so long ago that…none can remember. But the *word*…that unexplainable *emotion* that caused such suffering and anguish to our ancestors: that one mysterious word: *LOVE*.

I Am That I Am pondered.

No sensible unified thought emanated from what once was a chorus of melded minds.

Each broke from the bond and delved into long distant memories locked away in the vault of their intellects. They did so in order to understand that word, which drove humans to suffer tragically while protecting ones that are…

# SIXTY-FIVE

Zuzahna awoke, her limbs stiff. Every muscle ached. With the slightest movement, her body screamed in anguish. Her heart seemed to scream as well.

She was alone. In the wretched state of her disheveled and nearly broken physical body, each step taken up the staircase hurt. Her mental and physical suffering had taken its toll.

All she wished for was to collapse into bed and sleep. A thousand days of sleep, she thought, as she went to her knees in a four-limbed crawl because her legs alone would carry her no further.

At last she made it to the top landing, some four hundred steep steps from the cave. Crawling to a corner, she used her hands to grasp the stone walls and right herself. Taking trembling steps towards the door that was her safe haven, she noticed it was slightly ajar.

The key, worn these past two months around her neck for safe keeping, was not needed. She wondered, *Could it be him?*

She pushed on the massive door lightly with one finger, and it swung inward without a sound. The room was as she had left it, except for the tall sliding window leading out to the terraced gardens on the cliff's edge. The door was open. A cool and refreshing breeze ran through the opening, fluttering her matted and tangled hair.

*Could it be?* she thought, moving towards the opening and the sunlit gardens beyond. He was standing, his back to her, gazing over the precipice, appearing to be studying the falls.

Step by unbelieving step, she made her way, closer.

Constant warm updrafts from the cliff brought rolling mist from the falls. The mist clung to all the plants growing near the edge. It rested on Duhcat's dark hair. The sunlight reflected off of the tiny gleaming droplets upon his head and appeared to Zuzahna to create a halo.

She stood, unbelieving: shocked that he could be so callous. She questioned his motives and intent. She, in her exhausted and emotionally stricken state, became furious.

How could he stand there nonchalantly while she had been running for her very life? While she had lost her horse so dear? While her guardian and friend the wolf had sacrificed himself to protect her in her last exhausted dash to freedom? How could he not have helped her?

Zuzahna's mind ran a gauntlet of frenzied thought. In her exhaustion and shock, she struggled to understand.

He turned. His eyes made her step backwards, because she was not prepared to look into them.

Duhcat felt the many questions. He also saw the unhappiness on Zuzahna's face and in her body language. He saw that she was disgusted with him, because he was here, and she thought that he had not come to her rescue.

Duhcat smiled, brushing away the mental, seeking the emotional. He said, "Dear Zuzahna, you have made it home. Welcome."

She stepped backward again, as if in revulsion.

Duhcat went freely towards her, knowing her mind, wishing to give her comfort, needing her to comprehend that all that had transpired was for a purpose, for reasons she did not presently understand. Everything she had gone through was also of absolute necessity from his way of thinking.

He felt an imminent need to know if she was a survivor, and if she could learn to love others more than herself. In the past, Zuzahna had been undeniably wrapped up in selfishness and desires of personal gain, no matter the cost to others. She had manipulated men as if they were clay. She brought her own selfish desires into dark and moldy fruition. That very clay had inevitably sealed around her, trapping Zuzahna in her own creation.

He moved close and took her hands in his, saying, "I know it was very difficult. Everything you have just finished was absolutely necessary."

"You! You left Paint, the wolf, and you left me.... You left us! And you stand up here like some God, some all-powerful being who can cast his followers into the fray and be unemotionally concerned for the outcome! I lost two of my dearest friends out there! And you stand here with that enigmatic smile. A smile that says you know something: something I am not privileged enough to know!"

He attempted to console her, wanting to hold her, needing to tend her wounds as a father would an injured child.

"Damn you!" said Zuzahna, as he wrapped his arms around her and kissed her tangled hair. "Damn you!" she repeated, as his arms took some of the weight off her trembling legs. His presence made her mind reel backward in time, backward to a day so long ago she had almost forgotten: the day he had saved her life when she was a young girl.

It came flashing back to her, that distant past her conscious mind had forgotten but her subconscious mind knew, and within the tender hug, she felt once again that she was a young, homeless girl, living by her wits on the brutal streets of Nesdia—the memory opened like a picture book.

Now she realized in utter disbelief that she had risked a life, which all these years she had simply been borrowing. A life: a gift, given to her by the man who now held her without speaking, although she understood the unspoken message as clearly as if he had said the brutal words. In a nano, all became clear. Her trembling heart, her sobs, her rebellious mind, her exhausted body, all became still.

He said softly, simply, "I've never left you alone."

She looked. Her mind was unbelieving. She saw immense dark eyes. Eyes showing the pain she felt, eyes that drew her in. Eyes in which golden flecks swirled and which were, undeniably, her own.

"Come," he said. "I want to show you something."

"I can't walk another step."

"I know. I'll carry you."

Zuzahna gave way. Duhcat scooped her up and walked towards a wooden paneled wall.

The wall slid open, and a small closet presented itself. He stepped in with her in his arms, and pressed a button. Zuzahna felt an unmistakable rise in her stomach and heard the gentle hum and whisk of a high-speed elevator. The machine's whir slowed, and the fall was gently stopped. The door opened to a long hallway deep below the planet's surface.

Duhcat walked, carrying her, even though there were small, motor-powered vehicles standing nearby, unused. He walked, reveling in having her in his arms. Shortly they came to a door that held a small window. As it auto-opened, Duhcat walked through.

Two tables came into view. One was covered by a sheet in its entirety. Upon the other lay the wolf named Smoke.

Zuzahna looked at the friend she had resolved as lost. The wolf was breathing.

She asked, "Is he?"

"He is fine. His wounds have been repaired."

"Why the other table? Who ... or what ...?"

"Zuzahna, the wolf needed a donor. His heart had taken an arrow; it was beyond repair. Also, his liver."

Zuzahna gasped. "He will be all right?"

"Yes. He is recovering nicely."

Duhcat began walking again. Zuzahna, instead of feeling that he was a foreign and unmerciful force, relaxed and melted into his stride. It soothed her. "Where are we going now?"

"You'll see," was all he would say.

Not far down the corridor, another door slid open to a room that had obviously been cut from the same solid rock as everything here.

Paint stood inside.

She nickered, and Duhcat set Zuzahna down gently, on her feet.

Zuzahna stepped towards her lost friend. Stroking her beloved horse on both cheeks, she said playfully, "Has he been taking good care of you?"

As if she understood, the mare shook her head up and down, and Zuzahna burst out laughing, exhilarated despite her exhausted state; her two dear friends *lived*.

*Why?* she asked. She swayed as if to faint, and Duhcat swept her again from her feet. Duhcat looked towards Zuzahna. He paused, as if searching for words, words that could be readily understood but that would not come easily to him.

"Zuzahna, your trek ingrained primeval truths into your core. *You have learned!* And that was the issue at question: to *love others* or a cause more than yourself. You were given the daunting task of infiltrating the wild tribe's camp and learning all you could of their plans to attack the crescent cliffs where Tay and Estellene live. Then you had to escape with the information and survive to deliver what you learned.

"However, your job is not finished. You still need to trek three more days west. Then, you will give TayGor the intel you have gathered. Everything you have learned of the wild tribe's weapons, tactics, numbers, and plan of attack will be invaluable to Tay and Estellene. With the information you possess, Tay can conquer the invaders and stop them in their tracks. That is why I placed you at risk. To see what metal you were made from." Duhcat smiled disarmingly.

Zuzahna asked, "So I have passed your test?"

"Yes."

"You said someday you would tell me why, when I look into your eyes, I see only my own."

Duhcat looked to the floor and stammered words that were not words at all. Finally, gaining a semblance of composure, he said only, "To do that story justice, I must take you visually 3,450 years and seven days into the past. It is not a short tale. You need rest. When you wake tomorrow, ask me once again to share the unbelievable with you."

Zuzahna, feeling him squeeze her in his arms, felt safe and fell fast into a dreamless sleep.

## SIXTY-SIX

ZUZAHNA awakened. It took a moment before the reality of where she was sank in. She attempted to stretch her tight muscles, and they screamed in agony. She relaxed again, thinking back to the blur of the many days in flight, and to making it home, to Duhcat's fortress.

She then thought of him and their conversation.

The rooms were quiet. Outside she could hear birdsong muffled by the thick glass windows that faced the falls. She moved to sit up and failed in her first attempt. She steeled herself against the pain and tried again. This time she was successful and managed to swing her legs over the bed's side.

She noticed her feet first. They had been obviously doctored by Enricco. The blisters were bandaged as well as the cuts.

She stood on the pain-filled feet that had carried her the last few miles to safety, and she began to cry. There was no sadness. She cried tears of joy for having made it here, and for the fact that she could continue her trek to warn Tay and Estellene.

Walking painfully out of the bedroom, into which she could not remember being carried, she came to the big room with the tall, glass wall. The sky outside was a crystalline silver-blue. She called out, "Enricco?" There was only silence in response.

It was then that she saw the note. It was lying on a tall, wooden table by the door that led out to the terrace. As she walked to it, the glass panel slid open.

Zuzahna picked up the letter and walked out into the sunshine.

She read the letter slowly. The handwriting style was an ancient calligraphy she had seen only in archived documents from the distant past. The script was ornate, yet crisp.

*Dearest,*
*I am truly sorry. I couldn't wait for you to wake any longer. There are urgent matters that demand my attention. I must go. We will have our talk next time. Stay here until you are fit to travel. Take your horse. Leave the wolf. He has caretakers seeing to his every need. When you return, he will be yours again.*

*Thoughts of you, Enricco*

*P.S. It is Thursday 4 pm. At the time of writing, you have been sleeping for twenty-six hours. I did not wish to wake you.*

Zuzahna walked back through the open glass door and looked at the digital date keeper on the table. It was

Friday morning, 7AM. Was it possible that she had slept for over forty hours?

She went outside and through the terraced gardens, starting up the stairs to the pinnacle viewpoint and stopped on the first step. Her legs felt like they were tearing.

She shuffled back inside and ran a bath, as hot as she could stand. She found an ancient-looking cobalt blue jar full of mineral salt. She removed the matching glass lid and poured half the contents into the bath.

She then lowered herself into the steaming water and soaked until she was as red as a cooked lobster. Sitting on the edge of the deep tub, she left her feet in the water and allowed her body to cool off for a while, then she settled back into the steaming water.

After an hour of intermittent soaks and resting on the tub edge, she felt less stiff and began some simple stretches without pushing herself too hard.

When her stomach began to rumble, she went to the kitchen. Opening the cooler door, she saw that it was well stocked with just about everything she could possibly want. She pulled out a plate of fresh fruit and then went back out onto the terrace. She set the plate on the stone wall and ate while she looked out over the cascading whitewater.

He had saved her, for the second time, and he had also rescued Smoke and Paint. There was no other explanation. She had been ready to strangle him with her bare hands and may have tried, had she had any strength left.

Now he had disappeared! *How convenient*, she thought. He had promised to share an unbelievable story with her: a story that encompassed nearly four millennia... A tale she was forced to imagine...the story of why *her* eyes were *his!*

Zuzahna knew he was a mystery, and a man who controlled a vast network of technology, wealth, and information. His realm was unseen, yet power filled. She had spoken with him. He had held her in his arms; he had protected her, and had promised he would speak with her again. Zuzahna wondered why he had chosen to show such a focused interest in her.

Zuzahna walked back to the first of the several hundred steps that led to the viewpoint atop the rock pinnacle. She took the first step once more. Her muscles screamed in agony, but she continued to push the agony away, to place it in a compartment where it would hurt less. She made it as far as the fortieth step before collapsing. She vowed to try again tomorrow. As soon as she could conquer the stairwell, she decided, she would leave to warn Tay and Estellene.

# SIXTY-SEVEN

Taygor awakened to a dull throbbing sensation in his lips. His tongue was dry and hard. His chest was dripping sweat from the center between the cleavage of his breasts. He rubbed his eyes, wondering the time. The thin grey line along the horizon told him there was another hour or more before the first breath of morning light.

He lay still for a moment, attempting to hear into the night, to understand what had awakened him prematurely. *Something or someone had beckoned to him*, driving him from sleep. He could feel tension that was not normal. That tension was transferring a message—a message he could not decipher. He tried. The feeling became more acute.

Tay rose unwillingly from his bedroll and removed the cloth he had laid over the kindling the night before to keep evening's dew from saturating it. He lit the dry tinder, and the fire sparked and crackled cheerfully.

A screech owl spoke. The sound, which he would normally take in stride without alarm, startled him. Adrenalin surged, and with it, momentary flashes of blinding illumination: multiple frozen frames as if under a strobe light. In the frames, Zuzahna was running, a wild look in her eyes. He saw her staggering footsteps and heard the desperation in her rushing breath; her racing heartbeat pounded in his ears...

He whistled for Eclipse and began rolling his bedding, kicked the small fire apart, and dumped his camp bucket on it, dowsing it completely.

The fluid rhythm of Eclipse's approaching hoofbeats soothed Tay's querulous mind. He knew for some perplexing reason that the answer to his early-morning uneasiness lay upon the trail ahead: the trail that led towards the wild ones, and which he felt Zuzahna had taken some weeks before. The trail he and Eclipse hoped to soon pick up and follow.

He had found long strands of horse hair—tail hair—on certain branches and briars that swept the path he had ridden these past days. He had kept the tail hairs, which were of three colors and, when combined, convinced him that they were from Zuzahna's paint horse: the horse that had gone missing when Zuzahna disappeared. He knew for some unexplainable reason that she was near and that she needed him; he had been awakened by her need.

Eclipse sauntered gracefully towards him, appearing as if from nowhere, a shadow coming out of shadows. His beloved mount nickered nervously, without the normal relaxed exhale: sharing his uneasiness.

Within a minute, Tay had Eclipse saddled and his gear secured. The two beings, man and horse combined, broke into a fluid, adrenalin-filled gallop of muscle and mind.

## SIXTY-EIGHT

Zuzahna had been healing for three days before she finally made it up the staircase to the pinnacle of rock. She could see the smoke from campfires strung out along the river. *Ventras!* she thought.

She had promised herself that as soon as she could climb the stairs, she would leave to warn Tay. The truth was easily seen. Before her lay Ventras' net set to ensnare. She wanted to go, but native intelligence told her she needed to stay put. They would tire of the search soon, she was sure. She would watch, wait, and heal some more. Then, when the fires were gone, she would set out for Estellene's village.

Zuzahna went to visit Smoke and Paint, as she had been several times a day. After spending some time grooming her horse, she steeled herself and went to look in on the wolf.

He lay on a rolling table, his body covered with a blanket so that only his head was visible. The second table had been removed. Smoke's eyes were bright; he was obviously happy to see her, but his tail did not wag.

Lifting his coverlet out of curiosity, Zuzahna saw that Smoke's body was encapsulated in a kind of cocoon. But the envelope around him was nothing like anything she had ever seen. It shimmered and moved, pulsating as though it were alive. The colors reminded her of a glistening ocean. It looked like the cocoon was breathing, pulsing, massaging, and moving as if it were an organ.

She dropped the coverlet, pondering what she had seen.

"Hey boy! How you doing?" She stroked his head, and Smoke licked her hand affectionately. After a while, she said, "Thanks for what you did. You saved me from the arrows! Thanks, you are…so brave…so intelligent…and so beautiful. I'm honored to be your friend."

Smoke looked to her with the kind of admiration a young child has for a mother or father and then licked her hand tenderly. Then he drifted back into sleep.

Zuzahna walked out from visiting Smoke and into the corridor. She had never really noticed how vast it was. As she walked, she saw a large wooden door at the far end of the corridor. The door drew her forward by some magnetism she did not understand. Within the wood was a three-dimensional pattern of waves—translucent, deep, and mesmerizing.

Upon reaching the wooden door, she was compelled to reach out and stroke the wood lightly. She had expected her hand to ride the waves in the wood, travelling up and down on the crests and valleys, but the door was smooth as glass to the touch. Astounded, she pushed, and it opened easily.

Before her was a long room filled with shelves upon shelves of books under a very high ceiling. Some of the books were kept behind glass far up the walls, but even from where she stood she could tell they were ancient. She wandered around and found other glass enclosures housing items that appeared aboriginal in nature, including archaic tools and carvings, adornments, and what looked like crude and colorful clothing.

She walked the length of the room and was astounded by its immensity. Then, all at once, she realized the library—or perhaps it was a museum—was divided into categories of cultures. There was ancient Earth, Nesdia, Meantholia, Seven Galaxies, and many others.

Once Zuzahna realized the separation lines of different cultures, she also noticed that the highest shelves contained the works and histories of the most ancient, and, as the shelves descended, the subject matter became more modern. Finally, at eye level and below, were the recent histories and the studies of modern flora and fauna, religious doctrines, and many other subjects. The collection was astounding.

Upon closer scrutiny, she saw that in each categorically organized culture was a set of modern books all of the same design. She looked at the titles and was surprised to see they were all called *Emerging Sociopolitical-Religious Beliefs and Group Consciousness Core*. The author was Enricco Duhcat. Each of the series was a doctorial study on the different cultures.

Zuzahna wandered the library in a daze. When she approached the wall at the far end of the room, a panel auto-opened. Her curiosity drove her to slide through the small doorway.

She stopped and gasped. Before her, resting silently in the air, was a vast, shimmering ship of the same undulating blue-green color she had seen earlier around Smoke.

*I would like to see inside*, she thought, as she approached it. Suddenly she found herself inside the ship… standing in what appeared to be the bridge. Flabbergasted, she sat down in the well-worn pilot's seat and rested her hands on the arm console. The vid-screen came to life.

What played was a series of short vid-clips. They were all of a stunningly gorgeous woman with red-blonde hair and fair, freckled skin. The screen rolled to scenes of her playing in waterfalls and in the surf at pristine beaches, and gazing out a spaceship's window, gasping in awe at the wondrous celestial bodies that appeared to be right outside. The vid played for a while. When the woman spoke, Zuzahna detected the slightest hint of an archaic accent. Perhaps this woman had lived in the distant past, she thought.

Then the vid stopped. The last frozen frame was of Duhcat. He was holding the woman in his lap. Behind the two was the ship. Within the blue-green shimmering skin of the ship, she saw a subtly written word…a name she would never forget: *Intrepid*.

Duhcat's face, in the frozen frame, possessed a look not foreign to Zuzahna…it was the face she wore when looking at Tay as he held *her* tenderly in his arms.

*Who is this woman?* Zuzahna wondered. Then, feeling she had entered private memories that perhaps she wasn't meant to see, she thought, *I shouldn't be here in his ship.* At once, she found herself standing back in the hangar, looking at the beautiful craft and wondering what other mysteries it might hold.

*Unbelievable!* she thought, as she walked back to the elevator and rode it to the surface, pondering all she had witnessed.

# SIXTY-NINE

The end of her life: Zuzahna knew it did not matter. All that was important had nothing to do with her person. Only the message she carried had significance. *It does not matter!* she repeated to herself. *I would gladly sacrifice myself! I would gladly die helping Tay, Estellene, and the beautiful children to safety.*

In that state of mind, Zuzahna had set out for the settlement.

She was rested. She knew the trail. Paint was her old self.

The two of them ran as one being, hair flying in the wind; they ran with abandon. They ran from the wild ones, who were still searching.

Ventas had tricked her. He had obviously left hidden sentries scattered about the area. They had picked up her trail and were pursuing.

She prayed silently as her animal flew over the ground, hooves pounding. She prayed she could evade those behind, the ones who were responsible for threatening her new family.

# THE SEEDING SEVEN'S VISION

* * *

The four men on horseback pursued. They were gaining on the sorceress little by little. They knew they had a surprise for her ahead, and they pushed their horses hard, yet not *so* hard as to risk injury to them.

The surprise allowed them that convenience; it allowed each of them the confidence that they would indeed finally capture Zuzahna and bring her back to Ventras for her trial. She had proven her guilt by running. The trial was a formality. Then the games would begin.

Each man salivated, knowing she would soon be theirs intimately, if only briefly.

Each man thought back to all the times they had attempted tenderness with the woman, only to be summarily rejected, as though she were some puritan. None had been good enough for her. When they captured her, each man would have his turn with her, if he chose. Each of them thrilled at the thought, knowing she would be put to death, but not before their desires were satiated. Life in the wild tribe had simple rules: traitors lost all station, and she had betrayed the entire tribe.


The drumming, pounding, earth-rumbling, beating hooves rang in Zuzahna's ears. They echoed down the valley, becoming not just sound but substance: weighted matter, heaviness embodied in fear.

The morning was not cool. Paint's breath steamed plumes into the green landscape surrounding her. The horse instinctively knew she could not continue. She knew she would soon drop, broken by exhaustion, but still she ran, heart near the bursting point; she ran for love and because her mistress was afraid. She did not waste a step, never looking behind.

Zuzahna did not look back either. She prayed for a miracle, because she knew it to be her only salvation.

Within a straight stretch of the river trail, where the water threaded very close and where a rugged ridge of rock narrowed the valley into a tight little canyon, four other men on horseback suddenly appeared on the trail in front of her.

Zuzahna—not thinking, only reacting to the impediment before her—ran Paint towards an abrupt drop into the river below. She didn't know if she could clear the rock face, which sloped sharply to the water, but there was no time for thinking, only escape, or death.

Her pursuers reined up and stopped their mounts. Breathless disbelief waged a private war in each shocked mind. They watched Zuzahna and her horse swept downriver.

One of the men exclaimed, "She can't stay in the water long; it's cold as ice! All we have to do is follow her! Let's go!"

Brutally kicking the sides of their mounts, they broke into a run.

Tay heard the shouts and wondered who could be this far from camp. *Could it be the wild tribe?* he thought. Then he heard the pounding hooves and knew what was afoot. He could not tell how many riders there were, only that he was severely outnumbered. Old Sifu's words came to him—a childhood lesson from the past not forgotten.

Sifu's voice sounded in his head: *There are no rules when dealing with the ruthless and immoral. The only rule to live by is to be the one left living.*

Tay nudged Eclipse off the trail, into a dark space between several massive cedars that grew close by the river's edge. It was then that he saw her: eyes wide with fear, her hair in tangles. She swept by him, captured by the river's force, not noticing her guardian, her protector, astride his horse in the shadows.

Tay drew his sword and waited.


The sword came down in a circle, taking first one head clean off at the neck. The second neck was slashed as the arc continued, not slowed by the gruesome cleaving. The sword-tip sliced half through the second rider's neck. It continued in another semi-circle before flashing, its edges upright, and beginning a lightning arc driven by a powerful snap of the wrist into the azure sky. A vertical thrust changed the weapon's trajectory and then, with another flick of the wrist, it descended downward, effortlessly, its momentum and inertia cast upon the astonished onlooker's forehead while he was turning backwards in the saddle to discover the source of the chilling sounds he had heard from behind.

Three horses bolted, blood spurting from the twitching bodies of their previous masters—bodies that would be relegated shortly to the ground. Now the frightened horses were in control, and they raced past the five riders who were cantering in front. The front-riders reined in and turned in their saddles, trying to comprehend what had just happened. There seemed to be nothing but silence as they stared, for a frozen moment, at the visually startling scene. No man heard a sound except the pounding of his own heart in his ears. All saw the force that had turned upon them.

Tay and Eclipse bolted towards the five remaining adversaries, letting out a guttural, primeval roar. He rode into the fray of the five startled men, who moments before had closed upon Zuzahna, gloating. For a fleeting moment, the world to them stood still as they watched their destiny unfolding—destiny they had called upon themselves.

Tay's eyes knew. He knew. They were gone: seconds more, a few more sweeping flicks of the wrist, and Zuzahna would be safe.

Tay rode through the rabble, slaying, not looking down, thinking only of Zuzahna. One managed to unleash a wooden spear. It was deflected in a parried thrust, and the man, eyes bugging in pain and disbelief, fell.

Another of the four remaining strung an arrow and met with his ancient tomahawk. The hurtling weapon first smashed through the bow and then stuck deep into the rider's throat. No sound came from the man except the creak of his saddle as he slipped from it and the soft thud as the trail met with his body.

Three of the original eight remained.

Tay stopped Eclipse and pulled a miniature over-and-under crossbow from a leather holster attached to his saddle. He loosed an arrow, and it sailed into a man's forehead. Flipping the weapon, he cast another arrow as the remaining two turned to flee. It struck the temple of one, and then only one man remained. The man whipped his mount savagely and broke into a full gallop.

Tay let loose some rein, and Eclipse snorted and charged. The horse's competitive spirit, determination, and superior physical form quickly closed the gap.

Eclipse leapt from behind, striking the other horse's hind quarters with his front hooves. The horse reared and screamed. The rider fell, and his mount raced away without waiting for the fallen man to rise.

Tay brought Eclipse beside the man and stopped. Stringing another arrow and drawing the crossbow tight, he let the arrow loose, just as the wretched excuse for a human being began to plead and grovel. They had to die, and they had to die by his hand. He had not understood that before this instant, but it struck him now, the lesson taught in his childhood: *to be the one left living*. That was all that mattered.

Once clear of the bodies, he nudged Eclipse into a gallop and searched the river's blue-green current for Zuzahna. The river swept around a gravel bar that extended far out into the water. He saw Zuzahna, floating and clinging to her horse, just upstream from the river's bend.

Tay rode out onto the bar and into the water.

She saw him, and the fear left her eyes. It was replaced by admiration and love.

# SEVENTY

After dismounting, Tay walked into the river to meet Zuzahna. She smiled wide as he reached for her. Their hands and arms locked, and he pulled her up and out of the water.

"Tay, my darling, my savior, how is it you found me? I was praying for a miracle, I had no idea it would be you!" Zuzahna stood on her toes and gave her man a quick, tender kiss. Her wet hair dripped down the front of his clothes. Tay pulled her in tight, pressing her close. Zuzahna pulled away to grasp Paint's reins as the horse stepped near.

Zuzahna, caught in the moment, had almost forgotten. "Tay! The men! Ventras' men, they are riding...chasing me. They'll be here any moment!"

He said, without emotion, "They ride no more. I woke from a dream...you were fleeing some force. Fear showed in your eyes. It was barely first light when the dream woke me. I jumped up and started riding. I don't really know how I found you...perhaps it was because our lives have been intertwined, and connected deeply, intimately for so many years. My desire was unbelievably strong."

"What desire, Tay? To find me…or was there something…something more?" she asked. "Do you not still feel it? Your desire? You spoke in past tense." Zuzahna waited for his response.

Tay stammered, "I wished desperately to find you. I felt some kind of trouble would befall you if I was not by your side. I must admit, when I saw you float by my ambush point, I yearned for something more."

She shivered involuntarily, and she slid up near him once again, for warmth. "I'm so cold. The water chilled me to the bone. Do you have some dry clothes you could lend me?"

"Of course, me being so thoughtless, I…let's get a fire going and get you dried off."

They walked towards high ground as the two horses nuzzled and nipped each other affectionately. Zuzahna quipped, "She has missed the big dark brute."

"As *he* has missed her," Tay answered.

The man and woman looked into each other's eyes, saying no more. For the two of them, words were unnecessary.

Tay kindled a fire as Zuzahna stripped off her wet clothes, preparing to don the dry. He watched her body and movements, so familiar to him. She glanced back to him, smiling, knowing, and relishing his hungry look. He wore an expression she had seen a thousand times. His eyes spoke the truth. They painted a visual of the place she still held in his heart.

Tay un-stowed his bedroll and clothes, saying, "I have some extra jeans and a shirt you can put on until we get your stuff dried out."

"Would you mind just allowing me to use your bedroll? I promise I won't get it wet. I could towel off with your shirt. Then would you climb in with me? I need your warmth...I'm so, so cold."

Her eyes possessed a smoldering intensity. Tay felt powerless when she looked at him in that way. He felt he would do nearly anything she asked.

He dried her off with a clean shirt, and Zuzahna moved against him with each stroke of the cloth. If she were a cat, she would be purring, he thought.

Once dry, they climbed beneath the covers together. She was cold to the touch. She moaned softly as she pressed her mouth to his ear, saying, "Tay, you are always so like a furnace, so warm, so good...so nice. Thank you."

They woke as the birds began to sing of first light.

She clung to him, saying, "Oh, don't tell me we have to rise. I could spend a thousand hours in your arms and not tire in the least. I have longed to feel your embrace for...too long. I don't want to give it up...not just yet."

Soon the sun rose above the trees and shone in their eyes. "We must get moving. We have to go to River's Bend and convince the others to come with us," Tay said. "We must all move to the crescent cliffs...to Estellene's village. We must ready ourselves for the wild ones."

"Yes, Tay. I have much to tell you. I have just come from their camp. I lived among them, gathering information about their actual strength, tactics, and weapons. They mean to attack soon—and very soon."

"You've been among them?!"

"Yes, Tay. I was gathering information. Intelligence to bring to you. They have been trying to capture me so I couldn't warn you. They would have stopped me. They tried to kill me already...before you came. I just barely got away. The second time, I thought I was finished, but... you saved me. I had nearly given up all hope."

"Love, I would fight day and night, without rest. I would bleed to the last, seeing to your safety. If you truly know me, you at least know that much," Tay said, his eyes burning into hers.

Zuzahna shivered, feeling the impact of his message.

# SEVENTY-ONE

DENALI'S first day in Tay and Estellene's village was spent freely walking among the fields, meeting the children, swimming in the river, and enjoying each breath unhindered by oppression. She had felt at first as though an immense stone rested upon her chest. Each breath took effort. Every new person or animal was surreal and dreamlike. However, as the day moved toward evening, the weight slowly lifted, and with it the sense that all wonder before her could evaporate and disappear in an instant.

It was like her mind could not grasp that she was actually a part of this wonderful and heartfelt experience. She had difficulty shaking off the feeling that somehow she was only temporally visiting. That all too soon, some never-ending quagmire of gloom or duty bringing inevitable despair would call her from this wonder of lands, and this loving family of people and animals. She wondered how—after every black thing in her past was known—this very large and wonderfully loving family accepted her.

Denali walked along, reflecting. Her mind ran ahead; her was heart unsure. Her feet tested the new ground lightly, unbelieving at first, thinking, *This could all be just a dream.*

Towards evening, she laid the feeling to rest and cast away its loathsome company. She negated it, relegating it to the dark corners of her previous life. In this new life, she promised herself, she would prosper once and for all. She would become whole and bloom into a *real* person who possessed all the normal emotions instead of consuming bitterness. She swore silently that she would change. Denali longed to return to what she had been as a child, before darkness had claimed her.

That cold, heartless, lethal bitch into which her malleable youth had been extruded could *not* have a place here. She had been molded into a machine that created death. Her previous profession had stolen her from herself. It had stolen what she, in secret moments, sobbing beneath the covers, wished she could return to, to what she had been in youth. She had once had a talent for poetry and phrase, and a grasp of nature's voice, and these things had once brought happiness—happiness long since devoid within her deepest self.

Denali had been walking the river trail alone, pondering her revelations. She was enjoying, as never before in her adult life, sunset's colorful play upon the water as it rushed toward the ocean a few miles to the west. The trail came near a sweeping bend. Thousands of dancing violet, crimson jewels flitted about the water's surface, reflecting early evening light.

It was then, while enjoying the beauty nature so casually offered, that she saw the girl. The child was dressed very simply in a long, cream-colored dress with small dark-red roses embroidered along the hem. Her hair was dark and full of half-pipe waves that reached a bit below the shoulders. Denali's heart caught and then began to race.

She stopped, frozen in place. Her adrenalin spiked as some mysterious subconscious hope within pervaded her normally ice-cool persona. For a fleeting moment, she hoped for the impossible, her loss spurring on her imagination, a trick of a mourning consciousness longing for a dear one lost forever.

For a brief moment, Denali's heart ran backwards to childhood, and to the memory of a dearly beloved and lost friend who was still so painfully and deeply intertwined with her heart.

She gasped for air. For a moment, the apparition of the young girl, whose face was still turned to the river, appeared to be *Issy*. The memory of her one, her only, true love, and her death, flooded back painfully.

Denali thought back to her childhood, to the joy she had felt before reality had stolen her young life and turned it towards shadows.

She had become *death* strolling casually along, cloaked in the form of a stealthy and gorgeous woman—a woman whose path for many years past, was littered with evil bodies: those taken in, caressed, by her cunning wiles.

In the end, they all were dead, each and every one. The ones Duhcat had chosen.

They had wronged the people of Seven Galaxies. Denali thought, *I was the gatekeeper: the worst nightmare of those who did not follow Duhcat's rules.*

Denali often wondered who could possibly live with the secrets contained in the recesses of her clouded and disheveled mind. She wondered where she was to find peace from the nightmares of her past.

The young girl near the river turned towards Denali and said, "I've been waiting for you for so long. Now you are finally here, Denali!"

Denali's legs gave way. She collapsed to her knees, thinking, *The face! The voice.* In a desperate attempt to hold onto fleeting sanity, she asked, "How do you know my name? Did someone in the village tell it to you?"

The dark-eyed child moved cautiously, slowly, obviously taking in the pain and disbelief in Denali's eyes. Looking at her, she said, "I have known your name since my first day at Holy Names Orphanage. You remember. You befriended me when all the others shunned me and made fun of my appearance. But you were always different from the others."

"Stop this! Do not play with me! Forget your sick little game! Do not ruin such a beautiful and glorious day with absurdities! *Speak truth!* I demand it! *Who* told you my name?!"

Issy approached, half-step by half-step, soothing the stricken Denali with her words, offering them in kindness for the suffering friend before her.

Denali diverted her eyes and looked upon the ground, and then glanced up again as the footfalls came closer. She fell backwards in a weakness that was unfamiliar to her. She succumbed to paralysis, lying with her knees bent, her calves and ham strings numb.

She averted her eyes from the approaching girl again: the girl who appeared, unbelievably, to be *Issabell incarnate*.

"Denali, I was there that night."

"What night do you speak of, wretched haunting child?"

"The night Miranda killed me."

"What could you *possibly* know of that night so long ago? The night that stole my soul, the night that altered me and changed me into the monster I've become? What could you possibly know? You weren't even born until many years after that gut-wrenching, that heart-shredding, that soul-rending, that despicable sewage-filled evening! What could you, you black-haired little girl, possibly know?"

"I heard you come up the stairs. The night was black as a Raven's wing. There was no moon."

*"Up what stairs?"* Denali asked, in utter disbelief.

"The stairs to the rooftop."

"What rooftop?"

"The rooftop of the orphanage where you and I became friends. The rooftop Miranda cast me from."

"Child! Do not! Do not continue! *I swear! Do not!*"

Denali laid her face upon the ground. Memories flooded back: the distress, the loss, a beautiful and dear friend's untimely death. The only thing she had ever felt love for had been brutally stolen, ripped away, leaving a deep, sucking, black abyss into which Denali had been helplessly drawn, and into which her aching heart had plunged, free falling, spiraling out of control, downward, away from all that was kind and beautiful, away from all that was peace and harmony.

"You wish me to believe you are my dear and beloved...my innocent Issy? You think I could be deceived by your misdirected and sickly dark ruse?"

Not waiting for an answer, Denali screamed, *"Leave me alone!* Leave me! I swear you must leave me! Leave... me...be!"

Unsure, Issy stepped back. She had thought this reunion would be a simple affair: a look that would bring remembrance, and that they would hug and all would be well. The simplicity of a child had directed her approach, and she had failed miserably. Denali, her dear and beloved Denali, was summarily rejecting her.

Issy thought for a moment, her silence punctuated only by Denali's tortured sobs. The river sliding darkly over unseen obstacles, murmured soothingly.

"You came up to the roof. You threw the stolen key Miranda had used to unlock the door. You *saw* me! You called my name. I was by the big oak tree at the far end of the roof. You ran towards me, but I couldn't stay. I wanted to so badly, but I was forced to go! I wanted to feel you hold me once more before I had to leave, but I had no power to stay. When you rushed towards me, I was suddenly whisked upward and towards a brilliant light: a warmth, a special place that exuded love. I was in tears, my soul cast into sadness for being torn away.

"Don't you see? It *is* me, Denali! They don't call me Issy here, but you can. I want you always to call me by that name. Would you? I have dreamed to hear your voice utter it the way you did that day in the park. I have always loved the music of your voice, especially when it speaks the pet name you gave me."

Denali shuddered. Something rose from her tragic, shivering hulk, leaving the previously aghast and distrustful frame that had clouded her understanding. It rose as if it were a thin, trailing vapor. In an instant it evaporated, leaving behind hope—hope that the words this haunting apparition of a small girl spoke contained shreds of truth.

"What day in the park?" asked Denali, trying to understand.

"The hot August day you beat all of us in the footrace! The day we laid next to one another, sweating upon the grass, after Miranda and her crew left us alone. It was then that you took me flying. You took me with you. You were the wondrous swallow, and I was in miniature and *flew* with you. I sat straddling your blue-green back. We flew high into the mountains where the frigid snows bit at your wings, and then we coasted; your wings were tired. We coasted, gliding to the sea. The surf crashed and shot high into the sky, dashing the bluffs, and the great marlin rose from the depths, leaping, his sparkling jeweled body momentarily in flight. You *must* remember that day, Denali! *You must!*"

"I remember! How could I ever forget a day so brilliant in its youth and so *black* as it aged into nightfall? But how? How can it be true? You here as you were, a small girl, and me a grown woman, weathered by countless dark days and years on end with no one but myself? My best friend has been the solitude of loneliness. Since that day so long ago, the day my dear *Issy* was *murdered*, no one has entered my heart. I changed that day. Something broke inside of me. My poetry, my love of the flowing phrase, my admiration of nature's unending beauty and the inspiration to write of such phenomena left me as though it had all been locked away forever in an unbreakable vault, for which I no longer possessed the key."

"You spoke my pet name! The one you gave me so long ago. The name my *soul* has craved to hear your voice speak just once more! Thank you, Denali. When I was born on the ship coming here to the Virgin, Andarean and Estellene gave me the name Ellissy.

"From my earliest memories…flashes came of the friendship you and I shared as young girls. All that I just told you came from memories that I have not experienced since being born…they must come from somewhere deep inside my soul…from the past, from the bond we swore to each other."

Denali knew the bond spoken of by the young, dark-haired girl. She dared not believe it could be true.

Issabell fell silent for a time as Denali's mind reeled. Impatient, she looked deeply into Denali's eyes and began talking softly once more. "We call this planet the Virgin. I think it a very beautiful and special place," she said.

Her voice was the same, thought Denali. The inflection, the sweet sing-song melody she remembered, and the wistfulness that sometimes draped her words.

"I believe the Virgin births immaculate new beginnings," Issy continued. "Fresh starts for those who wish for another chance and for those who have unfinished business with loved ones they have left too soon. Perhaps many of us are here to rekindle, to heal, and to regain the happiness we lost upon our untimely departure from a previous life. Do you think that it's possible, Denali? For us to rekindle? To begin anew the friendship and love we lost so long ago?"

Issabell reached towards Denali's trembling left hand. Her pinky finger laced with Denali's and completed the intricate ballet of their much-practiced secret handshake. The pinky shake was one they had designed and kept secret from all others as young girls. It had been the promise...a bonding. It was the belief they each held as children...that they would experience "friendship forever."

With that simple yet heartfelt gesture, Denali's racing mind and heart settled. She looked at the little girl, with the waving black hair and dark eyes, the girl who claimed to be the love she had lost as a young girl.

Denali had attempted countless times to stow the memories of Issy away. She had tried unsuccessfully to bury the pain and suffering of her loss.

Issabell asked again, "Do you think we could? Could we find the friendship once again? The friendship that was so dear to us both, so long ago?"

Denali looked back to Issy and away from the river, pulling herself mentally out of the haunting memories of her past with strained effort. Tears would have begun flowing from Denali's eyes then, had she still been able to cry.

She said simply, "I would like to very much, *Issy*."

The little girl, dark eyes searching Denali's face, wept.

# SEVENTY-TWO

DENALI woke with a start as morning's sunrise filtered through the trees outside her window. She had just experienced a dream so poignant that if she hadn't just been asleep, she would have thought, for sure, that it was real. The mist outside was evaporating, rising ethereally. She rubbed her face, reflecting on the cruel absurdities the subconscious mind can play on the conscious.

It was then that she heard the sound.

Denali had spent little time in her cabin since being invited to live in Estellene and Tay's village. She adapted to her surroundings quickly. This sound was new—it sounded like a young child breathing.

Denali sat bolt upright. Adrenalin surged.

Next to her lay a young girl with a mop of black hair sprawled in half-curls upon the pillow.

*Issy? It can't be!* Yet here was her friend, lost so many years ago, now sleeping next to her. *How?* her mind screamed. *How could it be possible? The Virgin? New beginnings?* Her rational mind fought against the impossibility. She had longed to see Issy again yet knew such a fantasy could never come true...but here Issy was next to her in bed.

Memories of the evening before flooded back.

The two of them had talked incessantly through the night, both laughing and emotionally re-living their childhood, until Denali had accepted the totally unbelievable as truth. Issy *was* here! For some magically unexplainable reason, it was true.

Perhaps, Denali thought, the explanation was simply that Issy's soul, broken from their severed friendship, had magnetized to her own.


I Am That I Am watched the little girl sleep. The reunion was revered.


Denali was wide-eyed in joyous disbelief.


I Am That I Am felt all. Sentient emotions surfaced in the concert of minds that had for millenniums not experienced the most awakening of all human emotions: bliss.


Denali now experienced just that.
Denali swam in bliss.


Denali rose, hoping not to waken the child. She dressed quickly, not washing her face, only taking some water in her mouth to rinse away morning's breath.

## THE SEEDING SEVEN'S VISION

She then walked quickly towards Alex's cabin. She knew where he lived. She had seen him there at times, watching her as she passed by. He would be still in bed, she was sure.

Denali thought of knocking on his door and waking him. She reveled in the thought of slipping in beside him without a sound and lying next to him while he slept, waiting for him to wake naturally. There were so many possible wonders to explore now that the missing part of herself had been re-born upon Issy's return.

She stole silently up the two porch steps and lifted the catch carefully, without a sound. Swinging the door open slowly, she was surprised to see that Alex was not in his bed. The bed had been made.

She called his name softly and stood in the following silence. *Not here*, she thought, and then stepped back outside and closed the door again. She wondered where he could be. Surely in the village, or near. *Where?* A thought occurred to Denali that startled her. *Could he be with another woman?*

She walked towards the river, her mind racing. It couldn't be, she thought. Or could it? She had rebuffed each of Alex's advances for all the years she had known him. Surely no man would continue to retain even a shred of hope after her brutality. She had been unmoved, indifferent to the point of carelessness for his feelings or for how she might have hurt him.

The sun's early light fell through trees that draped the river's edge and leaned over the rustling water, stretching for the blue sky above. The dark trunks of trees and outstretched limbs were illuminated in places by the flickering patches of light that broke through the forest canopy and reflected off the water in spaces cherished by Denali. Birdsong clung to the air she breathed. The river's surface sparkled: moving colors of morning's light. Wisps of mist scurried from the fresh heat of the new day's light, disappearing as she walked, pondering her uncertainty.

Denali could see no one along the river and took the trail to the favored swimming hole, intending to dive into the deep, blue pool of bracing water and bathe quickly. Fall had turned the water cooler, and she prepared herself mentally for the plunge.

As she walked, she heard the splashing sounds of someone swimming, but no voices. Then she saw his glasses lying upon a rock with a towel.

Ducking behind a large granite boulder, she peeked, careful not be seen over the rock.

Alex was swimming across the deep hole, his back to her. Denali quickly ran upriver and slipped quietly into the water. Her intent was to drift unseen towards him, like a marine predator, eyes barely out of the water, forehead covered in wet, clinging hair.

She noticed he had turned and was stroking back across the river, oblivious to her presence. He was consumed by the exercise, turning his mouth to the sky only to breathe at regular intervals.

*He'll never even see me,* she thought.

She stroked downstream, nearer to Alex. When she was thirty meters upstream from him, she expertly calculated his speed and hers and then slid beneath the silver surface, swimming underwater.

When she saw him approaching, she went deeper towards the bottom, and as he swam over her, she reached up and grabbed his ankles for a brief moment, playfully.

Alex stiffened in her grasp as if he were expecting an unknown monster of the river to devour him.

*I plan to,* she thought. She let go and surfaced, smiling as she had done only rarely before.

Alex gasped. "Denali, you scared the hell out of me! I didn't even see you!"

"That was the plan, silly. Were you *truly* frightened?"

Alex noticed the language of her eyes. It had changed, and the change puzzled him. He could see her obvious humor at surprising him so thoroughly, yet beneath the joke was something he had not seen before.

Alex shivered. "Absolutely! What were you thinking? You could have caused me to have a heart attack!"

Denali noticed that his tone was sharp. He was stating the facts without tenderness or sentiment. She had weeded that garden, she thought. She had pulled out all the tenderness he had spoken in the past and laid it out into a place where, un-watered, it had withered and died.

She said simply, "I felt a need to test your heart, to see how strong it is before ..." Her voice trailed off wistfully.

"Before what?"

She ignored his question and changed the subject. "I found something last night."

"What did you find?" Alex asked.

Denali's face was wet from the river, but her eyes appeared to redden.

Alex was sure he could see the hint of a tear in those eyes, which were normally steeled from such a human emotion.

She did not answer immediately, just looked back to him, and into his eyes.

Then, in that moment, Alex was sure there were tears running down her flushed cheeks, melding with the river's current.

"What is it, Denali? What did you find last night?"

"I found a piece of myself, a facet that had been taken from me as a child. I was left with a wound so deep, so horrible. The memory has haunted me constantly. That void, and its blackness, stood between us. Remember, I swore I would never subject you to my darkness, and I warned you that I could never be good for you, that I would only cause you suffering and grief."

"Denali, you are speaking in riddles. Speak simply, please. What are you saying? What do you mean?"

She slid through the water, closing the distance that remained between them.

She came to him unlike any time before, without hesitation. She came upon him, smiling. *Enchanting.* He had learned to harden his heart against this woman and to distance himself from the feelings he held for her. He had kept them beneath the surface for so long.

Now, with her gaze, she melted his heart and exposed the feelings he had intentionally buried to save himself from the pain and suffering she had caused him through her refusals.

Denali slid through the water, a barracuda, a serpent, a lethal apparition that had frightened him before.

He saw the look in her eyes. Her eyes—those striking, blue-green eyes—were inches from his and coming closer. In them he saw softness and love. They closed as Denali's lips pressed softly against his.

\* \* \*

Denali lay wide-eyed in awe. Feelings that had been absent from her for nearly as long as she could remember came rushing over her: a tsunami of wondrous emotions sweeping her away into a place she had only dreamed of during the dark years of her life.

Happiness.

Alex stirred beside her and awoke.

"Alex," she said, in a tender voice, "will you walk with me? There is someone very special that I want you to meet."

He rubbed the sleep from his eyes and looked at her in adoration. "Sure," he said simply. He kissed her lightly on the cheek, rose from the bed, and began dressing. Denali dressed, too.

Soon they were walking down the path toward her cabin. The morning was still young, and the air was fresh and inviting. Denali sighed deeply, letting out with the breath a host of negative emotions from her past. With the next incoming breath, she embraced the future, and all the possible wonders before her.

"Alex?"

"Yes, gorgeous?"

"Thanks."

"For what, love?"

"For your patience, and your understanding. For giving me the space I needed and the friendship I didn't deserve."

"Slow down here, sweetheart, you deserve so much more than I've given you this morning!" He stopped walking and pulled her in tight. "Can I give you some more this afternoon?"

She answered him with a smoldering smile, a smile that said *yes!* He had fallen for her, in her darkness. Now, as a brilliant light began to blossom within her, he loved her even more.

They began walking again and soon arrived at Denali's little cabin.

"Come, I think she'll still be sleeping," Denali said.

They walked in, and Denali moved quietly to the bed and sat on the edge. A small, dark-haired girl was asleep in the bed.

Denali stroked the dark hair and said softly, "Issy...I want you to meet a very dear friend."

Issy stirred, and then her eyes shot wide open as if she had been shocked with electricity. "OH! Denali!" she said. "You *are* here! I was dreaming it was all a dream!"

Alex was puzzled by the tears he saw forming in the little girl's eyes. She began to sob, and Denali held her as a mother would hold an injured child, stroking her hair and saying softly, "There, there, I'm here. I'll always be here for you, my darling, *my Issy*."

Issy looked up to Denali, and the big sad eyes in the girl's small face brightened as she smiled. "You used my pet name. Will you always? I love the sound of your voice speaking it."

"Yes. Yes. I will. Always. I brought a dear friend to meet you. His name is Alex, and I have the strongest feeling that the three of us are going to be the best of friends."

"Hi, Alex," Issy said musically. A beautiful, strong smile spread across her face.

# SEVENTY-THREE

Tay had pondered the possibilities a thousand times and more. From the moment the wild tribes were dropped, he knew they would eventually foment trouble. However, he was surprised that the time here on the Virgin had passed so quickly and that the Northern tribe had migrated so far south so soon. Now that the threat was living and breathing so near, preparations would have to be made quickly. Tay had been training Estellene's people ever since coming to live with them. He had regularly drilled them on rudimentary horsemanship as applied to the battlefield, the arts of archery, the long staff, and the sword as well.

From his first days on planet, he had scouted the lay of the land for miles in every direction, familiarizing himself and drawing detailed maps that could be referenced by others less familiar with the surrounding terrain. As a student of military strategy, one stood in his mind—The Art of War: philosophy of Sun Tzu and the I Ching melded together. He understood well the importance of choosing a strategic area within which to stand, hold, and fight.

The cliffs and village were an excellently defensible site. Obviously, Leandra and the Fifteen had considered the possibilities and had chosen well. He found it hard to believe it had happened by accident. Saltwater sounds and bays surrounded the settlement on three sides. On the other side, mountains that were difficult to traverse at best made a fairly impenetrable wall on the fourth side. A pass cut through by the river running along their settlement was the only viable avenue for an army to approach.

Tay suspected Ventras would use cavalry in the attack. His observations and Zuzahna's intelligence gathering had taught them that the wild ones were training in horsemanship; at this point in time, Tay ruled out a seaboard assault.

The area that would afford entry to the northern tribe had very strong defensible positions. The river ran deep and swift through a narrow pass, with cliffs and steep slopes that made a sweeping bend. The level ground within this confined area was narrow and afforded sheltered ambush points.

The best advantage Ventras would hope for would be surprise. Also, if his army could make it through the cut and into open ground, they would have a sizeable numerical advantage. Tay resolved that he would not be surprised and that they would meet, lure, and decimate the enemy within the chosen ground. To accomplish this, they had to be prepared. They would show a weak presence to lure the overconfident enemy into their trap.

All the criteria on the surface may have seemed complicated to one less schooled, yet it was only a series of logical steps. Ventras' army was not trained in command hierarchy; hence, in a crisis, command would break and self-appointed leaders would follow their adrenalin-induced beliefs. Tay planned to help the illusion that they had an overwhelming advantage so they would rush headlong into attack, tasting blood and expecting the reward of many women, once they destroyed Tay and his vastly outnumbered army.

Every nuance had been thought through: the psychology of the enemy, the weapons they possessed, the lay of ground, the superiority of the opposing numbers, and lastly their lust for steel and gold, which they would have if they were successful.

The plan for the fight was simple, yet ingenious. Tay had engineered a powerful crossbow. The weapon was small, deadly, and easy to use. Ten of the weapons were mounted on a long horizontal pole that swung on a central pivot. All of the triggers were tied to a fanning set of ten strings, so that one person, at the proper time, could loose ten arrows at once.

Tay supervised the construction of six sets of ten. They would be placed strategically along the enemies' entry path and camouflaged by branches and brush until the proper moment. When the enemy was drawn into the chase and squeezed into a tight formation, where the land formed a funnel, sixty arrows would loose simultaneously.

Tay calculated that if only twenty-five percent of the arrows stuck targets, it would unsaddle a third of the attacking force. Some not wounded would be caught in the mayhem of tangled, thrashing men and horseflesh.

After the funnel area was a slightly wider area of tall grass. Tay, the blacksmith, taught young apprentices to pound out an ancient weapon deadly to charging cavalry. The "crow's foot" weapon came from ancient Persia on planet Earth. The gruesome device resembled jacks, from the children's game, but much larger. No matter which way they were strewn on the ground, the sharp points would stand in the air. Charging horses running across ground littered with a thousand of these nasty tools would plummet head over heels when their tender feet were pierced.

Tay had calculated fifty percent of the remaining riders would be fouled and would lose their seats. Many would be crippled in the fall, and those who rose would be mown down by the reloaded, pivoting crossbow banks.

What would be left, if all went well, would be approximately thirty riders. Tay would have fifteen well-trained cavalry troops on the field with another fifteen young men in reserve, just in case they were needed. He planned to lure the remaining enemy, once they regrouped, into a lined up charge. In order to encourage this, his small force would be spread out in an even line. Once the enemy committed themselves, the plan was to begin moving forward towards the point of contact while forming, at the last moment, quickly into a wedge on the move.

Tay and Eclipse would be the point. The idea was to break quickly through the line as the enemies' momentum carried them past their expected point of impact.

The third surprise would be revealed as they reeled their horses and fought to get them under control so they could reverse direction to charge again. In that moment of confusion, when they had no momentum and were still milling, the older teenage boys and girls would loose their longbows on the unsuspecting horsemen.

Those that lived would be met with hand-to-hand attacks from horseback. The grand finale would be to torch the tall, dry grass and let the prevailing wind carry the searing heat towards whatever enemy remained. This was a last resort, but if it was necessary, Tay was prepared to follow through.

Tay presented the battle strategy at a meeting that included all persons needed for the confrontation. Older teens on longbows would be directed by Alex, while the younger teens on crossbows would be supervised by Zuzahna. The grown men and some teenage boys would be on horseback.

Everyone in the group was excited at the prospect of a quick and imminent victory over a force vastly superior in numbers. Tay reminded everyone that timing would be critical, and that each and every person in the fight would have to focus and learn their part flawlessly.

Estellene asked, "Tay, what will my duties be?"

"You, I thought, would be excellent supervising the entire group on the ground."

"Dear Tay, I have been supervising them. They are all excellent archers and have within their groups an appointed officer. I assure you they can handle their part without my help. I would only be in the way."

"Then where do you see your talents fitting in?"

"My dear man, I will be riding on your left, within the wedge."

"Estellene, this is work for men; we would not risk you."

"Risk me? I will be protecting your left, as you will protect me."

"The men are stronger. They are better suited for the task," he said.

She looked at Tay, grinning, and asked, "Are they now?"

"Of course."

"I believe a contest should decide that matter," she said. "I challenge any of the men chosen to ride in the cavalry group. Who will accept my challenge?"

All the young men in the group, who were Estellene's children, glanced between themselves and then looked to the ground and shook their heads, declining. Not one of them had been spared the humbling experience in previous training.

Tay was unaware that Estellene had instructed all the children since the age of five. They were all competent, yet none could match their mother's skill, not even the oldest.

"Estellene, dear, please. You do not need to ride."

"You would agree, TayGor, that the most skilled of our people need to be chosen to ride as the fifteen who will be in the heat?"

"Yes, of course," Tay said seriously.

"Then we must qualify. I will be the first competitor. Who wishes to test themselves?" she asked again.

Gresham stepped forward confidently. Tay had instructed him aboard *Independence* and then on *Intrepid One*: he had a total of nearly eight years training. He was a competent martial artist and outweighed Estellene by forty pounds.

"Do you prefer weapons or hand fighting, Gresham?" Estellene asked.

"I think hand fighting should suffice to prove Tay's point," said Gresham, sounding a bit cocky.

Many of the young men and women could again be seen trading humorous looks. Some shook their heads, pitying Gresham as Estellene's chosen guinea pig. They had all been there many times and were thankful not to be the one bruised and embarrassed in front of so many that day.

The two faced off, first bowing in the ancient tradition.

Standing upright, Estellene smiled in confidence and said, "Please come."

Gresham, his face a mask of seriousness, moved in quickly, attempting to tie Estellene up and take her down.

Estellene, seeing his intent, moved gracefully and quickly towards the oncoming man. Bringing flowing hands and arms in a circular motion, she easily blocked Gresham's grab. When her sweeping block had passed the assailant's limbs to the side, she struck in the same motion: one hand to his solar plexus, the other to the throat. Estellene's forward foot had fluidly ended up behind Gresham's rear foot, and when her twin impacts hit home, he was not able to step backwards and away from the blows. He was lifted in the air and went flying backwards over five feet to land in an embarrassed heap on his rump.

Estellene had intentionally not hurt anything but the young man's ego.

Gresham jumped up and rushed in, intent to regain what he had lost in front of the entire village.

Estellene stepped aside quickly, one stride out of harm's way, while throwing a cranes-wing block and punching half-hard: three quick twisting blows to the tender, exposed area beneath Gresham's right arm. The punches were cast gently and timed to hurt but not to injure. They would bruise but do no serious physical damage. The blows resounded loudly in the drum of the Gresham's chest.

His rushing momentum led him to go flailing by, but Estellene had conveniently left one of her feet in his path. Gresham tripped over her foot and went to ground once more.

Everyone saw the grimace of pain when he pushed himself up and back to his feet.

More young men traded knowing winces with each other. Not one of Estellene's many older children in the room had been spared the same punishing lesson: all, at some time or another, had sparred with her.

Tay watched the entire contest closely, a quizzical look on his face.

Gresham, more cautious this time, got up and circled slowly. Estellene matched his movements. Gresham changed tactics, kicking towards her solar plexus. Estellene timed her movements perfectly, bringing her right forearm arcing down to strike the inside edge of his shin bone; then, spinning her wrist in a half-circle, she caught Gresham's air-born leg, trapping it resting on her wrist. At the same time, she came down with her left hand, striking another arcing blow to the suspended knee. She dropped the suspended leg. Her striking hand came up, impacting Gresham's throat, when he lunged involuntarily forward and his numb leg touched the floor.

Estellene's blows had all been restrained so that the young man would not be seriously injured or crippled. Nonetheless, Gresham choked, gasping for air, and for a brief moment his leg was paralyzed. Estellene took the embarrassed man easily in hand, finishing the contest by leaping forward and sliding to the floor on her side, one leg between Gresham's while the other remained on the outside. Trapping one of his legs between hers, she then rolled quickly to the right. Gresham was tossed like a rag doll onto his back on the floor.

Estellene came up from the momentum of her rolling spin on two knees, planting one of them into the fallen man's chest with just enough force to knock the wind out of him without breaking his sternum. With both hands in a striking posture, she asked. "Do you yield?"

Gresham, speechless from a lack of air, nodded frantically.

Estellene stood and offered her hand. She helped Gresham to his feet and then calmly asked, "Any other challengers?"

The other men all shook their heads or said quick *no*'s. Tay's mouth hung open in startled disbelief.

Estellene walked up to him, placed a hand on his chin, and closed his mouth. Then she planted an affectionate kiss on his lips.

When she broke from him, he asked, "Where did you learn Hung Gar Kung Fu?"

"Leandra taught me. She began my instruction when I was three years of age."

"And where, pray tell, did *she* learn the Ancient Art?"

"From your grandfather, dearest! When he was home on Seven, he instructed her personally. When on duty aboard the ship, he taught her by video. I have studied them as well, and have been instructed by Leandra personally my entire life before we came here."

"What other surprises may I expect from you?"

"Tay, you of all people should know that a woman mustn't give up her secrets. If she does, the mystery is gone. I can only tell you that I possess enough."

Estellene walked over to Zuzahna, placed an arm around her waist, and said quietly, "I guess that's settled."

Zuzahna had seen all the moves before—and a few that Estellene had not used. She looked at her new friend and said quietly, "Could you teach me?"

"Certainly, dear. I would love to. I feel certain you will be a natural."


From across the room, Denali took a long look at Estellene, in a new and brilliant light. She stepped forward saying, "I, too, challenge any man here." She looked directly into Tay's eyes. Her rare, subtle eye smile could be seen by him, and not likely by others.

Tay was silent. All the others were, too.

# SEVENTY-FOUR

Preparation for the upcoming and expected confrontation with Ventras' drastically larger force was all-consuming. Tay was everywhere at once—training in swordsmanship; battlefield horsemanship; and doctoring scrapes, bruises, and slashes in the ancient Chinese herbal medicinal art. He was happier than he had been in years.

Tay found that he shone in a crisis; his energy never left. His patience was unending. The thousands of questions thrown his way—sometimes many at the same time—never frustrated him. He moved with the strain like a giant sailing vessel rolling on powerful swells in a storm-tossed sea.

Everyone's life depended on a unified fighting force, each person flawlessly performing their part of an intricate and grizzly ballet. If one piece of the puzzle failed to fall into place at the proper time, or was damaged before it could be pressed into place, the consequences could be disastrous. He drilled his force relentlessly.

The teenage boys on longbows had to be able to string an arrow blindfolded and loose one after another in four seconds or less. If they failed repeatedly in the task, they were relieved until they had practiced profusely and were willing to give the trial another attempt.

The teenage girls manning the horizontal pivoting poles mounted with crossbows were broken into teams of three. The one among them with the hardest nerves, who was least likely to flinch, was given the task of pulling the trigger string. Tay drilled them day in and out on the reloading sequence so that they could be fast enough to fire not a single volley but two.

He worked the fifteen who were to ride into the final fray on horseback until they dropped into bed every evening so tired that they longed to die in their sleep and not suffer another day's training.

Despite the hard work, everyone was happy and upbeat. They all knew that as a cohesive team, they could prevail. Each person understood that the lives of all others, not just their own, depended on split-second timing, accuracy, courage, and an unfailing determination to win. Anyone who showed the least reluctance to present absolute mercilessness to the enemy was withdrawn from training and placed in the food-preparation team.

Andarean's people astounded TayGor. The strength, stamina, vision, attitudes, and reflexes of all were uniformly superb. They also showed no fear. Courage exuded in their countenances. Tay heard no negative speak, no rumors of doom.

Andarean, from all he could see, had been successful. If there was such a thing in the vast unexplored Universe as a perfect race, Tay was convinced that he had them as his small and brutally outnumbered army.

They were, for the most part, adolescent children, but they carried the weight of well-conditioned and trained soldiers in every facet of their duties. Tay was truly honored and amazed. He sent silent prayers of thanks to their Father Andarean, hoping in fleeting moments of rest that wherever Andarean's gentle, peace-longing spirit cruised, he would be honored by his children.

Each and every child, from the smallest to the largest in size, knew they were coming up against the force that had brutally slain their loving father. Tay could see the determination in their eyes. The desire to punish the ones responsible for Andarean's unfortunate death was a force within in each one of them.

Soon, the small army's mettle would be forged in battle. Tay had visualized the confrontation in his mind a thousand times. He prayed silently that all would go as planned and that not one of his people would be sacrificed. It was something to ask for—something he knew his grandfather demanded of him. No detail was overlooked. He drove himself harder than any of the others. All must be ready, he thought.

The wild one's force could show themselves at any time.

# SEVENTY-FIVE

The day did not come any sooner than Tay had expected. He had been training his people for seven days when his scouts came thundering in on horseback, announcing that the army of wild ones were less than ten miles away upriver. They would be in position by the morning.

Sentries were sent out to ensure they would not be surprised by a night attack.

Tay felt sure Ventras would not risk attacking on unknown ground in darkness. Ventras would also want to rest his men and possibly do some scouting. All things considered, Tay felt the battle would be some time the next day, but he wanted to make sure they would not be surprised. The massive dogs were set out as roaming sentries; they would alert at the least hint of danger.

The village scarcely slept that night. Tay changed the sentries every four hours and patrolled the village perimeter himself to ensure none fell asleep on their watch.

In the morning, the scouts rode in and breathlessly reported that Ventras' force had broken camp five miles upriver and were heading towards the crescent cliffs. The heat could begin in less than an hour.

## THE SEEDING SEVEN'S VISION

Tay called everyone together quickly on the premise of giving final instructions. He intended nothing of the sort. Instead, he wanted to look each soldier in the eyes, and to instill the calm confidence of leadership. He also wanted everyone to understand their common goal.

He began after everyone was quickly gathered.

"We haven't much time, so I will be brief. Each of you knows we are vastly outnumbered. However, I wouldn't trade any one of you for *five* of Ventras' men! We fight for freedom! We fight for peace and prosperity! We fight to protect one another, our home, and all that is worthy and just! That is our creed.

"Those who come believe our numbers are small... *they* do not know us! We are victors, even before the fight begins! For every dark thing that crawls out of the slime of immorality, we are light! Each and every one of you will execute your part without fail, and we shall walk through this day unscathed, I promise you!

"To each of you, I give thanks. I am honored to fight with you, just as my grandfather, the legendary Admiral Gor, would be, too. And he is here! Each one of you has his spirit, his morals, his courage! Do not ever forget that he walks beside us with every painful step we take. Some of you are young, but do not let that dissuade you. With the skills you have learned and the lightning strike of surprise, Ventras will fail. Then...we shall live in peace!

"TO YOUR STATIONS!"

# SEVENTY-SIX

Fifteen riders mounted on lightly armored horses stood in the open field, creating what appeared to be a staggered, disorganized line with many holes.

They waited. Their horses nickered nervously. Each of the riders shared knowing, confident glances with one another. They were the team: the fifteen chosen to ride against the many of the wild tribe.

The incoming horsemen of the wild tribe arrived, riding at a slow walk, evidently sizing up the foe. Their heads were held high, sure of an imminent victory over this much smaller force.

"Hold," Tay said softly, in a low tone that would not carry to the enemy.

The fifteen waited.

Ventras, wearing the cougar's hide and head, rode in front of the enemy column with two others, one on either side. Sunlight shone into his piercing, steely blue eyes.

Two people in TayGor's group recognized those eyes: Tay was one, and Denali was the other. Tay caught Denali's glance and, in the unspoken message that passed between them, he knew she meant to kill Ventras.

At that moment, Ventras, as if feeling a cool wind, stiffened and pulled his cloak about him. He motioned for his force to stop.

Tay could see him gesturing, evidently giving orders, yet he was too far away to be heard.

Ventras soon broke from his group and rode onto a small, grassy knoll. It was a good vantage point for a coward, thought Tay.

He looked again to Denali and caught her eye. He saw in her glance the intent, the ruthless hatred for the man who had forced her to kill Admiral Gor, and then darted, drugged, and raped her before imprisoning her for life.

Tay shook his head from side to side, telling Denali, without words, to hold within the group; she was not to seek her private vengeance and attempt to kill Ventras.

Denali saw Tay's look and heard the silent command. She nodded ever so slightly in acknowledgement.

Ventras' force began to move. They gained momentum until the beating hooves of their horses filled the air, sounding a thousand drums. Dust flew behind the riders, obscuring Ventras from view.

Tay judged the distance. He wanted them close, but not so near as to risk enemy arrows reaching his small army. A moment later, he gave the signal. The fifteen turned and broke into a thundering, pell-mell gallop that would have appeared, to the much larger force of the wild tribe, as if they were fleeing.

The wild ones whipped their horses mercilessly, driven by the lust for young women, and for steel and other precious metals. They thought of the many beautiful horses they would capture, and of the prime land they would acquire: a land more beautiful and lush than any they had seen in their vast journey. They rode with abandon, desire spurring and clouding their minds. They were blinded by dark passion as they chased Tay and his small group.

Soon the valley narrowed. The river swept in a tight arc around a protruding rocky ridge running downslope and very near the water's edge.

Tay's group broke into triple file and made for the narrow opening, which was squeezed on one side by the river and on the other by the rock. Tay led them into the funnel and, shortly, the fifteen riders came into another field that opened up gradually. Tay led them further on out into the valley before he signaled a halt and turned his group to face the onslaught of nearly eighty ruthless, frothing riders.

Serrenda, a girl twelve years old, waited with her arm in the air. The drill had been practiced many times before with a moving target. She waited to unleash the arrows, with her signal. She had been chosen by Tay for her timing and fearlessness. Her golden-blonde hair fluttered, reflecting the sunlight through its waving strands.

All the crossbows pointed not across the path but angling into it. Sixty hammered steel tips glistened in the sunlight. Their focused fire would riddle the air in a small area just as the men on horseback came through the narrow point on the trail.

The fifteen waited.

The wild ones appeared, unknowingly racing into the trap, and the young woman's hand dropped.

The air bristled. The hissing feathers seemed to claim their victims even before they hit them. Grizzly shafts protruded from many of the screaming, startled men. Horses tumbled one after the other, and men flew through the air, landing in broken heaps. The remaining horses bolted, stirring up an obscuring dust cloud.

Pain-filled and gruesome screams emanated from the scene as the bolting horses crushed men on the ground. Others stumbled over the bodies of men and horses that littered the area. Mayhem had been unleashed. Tense moments passed.

The wild ones who had remained in their saddles looked at their fallen as the breeze cleared the dust from the scene. Startled by the magnitude of damage wrought, they quickly regrouped.

Nearly fifty of them remained. They began riding towards Tay again, hate showing in their eyes. They knew that even their diminished number could easily rout the much smaller force.

However, Tay and his group had picked their way carefully through the field, taking a safe, serpentine path. They knew what awaited the oncoming force.

Ventras' riders plunged headlong towards Tay's group, unaware of the brutal crow's feet until it was too late. Horses tumbled. More men, thrown from their seats, were crushed and broken.

Not more than thirty riders made it through the minefield in their saddles. Those on the field who could rise staggered in stunned circles, attempting to find a horse, but there were few to be found. Dazar, the wild ones' leader, regrouped his weakened force and began the charge again. They rode in a line towards the fifteen.

Tay signaled, and the fifteen broke into a gallop, riding in a line towards the oncoming rush of men and horses.

Just before contact, and upon Tay's signal, his line condensed itself quickly into a compressed wedge. Tay and Eclipse were the spear's head. Denali and Estellene rode beside him, only a half a horse-length behind.

Eclipse's dark, powerful body seemed to whisk the group forward. His eyes showed a focused determination that was near human. His breath could be heard surging above the din of pounding hooves.

They rode into the wild tribe's line and crashed through them like an avalanche down a sheer mountain face. They were a giant shield of humans, horses, armor, and weapons glinting in the sunlight, each of them protecting one another in their tight formation.

To those watching, the sight brought the joy of confident, happy tears. Tay shone as a beacon to all.

More wild ones fell. Those still riding had to rein up and stop for a second while they reformed and began to turn their mounts around. In that instant, twenty longbows, hidden in the trees and held by teenage boys and girls, were unleashed upon them. Almost immediately, before the wild ones could regroup and charge, they were pummeled again by the fleet, merciless shafts that sang through the air.

What came away from the unexpected assault was a mere ragtag group, many of which were wounded. No longer did victory shine in their eyes. Dazar's one eye saw, and his mind knew. He took his chance: as the dust from the charge rose, obscuring him, he heeled his horse away and raced into the river.

## THE SEEDING SEVEN'S VISION

The fifteen waited by the rock and watched the group of adolescent girls reloading the crossbows. They had been pivoted to point downfield towards the remaining wild ones. Tay gave the signal, and once more the bows that had been hastily reloaded sang, strumming the air with their strings. Feathered arrows, screaming as they flew, took down a few more targets.

Of the nearly eighty that had begun the ill-fated attack minutes before, less than twenty remained in the saddle. Some fell as they picked up more crow's feet, and others fell from wounds that had turned their mounts red.

A final small group continued the beleaguered attack in desperation. Tay, Estellene, and Denali circled them. To those watching, they resembled three giant, four-legged birds of prey with wings of steel.

It was over quickly.

Afterwards, the wild ones on the ground who were still alive were dispatched without feeling, and those who had managed to run or stagger away on foot were run down and slaughtered without mercy, or passion.

The field was then quiet, except for the rushing breath of animal and man, and the shuffling steps of the horses as their legs brushed the grass that was now crimson in many places.

Awestruck, they all heard one set of horse hooves beating. Every one of the mounted riders looked upriver. Dust swirling in the air made visibility poor.


Denali broke from the group, turning her mount in the direction of the sound.

Ventras was fleeing.

Denali signaled her horse and broke into a gallop.

Tay shouted, "Do not kill him, Denali! He is fleeing."

"Okay," was all she shouted as she galloped away, appearing grown from the animal, as if they were not two separate entities but one throbbing beast that craved blood.

Tay wondered whether she would obey his instruction. He also felt an odd sort of pity for Ventras, knowing that a quick death on the battlefield would have been more pleasant than whatever the woman he had come to respect, accept, and admire had in store for the scourge named Ventras.

# SEVENTY-SEVEN

Denali willed her horse to run harder, not by whipping the sweating animal but by nudging and squeezing with her legs at each stride. The trees and ground flew by in a blur. The wind feathered through her eyelashes, and the pressure on her eyes made them water, magnifying the haze.

In all, she was caught in a time nine years in the past. Through the blur that surrounded her, she saw at the center of her focused vision a small round hole of clarity. It was all that mattered: it was Ventras.

The man she was running down whipped his horse without mercy. Dust flew from the beleaguered animal's stride and clumps of damp sod flew off the horse's rear hooves, propelled skyward.

Ventras' seat was unbalanced. His frantic attempt to escape showed in his position and movement. His horse, instead of concentrating on its flight, often threw its head slightly from side to side, complaining of the man's incessant torture.

Ventras looked backward often, fear displaying in those sideways glances. Every time he glanced backward, he saw that Denali and her mount had gained a full stride. The gap between them was rapidly closing. The fear in his eyes increased with each look cast behind. He knew; she knew.

Shortly, the nine years of Denali's hate, which had been carefully and unemotionally built stone by stone, day after day, year upon year, would have its release. She relished the thought. She longed to hear his screams. Denali desired his agony. What he had taken from her years before, she could taste. A bitter flavor rose on the back of her tongue: resentment and shame—the spice brewed by the fleeing man before her, so long ago.

Denali held the reins in her left hand. Without breaking stride, she reached down with her right and slipped a short spear from its resting place. Sliding her hand up the shaft just short of the center point, she tucked the butt under her arm, up high where it rested snugly, held tight directly beneath her shoulder.

Denali was so close she could smell the commingled sweat of Ventras' horse and his fear. She enjoyed knowing his brain was screaming in fright; she longed for it to scream in agony.

*Shortly!* she thought. Like a wolf sensing a near kill, Denali's hunger burned into her. Primeval saliva wetted her tongue, which moments before had been paper-dry. Her breath rushed faster. Adrenalin spiked as she came near to the striking distance.

Fleeting seconds later, her horse's head was even with the left hindquarter of Ventras' faltering mount. He viciously swung his crop away from the tempo it had been ruthlessly playing on his horse and aimed for her horse's head. It missed by an inch.

At the same moment, Denali plunged her spear's point into Ventras' calf and then lifted with all her strength, keeping the butt of the spear under her arm and pivoting it, her right hand acting as the fulcrum. She flung his leg up and then lunged the spear forward as Ventras' leg was even with his seat.

Ventras lost his balance and spun away from her, sliding out of the saddle, his right foot still caught in the stirrup. The horse reared sideways, its exhausted body unable to correct for the man's drastic change in position. The horse took a couple more strides in a tight, right-handed circle, attempting to compensate, and then it fell, landing on Ventras' right leg and pinning him to the ground.

The fallen horse's eyes were wild and bulging. The day was hot; still, the overheated animal's breath steamed.

Ventras' eyes were filled not only with fear but with disbelief as well. He spoke her name with an insincere kindness. He was attempting an ill-fated reconciliation. His eyes pleaded, wishing forgiveness, longing for mercy, and of revenge, forgotten. All the things Denali could *never* deliver to him.

She circled him, looking into those steel-blue eyes.

"Ventras…it looks as though you're trapped beneath your horse. Can you get up?"

"No! My leg is caught. Help me! Please!"

Denali only looked at the man who deserved no pity. His headdress made of the cougar's head had fallen away. What she saw should have drawn her pity, but her heart was hard as granite.

He was disfigured. Old scars, un-stitched, had healed, leaving welts. *The cougar's slashes*, her mind said. Between the scars, the skin was mottled with dark-brown and nearly black blotches, which created thick, rough patches. Between them the skin was thin and red, blood veins shone through thin patches of skin, revealing the desert sun's brutal damage.

"Ventras...what happened to you, the picture of aristocracy, the noble legislator, the man of power and the hour? You are hideous! Do you know how you look? You could get a job as a circus freak, if we only *had* a circus. Your farce is lying on the blood-red field back there." She gestured with her hand to the battlefield behind.

Denali...I will change! I'm so sorry, I...wasn't in my right mind...the asteroid, the stress. The responsibility for the people. I...I...forgive me, please! Will you? I promise, I'll only do *good* from now on. I've learned a great lesson today. Really! I'm truly sorry. Have mercy on me! Look at me! I can be no threat to you! I'm finished, washed up, broken. That's what you wanted, wasn't it?"

"Forgive? Is that what you asked?"

Ventras nodded frantically.

"Broken? Is that how you described yourself?"

The frantic nodding continued.

Denali took the spear's sharp edge and sawed lightly at his horse's girth strap until, after a few minutes, the strap parted.

Ventras' horse, now free of its burden, staggered to its feet and bolted.

"Oh! Thank you, Denali!"

"Is your leg broken, Ventras?"

"No. No, it seems to be fine. Thanks you so much for freeing me. I am forever in your debt. I don't deserve your kindness." Ventras stood.

"No. You do not."

Ventras looked perplexed. He wondered what lie would work the best.

Denali said coldly, "You'd better start running, Ventras."

"What?"

"RUN!"

Ventras' eyes flitted to his saddle lying on the ground. He was obviously looking for some unseen weapon.

Denali wasted no time. She said, "I TOLD YOU TO RUN!"

Ventras looked at her in disbelief and stood frozen as it dawned on him: all his desperate lies and psycho-babble had not softened her a bit. He made a move towards her in aggression, and Denali heeled her mount. The horse lunged forward, and she ran over top of the oncoming man.

She heard some small bones snap. The foot or a hand, she thought. Nothing serious, nothing that would cause a lifetime of pain.

Ventras jumped up, swearing like a pirate.

She said once again, "RUN!"

Ventras faltered, his steps quivered in uncertainty.

Denali swung her spear sideways, and the sharp edge cut brutally deep into his shoulder. "Are you deaf?" Denali asked mercilessly.

Ventras saw the futility, yet what choice did he have. He turned and fled. Denali allowed him to gain fifty or sixty meters head start before she took off after him. She galloped alongside, brushing him and knocking him to the ground. He tumbled head over heels and made no attempt to rise.

As he lay, writhing in pain, Denali cantered the horse over top of him. She heard the snap of ribs and felt one of the horse's hooves step on something hard and fairly solid. There was a grizzly crunching sound and a sharp, piercing shriek from below.

She spun her horse and looked at Ventras. He was grasping his right knee, moaning in agony.

"Hurts, doesn't it?" Her rhetorical question went unanswered by words, but his anguished cries told the story well.

Denali led her horse to a small tree nearby and tied the animal to it. Walking back, she saw that Ventras had made no effort to rise.

"Tay must *really* like you, Ventras."

The writhing man managed to say, "What do you mean?"

"Well, he made me promise *not* to kill you! Actually, this is a much better healing process for me: so much more drawn out, so much more rewarding. *Death* would be too quick a cure for what ails you, you stinking piece of filth!"

Denali stabbed Ventras with the spear in the back of his unbroken knee and twisted the shaft. She could feel the joint separating as he screamed and rolled futilely away. She did the same with both ankles as he attempted to escape in a desperate, fast-moving crawl.

Finally, Ventras lay helpless, bleeding. There was no physical fight left in him.

Denali went back to her horse, untied it, and swung into the saddle. She walked the horse to Ventras. He squinted from the sun or the misery—she could not tell—and looked up at her.

"Your wounds are not fatal. You will live. Most likely, you will have to crawl back to your dark den. If I ever see you, or any of your kind, near my village or *my* family again, I will find you, and our conversation will not be nearly as pleasant as it was today!"

# SEVENTY-EIGHT

Alex watched from the sidelines. Issy stood with him. He had directed the boys in the longbow attack, and then, afterward, when the dust created by their spectacular victory had settled, he found that Denali was no place to be seen.

He rushed out and shouted, "Denali?!" at the top of his lungs, his heart pounding, fearing she could be a casualty of the conflict. Issy ran right behind.

Tay rode up on his big beast. The horse's coat was wet with sweat. Every muscle in the magnificent animal bulged and rippled. Eclipse, with Tay aboard, sauntered near and nudged Alex affectionately.

"Denali? Where is she, Tay? I don't see her."

Tay pointed up river and cupped a hand to his ear. Over the excited animal's stuttering footsteps and the talk of the people, Alex could hear the distinct sound of pounding hoof beats, diminishing as they gained in distance from his ears.

"She's gone?" Alex asked in disbelief.

"Chasing an old demon, I think," answered Tay. "Here, take Eclipse. You may catch up to her on him. I doubt any other horse would."

Alex looked to Tay, and then at the big black monster who stamped and pawed the earth as if he knew, telepathically, that the challenge had been made: he would need to close the distance between Denali and the unknown demon she pursued.

Issy said frantically, "Go, Alex! You mustn't leave her out there alone! Promise me she'll be all right!"

"I promise, Issy! I promise!"

Tay swung down from the saddle and said, "Settle, Eclipse. Be good to Alex. Take him safely and quickly to his destiny." Tay smiled disarmingly, as if he knew the quandary Alex's heart ran. As if he knew, in some way, that Denali had embraced Alex, and that Alex would do anything—even risk his own life—not to lose her.

Tay helped Alex with a stirrup and then assisted him in swinging into the massive horse's seat.

Tay held the hackamore tightly and then breathed one deep, long rush of breath into Eclipse's flared nostrils. He said quickly, "Take care of my best friend. Do you understand?"

Eclipse let out his trademark answer, a shrill squeak, and then turned and bolted towards the sound of hoof beats in the distance.

"Hold on, Alex! You'll be all right!"

Alex sat astride a beast he had only ever admired before. Eclipse's gallop was a fluid dance. Trees became a rushing mass that waved in undulating patterns as he and Eclipse bolted by. The wind in Alex's eyes made them water profusely.

He held on for dear life, being a novice in equestrian training. Fear for Denali's safety was foremost in his mind; her safety came before his own. She was the woman of his dreams. He had no idea what demon she might be pursuing, only that he needed to be near her, to do what he could to ensure she would not be harmed, and to ensure that her demons would not steal her from him once more.

Alex focused his vision on a tunnel before him. Nothing else mattered except that he find her—safe and unharmed.

Denali had finished watering her horse and was riding away from the sound of the river. She preferred to stay in the shadows of the forest along the river, just in case some of the wild ones were still lurking about. As she headed for the trees, she heard the pounding drum of a horse's hooves. A moment later, to her utter surprise, Alex bolted by on Eclipse. *What in the world?!* she thought.

She set out from the trees in a hard gallop, yelling his name at the top of her lungs. He turned slightly in the saddle, saw her, and reined in Eclipse. He rode a half-circle through the tall grass of the field, turning towards her.

Denali smiled wide as he came up alongside her.

"Wow, Alex! You cut a fine figure riding that big, dark beast."

"Denali! Issy and I were worried sick about you. Tay said you were chasing an old demon... What in the world does that mean?"

"Don't you worry your sweet head about it, love. I won't be chasing anything but you from now on. Race you back to your cabin!" Denali gave up some rein and nudged her mount. She bolted off before Alex could even think about what she had said.

Eclipse got the message and tore off after her. Within moments, they were galloping side by side, hair flying, smiles breaking, hooves pounding pell-mell.

Alex kept a tight rein on the dark brute, and let Denali win.

# SEVENTY-NINE

Tay stood watching Alex be carried away by Eclipse. He turned and looked for Estellene. She was cantering her horse, cooling it from the fray. He looked for Zuzahna, and saw her with the young girls who had manned the crossbow line.

The children were obviously in shock; they had never before witnessed such brutality. Leadership pulled him in many directions: to the children, to Estellene, to Zuzahna, to Alex and Denali, and to his brothers in arms. Tay stood, sunlight illuminating the highlights in his auburn hair; he stood tall and dark. He stood as a beacon of light for all that watched.

He was their leader.

Wondering what he should say...doubting, as any human does at times, his ability to form the proper words to fit the moment—appropriate words—he began.

"Brothers and Sisters...today marks a monumental achievement. Each and every one of us has played an integral part. Each of us has bought, with our pain-filled efforts, freedom!

"Freedom for the ones we love. Freedom for the ones we cherish! This day has forced brutality from us. This day has shown each and every one of us here, each member of our family, that we can indeed be brutal when protecting one another and our home, when it is imperative.

"We have fought not only for ourselves. We have fought for one another. We have learned our *power*. The *power* of unity, the power of combined and concerted effort, the power that can be unleashed...unleashed when we love one another without reserve, and when we understand and feel love: a love for which we would gladly sacrifice ourselves to protect ones held dear! Then we know *true bliss!*

"We have *only* matched the brutality of our enemy, and we have prevailed! We are the victors! Light—not darkness—is our mantle, and if to shed light upon this Virgin planet we must meet the wild hoard, then we will become *devastation* to them! As we have today, we will do what is necessary to ensure our family is safe!

"Fifteen rode onto the field. I chose the number fifteen, to commemorate the foundation and spiritual leaders of our society. We have all read of our distant culture, the culture that gave birth to us, a culture that was governed by fifteen selfless leaders with the common people's best interests at heart. AND SO ON THIS DAY—THIS DAY OF OUR VICTORY—I WISH TO COMMEMORATE AND UPHOLD THE VALUES THAT ALLOW US TO BE A FREE AND PROSPEROUS FAMILY! To the fifteen, I say we dedicate a festival. Shall we call it the Festival of Fifteen?"

The valley roared.

"Fifteen days of celebration and homage! Fifteen days where we will work little, and dance and eat. Fifteen days dedicating ourselves to knowing our brothers and sisters. Fifteen days of thanksgiving. We have prevailed! We will now *know*, and *live* in peace!"

# EIGHTY

Ventras was crawling, once again. The agony of his predicament etched hatred into his beleaguered mind—hatred for the one called TayGor, the one responsible for his pain.

Ventras' thoughts drifted backward into the past, to the torturous desert. He attempted to pull from deep within the metal that had seen him out of that desolate furnace and to the clear, cool pool of water at the foot of the rock face, to the place where he had slain the cougar. His iron will and his hatred of TayGor had allowed him to survive and to make it out of the desert. He *would* survive this day. He would have his revenge. The thought of TayGor on his knees before him, begging to be spared, spurred him on, allowing him to relegate the agony and pain of his injuries and wounds to a compartment again. The misery was locked away. Without it, he could continue on.

He could make it back to his village...to his people. There, he would heal, and then train the children. He would train the ever-hungry, dirty, unruly pack in hatred. He would infect them with his own. And one day in the future...one glorious day, a day he would dream of for years to come, while the children of the wild ones slowly grew towards adulthood…they would swarm Tay's village with a force that so vastly outnumbered Tay's own they would easily take the valley of the crescent cliffs and the precious steel that could be made there.

Then, Ventras thought, he would finally achieve his life's destiny: he would preside over the entire planet! *He* would be the one in power. He would regain what TayGor had stolen from him: his victory on Seven! TayGor had stolen his life's work.

On Seven, Ventras had fought, killed, cheated, and maneuvered to rise in power, to become the ultimate force: the ruler of all Seven Galaxies. Just when his plans had seen fruition, TayGor had somehow escaped the penal moon, and in the blink of an eye he had stolen all that Ventras had achieved.

Ventras' face was pale from his loss of blood and etched into a fearsome mask, scored by deep crevasses of suffering. Misery ebbed and flowed. The tide of suffering was kept at bay only by his hatred for the one he believed, in his degraded mental state, to be responsible for his pain.

Ventras could never admit to himself that the black acts of his past had cast him into suffering once more. The cause of his misery was once again his own greed and unquenchable thirst for ultimate power. Tay and his village's victory was only the effect. Ventras, in the haze of his thinking, found only hate. He would never fault himself. In Ventras' twisted mind, he believed himself to be faultless; he easily justified his actions and blamed those who stood in his way. He could never dare admit that at this time, a time he crawled through slowly on crippled legs, he was living a destiny of his own creation.

At last, worn out and weak from losing much blood, Ventras gave up. He laid in the shade along the river, listening to the rustle of late summer's breezes stroking the leaves of the trees. He saw the fluttering green canopy above him, and the great blue beyond. The light flickered and danced upon his prone form.

The journey before him, to his village, was nearly a week on horseback. The realization dawned within his pain-filled mind that there was no way he could make it home crawling; the distance was too great, and his injuries were too severe.

He lay upon the soft, warm earth and his mind traveled backward in flashes. He saw his life in reverse. He reveled in what he had, through Machiavellian moves, accomplished. *I was destined to be a great and powerful man!*

"It cannot end here!" Ventras shouted to the open spaces and to the sky above. But somehow Ventras was not convinced that this place along the river would not become his final resting place, and that his dreams of conquering TayGor might never come to fruition.

His headdress of the cougar's hide and skull lay in a dirty mess. He had been dragging his most prized possession along, tied by a lace of leather that was looped around his neck. Ventras looked to his mantle, the mask that had awed the wild tribe, the mask he had constantly hidden behind so as not to be recognized by the evil ones he had first imprisoned in the penal moon back on Seven Galaxies and then, by fate's strange turn of events, come to rule upon this new planet.

Ventras was drifting in and out of delirium caused by fatigue and blood loss.

In the distance, he thought he could hear the unmistakable sound of horse's hooves growing louder. He reached for his headdress and donned the filthy mask. Through his bleary eyes, he could make out a horse and rider in the distance.

Denali? His mind screamed the question, fearing she had only been toying with him, letting him crawl in agony. Was she now coming to finish him off? His mind reeled in unanswered questions. The rider grew in size and clarity as they came nearer.

Soon Ventras could see it was not a woman but a very large man on horseback. Another horse was being led on a tether behind the rider. Ventras squinted, trying to make out the man's face, and soon he realized it was *Dazar*!

Dazar had obviously escaped the slaughter. He had always been a crafty one, thought Ventras.

The man reined the horse to a stop and took in Ventra's pitiful form. "Shaman! What happened to you? I didn't see you fighting in the battle, or the massacre as I've come to think of it."

"No, I was set upon by several warriors from TayGor's force," Ventras lied. "They wounded me severely and then left me for dead. I have been crawling ever since, trying to make it back to our people. I fear I can go no further without help. Will you help me, old friend? I see you have a spare horse I could ride."

Dazar's quick, calculating mind ran the question through, weighing it as he did everything, in relation to his desires. It was true that he had never liked the shaman. The shaman had taken from him some of his authority over the tribe. Dazar had resented the man. Now, here, with no witnesses, he could easily slay the shaman. He was tempted to do just that, but the problem was not quite so simple.

All of the younger men from the tribe had been brutally slain in the battle. He and the shaman were the only survivors. Back in the village, there were only very old men, women, and children. The simple fact that the tribe needed to grow into a large and powerful force made slaying the shaman impracticable.

Who would breed the women? Dazar thought.

Surely the tribe needed genetic diversity, and the shaman had many strong qualities. He was firstly a survivor, and he also possessed a determined ruthlessness and hatred for TayGor, qualities that—when combined with Dazar's—would spawn a tribe of large, physically powerful and intelligent fighters: a successful army that could defeat TayGor and take his precious land.

Within a few short seconds, Dazar's calculating mind had run the gamut of possibilities. His dislike for the wounded shaman did not supersede his desire to conquer TayGor. He needed the shaman's genetics; the tribe needed them.

"Come, Shaman! I will help you onto your horse! We will ride together towards home…to our people."

# EIGHTY-ONE

TAY walked up to Estellene, who sat still, astride her mount.

"Come," was all he said.

She dismounted and looked for Zuzahna at the same moment that Tay and Zuzahna's eyes met. The pair walked towards her.

"Let's clean up, and the three of us can hike to the cliff-top. The others can take care of the horses and have instructions on disposing of the wild one's bodies."

They walked to the river and swam in the clear, cold water, refreshing themselves from the fray, cooling not only their physical bodies but their nerves as well.

After drying and changing into fresh clothes, they hiked the path to the top of the crescent cliff.

All during the swim, the hike, and then while sitting down, winded, at the summit, Tay had noticed Estellene exchanging knowing looks with Zuzahna. It seemed to him they shared some bit of levity and were keeping it from him.

The festival had begun. A huge bonfire had been started and many of the children as well as the grown-ups could be seen dancing to music.

The setting sun, as always at this time of day, played its light upon the scene, changing colors from brilliant to muted violets and greys. A pair of coal-black ravens swam lazily in the warm updrafts above the cliff. Once in a while, Tay could hear the brush of their wings stroking the changing sky.

"All right you two, what's up?" Tay asked, wanting to be let in on their little secret, whatever it might be.

Estellene and Zuzahna looked to each other once more and then slid up, one on either side of him, brushing their warmth close until he was nearly walled in by the two smiling women.

A more gorgeous sight he had not seen, he thought. The two of them smiling together.

They spoke in unison, one into each ear. "We're pregnant, Tay!"

Preview the next book in the series:

# THE SEEDING III
# QUEST FOR STEEL

*Available in August, 2013*

# ONE

Waking at first light, Tay dressed quietly and then stole out of the house, so as not to wake Zuzahna and Estellene. They needed their rest, he thought, as he picked up his favorite fly rod from the tool shed and walked towards the river.

Mist blanketed the meadow in an undulating sheet of white-gray. The sound of the distant surf crashing filled his ears with a roar. *A storm must be coming,* he thought. Normally the ocean surf could not be heard so loudly this far inland.

A thin, gray line formed on the eastern horizon, and Tay turned to see the silhouetted cliff against the lightening morning sky.

This place, he thought, brought such peace, beauty, and love. Happiness abounded here.

Though, at times, his more daring side craved the unexplored mysteries of an unfamiliar night sky. To be aboard *Intrepid One*, searching out the vast unknown surrounding the Virgin.... The idea was compelling, but duty to his new family tethered a spirit that dreamed of another time in the future—a time when he would be less needed here, and would be free to roam the stars once again.

The ship was orbiting the planet, in hibernation mode under Full Stealth Cloak. Tay had not set foot on her since landfall on the Virgin. He was content. His itchy feet had grown into roots, intertwining within a family that was extraordinary.

When he pondered the depths of each member—their intelligence, beauty, strength, and compassion—he was astounded. The complete lack of jealousy and the other elements comprising the base nature of man were missing from his family, the family Andarean had masterfully created—a family Tay had become patriarch of since Andarean's tragic death. Within Estellene and Andarean's children, he had made his home. He had never been happier.

All the previous thoughts wafted through Tay's mind as he enjoyed the sound of his footsteps along the trail that led to the river. He knew the sea run trout were in. They were following the spring salmon up the river, readying to plunder egg stashes laid by pairs of the spawning, giant fish.

The big trout would be hungry. The springs had not yet begun to run. They were waiting in the river's mouth and in the tidewater for the first fall rains. Then they would make their one-way journey, a few hundred miles inland, to procreate in their instinctive and intensely suicidal way.

Tay had seen the giant springs jumping in the evenings, when he came to watch the setting sun play against their bodies as they cast themselves airborne for a nano. It was a gorgeous sight, one he never tired of admiring;

when they splashed down, they sent concentric rings of ripples racing in all directions.

A pair of ravens jumped up from the tall grass as he walked by. Startled during their morning foraging for fallen seed heads, they leapt into the air, their coal black wings glistening in the early morning light, showing the dappled signs of old age. Rushing air, streaming through their powerful, feathered wings, spoke softer than it had in the years past. It was a familiar and wondrous sound. It was a sound unlike any other.

They beat their way higher, and upon reaching the cliff's upper ledge, locked their wings and slid effortlessly, graceful, gliding silhouettes, dark against a backdrop of silvery blue.

Tay stopped to watch as they made way, circling higher, towards a vantage point where they could watch his movements easily. He often left them some of the fishes' innards when he was done and had cleaned his catch. They waited patiently for the tasty bounty that they could not so easily obtain without his help.

Smiling to himself, he continued down the river trail to his favorite deep-water hole.

The ripples' peaks reflected meandering strips of sunrise; deep blue colors blanketed its surface as well. Tay could see swirls, created in the dark water below and rising on the lazy current. The fish were coming alive, as the morning light brightened and insects began to fly and dip into the water. The trout would soon be rising. Then the fun would begin, he thought, smiling inwardly.

Casting out into a ripple, his pole immediately dove towards the water. What he expected was a fast run of line off the homemade spool. Instead, when he jerked the rod, setting the hook, a monstrous dorsal fin broke the surface, and one of the biggest spring salmon he had ever seen launched from the dark water into the air. The massive fish shook its head wildly in a frantic attempt to free the hook.

Tay's heart leapt. He thought of the meager line on his reel and the lightness of it. The big fish turned and began running downstream towards open water, using the river's current to rapidly strip line from Tay's reel. Thumbing the reel to slow down and tire the fish, he ran downstream as fast as he could, reeling when he found slack.

The river's mouth was several kilometers away. Once in the open water, there would be no stopping the giant, Tay thought desperately. The big spring showed no sign of slowing down.

Running, trying desperately not to lose his footing on the slippery and uneven rocks, Tay silently thanked his teacher Sifu for the intensive training he had undergone for years. Without it, he thought, *this* would be absurd.

The salmon, as if understanding that Tay was running, or hearing his crashing footsteps on the rocks, began to increase his efforts. No longer was Tay reeling. He was thumbing the reel's spool, attempting to wear down the escaping, massive, sea-born slab before it reached open water.

Tay was losing line at a rapid rate. The skin on his thumb smoked as friction burned into his consciousness. The big fish just kept steaming, showing that he had no intention of being eaten by this strange two-legged creature who had tricked him into biting the hook. It had been craftily concealed from view, hidden inside what seemed a tasty treat in the meager morning light.

Tay was breathing hard, sprinting as fast as he could while managing the pole and the beach's obstructions. He jumped over fallen logs and tide pools filled with startled sea creatures.

The river's mouth came into view. Glistening ocean rollers moved towards the big sand bar and rose cresting and breaking in a show of white foam and sea green and blue.

*I must stop him before he reaches the open water!* Tay thought. Yet when he looked at his reel, there was little line left on the spool. The beach became sand instead of rock. Tay poured on all the speed he could muster. The line on his reel still sang out.

The big fish was leaving, and taking with him all the man's valiant effort. Tay could see the huge dorsal fin just nearing the rounded curve where the river's mouth met the crashing surf.

Just then, about a half a dozen seals rounded the point. They were coming upriver for a morning feast. Abruptly, the big fish turned and fled the pack, heading straight towards Tay. He was obviously attempting to lose the sleek marauders in shallower water.

Tay reeled like a banshee while running backward, keeping the line tight. He winded, stopped next to a small inlet in the beach, and watched the drama unfold before his wondering eyes. The seals had obviously seen the flashing color of true coin. They were following the big fish and rapidly gaining. Tay reeled franticly. The big salmon was tiring, enabling him more control in directing the fish.

At once nearing the little inlet, the giant fish seemed to sense safety from the hunters following so close and headed into the small, protected pool. In the shallow water, the big spring's back was a third out of the water. The prowling seals were too large to make fast way into the shallows. They saw Tay and obviously decided hunting would be easier farther upriver. They turned, reluctantly giving up pursuit, and disappeared beneath the surface.

The massive fish was larger than any Tay had seen before. The rising sun played jewels of shifting light upon its body. Setting his fly rod down between two large rocks, he wedged another on top of it. Walking around the small pool, Tay rolled two large rocks into the water at the narrowest point of the inlet, effectively blocking the only exit.

*I've won the contest! He is mine!* Tay thought excitedly, panting from the exertion. His prize lay languidly in the pool, obviously worn out from the contest. The salmon's gills pumped rapidly, working to replace oxygen that had been overused in frantic flight.

Tay sat on a large boulder next to the glistening pool and admired the massive fish. This one would make a hefty meal for the entire village.

Then, in his admiration, Tay began feeling something greater than the victory. He felt the challenge won growing into compassion and respect-filled awe. The heart of a hunter softened. Tay reached into the water and quickly twisted the hook free from the great salmon's upper lip. As if charged by electricity, the fish flopped and leapt, thrashing in the small pool and soaking him with the salty water.

Soon the water was once again calm as the big spring realized the futility of his struggle. There was no way out.

Two shadows passed across the pool, and Tay looked up. The pair of Ravens coasting in the air above and to the east were admiring his prize as well. Looking into the salmon's eyes, he could see it react to the passing shadows. He wondered how many times, as a young fingerling, the salmon had survived near misses from birds of prey.

All at once, as the rising sun brightened the rocks on the beach, Tay's thoughts brightened as well. This salmon was a specimen larger than he had ever seen. He was awed by this opportunity to observe the impressive creature. Then, in a flash, he realized what he was destined to do.

Rolling the rocks back out of the small entrance, he stepped into the shallow pool and placed one hand along the fish's side. It turned and in a flashing streak, disappeared into the deep water beyond.

Tay sighed deeply, feeling exhilaration from the challenge and from the inspired decision to set the captive free.

The Ravens circled lower, chanting their dismay in rasping voices. Tay heard them speak of unearthly disbelief. He smiled wide, looking up to the dark, airborne forms and said, "Not that one. I'll find you some . . . a bit less magnificent."

With that, he moved the rock, picked up his pole, and walked back up the shimmering river towards his favorite deep hole.

CPSIA information can be obtained at www.ICGtesting.com
Printed in the USA
BVOW071142270113

311619BV00001B/1/P